Sign up for our newsletter to hear
about new and upcoming releases.

www.ylva-publishing.com

Other Books by Jazz Forrester

Shifting Gears

Jazz
Forrester

BREAKING
from
FRAME

Dedication

To all the Claires out there.

Chapter 1

March 17, 1969

Suffering From Nervous Headaches? Ask Your Doctor About Anacin Fast Pain Relief!

Claire sighs. Nervous headaches—not even close to her biggest problem today.

She squints at the poster, tilting her head. It's been here in the waiting room of the doctor's office since she was a child, with the same pretty cartoon nurse holding a bottle of medicine on a faded pink background. Back then, Claire had looked at it as a kind of role model. Her own mother trained as a nurse, though she stayed home to raise Claire and keep house rather than working as one. She's now happily retired, having never worked a day in her life.

Today, the well-kept woman on the poster looks down at Claire judgmentally.

Swallowing down the pang of anxiety, Claire casts her eyes around for a distraction. The waiting room is busier than usual—almost every seat is full. There's a man dozing off in a chair near the door, wearing perhaps the most obvious toupee Claire has ever seen. It looks like he's skinned a small Yorkshire terrier and glued it to his head. A person to her left is coughing wetly. There's a very unhappy toddler somewhere behind her. Cold and flu season is just winding down.

Claire would normally have waited until her birthday in July for her yearly check-up, but she has something important to ask today. Though she's been dreading it since she made the appointment, she just couldn't stomach waiting another four months.

"Mrs. Davis?" a nurse calls from the front desk.

As the sleeping man starts to snore, Claire wonders whether he realizes that his toupee is two different shades of brown. Is it only Claire who sees it? Nobody else is giving it a second look. Is she the odd one out? It wouldn't be the first time.

"Mrs. Claire Davis?" the nurse repeats, with a note of annoyance.

With a jolt, Claire finally recognizes her name being called. She stands so abruptly that she jostles the woman to her left with an elbow, sending the woman's magazine tumbling to the floor.

The woman tuts quietly, glaring at Claire as she bends down to pick the magazine up.

"Sorry," Claire says, gripping her purse with all her strength. The nurse who called her name has her eyes on a clipboard, flipping through it with a harried look. "I'm Claire Davis?"

"Dr. Martin is running late today. He appreciates your patience, but it's going to be a while longer," the nurse says. Her smile is kind, but tired.

"Oh," Claire says. The bubble of dread in her chest doesn't deflate—it only grows bigger. "Of course. No problem at all."

The blue plastic chair creaks as Claire sits back down. The woman to her left opens her magazine again, muttering disapproving words under her breath.

Claire tangles her fingers in her pearl necklace, tapping it against her front teeth. It helps to quell the restlessness, the constant *tap tap tap tap* matching the frantic energy in her body, but soon the woman to Claire's left clears her throat pointedly, looking at the source of the tapping with a disapproving frown.

Claire quickly sets her hands in her lap.

The woman goes back to her magazine. Bereft of anything else to fidget with, Claire grabs a magazine of her own. *VOGUE*, the cover proudly proclaims. *American Fashion Issue.*

Claire gnaws on her lower lip. Her husband doesn't approve of having fashion magazines in the house. His mother makes most of Claire's clothes to spare him the cost of dress shopping, so there's no need for Vogue.

But Pete isn't here right now.

The woman on the cover of the magazine is beautiful. She's a blonde bombshell, with her hair styled long and straight to frame her face and a chic neck-scarf under a stylish jacket. She's sophisticated. Modern. She's everything Claire isn't, really. Claire's hair is a mousy brown, and a bit unruly—by the end of any given day, curly strands of it have usually escaped from whatever style she's wrestled it into. She's too tall for her own good, leaning towards gangly and thin, never quite fitting properly into her dresses. Sometimes she thinks it's a miracle that she managed to get a husband at all.

Claire turns to the first page. *Beauty That Works For You!*

New hairstyles. New makeup trends. Everything up and coming for the modern woman at the turn of the decade. Claire flips page after page, taking in woman after beautiful woman showing off clothes that look terribly uncomfortable. Claire can't imagine herself wearing them—how ludicrous would she look doing dishes in a draping black cape over wool pants? Planting tulips in the garden, caked with dirt, while sporting that colorful and expensive floral pantsuit? She can practically hear what Pete's opinion would be: *Too revealing. Too tight. Pants are for floozies. Hippie clothes.*

The next set of pages advertises something called the Mark Eden Developer—guaranteed to increase your bust in eight weeks or less. Claire scoffs as she flips the page over. As much as Pete would probably love for her small bust to grow, she doesn't have the time for that kind of silliness. Next is a two-page spread where a model shows off what she can only assume is some kind of fancy lingerie. It's a mess of tiny straps, hardly any actual fabric at all to cover her, and Claire has no earthly idea how the woman got into the thing in the first place. She tilts her head, twisting the magazine back and forth to puzzle it out. Is there some kind of mechanism at the back, or did she somehow maneuver her legs through the labyrinth? And how on earth could the woman have gotten *out* of it?

Claire is holding the magazine fully upside down when she hears her name again.

"Mrs. Davis? If you'll follow me?"

Claire almost rips the magazine in two. She fumbles it, catching it with a bent cover, and the woman beside her tuts disapprovingly again. Claire swallows down the urge to tell her to mind her own business. No need to cause even more of a scene.

The transfer to the doctor's small private office is just an opportunity for more waiting. Claire sits gingerly in the second plastic chair, and lets her gaze wander over more posters on the walls. The one that catches her eye features cartoon renditions of various fruits and vegetables, dancing around an energetic-looking couple.

Eating Right Keeps You Swingin'!

It's funny to think about little cartoon apples and carrots swapping spouses, having wild nights with the local cucumber or bunch of grapes. In that case, would a salad classify as some kind of key party?

Claire snorts. If only Pete knew that healthy eating would lead to *that*, he'd never eat fresh produce again. If any couples in their suburb seem to be engaging in the *swinging* trend, Pete insists on not inviting them to the neighborhood barbecues anymore.

Claire nearly jumps out of her skin when Dr. Martin strolls in, stopping only to put out his cigarette and wash his hands.

"Well now, Mrs. Davis," he says, sitting heavily and flipping through Claire's chart with his damp hands, "bit early for your checkup, isn't it?"

Claire clears her throat. It's now or never.

"Yes. But there's something I wanted to ask you about," she says. Her heart is starting to pound, and not because of the startle. The room smells like antiseptic and cigarette smoke and Dr. Martin's cologne. Her fingers are so tight around the strap of her handbag that she's sure she's going to rip the darn thing off in a minute.

"Oh?" he says, over the noise of his rolling chair. He approaches with a tongue depressor. "Say *ahh*."

Claire does as she's told. The doctor examines her mouth, makes a small noise of satisfaction, and scribbles something on her chart.

"Yes. It's about..." Claire swallows hard past the dry wooden taste, watching his messy scrawl across the paper. "You know that Pete and I have been trying for a baby for some time."

"Ah, yes." Dr. Martin slides across the room on his chair again, grabbing the blood pressure cuff. "No success on that front yet?"

"No. No, and..." Claire takes a breath. She's edging around the truth, now, and it eats away at her stomach. "I thought—*we* thought, as it's been so long, I might be getting a bit too old to be carrying children. Don't you think?"

"Twenty-eight? A bit far along, but not unheard of," Dr. Martin says. He fastens the cuff, pumping it up quickly.

Claire can taste her heartbeat. It races at the tips of her tingling fingers. This is the moment of truth. Her voice feels thin and uneven, but she forces the words out. "I'm turning twenty-nine this year. I read in the Ladies' Home Journal that fertility goes down after thirty. There can be birth complications. Issues with the mother's health. I thought, just to be safe... that perhaps it's time we stopped trying?"

"Stopped trying?" Dr. Martin repeats distractedly, squinting down at the dial.

Claire bites hard at her lip as the pressure on her arm increases. The words tangle on her tongue, tumbling out fast and nervous. "I hoped you could talk to Pete about it. Tell him that childbirth gets more dangerous the older the mother is? He'd listen to you."

Dr. Martin's moustache twitches. He leans back in his chair as he unfastens the cuff, his thick brows knitting into a frown. "I wouldn't take medical advice from some silly women's magazine, Mrs. Davis. It might be more difficult after thirty, but it's no reason to stop trying, is it? If you're struggling to conceive, I'd rather send you to a specialist who can sort out what's going on."

"No!" Claire interrupts. She shouts it, in fact, so abruptly that Dr. Martin startles and almost drops the cuff. Claire clears her throat, straightening her posture into something more demure. "Sorry, I just don't think that's necessary. Please."

If some specialist figures out what's wrong with her, what's keeping her from conceiving, this period of luck will come to an end. That's the last thing Claire wants.

Claire Davis has a good life. She has a nice house, and a husband who provides. She spends her days keeping their things clean and making sure dinner is on the table when Pete gets home. She should have absolutely no complaints, least of all that her husband wants children. She should be thrilled at the state of her life. Blissfully happy.

She should *not* be terrified by the very prospect of a potential pregnancy.

"You've got plenty of time to start a family," Dr. Martin says. There's a hint of reproach in his voice that makes Claire squirm. She can only hope that he puts it up to the cold stethoscope being pressed to her chest. "But perhaps you do need a bit of help. I'll talk to Peter about a specialist referral when he comes in for his physical."

"Oh, I don't want to wait that long," Claire says. She clenches her fingernails into the palm of her hand until the dull pain stops her breakfast from threatening to reappear. She's been trying to curb the habit, but it's just about the only thing that soothes the chaos in her mind. The light scabs there only just healed after Pete forgot their anniversary last week, and now she's threatening to re-open them. "I think I'd rather talk to him about it myself, if it's all the same to you."

She'll do nothing of the sort, of course. Pete doesn't even know that she's here today, let alone what she's asking for. He's wanted a family since they were going steady in high school. They've been trying since the day of their wedding, but with each passing year Claire's feeling on the subject of children has shifted from mild discomfort to outright dread. Every month she gets her usual cycle is a relief, even though Pete's disappointment always follows swiftly.

If Pete knew she had asked this? If he knew she wasn't only failing him as a wife, but was actively looking to stop trying?

Dr. Martin takes the stethoscope out of his ears, making another note on her chart. "You do that, then. As for your habits, are you eating well?"

"Good and healthy," Claire says.

"Getting a bit of exercise?" Dr. Martin says, making an x on his sheet. "And adequate sleep?"

"I think so."

Dr. Martin scribbles some more. Claire wishes she could see what he's writing, but his penmanship is indecipherable from this distance. Instead, her attention is drawn to his necktie. It's a pale blue, and there's a stain just below the knot. It's bright yellow, like maybe he spilled mustard on it during his lunch, and the more Claire stares at it, the more it seems to resemble the state of Massachusetts. It even has a few little splotches underneath that could be the islands off Cape Cod.

Mustard-chusetts. All it needs is a tiny Dijon Mayflower, sailing across the ocean of Dr. Martin's tie.

Claire chuckles under her breath. When she finally looks back up at Dr. Martin, he's frowning, and Claire realizes he's been trying to say something to her. There's a small piece of paper in his hand, which he's trying to hand over.

"Sorry," Claire says, straightening her posture and averting her eyes from the distracting stain. "Could you repeat that?"

"I was saying, I think you might be struggling with some anxiety. These will help," he says. "Take one with each meal."

Claire takes the paper; scrawled across it in messy writing is a long and complicated word. *Chlordiazepoxide*.

"Are you sure these are necessary?" Claire asks. She's not sure what she's being prescribed, exactly, and even when it's coming from a doctor, she doesn't like the idea of taking something blindly.

Dr. Martin waves her off. "It's easier to conceive when you're relaxed. Malaise can throw off the body's rhythms."

"Then maybe it's Pete who needs the pills. He's got no rhythm at all," she says, chuckling. "Two left feet."

The doctor doesn't laugh. He frowns deeply, and reaches for his prescription pad again. "Are you sure you're sleeping enough? Maybe I should prescribe you something for that."

"No, that really isn't—I'm sorry," Claire says. Another nervous laugh bubbles up from her chest. "Just a bad joke."

Thankfully, Dr. Martin puts the pad down, though he's still frowning. "Right. Well then, besides a bit of a rapid heartbeat, you're in good health, Mrs. Davis. We'll see you again soon, and you can tell me how the medication is working."

He stands, opening the door for her, and Claire hops down from the examination table feeling duly chastened.

The walk home is a long one. The doctor's office is further into town than she usually goes, and it took her almost an hour to get here. She has no intention of going to the pharmacy—the prescription is crumpled in the bottom of her purse and she plans on it staying there, but she does have to stop at the grocer for her weekly shop before heading back to their little suburb of Acacia Circle.

Her feet don't take her straight to the store, though. She meanders through the park instead. It's a perfect early spring day, and women are out and about. They socialize with friends, push prams, and lay out picnics for their young families. As always, Claire feels no desire to be among them, caring for her own future children. Observing is enough. More than enough, in fact—it's a reminder of Claire's brokenness.

It's not only Pete that she's not doing right by, in hesitating over motherhood. It's also her own mother, who has always wanted grandbabies and is cursed to have only one child who could give them to her. Even though she lives in Florida now, thriving in her second marriage after Claire's father passed, she still asks about the status of Claire's womb every time she phones up.

Once upon a time, Claire might have been inclined to stop and sketch on a day like today. Maybe capturing these idyllic little family outings could magically make her want what they have. But it's been a long time since she had a moment to draw in the park, the way she did when she was a teenager. She doesn't have the time for that kind of frivolity anymore. She has a house that needs keeping.

So, Claire keeps walking. She finds her way to her usual grocer, pushing her squeaky cart aisle by aisle and grabbing things by memory. She hardly ever needs to write a list anymore—Pete is a creature of habit. He leaves the same amount of cash for groceries every week, and Claire has the necessities down to an art. It's so second-nature that Claire often ends up lost in thought until she hits the checkout.

A bag of frozen carrots. Two packs of bacon. There are two toddlers wrestling in a cart in the middle of the aisle, while their tired-looking mother is distracted by a sale on frozen TV dinners. They remind Claire of Tom and Jerry—one slightly larger than the other, bonking his sister insistently on the head with a box of Cream of Wheat while she gnaws on his arm. Being an only child, Claire has always wondered what having a sibling might be like, but passing their cart makes her reconsider. A few lonely days in childhood are probably better than being smacked about the head.

A carton of eggs. A quart of milk. There's a display of Ovaltine set beside the milk refrigerators, and Claire picks up a box out of pure nostalgia—she used to love the stuff, until she got too old for it. Pete probably wouldn't notice if she bought some. He never checks the cupboards. After a moment of consideration, Claire sets it in her cart.

Three cans of mushroom soup, and one of peas. Claire ducks around a woman with a cigarette in her hand, and the smoke makes greyish swirling patterns as it rises towards the ceiling. Claire tries not to wrinkle her nose as she grabs the cans. She's always been glad she never started smoking. The smell of it is unbearable. Next is a box of puffed rice...

As Claire rounds the corner into the cereal aisle, her mental list skids to a halt.

There's someone in her way.

This shouldn't be such an obstacle. Claire could easily scoot past like she has in every other aisle, but this time her feet seem to have rooted themselves to the linoleum. The woman is unlike any person Claire has ever seen in real life, and she finds she's unable to do much besides stare.

The woman is fairly young, probably around Claire's age, and arresting to look at. She's much shorter than Claire, not helped by the fact that she's in flat-soled sandals; Claire can see painted toenails, a deep navy blue, which shouldn't be an interesting fact but somehow seems fascinating. Her legs are also bare, no stockings in sight, all the way up to the knee-length hem of her black slip dress. A leather belt cinches it to her waist, and the long sleeves drape a bit as the woman stretches up to reach futilely for a box of Sugar Crisp tucked away on the top shelf.

Her face, when she turns towards Claire, is entirely unfamiliar. Sharp features, highlighted with the kind of hip makeup that Claire only sees in magazines. An aquiline nose with a strong, angular bridge. Dark olive skin, dramatic almond-shaped eyes, and black hair hanging loose and straight around her shoulders. This woman is glamorous. She looks carefree and stylish. European, maybe? It's a struggle to guess at where she might be from.

Claire can't stop looking at her. She looks like she belongs on a beach somewhere. She looks like a catalog model, like those ladies in Vogue Magazine. No…even better. The women in Vogue don't have such a perfect curve to their waist. They don't have that kind of generous bustline. They don't have the same subtle smile, or those warm brown eyes.

Warm brown eyes which are staring directly at Claire.

"Sorry. Do you need me to move?" the woman says.

Claire's mouth opens and closes once or twice before she finally remembers her manners. She springs into action, scooting her cart to the side of the narrow aisle.

"Oh no, I can fit. See?" Claire gestures down at her cart, smiling widely. She feels silly when the woman only nods, the corner of her full lips quirking. The almost-grin makes Claire's smile feel all the more forced. Claire is sure, somehow, that this woman's real smile would be dazzling. She can imagine how she might draw it.

The woman goes back to her task, stepping up onto the bottom shelf to boost herself, but she only succeeds in knocking the box backwards and further out of reach.

"Do you need some help?" Claire says tentatively.

The woman hops down from the shelf, flicking her shiny hair out of her face with a frustrated sigh and turning to Claire. "Help?"

Claire points up to the tipped-over box. It's well within her own reach. "I could get that for you?"

The woman's expression clears. She looks surprised, but she moves aside, nodding. "Oh. That'd be swell, actually. Thank you."

Claire abandons her cart, stepping closer to the woman. The top of her head barely comes past Claire's chin. She would usually expect to smell someone's perfume, standing this close, but the woman doesn't seem to be wearing anything too strong—just a light herbal scent. Shampoo, maybe?

Claire plucks the box easily from its place, handing it to the woman with a tentative smile. "Here."

"This is what I get for not wearing heels today, right?" the woman says, dropping the box into the basket sitting on the floor near her feet. It lands haphazardly next to some milk and a loaf of bread. Her voice is low and a little throaty, but her accent sounds local, not European. "I wish I had your height."

"No, you don't. Trust me," Claire says, with a self-conscious chuckle. "Try being the only girl in the back row of every school photo. There's no blending in when you're taller than most of the boys."

"Why would you want to blend in?"

"I..." Claire says. Her words trail off as she actually absorbs the question. She can't say she's ever been asked such a thing before, let alone in the middle of the cereal aisle, and she's not sure how to respond. It feels as if it should be obvious.

Blending in is just what one does, isn't it? Claire used to stick out like a sore thumb as a child. Her parents wanted a simple, sweet little daughter, and instead got a gangly daydreamer of a child who had to be pushed into the appropriate ladylike behavior. Even now, over ten years into marriage and long past her tomboy days, Claire still stumbles through the everyday steps that every other housewife in the country seems to dance through. She never says the right things, never wears the right clothes. She never quite fits.

The woman is still looking at her like she expects an answer.

"Every painting needs a background?" Claire blurts.

The woman's expression changes. Claire wishes she could read it, but she truly has no idea what might be going through that lovely head. The woman's dark eyes brush over Claire from head to toe, and all at once she wishes she had kept her mouth shut. And maybe worn a nicer dress. Next to this woman, Claire might as well be a lanky teen dressed in a paper bag. She almost wants to move behind her cart again just to have some semblance of cover.

Before she can follow that impulse, the woman smiles.

Claire was right. It's absolutely stunning. It changes her whole face from something uncannily beautiful, like some marble statue behind glass at a museum, to something that feels *real*. Her eyes crinkle at the corners. One of her canine teeth is very pointed, almost sharp, while the other is slightly shorter, like it's been sanded down by tooth grinding. It lends a slight crookedness to her grin that only makes her more interesting.

It's a marvelous smile. Claire is tempted to try to commit it to paper. It's more than a passing thought, this time—it's an urge. She can feel the weight of the pencil in her hand, and the wrist movements it would take to draw the sharp line of her jaw. It's like stretching a long-neglected muscle.

Claire has no idea what she did to earn that smile, but it's sunshine breaking through clouds.

"My advice?" the woman says, leaning close. Her smile is conspiratorial now. "Don't bother with the background. Some people belong at the front."

Claire blinks silently while the woman gathers her basket, hanging it over her arm.

"Thank you for your help," the woman says. She slips past Claire, headed towards the checkout, while Claire is still rooted to the spot.

"You're very welcome," she says faintly to an empty aisle.

Chapter 2

The rest of the shopping takes longer than usual. Claire forgets things she normally wouldn't, having to double back once or even twice to each aisle as *'Don't bother with the background'* echoes in her mind. She fumbles her groceries into paper bags at the checkout, and, as the cashier takes her cash, all Claire can think is *'Some people belong at the front'*. By the time she makes it all the way home, it's almost noon.

She's lost in thought and midway through unloading the groceries when the kitchen phone rings.

"Davis residence," Claire says distractedly, tucking the receiver against her ear as she stacks cans into the cupboard.

"Hi, honey," Pete says across the crackling phone line.

Claire's hand stops mid-air, a can of peas clutched in her fingers. Her husband calling from the office is quite out of the ordinary. "Pete? Is everything all right?"

"Just wanted to warn you I'm going to be home a little late tonight. We've got a big sale coming up, and they want a presentation at six. Expect me at seven-thirty."

"Oh. All right," Claire says, mentally adjusting her cooking schedule. "Is that all?"

"And Mom wants to come over for dinner tonight, so I'd like you to make something nice," Pete continues, crushing Claire's shifting plans into dust with just a sentence. "She'll be by around the same time."

Claire's stomach drops, and the can of peas along with it. It almost hits her foot, and she twists and dances out of the way as it rolls across the floor, gripping the phone tightly. "Your mother is coming? You didn't tell me that this morning. And your father, too?"

"Of course."

"I didn't plan for that," Claire says. She picks the dented can up, already running through a mental checklist of the ingredients in her cupboards. She has nothing suitable for a dinner party for four, especially to the standards of Rita Davis. "I already did the shopping, and I don't have any budget left."

"I'm sure you'll whip something up," Pete says easily. "You always do."

"Does she like pea soup?" Claire says, growing desperate now. With some fresh bread, it could be a nice last-minute supper.

"You're not making soup," Pete says. There are voices in the background of the call. "We don't want to drink our dinner. I have to go, honey. I'll see you tonight."

Claire digs her fingernails into the soft skin of her palm again, finding the same scabbed grooves from earlier in the day. The pain grounds her. She swallows down the frustration, and nods.

"Yes, dear."

The phone cord is stretched across the kitchen, and in her tizzy Claire has apparently gotten herself tangled in it. For a few moments after Pete hangs up, Claire simply stands in the jumble she's made.

There's no chance that she's going to get something on the table that Rita won't turn up her nose at. If she had more than eight cents left in her budget she could walk to the store again and get something up to her mother-in-law's standards, but that wouldn't leave her much time to cook, and the pennies sitting on the countertop won't get her far. She never should have gotten the Ovaltine, or dallied in the park.

After quietly untangling herself, Claire puts a record in the player. She turns the volume up enough to be heard in the kitchen, and she turns the faucet to get a start on the dishes left over from breakfast. While the sink fills, she leans forward onto the countertop, letting her breath out slowly until her lungs start to burn.

Rather than cheering her up, the upbeat, familiar pop song playing from the den grinds against her nerves. She wonders, in some idle part of her brain, how long she could actually go without air. A minute? Two? How long before the world goes black?

Three sharp knocks on the front door startle Claire enough to inhale again.

She waits a beat. She turns off the faucet, and tangles her fingers in her necklace—the pearls are cool and smooth under her worried touch. She doesn't feel up to entertaining this afternoon. Perhaps if she's quiet enough, they'll think she's out.

She stays stock-still, straining her ears, until the knocks sound again.

"Are you going to leave me waiting on the doorstep like a vacuum salesman?"

Claire relaxes somewhat.

Martha Robinson from across the street is maybe the only person in the neighborhood that Claire would consider a friend. She's always had a penchant for midday visits, but lately she's been coming over more frequently. Martha and her husband Walter announced her pregnancy a few months ago, and Pete has been effusive ever since about how wonderful it all is. How well Martha is doing as a wife. How perfect a mother she'll be.

There's no way that Martha doesn't know Claire is home. She knows everything in this neighborhood. Luckily for Claire, Martha could just be the solution to her dinner woes.

Claire re-affixes her smile, and heads to the door to let her in.

"Martha! Good afternoon," Claire says.

"We have new neighbors," Martha says before she's even crossed the threshold. She's on the stoop poised to come inside, framed by the yellow acacia tree that gives their street its name. It towers in the center of their cul-de-sac, taking up most of the grassy circle there. It's just starting to explode into its golden spring flowers.

The moment Claire moves aside, Martha heads straight to the kitchen table to make herself comfortable. Her hand sits perpetually over her belly, framing the baby bump under her dress—she's only barely started to show recently, and, ever since, she's made sure to emphasize it.

"New neighbors?" Claire says, setting the kettle on to boil for some tea. "Whereabouts?"

"Look outside."

A quick glance out the kitchen window reveals that Martha is right. There's a moving truck parked in the driveway of the bungalow next door. It must have pulled in right after Claire got home. The movers are just opening the back of the trailer.

She hadn't even been aware that the house was for sale. She certainly hasn't seen the original owner in some time, a quiet elderly widower that

Claire used to have pleasant conversations with at the mailbox. It's been under renovation through the winter, and Pete complained endlessly about the painters' trucks parking on the street all through Christmas. Claire hasn't seen a For Sale sign on the lawn, though.

"We should be hospitable. Go over and say hello," Claire says, craning her neck to get a better view. She can't see anyone in the front yard.

"I'm making cookies. I'll bring them by once they've settled. Who do you think is moving in?" Martha asks. Her foot bops gently in the air to the beat of the song from the den. "That house can't have been cheap. It's the only one on the street with a pool."

"Another retired couple?" Claire suggests.

Martha scoffs. "With three bedrooms? Too much space for that. I'll bet it's a family. Some richy-rich lawyer from the city and his pretty little wife. Everyone who's anyone is leaving San Francisco for the suburbs. I'll need to make sure Walter's eye doesn't wander."

Claire hums. She isn't concerned in the least about Pete's eye wandering.

"Neighbors aside, it's a stroke of luck that you came along today," Claire says, turning her attention away from the window as the kettle starts to whistle. "Pete's parents are coming for dinner tonight, and he's only just told me."

Martha makes a sympathetic noise. "Oh, you poor thing. And I'll bet you don't have anything ready?"

"You know how critical my mother-in-law is," Claire admits.

For Martha a change in dinner plans would only mean a quick jaunt to the store in her station wagon with her husband's checkbook in hand, so she's always been helpful when Claire needs to borrow something. She's even given Claire a lift to the big box store further into town a few times, on account of Claire not having a driver's license. Pete has always insisted she doesn't need one, but on a day like today it'd sure be nice.

"These husbands of ours—Walter did the same to me just last week. We just have to grin and bear it, don't we?" Martha says, standing up and abandoning her untouched tea. "Come on, you'll shop in my pantry. I've got enough to feed an army."

"You're a peach," Claire says, breathing a sigh of relief. "What would I do without your help?"

"Struggle endlessly, I'm sure," Martha says, with a light laugh.

It's meant as a silly joke, of course, but Claire can't help but feel the sting of truth in it. She really would struggle without Martha. Pete's expectations are high. They should be, of course, as the breadwinner of the household, but Martha's help is sometimes the only reason Claire can meet them.

Martha has one of the nicest houses on the block, and a happy husband. She's younger than Claire by four years, though Walter is a bit older than Pete. She has a lovely figure, where Claire has always been long-limbed and thin with no curves to speak of. Martha's red hair is always in a tidy beehive. If there were a class somewhere on how to be the ideal wife, Claire would be the cautionary tale; Martha would be the exemplar.

As she follows Martha across the street, Claire's mind drifts again to the grocery store.

Why would you want to blend in?

An easy thing to say, coming from someone as pretty as that cereal-aisle woman. Standing out has never gone well for Claire. Standing out meant scoldings, and judgement. It meant rocking the boat for no reason. Ordinary people aren't destined for the spotlight. Martha, maybe, with her effortless perfection, or someone like that glamorous woman from the store.

Claire needs to keep her head down.

※

A chicken is in the oven and the table is set by the time Rita arrives. The house is perfumed with cleaning products, Claire's hair and makeup have been fixed after her stressful and sweaty afternoon, and she's wearing the newest dress Rita sewed for her a few months ago when the doorbell rings.

"You must have lost weight again," Rita says, before Claire can even get out a greeting. She steps past Claire and into the foyer, handing over her coat and plucking at the places where the fabric of Claire's dress is loose over her chest. "I tailored this perfectly, and now it's hanging off you, dear. Send it over later this week and I'll make some alterations."

Claire frowns. Rita says this kind of thing often, but Claire has been the exact same size for the last ten years. Rita's dresses just never quite fit.

It's as if she makes them for curves that she's hoping Claire will magically grow, and then clucks with disappointment when they don't appear.

"Thank you, Rita," Claire says, stifling a sigh. "Pete should be home any minute, and dinner will be ready in a jiffy. Why don't you make yourselves comfortable in the den?"

"What's for supper?" Pete's father says, following Rita to the den while Claire hangs their coats. He hardly looks Claire in the eye.

"Something substantial? I hope you're not feeding my son some kind of rabbit food," Rita says. While Pete's father sits heavily on the couch, Rita doesn't join him—she walks towards the nearest shelf, swiping her finger across it.

Claire lets out a small breath of relief when the finger comes away without a speck of dust.

"Only if rabbits eat roast chicken," Claire says.

Pete's father is already absorbed by the television and pays her joke no mind, but Rita's lips purse.

"Make sure you eat plenty," Rita says. "If you're going to be having my grandchildren, you're going to need some more meat on your bones. We make healthy babies in this family."

Claire grits her teeth. After this morning's appointment, the very mention of grandchildren makes her stomach roil.

It's not that Rita is viciously unkind, exactly, but she's never been warm with Claire. Rita is capable of it—she dotes on her existing grandchildren, and she's more affectionate with her four sons than Claire's mother ever was with her only daughter. But there's always been a layer of ice between Rita and each of her sons' wives. Claire has always suspected that she resents the women who took her boys away.

"I should run and check on dinner," Claire says. "If you'll excuse me for just a tick?"

She ducks out of the room before anyone can protest. Her hope that Pete might be home before Rita arrived is dashed, but she can at least retreat to the safe haven of the kitchen until he gets here. The blast of hot air against her face when she opens the oven door to peek at the chicken makes her wince, but she stays there for a few extra moments until her skin starts to tingle.

For once, the sound of Pete's car pulling into the driveway is a relief.

Dinner is a strain on Claire's patience. Rita comments on the cooking—too much salt, and she prefers corn to peas. She points out a stain on the tablecloth. Towards the end of the meal the spotlight is taken off Claire when Pete announces his recent promotion at work, but by the time the dishes are done Rita has already insisted on taking Claire's measurements for the hundredth time and bringing the dress home to fix.

The dark and quiet of the bedroom is a balm once the company has gone home and Pete has fallen asleep. Claire goes through her usual quiet routine, brushing her frazzled hair out of its updo and removing her makeup. Every piece of jewelry has its place on her vanity, and the orderliness of it calms her.

Lost in thought, Claire glances out the window at the neighboring yard.

She's gotten used to it being dark, but tonight the pool lights are on. There's lawn furniture out—two reclining chairs, and a table with an umbrella. The windows are lit up. Occasionally a dark silhouette passes by the sheer curtains, but Claire can't make out any details.

Tomorrow, Claire should go meet the new neighbors.

Chapter 3

"Honey! Where's my good tie?"

Claire flips Pete's eggs, turning the burner off and reaching into the oven for the bacon. "It's on the hanger behind your suit jackets, dear. Right next to your other ties."

"Don't be smart," Pete calls down the stairs. "Why aren't they in the drawer?"

"I've started hanging them, remember? To stop them wrinkling?"

"I want you to put them back," Pete says, his footsteps thundering down the stairs. "I liked them where they were."

Claire sets out the Tuesday morning paper next to Pete's bacon and eggs, pressing her usual quick peck to his cheek as he sits down to eat with his good tie now fastened. He smells strongly of aftershave and hair oil, as always.

"Protests again," he says, putting on his glasses to gesture at the newspaper headline. "At the college, this time. Going to be more of that going into the '70s. Hippies and fruits. Soon it'll be draft-dodgers."

"Nobody wants to be drafted," Claire says.

"Then they should be signing up, so we don't need the draft in the first place," Pete says. "Serving their country, instead of running to Canada with their tails between their legs."

Rather than speaking the first thought that comes to mind—*I don't see your enlistment papers in the mail*—Claire presses her lips together and hums wordlessly. Pete often talks this way, and Claire knows he just needs a wall to bounce against. Whether she agrees or not, he'd never expect her to have an opinion on the matter.

"Bunch of degenerates. This is why we don't live in the city. Don't want to be raising kids in an environment like that," Pete says.

Claire's stomach lurches. She almost pours coffee all over Pete's lap but catches herself just in time.

He doesn't even notice. He just flips to the sports section, snorting loudly. "Look at this—at this rate, the Mets are going to the top of the league again this year. Someone's got to give them a run for their money."

"Quite right," Claire says quietly, refilling Pete's coffee cup with a steadier hand.

By 8:15 Pete has bustled out the door with his briefcase and lunch bag, and Claire's shoulders relax as his noisy black Cadillac trundles out of Acacia Circle. She never feels quite settled into the day until he's off to work.

First on Claire's to-do list today is to make a welcome gift for the new neighbors. The leftover chicken from last night's dinner makes a perfect quick and easy casserole, and while it's baking and cooling Claire fixes herself a bowl of shredded wheat and finishes up the dishes. Once she finds herself with a few minutes to spare between dusting and ironing, she puts on her nicest dress and picks her way between the lawns with the casserole in hand.

It's a lovely day to be outside. The sun is shining in a vivid blue sky, warm without being too hot yet. The honey-sweet smell of acacia is in the air. The birds that nest in the tree are singing, fluttering around each other in a state of spring twitterpation. With most of the husbands in the neighborhood off at work, the birdsong isn't interrupted by the sputtering of lawn mowers at this time of day.

It looks like Martha might be right about the richy-rich theory, at first glance. The car that Claire passes in the driveway is a Mustang, a powder-blue convertible with beige leather seats. To have a sports car with no backseats could mean that the new couple doesn't have children, or that the lady of the house doesn't drive, like Claire. Either way, the idea of having a kindred spirit in the neighborhood is a nice one. The Mustang is shined up like a new penny inside and out. The man who drives it must take a lot of pride in keeping it nice.

There's loud music coming from an open kitchen window when Claire climbs the three steps up to the bungalow's porch, something mellow and haunting with a female singer. It's completely unfamiliar, but intriguing.

Claire adjusts her tight grip on the casserole dish as she knocks soundly on the door. They're a double set, wood with clouded glass inserts that obscure the movement inside.

The music stops.

The act of bringing a welcome gift should be an innocuous one. It's something Claire has done dozens of times for families moving into their suburb over the years they've lived here. A slight deviation to her daily routine, but not an unfamiliar one.

This feels different, somehow. Claire's skin tingles with nervous anticipation. Like the very hair on her arms is standing up, waiting, until the doorknob turns.

The woman who answers is nothing like Claire expects. She doesn't have a child on her hip. She's fashionably dressed in a blue pinstriped minidress, with long, dark hair and olive skin and large brown eyes that look at Claire with some interest. She's young, and clearly not retired. She's also startlingly familiar.

The woman from the grocery store.

For a moment, Claire wonders if she's hallucinating. Is it possible that she's thought so often about the woman who gave her that strange advice that she's conjured her here, in the form of her new neighbor? It wouldn't be surprising, but no matter how many times Claire blinks, that lovely face doesn't waver.

"It's you!" Claire blurts.

The woman looks taken aback for only a moment. Her expression schools quickly into something more neutral, her eyebrows raising slightly—her brows are as thick and dark as her hair.

"So it is," the woman says. That same half-smile quirks at her lips, and Claire knows that her eyes haven't deceived her. It *is* the same woman.

But does she remember Claire at all? She could be humoring Claire by being polite, having no recollection of their short conversation at all.

"I mean—I'm sorry. I wasn't expecting—" Claire clears her throat, fumbling with the glass dish in her hands. She holds it out like it's a bomb about to go off. The aluminum foil on the top crinkles, and the woman looks at the gift curiously. "I just wanted to say hello, and welcome to Acacia Circle."

The woman's smile grows slowly at first, while Claire's heart races. As it turns into something more genuine, Claire gets another flash of those uneven canines.

"That's very nice of you. I wasn't expecting a welcoming committee," the woman says, taking the dish from Claire's hands. She sounds confident, in yet another contrast to Claire's nervous shrillness.

"No committee," Claire chirps, clasping her hands tightly in front of her. "Just me. I'm number sixty-three, right next door."

"What a small world. I just enjoyed a bowl of that cereal you helped me get," the woman says, setting the casserole down on a table just inside the door.

So she *does* remember Claire. It's gratifying to have, in even the smallest way, taken the woman's advice—she stood out just enough to be remembered. "I'm very glad."

"It's nice to properly meet you, Miss....?"

"Davis," Claire says quickly. "Mrs. Peter Davis."

The woman chuckles lightly. To Claire, it sounds like wind chimes. Soft and lovely. "I didn't ask for your husband's name."

"Right," Claire says. She shifts from foot to foot. "It's Claire. I'm Claire Davis."

The woman's smile lights up her eyes, this time. "It's lovely to meet you, Claire. I'm Jacqueline."

Jacqueline extends her hand between them, as if she wants to shake hands. Claire hasn't been offered many handshakes in her time—that's Pete's domain—but she accepts this one. Jacqueline's grip is firm and confident, like her voice. Her hand is dry where Claire's is clammy, and it's surprisingly large, matching the size of Claire's, rather than being engulfed by it.

Once again, Claire's fingers itch for a pencil. Hands are one of the toughest parts of the body to master drawing, and Jacqueline's would be a unique challenge. The taper of her long, slender fingers, with rounded knuckles. The tendons flexing as she shakes Claire's hand. The blunt shape of her short nails.

What is it about this woman that makes Claire want to pick up a sketchbook again?

"Where did you move from?" Claire says, fishing for anything that might prolong the conversation.

"San Francisco."

"Goodness," Claire says, with a nervous laugh. "My husband says it's more dangerous the closer you get to the city. You must be glad to have moved somewhere so safe."

Jacqueline hums noncommittally. She looks amused, likely because Claire is inexplicably still clutching her hand even though the reasonable timeframe for a handshake has ended.

She pulls her hand back quickly, holding her arms stiffly at her sides. Jacqueline is such a stark contrast to Claire—Claire in her outdated floral dress, with her pale skin and her freckles and her dull, frizzy hair. It's hard not to see the difference between them as a gulf.

The moment grows awkward. In a daze, Claire forges forward with the next conversation topic she can think of. "Is your husband at home? Maybe once you're all settled in, we could all get together. We could do fondue?"

Jacqueline's smile fades a little. Her shoulders straighten; she seems to get a bit taller. "I'm not married."

Claire blinks owlishly.

How has a woman as beautiful as Jacqueline not been snatched up? Claire has rarely known any woman, let alone a woman who looks to be her own age, to be unmarried unless she's a widow. Her mother waited four years to remarry after her father died, and that had been considered a bit too long. And besides that, Claire has no earthly idea how an unmarried woman of such ambiguous origin managed to buy a house in this neighborhood. Does she manage her own finances? Have her own *bank account*?

"Oh. Gosh, I'm sorry for assuming," Claire stammers. Claire can't hear any children in the house, either. Pete will be pleased by that.

Martha will have a field day.

Jacqueline's smile doesn't quite reach her eyes this time. They're a very dark shade of brown, like some kind of expensive and glossy wood. The iris and pupil are nearly indistinguishable from each other, split only by occasional flecks of dark amber. They look endless. "It's fine. I realize a single woman buying a house is a rarity."

It is a rarity. An impossibility, even, in this neighborhood. Jacqueline truly is a singular woman, the likes of whom Claire has never met before.

"Well. I'm sure you'd like me out of your hair, then," Claire says, forcing a smile on her face despite the disappointment. If Jacqueline had a husband, Claire would have a comfortable excuse to get to know her better. "Surely you have better things to do than spend your time with a boring old homemaker like me."

Jacqueline's shoulders relax a little, but a furrow forms between her thick brows. "Why would you think that?"

Claire blinks at her again. Much like their first meeting in the cereal aisle, every twist and turn in this conversation has been completely unexpected.

"Honestly, I'm not spending my time with anyone just yet," Jacqueline says after a pause, perhaps seeing Claire's confusion and taking pity. She leans against the doorframe, crossing her arms over her chest. "It's hard to get to know people in a new place."

The movement draws Claire's eyes down to Jacqueline's bust, but she wrenches them back up as quickly as she can before it becomes inappropriate. Something in her belly is fluttering madly.

"Maybe you should have a housewarming party," Claire says.

Jacqueline's head tilts curiously. "Do you think that's something people would actually come to?"

"Oh, we love a neighborhood barbecue. It'd be a great way to introduce yourself," Claire says. Her voice has gone up in pitch again, and she clears her throat quickly. "Just stuff an invite in every mailbox."

"Would you stop by?" Jacqueline says. "It'd be nice to see a friendly face."

"If you're sure you'd want me there," Claire says, probably a bit too eagerly.

"I wouldn't offer if I didn't mean it." Jacqueline smiles, tucking a bit of hair behind her ear. The movement reveals a small tattoo on the outward edge of her wrist—it looks like the branch of a tree, but Claire can't see the details without asking Jacqueline to push up her sleeve. She can't take her eyes away from it.

She's never seen a woman with a tattoo before. She's never really seen a tattoo up close at all. Dazedly, Claire wonders if the inked skin is a different texture than the rest. Would it feel raised under her fingers, or smooth? The thought is as fascinating as it is shocking.

"Then I'll be there," Claire says, dragging her eyes away from Jacqueline's wrist. She really should be asking Pete first—he'll be livid if he decides not to attend and she's already agreed—but she can't fathom saying no. The fluttering is coursing through her, driven by something panicky and strange, and her hands are starting to shake. "Should I bring anything?"

"Just yourself," Jacqueline says warmly.

"Sounds swell," Claire says, already backing away and down the front steps. She needs to get back home, before she makes any other promises she might not be able to keep. "Just swell. It was lovely to see you again, Jacqueline, and I'll—I'll see you at the party."

Claire darts back home as fast as she can without jogging. Only when she's in the safety of her own kitchen does she sink into a chair, putting a hand to her chest where her heart beats wildly under stiff fabric.

Strange.

She finds a handwritten invitation in her mailbox the next morning. Jacqueline's writing is slanted and just a bit messy, and Claire finds herself staring at it for much longer than it takes to read the short, scribbled note with the date and time.

Chapter 4

When Claire enters Jacqueline's house for the first time, on Pete's arm and dressed in her Sunday best, the party is different than she expected.

She's no stranger to neighborhood parties. Usually they're daytime gatherings, where the men conglomerate to drink beers and talk about grilling techniques while the women fuss with the potluck table and tend the children. They're over by sundown, and Claire always makes her famous potato salad. It's a formula she knows by heart.

As written on the invitation, Jacqueline's party is adults-only, and it's not a potluck. It's only now getting into full swing at half past eight. They've arrived over an hour late, as Pete had grumbled and dragged his feet about attending just as she suspected he would, and the atmosphere is strange. The lights are dim, the rock music is so loud that it seems to make the air vibrate, and the house is packed.

Jacqueline's house is what Claire might call *artsy*. The walls are white interspersed with grey brick, with blue carpets in the living room and eclectic, rounded furniture. It's decorated as if Jacqueline has transposed it right from the pages of an interior design magazine. Claire can only imagine what a pain it would all be to keep clean. She has a hard enough time with her own house, with its darker palette of reds and oranges and wood paneling.

It seems like the entire suburb is here, drinking and eating catered hors d'oeuvres. There are quite a few couples milling around whom Claire has only seen in passing, and even several that she doesn't recognize at all—Jacqueline really must have put an invite in every mailbox within a few blocks. Pete likes to stick mostly to the small group of families in their cul-de-sac. It's a warm night, and the unfamiliar people seem to have conglomerated in the backyard, splashing around in the pool and making a ruckus in various states of undress.

"This *Jacqueline* should be more careful with who she invites," Pete says darkly.

Claire *tsks*, tugging his arm as they wander into the common area. "Peter. She's just trying to get to know everyone."

From the living room, Claire has a better view of the pool through the sliding backdoor. Two people in the water are kissing in a way that Claire can only identify as 'sloppy'. The people around them seem unperturbed. In fact, a few are cheering them on.

Claire averts her eyes. Her face feels warm.

Jacqueline is nowhere to be found, but Pete quickly spots Martha and her husband Walter sitting stiffly on a large sectional couch in the conversation pit. They're usually the neighborhood hosts, as they have a large yard and the biggest grill, and they don't seem to be enjoying the new dynamic.

"Walt!" Pete shouts over the music. It's even louder here, near the record player.

Walter stands, grinning widely and giving Pete's hand a hearty shake. "Petey! Some party, huh? Martha and I really scratched our heads when we saw that it started at seven."

"Babysitters are making a killing tonight," Pete says. "Have you met this Jacqueline person yet? I'd like to give her a piece of my mind about the music."

Claire tries not to flinch. For some reason, Jacqueline's name said in Pete's voice with such distaste feels like a slap to the face.

"Not yet," Walter says. "We weren't sure we were going to come at all, but Martha wanted to see the inside of the house after all those damn renovations."

"It's not to my tastes," Martha says, one dainty hand pressed to her belly. "Very modern. And did you see the nonsense going on in the pool? She's invited the *swingers*."

Something hot and uncomfortable forms in Claire's belly. She clenches her hand, pressing her nails lightly into her palm—as usual, it eases the feeling.

"Claire doesn't need to hear about that," Pete says brusquely. "Why don't you two ladies grab us some drinks?"

Martha scurries off right away, and Claire follows her to the kitchen. It's just as crowded as the living room, with the countertops hosting several buckets of ice full of cans and bottles.

"What did you mean by that?" Claire says, sifting through a bucket to fish out a cold beer for Pete. "She invited the swingers?"

"Don't you see them?" Martha says, nodding towards the large window facing the pool where boisterous laughter and splashing are filtering in. "They put the whole neighborhood to shame, swapping spouses and-and doing *illicit substances*." She says those last two words in a hushed whisper that Claire has to lean in close to hear.

"I know what a swinger is, Martha," Claire says a bit snappishly, clutching the chilled can to her chest. "But you really think that's what they're doing? At Jacqueline's invitation?"

Martha makes a face. "Our hostess is from San Francisco, I hear. Urban people aren't like us. Those parties are nothing but drugs and debauchery."

Claire glances around. She doesn't see any drugs, just beers and cigarettes. "I don't think she's like that. She seemed too nice. She invited *everyone*, she didn't have any way of knowing who was who."

Martha heaves a little sigh, shaking her head. "I hope you're right. Hopefully she learns a lesson tonight in who to avoid."

Pete and Walter are deep in conversation about lawn care when they return with the drinks. Claire keeps an eye on the goings-on around them—the pool has gotten progressively rowdier, and she could swear that the pile of fabric on one of the deck chairs is a stack of bathing suits—but still no Jacqueline. Not that Claire is overly interested in her whereabouts. She's just wondering where the hostess is, at her own party.

When Claire excuses herself to use the bathroom, she's grateful that Pete is distracted enough by complaining about the party that he only nods briefly at her when she slips away.

It's much quieter in the hallway Claire ducks into. The house is a bungalow with a swinging door between the common space and the bedrooms, and the loud music and lights are less pervasive here.

She takes a deep, calming breath. There are five closed doors in this hallway, and she's not sure which is the restroom—she's just considering knocking on the nearest one when it spills open, and the object of her fascination stumbles out with someone else in tow.

Jacqueline looks just as stylish as she did when Claire met her. She's wearing a dress again, and again it's so unlike Claire's starched floral shirtwaist that it might as well be a different thing entirely— it's short and boxy, a navy blue number with little white sleeves and a hem that ends just above her knees. She's wearing shoes this time at least, bright yellow sneakers, with tall socks instead of nylons. One of the socks is pushed halfway down her calf.

Claire also recognizes the woman Jacqueline is with, surprisingly. Susan Wilson. She moved in a few streets over with her young husband about a year ago, and she occasionally attends the ladies' book club that Martha runs once a month. Her tiny dog yips every time Claire walks past on her way to the grocery store.

Claire notes with distant concern that she's fairly sure she saw Mr. Wilson heading to the pool.

Susan is giggling, twisting her auburn hair up into a bun, and Jacqueline has a light pink mark on the underside of her jaw. It feels as if Claire is intruding on something, but when Jacqueline's eyes fall on her, her face brightens considerably.

"Claire! You came," Jacqueline says loudly. The brilliant smile she trains on her sears itself into Claire's memory.

Susan snorts, and then starts to giggle as if Jacqueline has said something hysterically funny.

Jacqueline elbows her in the side. "Don't be crass."

Susan shrugs, still smiling, and she finishes with her hair and squeezes Jacqueline's arm before shouldering the door open as she heads back to the party. "Find me later, if you get bored."

The music gets loud, before muffling again when the door shuts behind her.

Claire can't quite parse their interaction, but Jacqueline and Susan must be getting close already. It makes that hot and uncomfortable thing in Claire's stomach expand even further.

That's what Claire gets for being late—Jaqueline is already making fast friends with other people.

"I'm sorry about her," Jacqueline says, watching Susan disappear through the swinging door with a strange expression. She rubs at her jaw, managing to swipe away whatever pink smudge was there. She's fidgeting with the fingers of her right hand, but she stops when she sees Claire looking.

Claire waves her off. "Oh, don't be silly. She seemed nice."

"That's one word for it." Jacqueline fiddles with her hair, now, which is loose and cascading over her shoulders. "You know, I wasn't sure if you were going to turn up."

"You weren't?"

"You practically ran away when I invited you."

Claire winces. "I'm sorry about that, I just—I remembered that I had a cake in the oven, and I didn't want it to overbake, you know? Pete hates dry cake."

It's a terrible excuse, and an outright lie. Thankfully Jacqueline takes it at face value. "Pete is your husband, right?"

Jacqueline steps towards the door to the living room, like she's expecting Claire to lead her to him for an introduction, but suddenly the idea of introducing her to Peter sounds like the worst idea in the world. With a sudden ferocity, Claire wants to keep Jacqueline to herself. Her own private acquaintance. One small thing in her life that Pete can't influence.

"No," Claire blurts. In a wild burst of panic, she reaches out to touch Jacqueline's arm before she gets to the door. Her forearm feels searing hot, in the moments before Claire snatches her hand back and clenches it into a fist.

Jacqueline frowns. She doesn't seem bothered by the inappropriate touch, but instead understandably puzzled. "No?"

"No, I mean—I mean, yes, he is my husband." Claire swallows hard, digging her nails in until her arm starts to shake. "I think he's busy."

Claire has no idea what kind of hysteria has gripped her. She feels manic, like she's completely untethered from what's appropriate—she only knows that she doesn't want to go back out to the party, and she wants Jacqueline to meet Pete even less.

Jacqueline merely nods, rubbing her arm where Claire touched it.

"Sure," Jacqueline says softly. "Do you want to go get some drinks instead?"

Claire gnaws on her lower lip, but she lets it go quickly before it ruins her lipstick. In truth she'd rather stay here, but she shouldn't be bossing the hostess around in her own house.

"You know what, it's a bit loud out there," Jacqueline says, glancing towards the door as if she can sense Claire's thoughts. Music and voices are audible through it and, distantly, a raucous shout, but Jacqueline doesn't seem bothered by it. "Not a great place to talk. Follow me?"

She leads Claire instead to one of the other doors at the end of the hallway, beyond which looks to be the beginnings of an office—there's a desk and chair, and a long table stacked high with cardboard boxes. It looks like Jacqueline threw a lot of her things in here to make room for the party.

Across the surface of the desk are scattered several expensive-looking cameras and film canisters, along with what looks like a disassembled tripod. The canisters are each labelled with a name and date. Claire picks one up, reading '*Jacqueline Callas—16 March, 1969*'. The day before Jacqueline moved in.

Jacqueline Callas. A lovely name, and perhaps a clue as to her origins—is it Spanish? Italian? Claire isn't worldly enough to guess. She files the information away, setting the canister down.

"Do you really know how to use all of this?" Claire says, hovering awkwardly until Jacqueline pulls out the desk chair and indicates she should use it.

"I should hope so. It pays the bills."

Claire sits, carefully arranging her skirt. "So you're a photographer? No wonder you look so fashionable all the time."

Jacqueline smiles. Since there are no other chairs in the room, she perches on the edge of the desk. She straightens out her socks, and then her feet swing back and forth; there's a dark freckle on the smooth skin in the middle of her left knee. "That's sweet of you to say."

"I don't know many women around here who work," Claire says. She tears her eyes away from that freckle. It's like a magnet for her eyes. "Or who can buy a house on their own."

"I was lucky. I paid in cash, and the family was looking to sell quickly to the highest bidder," Jacqueline says, with a wry smile. "It took ages to find a realtor who would even look twice at me. And photography is more like a hobby I sometimes get paid for. It hardly feels like a job sometimes."

Claire presses her sweaty hands into the starchy material of her skirt. Jacqueline is being perfectly polite, volunteering information and asking questions, but somehow that doesn't calm her nerves.

"I don't even have time for hobbies anymore. That's married life," Claire says with a quiet chuckle.

Jacqueline's smile melts into a look of mild concern. "Is it?"

"I mean, it takes so much time to do everything I need to do," Claire says hastily, suddenly aware of just how uninteresting she must sound. She worries at her pearls, lifting them to her mouth and tapping one against her teeth. Pete hates it when she chews on them—Jacqueline surely feels the same, and that thought makes Claire drop them again.

"Such as?"

"Clean, and cook, and—and take care of Pete. Mend clothes. Tend the garden."

Jacqueline's legs stop swinging. That furrow between her brows is back. "There must be something you like to do, beyond all that."

Claire's mind races. Everything that comes out of her mouth seems only to reiterate her own dullness, in contrast to Jacqueline. Jacqueline the photographer, the bohemian city dweller. Jacqueline the enigma. "I do enjoy gardening. And the ladies in the neighborhood sometimes do a book club?"

"That sounds fun," Jacqueline says. Her tone is polite, but it's clear she's not interested in a ladies' book club.

Claire swallows hard. She traces along the edge of a photo frame—it's face-down, so she can't see Jacqueline's work. She's desperately curious about it.

"I...like to draw," Claire says haltingly, fishing for the only thing she ever felt she was particularly good at. Art classes had been her favorite part of the day once upon a time, but by senior year Pete was taking up most of her free time. "And paint. At least, I used to. I won a drawing competition once, in school. Before Pete and I started dating."

Claire is grasping at straws, but Jacqueline's smile turns softer.

"Every painting needs a background," Jacqueline says warmly. "I should have guessed you were an artist."

Claire laughs. It's a horrible nervous braying thing. "Oh, gosh, I wouldn't call myself an artist. It's not like I was making a career out of it, like you. It was just a silly distraction."

"Did it make you happy?"

"Yes," Claire says, with hardly a thought. It *had* made her happy. She'd sit and sketch for hours, using it as an excuse to go for long walks in the park once her parents had deemed her too old to run around playing and scraping her knees. Her bedroom was full of watercolors, until one day it wasn't.

Jacqueline leans a little closer, like she's sharing a cheeky secret. "Then it wasn't silly."

Claire isn't sure what to say to that. Her hands are shaking again, for some reason. It seems to happen every time Jacqueline looks at her for too long with those beautiful, inscrutable eyes.

"I think I'd like to take you up on that drink," she says, casting her eyes downward. They fall on that darn freckle again. It's like a single drop of brown paint. Claire wants to smear it with a brush. Or with her finger, even.

Jacqueline is sliding off the desk and halfway to the door before Claire has shaken herself of that strange urge. That light, herbal scent washes over Claire as Jacqueline moves past her—it's definitely too soft to be perfume. "Sure. I'll be right back."

"Oh, you don't have to get it for me," Claire says, standing up so quickly that the chair rolls across the carpet.

"We can go together," Jacqueline says.

Reluctantly, Claire trails her back out to the living room. The noise of the party hits like a wall, and she grits her teeth against the onslaught of it as Jacqueline leads her towards the kitchen. Claire sticks close, hoping against hope that she can sneak through.

Just before the threshold, something catches her arm.

"*There* you are."

It's Pete, of course. His cheeks are red. Claire isn't sure if it's due to the beer, or the fact that the kissing in the pool seems to be a group activity, now. Just a glance is enough to make her own cheeks heat up.

"These people are embarrassing themselves," Pete says gruffly. "Let's go."

"But we only just got here," Claire protests.

"And now we're leaving."

"Where are Martha and Walter?" Claire asks, casting her eyes around. She doesn't see them anywhere in the living room.

"Home, where we should be. This party is a *zoo*."

Pete is cut off when Jacqueline appears at Claire's other elbow with a drink in each hand.

"Everything peachy over here?" Jacqueline hands one of the drinks to Claire, her eyes lingering on Pete's grip of Claire's upper arm.

"This is Jacqueline," Claire says quickly. She clutches the glass so hard that she worries it might shatter.

"So you're the one in charge of this madhouse," Pete says, dropping Claire's arm. He takes the drink from her, setting it down on an end table.

Jacqueline's eyes narrow. Though she's smiling, it doesn't quite look friendly. "You must be Pete."

Jacqueline holds out a hand to shake.

Pete stares down at it. He looks flummoxed; Jacqueline offering a handshake to Claire when they met was one thing, but Claire can hardly believe the brazenness of *this*. She's never once in her whole life seen a woman extend a handshake to a man, uninvited. Maybe in the city things are different, but here in Acacia Circle? And to *Pete*? He's the most traditionally-minded man Claire knows.

"Is this what parties are like wherever you're from?" Pete says, rather than accepting the shake. Claire gets the feeling he's referring to more than just her previous city of residence.

Jacqueline drops her hand, along with her smile. "Not at all. I'd actually say this is quite tame."

The pain in Claire's palm gets sharper than usual. When she glances down, opening her hand, her scabs have turned into four red grooves in the skin again. Two of her fingernails are tipped with crimson.

"Tame?" Pete says. His voice raises almost to the volume of the music. "This is a nice neighborhood you're disrupting, you know that?"

"Nice is in the eye of the beholder," Jacqueline says, never for a moment losing her confidence.

Pete is bristling like a porcupine, while Jacqueline seems unbothered. There's something of a battle of wills happening, and Claire is astonished to see that Jacqueline isn't standing down. It's Pete who finally cedes the silent impasse.

"It certainly is," he scoffs, putting a firm hand on Claire's back to guide her away. "Consider any of our future invites rejected. Come on, Claire."

Claire keeps her eyes on the floor as she follows Pete to the door. He's just opening it to storm through when she braves a quick turnaround.

Jacqueline is still standing in the wide arched doorway to the kitchen, drink in hand; she raises it to Claire.

Claire waves back. She wiggles her toes inside her sensible shoes, and clenches her fist tight as Pete pulls her out the door.

Pete doesn't give outright instructions not to see Jacqueline again. He does rant about the party for close to an hour after they get home as Claire applies an ointment to her tender palm, but she tunes a lot of it out. She catches words like *shameless* and *foreign* before he finally turns off his bedside lamp and goes to sleep.

And if he hasn't given outright instructions, Claire wouldn't be breaking them by visiting Jacqueline again. Would she?

Claire sits at her vanity by the window for longer than she should, watching the light and movement in Jacqueline's living room windows as the party continues without her.

Chapter 5

"Hey there, neighbor," Jacqueline says, obvious surprise turning to a smile as she opens her front door on Monday morning to find Claire on her doorstep holding a Tupperware full of freshly baked muffins. "I was wondering if I'd see you again. I got the idea your husband didn't like my party much."

Claire has been scouring her mind for days now for a way to atone for what happened at the housewarming party, and this seemed the most reasonable solution. Baked goods. A normal, neighborly thing to do. Pete had been so rude. Jacqueline didn't deserve it, no matter who came to her party.

Jacqueline herself is wearing pants today, a dark maroon velveteen fabric with a belt, and a black silk shirt. Once again, she's barefoot. She looks daring and naturally fashionable.

Claire smooths her hand over her pleated skirt, feeling just as frumpy as usual next to Jacqueline. "Yes, I wanted to apologize for that. Pete is—when he gets tired, you see, he—"

"I understand," Jacqueline interrupts smoothly, saving Claire from needing to stammer an excuse. She points to Claire's hands. "Are those for me?"

Claire had forgotten that she was holding the muffins. She thrusts them into Jacqueline's hands. "Yes! Blueberry bran. I hope they make up for our impolite exit."

"Sounds delicious," Jacqueline says, pulling up the corner of the lid to peek inside. "Do you spoil the whole neighborhood like this?"

Claire doesn't know how to answer that. The truth is that the first move-in casserole was customary, but Claire isn't usually prone to baking for the neighbors unless there's a potluck.

Thankfully Jacqueline lets the question lie. She moves aside after a moment, gesturing into the house. "Why don't you come in for a minute? I'll fix us that drink we missed out on."

Claire hesitates.

She should really be getting back home. She has laundry to fold, and dinner to get started. She'd been planning to give the bathroom a good scrub. The front flower beds are in a state, and she really needs to get them in order so she can start her spring planting.

But Jacqueline's house looks so inviting. It's just the two of them this time, no rowdy partygoers or irate husbands, and Claire so enjoyed their last brief conversation. Jacqueline is an enigma, and Claire has only caught glimpses of her over the last week through the kitchen window as Jacqueline gets into her car and jets off for the day. Claire wants to know more.

She steps inside, and Jacqueline closes the door behind them.

The house looks quite different when it's not littered with empty beer cans. Jacqueline has cleaned up so well that there's no indication there was a party here at all. The air smells warm and spiced, like a scented candle Claire can't identify.

"If you're looking to get your dish back, I'm afraid you'll be disappointed," Jacqueline says, leading Claire towards a breakfast nook in the corner of the kitchen. "I've been practically living off your casserole, and I haven't gotten around to washing it yet."

"Really? You liked it?" Claire says, twisting her fingers together.

Jacqueline breezes past the nook towards one of the cupboards. She seems to have made a lot of headway in unpacking—the shelf hosts a truly startling array of liquors next to the glasses. Taking up a large piece of counterspace is, staggeringly, a brand-new Amana microwave. Claire has seen commercials, but she's never seen one in person. She can't even begin to imagine how much it cost.

"It was delicious. Though I can't cook to save my life, so maybe my opinion counts for very little," Jacqueline says.

"I'm sure that isn't true," Claire says quickly. "You can just keep the dish if you'd like. I have three."

"Three?" Jacqueline remarks, leaning her hip against the counter. "You must make a lot of casseroles."

"Pete usually gets me kitchen things from the department store for Christmas. He doesn't know what I already have, so he just grabs something off the shelf," Claire says, chuckling lightly. "It's been casserole dishes the last three years in a row."

Jacqueline doesn't join in on the laughter. She looks at Claire with some concern, actually, with her hand suspended halfway to the cupboard.

Claire has joked about this same thing with Martha countless times. Walter isn't terribly observant either—Martha has a closet full of scarves she never intends on wearing after a decade of Christmases with him. Claire has never had a second thought about it before, and it makes her suddenly self-conscious.

"Right," Jacqueline says, shaking her head a little. Her expression clears. "What can I get you to drink? Coffee, tea, wine, beer? I have some liquor left from the party if you need a pick-me-up."

"Tea is fine," Claire says, smoothing her hair nervously. She went with a different look today, a knot at the base of her neck with the top slicked down with hairspray instead of her usual more voluminous coif. It's a bit more modern. Pete looked at her strangely this morning, but Claire had told him it was because she was going to be working on the garden. Foolishly, she hopes that Jacqueline will notice.

Jacqueline turns the stove knob underneath a shiny kettle. "Are you sure? I can put a nip of whiskey in it."

"I don't actually drink very much," Claire admits. "It makes me act senseless, and Pete—well, I don't want to embarrass him. He says I get too loud."

Jacqueline pauses again. Her brow furrows.

Claire has the wild, unsettling impulse to press her fingertip against the divot it creates in her forehead.

"There's nobody to embarrass here, Claire."

Claire's face feels hot, though she's not entirely sure why. Her stomach is in knots. A silence stretches out between them that makes her want to run for the door. Instead, she tangles her fingers in her pearls.

Jacqueline smiles softly. She grabs two mugs and a box of teabags, setting them on the table. "Tea it is."

"I'm sorry," Claire blurts, already wishing she hadn't said anything at all.

Jacqueline opens one drawer, and then another—in a third, she finally finds the spoon she's looking for, holding it up victoriously. "Sorry for what?"

The pearls roll under Claire's fingertips. She presses them hard against her breastbone. "I realize that I can be terribly awkward to talk to. Martha sometimes tells me that I say the oddest things."

The kettle is boiling—it must have been hot already. Jacqueline pours water into Claire's mug, and it slowly turns dark pink as the tea steeps. It must be some kind of herbal blend. "Who's Martha?"

"From across the road," Claire says, nodding in the direction of the house. She stirs some sugar into her mug. "Martha and Walter? They were at the party."

"Ah," Jacqueline says, just as Claire is blowing on the hot tea to take her first careful sip. It's a delicious and fruity blend. "The one with the stick up her ass."

Claire snorts into her mug, spraying tea across the table. She manages not to inhale it, but it spills over the sides of the cup as Jacqueline smiles again.

Claire probably shouldn't laugh. Martha is her friend, and she shouldn't be tickled by something so vulgar. But she can't help but react to the truth of it. Martha is very uptight at times, and her reaction to Jacqueline has been especially so.

"Sorry. If she's your friend, I shouldn't be so rude," Jacqueline says, though in contrast to her words she seems delighted. She passes Claire a handful of napkins. "She brought me cookies the other day, but I think I unsettled her a little."

"No, it's all right," Claire says, coughing a little. "I know what Martha is like unsettled. I can't imagine she was very welcoming."

Claire mops up her spilled tea, her lip caught between her teeth, focused entirely on making sure the surface of the table is clean, and when she's finished she's startled to see Jacqueline watching her with an intense expression.

"Do I have something on my face?" Claire says, reaching self-consciously for her purse and compact mirror.

"No, no. Your face is fine," Jacqueline says. She moves as if to put a hand over Claire's to stop her reaching, but she stops just short. Claire wishes she hadn't. "Sorry. I'm only thinking that—you know, you're very different, Claire."

Claire's stomach sinks. She thinks of her house, in all its dull normalcy. She looks down at her clothes—the plain blue pattern on her dress, her clunky brown shoes. She *is* very different from Jacqueline. Jacqueline is calm, and confident. Jacqueline is effortlessly stylish and appropriately feminine. She's everything Claire has never quite succeeded at being.

"Yes, I must seem dreary when you're used to living in San Francisco," Claire says, trying to sound light and airy. "I feel like a drab old lady next to you. You look like you walked out of Vogue Magazine."

"Me?" Jacqueline says, leaning forward towards Claire with a frown. "No that's not—I meant you're different from *Martha*."

Claire's brain stutters to a halt.

"Oh," Claire says blankly.

It's Jacqueline who now seems to scramble. "I'm sorry, that's not what I—it's in a good way. I met a lot of the people in this suburb at the party. And besides the partiers who took over my pool, they're all either…well, there's a certain—"

It's odd, seeing Jacqueline flustered. It calms Claire down a bit.

"They're all horribly boring?" Claire says. She's usually tight-lipped about her opinions, but it slips out of her, eager as she is to impress.

To her delight, Jacqueline laughs. It lights her whole face up, and she visibly relaxes as Claire gets a glimpse of her uneven canines. "Yes, actually. I was trying to be diplomatic, but you took the words right out of my mouth."

Making Jacqueline laugh, even for those few seconds, somehow becomes one of the proudest moments of Claire's life. She wants to do it *more*. She's hungry for Jacqueline's attention in a way she isn't used to.

"My husband likes to socialize with the neighbors, but he avoids the swinger types. And as for me…" Claire pauses. "Martha is my friend, but she can be…a bit controlling, at times. You should see her at book club. She never lets anyone else choose the books."

"I'm not surprised," Jacqueline says. The corner of her mouth quirks. "You know, you're the only person who's really been nice to me since I arrived."

"You seemed to be getting along just fine with Susan Wilson," Claire says. The words feel a bit too sharp, but Jacqueline only hums, tracing a circle around the rim of her mug.

"Susan's interest in me faded pretty quickly. I think most of the women in the neighborhood assume I'm here to steal their husbands."

"Well, you can have Pete," Claire says.

Her heart soars when Jacqueline laughs again. Can one translate a laugh onto paper? Is there some visual medium that can capture the way Jacqueline's makes her feel?

"See, you're funny," Jacqueline says. "You're quick. I wasn't expecting to find someone out here so good to talk to."

Claire is sure her face is glowing. Jacqueline's attention is a hot spotlight, and one Claire doesn't quite deserve—it doesn't make sense for such a lovely woman to think Claire is interesting, to look at her like she's a puzzle worth solving.

Claire can only hope that Jacqueline never discovers just how untrue that is.

"Oh, I don't know about that," Claire says, hiding her nerves in her mug. The tea is still so hot that it threatens to scald her tongue.

"I hope Pete appreciates you," Jacqueline continues. "How long have you been married?"

Claire picks at the string of the teabag until it splits into tiny strands. "Eleven years. He asked me to go steady in junior year, and he proposed right after graduation."

"High school sweethearts," Jacqueline says. "Sounds idyllic."

Now that Claire is saying it out loud to someone like this, it doesn't seem idyllic. Here sits Jacqueline, who lives on her own, who throws parties without a husband, who provides for herself and drives a Mustang, and Claire hardly leaves the house unless it's to walk to the supermarket or go to book club. She doesn't even have a learner's permit.

"It's not near as interesting as your life," Claire says, taking another overly large gulp of tea. "You must do a lot of travelling."

"My family is from Greece, but they all live here in the U.S. now," Jacqueline shrugs. "I've only been a few times."

"Oh, no, I meant that—I can't imagine there are too many job opportunities for photography around here," Claire corrects quickly. The tidbit about her background is new, and Claire tucks it away. She's never met anyone Greek before.

"Ah. Yes, I used to do more travelling. I'm trying to slow down." Jacqueline chuckles to herself, but there's no joy in this laugh—it's almost bitter. "Life became a bit of a whirlwind for a while. Now I only take gigs I can drive to."

"Is that why you moved here?"

Jacqueline hums noncommittally. "One of the reasons."

The subject changes swiftly after that. The conversation turns to easier things, and by the time Claire gets home she finds she needs to sprint through the chores she ignored during those two lovely hours just to get dinner on the table in time.

She doesn't tell Pete about her excursion.

Pete complains about work over his chicken Kiev, only stopping to tune into the evening news. Claire settles in to mend some socks while he talks over the anchor's coverage about NASA, but it's harder than usual to focus her attention. Her gaze keeps sliding from her stitches to the window, watching the way Jacqueline's pool lights cast blue-white ripples across the side of her house.

Chapter 6

Claire doesn't mean to snoop. She's not one of the neighborhood ladies that watches the movement of every family like a hawk, craning through her windows and over fences like Martha does. Claire prefers to keep to herself.

But Jacqueline's front door is so visible from the kitchen window, and Claire is only human.

Jacqueline backs her Mustang out of the driveway a few times in the following week with her long hair tucked under a driving kerchief, often with a passenger seat full of camera equipment. Claire never sees another car in the driveway, so no friends or family visiting—just Jacqueline.

Claire would like nothing more than to pop over for another visit herself, but she can only spare the time during the weekdays when Pete isn't home, and she has no idea if Jacqueline would welcome it. They had such a nice time together during their last brief visit, didn't they? Claire had thought it was nice, at least. The nicest afternoon she's had in ages.

But does Jacqueline feel the same?

She's mulling over this conundrum while throwing together some biscuits on a drizzly Friday when she scoops a measuring cup into the flour tin to find that it's nearly empty.

She must have used the last of it to make Jacqueline's muffins last week. Normally she'd go straight to Martha for this sort of thing, but an idea strikes now that she can't ignore.

"Claire," Jacqueline says warmly as she opens her front door, leaning on the frame as if she has all the time in the world. She's in a striped skirt and shirt combination this morning, loose and comfortable, with her dark hair pulled up into a knot and little wisps falling on either side of her face. "This is becoming a regular occurrence, I see. To what do I owe the pleasure?"

"I'm afraid I've run out of flour," Claire says, holding out the empty measuring cup like a shield from under her umbrella. "I was hoping I could borrow a bit?"

A crease forms between Jacqueline's brows. "You know, I don't think I have any flour in the house. I'm not much of a baker. Or a cook."

"Oh," Claire says, deflating like an old balloon. "That's...quite all right." She finds herself at a loss for what to say next, but Jacqueline is the one to keep the conversation going.

"In fact, I tried to make scrambled eggs this morning, and I burnt them so badly that I might just throw out the whole pan," Jacqueline says. The fact that she's not closing the door in Claire's face is encouraging enough that Claire doesn't excuse herself and go home right away, like she probably should. She clings tighter to her umbrella.

"Oh, don't throw it out," Claire says, waving the suggestion off. "All you need is a bit of baking soda."

"Clearly I'm also not much of a cleaner," Jacqueline says, chuckling. Claire can now see that she does indeed have a few streaks of black on her shirt. "Can baking soda really fix it?"

"I'd be happy to show you," Claire says.

Jacqueline doesn't answer right away. She looks confused, as if Claire's offer doesn't make sense to her; after a moment her expression clears, and once again Claire can't guess at her thoughts.

"That'd be quite a magic trick," Jacqueline says, standing aside and ushering Claire in. "I'd love to see it."

The house is much the same as it was last time, still smelling like that warm and comforting scent—cinnamon, maybe, or sandalwood. She must ask Jacqueline where she gets her candles from. Claire folds her umbrella, and while Jacqueline hangs it for her on a hook near the door, she gets a better look at the newest décor. The furniture is much the same, but the walls are no longer bare. The living room is now lined with framed photographs, and Claire's curiosity burns as they pass the doorway and head instead towards the kitchen.

"Tell me," Jacqueline says, reaching the stove and holding up a frying pan crusted with blackened egg remains, "is it a hopeless case?"

Claire can't hold in her gasp. She takes the pan from Jacqueline, holding it upside down over the sink and shaking it a bit—none of the gunk even budges. "Good *Lord*—what happened?"

Jacqueline laughs, leaning against the counter. "I got a phone call, and turned my back. Though I'm not sure they would have been any good even if I hadn't been distracted. Like I said, I'm lousy in the kitchen."

A phone call. It's hard not to wonder who has the privilege of speaking to Jacqueline so easily, to just ring her up on a Friday morning like it's nothing. Claire isn't sure she'd be brave enough to do that even if she did have Jacqueline's phone number.

"Oh, I must have done that a hundred times," Claire says. "My mother has a habit of calling at the most inopportune moments."

"If it had been my mother on the phone, it would have been a much shorter conversation," Jacqueline says. Her smile is small, almost nonexistent, but her eyes have crinkled at the corners.

Claire fills the pan with water, setting it on the stovetop to simmer. "Oh? Is she not a conversationalist?"

"I haven't spoken to most of my family in some time. I left home quite young," Jacqueline says.

"How young?"

"Fifteen."

Claire almost knocks the pan clear off the stove. She grabs the handle, moving it back into place as it starts to bubble. "Fifteen? What kind of mother would let her daughter move out by herself when she's only a teenager?"

"It's...complicated," Jacqueline says, rather vaguely. She's looking not at Claire, now, but somewhere to her right. Her jaw is tense.

Realization stabs at Claire's stomach.

"Not that I mean to meddle," she says, hurriedly shutting off the stovetop before the pan boils over. "For Pete's sake, you asked me to fix your frying pan and here I am prying into your life! I'm so sorry, Jacqueline." Claire only notices that her hands are unsteady when Jacqueline hands her an open box of baking soda, and she scatters some onto the countertop by accident. "Oh—darn."

Jacqueline wipes up the spilled powder quickly with her hands, brushing them off over the sink. "It's all right. I just don't like to talk about my family much, if that's all right with you."

"Of course. I shouldn't have," Claire stammers, her fingers itching to grab at her pearls, "it was in poor taste. It wasn't my right to—"

"Claire," Jacqueline says clearly, putting a hand on Claire's wrist, "it's all right."

Jacqueline's hand moves away almost as quickly as it came, but even those few precious seconds bring a calming effect like Claire has never felt. No talking-to from her mother, no number of pep talks from Martha, no amount of stern reminders from Pete that she's working herself up, have ever calmed her so effectively as Jacqueline's hand gently clasping her wrist.

Claire's shoulders unclench. She sets the baking soda down, taking a deep breath through a chest that's only just starting to relax. Her incessant worries—that Jacqueline would have no interest in seeing her, that Claire had somehow made up their whole last pleasant meeting in her head—finally melt away.

"All right," Claire says.

While the pan soaks, Jacqueline makes some tea. The time passes just as pleasantly as it did the last time Claire was here, and by the time she's scrubbing the pan and showing Jacqueline the way the blackened eggs simply slide off the surface, she's quite forgotten why she ever thought popping over for another visit would be a bad idea.

"You're a miracle worker," Jacqueline says, drying the salvaged pan with a tea towel that looks completely unused. "Look at that. What would I have done if you hadn't stopped by?"

"Why don't I give you my telephone number?" Claire blurts, before she can lose her nerve. "In case you have another cleaning emergency. Or if you need a cup of sugar, or—or some milk." She hopes dearly that Jacqueline will reach out for more than just inadequate groceries, but it's as good an excuse as any, isn't it?

"That's very thoughtful," Jacqueline says, after a pause. "I should offer you mine as well, shouldn't I?"

"If you'd like," Claire says, eagerly.

"Let me grab a pencil from my office."

While Jacqueline strides towards the hallway, Claire's attention wanders to the arched doorway into the living room. She can see the framed photographs even better from this angle, and she takes two quick steps towards the nearest one.

"Did you take all of these?" Claire says, squinting at the composition. It's like a scene from a dream—a fuzzy city skyline at night with two figures in the foreground, dark shapes outlined by warm light. They have no distinguishable features, but they're intertwined like lovers. She can recognize the Golden Gate Bridge, blurred in the background.

"I know it's a bit gauche to decorate with your own work, but I've never claimed to be classy," Jacqueline calls from the direction of the office. The hallway door is propped open, and Claire can hear her rustling through desk drawers.

Each of the photographs is unique. Some are cityscapes, and others are clearly from professional studio shoots. Some look candid. Claire's interest is drawn most to the ones with human subjects as the central point. They're all taken from afar rather than close-up, and often the features of the subject are obscured in some way. An artful angle or shadow. A length of sheer fabric. A contrast of color. There's a sadness to the way they're framed. They're distant and untouchable. It's been a long time since Claire considered herself an artist, but they tug at something in her that she can't explain.

"They're beautiful, Jacqueline," Claire says quietly. She's come upon a small grouping of pictures all taken at what appears to be various parties. Jacqueline has managed to capture quite a lot despite imperfect lighting and a haze of smoke. The people in them are in various states of revelry, reminding Claire starkly of the ruckus in the pool last weekend.

Claire is all set to move on when her eye catches on one frame in particular.

In the center of the party photos is a shot of a woman wearing what Claire can only describe as *menswear*. She's broad-shouldered and short-haired, not a coiffed and teased pixie cut but shorn close to her scalp at the sides, more like something you'd see on a military man. She's sprawled comfortably on a large couch with her legs wide apart, in tight pants and a golf shirt with an ascot tied into the collar.

Claire might have thought she was a particularly handsome man from afar, were it not for the obvious swells under the shirt. A certain softness to the face. She's caught in motion, a beer bottle hanging from her fingers and a cigarette between her lips. A gorgeous long-haired woman is leaning against her arm, smiling coquettishly and lighting the cigarette with a match in a way that should be mundane but instead feels marvelously artistic.

Claire's breath fogs the glass of the frame as she leans in to absorbs every detail. She's never seen a woman so effortlessly, joyfully *unfeminine*. Just looking at it feels a little bit vulgar, like she's intruding on something private.

"They could be better," Jacqueline says, coming around the corner with a pen and a pad of paper in her hand. "But life's all about learning, isn't it? And please, you should call me Jackie. All my friends do."

Claire jumps back, quickly putting space between herself and the portrait. Being caught staring at it so avidly feels shameful, somehow, but that shame is eclipsed quickly by a single word.

Friends.

"I think they're wonderful," Claire says. She glances back at the photo, and Jacqueline follows her eyeline.

"Ah. You've found my candid collection," Jacqueline says. Claire could swear that Jacqueline's cheeks have gone a bit pink. "This is where my career started. I'd bring my camera to parties, and people started paying me to develop the pictures. I liked it so much that I started taking courses."

Claire steps closer to the wall again, making a show of looking at all of the photos while mostly just staring at the one. "Are they friends of yours?"

"Yes. It's the kind of thing I like to shoot best, but it doesn't always sell very well," Jacqueline says. She gives no further information about the woman in the picture, though Claire is burning with curiosity.

"You know such interesting people," Claire says, folding her hands together with a self-conscious titter. "I can only imagine how tedious you must find me."

"You keep saying things like that," Jacqueline says suddenly. Her head tilts. "You're very hard on yourself. Why is that?"

Claire flounders. Her mouth opens and closes, but no words are forming. She has no idea how to answer that question—she's having trouble even understanding it. Nobody has ever done anything besides agree with her self-assessments before.

"I don't think you're boring, Claire," Jacqueline says, once it's clear that no response is coming. Her smile is full of an understanding that Claire can't wrap her head around. "But I do think you should be kinder to yourself."

Claire shifts from foot to foot. She tangles her fingers in her pearls. Jacqueline is still looking at her, not seeming compelled by the usual guard-rails of social interaction that Claire is used to. She seems to operate outside of everything Claire has ever known.

"All right," Claire says. "I'll try. Jackie."

She heads home soon after with a promise to give Jackie a call soon. Just before she reaches her own front door, she catches the telltale movement of Martha's curtains across the street.

In the end, Claire doesn't even make the biscuits.

Chapter 7

"Claire? Devilled eggs?"

A tray full of canapes floats into Claire's vision, disrupting the view of Jackie's house through Martha's front window.

"No, thank you," Claire says. She leans around Martha's belly, trying to sneak another glance. The roof of Jackie's convertible has been pulled down, so Claire expects to see her coming outside at any minute, but soon her view is obstructed again. Martha's sitting room is starting to fill up with the neighborhood ladies arriving for book club.

"Are you sure? You love my devilled eggs," Martha says. The tray waves in front of Claire's face again, and Claire is relieved when several other hands reach for it, deferring Martha's attention.

"I don't know what you put in these, Martha, but they're amazing," Susan Wilson says, taking the seat next to Claire as she shoves an egg into her mouth. She's the only woman in the room wearing pants, and it doesn't seem to bother her. She's a little bit like Jackie in that way—a little brash, a little open and uncouth. Maybe that's why they seemed to get along so well at the party.

But she lacks Jackie's kindness. She lacks that mystery, that unexplainable *something* that makes Claire need to know Jackie. Susan is an open book, easy reading, and Jackie is an elegant diary with a big, shiny lock on it.

Normally Claire wouldn't pay Susan much mind. Today, her interest is piqued. How close have Susan and Jackie gotten, exactly? Jackie claimed that Susan had lost interest in their budding friendship, but what does Susan think?

"What's the book for today?" Susan says, leaning close to Claire conspiratorially. "I had a busy week, and I forgot to pick it up."

"Little Women," Claire says.

"I guess I'll just have to partake in the gossip instead," Susan says. She grabs a few Vienna sausages on toothpicks as Martha passes, lowering her voice. "Don't tell Martha I didn't read it."

"I won't. But, um. Speaking of gossip," Claire says, doing her best to channel Martha's easy way of prying out juicy tidbits of information, "We have a new addition to the neighborhood?"

"We do," Susan says. She's picked up one of the scattered paperbacks and is peering down at the synopsis on the back cover with narrowed eyes as she chews. She doesn't seem particularly interested in talking about Jackie, which makes no sense at all.

"I saw you getting along rather well at her party?" Claire says.

"With Jacqueline?" Susan says, tossing the book back onto the table and picking over the tray of aspics Martha just put down. "Oh, she's a gas. But I won't be socializing with her regularly, obviously."

"Why not?" Claire asks. She can't imagine not wanting to see Jackie all the time, if given the chance. Why on earth would Susan not want to associate with her? It certainly isn't *obvious*.

"She's not exactly normal, is she?" Susan says airily. "You were at that party. A dalliance now and then is one thing, but it's quite another to make a lifestyle out of it."

Something unfamiliar rises behind Claire's ribs. An indignation, on Jackie's behalf, for the judgmental tone in Susan's voice. Before she can think, Claire's mouth opens. "Wasn't your husband in the pool?"

Susan looks at her sharply. More than anything she looks shocked by Claire's sudden and uncharacteristic gall, but before she can retort one of the chairs opposite the couch is taken up by Dorothy O'Neil. She lives next to Martha, and she's never missed a book club meeting.

"Are you talking about the housewarming party last week?" Dorothy says. "Can you *believe* how rowdy it was? That woman should be ashamed."

"Ashamed of what, exactly?" Claire says.

"A single woman of her age, moving to a nice place like this? She's not going to find herself a husband here," Martha says. She sits in the easy chair just to Claire's left, adjusting herself more comfortably with a hand over her belly.

Dorothy titters. "Maybe she's looking to be a mistress."

Another woman pipes in—Louise, who lives around the corner. She's always been nice enough to Claire, if a bit dull, but she certainly isn't being very nice now. "And have you seen how *dark* she is? Don thinks she's an Italian."

"She's Greek," Claire says, but her voice is lost in the group.

"You'd think her realtor would have warned her this is too nice a neighborhood for that kind of thing," Dorothy says.

"And have you seen her car? Some rich man bought it for her, no doubt," Louise says. "Only a floozy needs to drive a car like that."

Martha clicks her tongue. "Hang on to your husbands, ladies."

Four pinpricks of pain erupt against Claire's palm. She hides her balled fist between her thigh and the arm of the couch. "Have any of you even spoken to her?"

"Why would I want to speak to a woman like that?" Martha says. "I said hello when she moved in, and that was enough to know she's bad news."

The other ladies cluck in agreement. Claire looks to Susan, but Susan says nothing—she only takes the glass of punch offered to her by Martha, watching the conversation over the rim of her glass.

They hardly even talk about the book, in the end. The full meeting is taken up by gossip, which thankfully shifts from Jackie to other targets quickly enough, and once the other ladies have left Claire finds that she's not very enthusiastic about helping Martha clean up.

"What's eating you?" Martha says, after Claire has unhelpfully moved the same tray of empty teacups from place to place three times.

"Sorry," Claire says, leaning against the couch. She feels deflated, like she's spent the last two hours holding a heavy weight. "I'm a bit bothered by all the gossip, I think."

"We always gossip," Martha says, handing Claire a small garbage bin. She starts gathering napkins and leftover food to put in it, and Claire trails her.

"I don't think Jackie deserves it."

Martha stops so suddenly that Claire walks straight into her back. She turns, levelling Claire with a furrowed brow. "*Jackie?* Since when are you so familiar?"

"Jacqueline," Claire corrects quickly. Her stomach does a little twist. "I just think she's an interesting addition to the neighborhood, that's all."

"Interesting is one word for it," Martha says. She starts gathering garbage again, and Claire holds out the bin to make it easier.

"What word would you use?"

"Disruptive."

"Sure, her party was a bit much," Claire says, putting the bin down near the door when Martha has finished collecting, "but she's really very nice."

"And how would you know that?"

Normally, Claire would easily share something so inconsequential with Martha. They're friends. They share burdens around housework or cooking, irks about their husbands or their in-laws. Being honest about her tea with Jackie should be no different, but something stops Claire this time. The sharpness in Martha's tone. The memory of Martha's curtains fluttering closed as Claire returned home after her last visit.

"We've talked at the mailbox once or twice," Claire says.

Martha hums, but she doesn't sound convinced. Claire sets the garbage bin down, and she bites her tongue.

"I really should go," Claire says, grabbing for her purse. "I have a huge shopping list for Easter."

Martha's face turns more sympathetic. "Oh, dear. Is the whole gang coming like usual?"

"All three of Pete's brothers, and their families. Of all the holidays in the calendar year, I might just dislike Easter the most."

It's not that Claire objects to the tradition of Easter, per se, but it's the holiday in Pete's family rotation which Claire is expected to host. Thanksgiving and the Fourth of July fall to Pete's two older brothers and their wives. Christmas is always hosted by Rita. Pete's younger brother Alan, being the baby of the family, is lucky enough to not be expected to host anything besides the occasional birthday or family cookout.

Hosting for Pete's family means a house full of nieces and nephews, running about and knocking things over. It means the usual criticism from Rita. It means trying to make conversation with her sisters-in-law, with whom she has almost nothing in common. And worst of all, it means she needs to shop for a meal to feed sixteen people and carry it all home by herself.

Pete left extra money for the shopping, at the very least. Claire tucks it into her purse, and she's just heading out the door fully prepared for a terrible afternoon lugging ham and potatoes home when she hears a shout.

"Claire?"

It's Jackie. Her hair is tucked up under a kerchief, and she has a set of big sunglasses on her face. Claire was right—she's about to get into her car, and she waves at Claire from the opposite side.

Claire waves back. Jackie looks genuinely happy to see her, which wipes away the annoyance of the morning. "Afternoon! Heading out for a drive?"

"Heading to the store, actually," Jackie calls back. "I'm short on groceries."

"Oh, how funny. That's where I'm headed," Claire says.

"You aren't walking there, are you?" Jackie says, putting a hand up to further shade her face from the sun.

Claire herself just squints into it—Pete has always said that sunglasses make a woman look too uppity.

"I usually do."

"The nearest grocer is two miles from here," Jackie says incredulously. "Why don't you let me give you a lift?"

"Oh, I couldn't do that," Claire says, though she very much wants to.

"Why not? I'd like the company. Besides, what if I have to grab something on the top shelf?" Jackie says. She flashes a cheeky grin as she sidles around the car to open the passenger side door. "I might need you."

Claire stifles a giggle. She has very little willpower when it comes to the new neighbor, it seems. And besides, hitching a ride will cut at least two hours out of her busy day. "In that case, I suppose I have to help."

"Hop in," Jackie says, rounding the car again and sliding into the driver's seat. "I'll even let you drive back, if you want."

"I don't drive," Claire says, bounding over the slight dip between their lawns. As she makes her way around to the open passenger door, the sunglasses hide Jackie's eyes from her, so it's difficult to read her expression.

"Not ever?"

"No. I don't have a license. I'm too clumsy to operate a vehicle," Claire says. She settles on the beige seat—the car smells like fresh leather, warm and rich in the spring sun. "I used to crash my bicycle so often that my mother made me wear knee-pads."

Jackie's eyebrows raise behind her sunglasses. "How often is *often*?"

"Weekly," Claire says, chuckling as she fastens her seatbelt. "I hated how my skirt would blow up, and when I tried to fix it or hold it down I'd end up getting all tangled up."

"That sounds more like you needed to wear pants," Jackie says.

"My mother would have laid down on the train tracks before letting me wear pants."

Jackie snorts. "Haven't you ever wanted to learn to drive?"

"Of course, but it'd be wasted on me," Claire says. "Pete will never buy me a car. He says I don't need one. And he'd certainly never let me drive his Cadillac."

Jackie hums. She reaches to put the car in reverse but hesitates when Claire gives her a pointed look. After a pause, she fastens her own seatbelt as well before backing out of the driveway.

The drive to the store is thrilling. Claire has never ridden in a convertible before—the wind is bracing, cool and fresh on her skin. Jackie's driving kerchief doesn't quite keep the long ends of her hair from swirling around her face. The unpredictable motion of it is mesmerizing to watch. Even if it impedes Jackie's vision, she drives confidently. Almost too confidently, in fact, such as when she sails through a yellow light as it turns red without paying any heed to the honking of cars in the opposite lane, or when she takes a corner so hard that Claire is glad they're both wearing their seatbelts.

They make it to the store in one piece, at least, and Claire can't be too judgmental when she herself has never driven at all past a few mandatory lessons in high school.

"What's on your list?" Claire says, pulling out her own while Jackie grabs them each a cart. While Claire can find her normal items by memory, an Easter dinner requires a few new things, and she unfolds the square of paper with her ingredients on it. Ham and tinned pineapple slices, bread rolls, potatoes…

"List?" Jackie says, grabbing at a bag of potato chips on the first aisle cap they come across. "That takes all the fun out of it."

"The fun? Out of groceries?"

"I like to mix things up," Jackie says. She turns into the first aisle, grabbing a can of tamales in red sauce and peering down at the label. "Have you tried these?"

"Pete doesn't like ethnic food," Claire says. "We have a dinner rotation."

Jackie throws the can into her cart with a noise that sounds like a sigh. "And you actually know how to cook, so you don't need to grab ready-made all the time like me. Part of why I never learned to cook back home is that my apartment was surrounded by restaurants. I miss that."

"We have some decent restaurants here," Claire says.

"Diners and malt shops," Jackie says. She sighs wistfully, looking down at a box of instant mashed potatoes. "You have no idea what I'd do for some decent sweet and sour pork."

Shopping with Jackie is entirely different than doing it alone. She examines the shelves slowly, picking things seemingly at random. Claire doesn't need to daydream or distract herself to get through the ordeal. Jackie makes it fun. She makes a game out of the aisles, picking up odd assortments of items and challenging Claire to come up with a meal out of them.

Jackie does end up needing Claire's help to get a box of minute rice on a high shelf. It feels almost chivalric to reach up and grab it for her, which is oddly pleasant. By the end Jackie's cart is piled with a mix of frozen meals and expensive coffee, with half the items being things Claire has never tried. She even inspires Claire to do something she hasn't ever done before—pluck something new off the shelf herself. Inspired by Jackie's mention of sweet and sour pork she grabs a can of chicken chow mein, advertised by the bright blue packaging as *inspired by traditional Chinese cuisine.*

"Do you miss living in San Francisco?" Claire says as they line up at the cash register, pulling out her checkbook. "It must have been hard to leave. I've always lived within an hour's drive of where I was born."

"Sometimes," Jackie says. She moves her cart forward, flashing the cashier a small, polite smile—smaller than the one she usually points at Claire, which is somehow gratifying. "I left for a reason, but I do miss some things. Good food. Easy gigs. Some of my friends. And the ocean. God, I miss the beach."

It's an odd distinction to make—*some* of her friends. Who are the friends she doesn't miss?

"The ocean isn't terribly far from here," Claire reasons. "You could take a drive? Santa Cruz is only an hour or two. I hear they have a roller coaster."

"It's not the same. I used to be able to walk to the shore," Jackie drawls. "It's why I bought a house with a pool."

It's hard not to wonder why Jackie moved here at all, if she loved the city so much. The question burns in Claire, begging to be asked, but too soon the cashier is starting to punch in their groceries, and it gets lost in the shuffle of bagging and loading and the thrill of driving through town again.

Claire makes the chow mein for dinner that night. Pete absolutely hates it.

Chapter 8

April is a busy time at Pete's work. Things get more hectic for him after Easter with people buying new cars for the summer, and it means he needs a perfect house to come home to—Claire's time is usually taken up with deep cleanings in late spring.

Lately, though, at least a few hours a week are taken up by Jackie.

Claire makes excuses, at first. She ensures that she always has a solid reason to visit, with some food to share or a question to ask, but it becomes much easier after her third straight day crossing the lawns, when Jackie finally tells her that she's welcome to come socialize anytime.

Each day she knocks on Jackie's door means experiencing something new. Mixing champagne with orange juice over fresh bakery pastries for breakfast. Watching Jackie pop the hood of her Mustang and change the oil, with the femininity of her outfit—a sleeveless jumpsuit with a loud blue and yellow pattern—clashing with her grime-stained hands in a thrilling way. Going through Jackie's extensive record collection, most of which Claire has never heard before.

One such new thing is revealed two weeks after Easter, when Claire knocks on Jackie's door only to be met with silence.

Strange. Jackie's car is in the driveway, so she should be home. Claire knocks again, and this time she can just barely hear Jackie's voice carry through the wood.

"Claire?"

The fact that Jackie knows it's Claire knocking—that her visits are regular and anticipated enough for that to be her assumption—makes her a bit giddy.

"It's me," Claire calls back, glancing behind her to Martha's house across the road. There's a gap in the curtains, but she can't see if anyone is behind them. It tinges the giddiness with a bit of worry. "Are you alright?"

"The door's unlocked," comes Jackie's muffled response.

Claire hurries inside, closing the door behind her, and follows the sound of Jackie's movement to the kitchen.

Jackie is seated in the breakfast nook, surrounded by white papers and greenish herbs. She's rolling one of the papers into a long, fat cigarette shape, and when she looks up Claire can see dark circles under her eyes. Her smile is genuine, even if it doesn't quite light her face up like usual.

"Morning," Jackie says, running her tongue along the edge of the paper to seal it. She scrunches up the ends, holding it out to Claire. "Want to share?"

The papers, the herbs, the strange smell hanging around the kitchen—the combination of everything she's seeing finally sparks Claire's brain, and she gasps.

"Is that *marijuana*?" Claire hisses, looking nervously over her shoulder as if the police might knock the door down at any moment.

Jackie hardly reacts to Claire's outburst. She sweeps the leftover cannabis into a baggie, tying it up and putting it into a mason jar. "It's a little harder to get out here than it is in the city, but luckily I brought some with me."

"But it's illegal," Claire whispers. The feeling of being watched has only intensified—if Martha were here, she'd no doubt have something to say. Several things, most likely, and none of them flattering.

"Lots of things are illegal, Claire," Jackie says quietly. Even through the film of Claire's anxiety, the moment feels suddenly heavy. Jackie's brow is furrowed as she taps the joint on the table, like she was just reminded of something she'd rather forget. "You can leave if it makes you uncomfortable. I won't hold it against you."

"I don't want to leave," Claire says, sure at least of that one thing. Claire never wants to leave. She only goes back to her own house after their visits because she needs to get things done before Pete gets home. If she had her way, she'd spend her whole day here.

"If you're sure," Jackie says. She grabs a silver lighter, flicking the cap off and heading towards the living room. "I don't usually indulge, but I had a rough night. I'm going to get blazed."

"A rough night?" Claire asks.

Jackie throws herself onto the plush couch and flicks the lighter. The tip of the paper glows orange, and Jackie take a deep pull on it, holding the smoke in for a few seconds before exhaling it all in a strange-smelling cloud.

"My mother called."

Claire has never seen Jackie so disheveled before. She has not a stitch of makeup on her face. She's still in her pajamas, a blue gauzy robe over a silk negligée, and she's sprawled across the couch with the joint in her hand as if she doesn't have a guest over. It's exhilarating to be trusted with this side of her. Claire wonders if anyone else gets to see it, besides her. She hopes not.

"You aren't close with your mother, right?" Claire says, carefully perching on the cushion near Jackie's bare feet. Her scarlet toenail polish is chipped.

"That's an understatement," Jackie says, flicking ash carelessly onto the carpet. "Have you ever met a Greek Orthodox mother?"

"I can't say that I have," Claire says.

"She's been trying to get my inheritance renounced. Thankfully my grandfather left a will, but my mother got it tied up in litigation for a few years."

Claire folds her ankles demurely, resisting the urge to clean up the ash. "Why would she do that?"

"She doesn't approve of my lifestyle."

"What, just because you're not married?" Claire scoffs. "That's absolutely ridiculous."

Jackie laughs bitterly. She takes another puff—the tip of the joint glows orange, and the smoke rises towards the ceiling. "Among many other grievances. C'est la vie."

"I'm sorry, Jackie."

"It's alright. This is helping. And I'm glad you came to see me today."

Jackie does seem much more relaxed already. She isn't acting wild or crazy. She's just sitting with her head lolled back on the headrest of the couch, humming quietly to herself. The smell is odd, but not harsh and sharp like cigarette smoke. Claire has always associated drugs with hard partiers or beatniks, but Jackie is...well, she's *Jackie*.

She hasn't steered Claire wrong yet, right?

"I want to try it," Claire says decisively.

Jackie cracks one eye open. It's slightly bloodshot. "Try what?"

"The...the reefer," Claire says.

Jackie snorts. It turns quickly into a giggle, and her feet worm their way under Claire's thigh. The warmth of them seems to burn. "Reefer. Haven't heard that one in a while."

"I've liked all the other new things you've shown me," Claire says, watching the smoke curl lazily from the tip of the joint. "I trust you."

Something comes over Jackie's face, then. A tension, maybe, like a raincloud darkening the light in her eyes. But it passes quickly. Jackie sits up, handing the smoldering joint over to Claire.

Claire raises it to her mouth. It seems silly, but the part that Jackie touched to her lips seems warmer than the rest.

"Take a small drag. It's probably going to make you cough," Jackie says.

It does, in fact, make Claire cough. There's a heaviness to breathing the smoke in that she didn't expect. It's a little bit acrid, but it isn't as horrible as everyone has always made it sound. Jackie rubs her back throughout, helping her through the coughing fit. When Claire hands the joint back, she feels rather accomplished.

"I don't feel any different," Claire says. Her voice a little rough, and her eyes are watering from the coughing.

Jackie chuckles, taking another puff herself. "Give it a minute."

A few minutes and a few lungfuls later, Claire can see what Jackie means.

Her skin feels strange. It's slightly more sensitive than usual, and tingly in some places. Everything is just a little bit brighter. She can't seem to control the things that come out of her mouth, and the heavy, anxious feeling that usually sits in her chest—always present, in some way, in every facet of her life—is completely gone. The world is just *swell* all over, and the jaunty, unfamiliar record that Jackie puts into the player makes Claire want to move her body.

Setting the joint at the edge of a crystal ashtray on the table, Claire lets her shoulders twist to the beat of the latest song. It's upbeat and fun, and it fills her chest like a balloon. "What is this music?"

"The Supremes," Jackie says, picking up the joint Claire just abandoned. She takes a long drag. Her foot is bopping, jumping to the song even if the rest of her is still. "Aren't they great?"

"They're *amazing*," Claire says. She jumps to her feet, her hips already starting to twist. The song is too good to stay sitting—it feels like it's inside her, zooming through every last one of her veins right to her heart. "Jackie, let's dance."

Jackie laughs, falling back against the couch cushions. "You have fun. I'll just stay here, if you don't mind."

Claire keeps moving. The self-consciousness she might have felt about dancing in Jackie's living room can't seem to get its hooks into her—now that she's started, she doesn't want to stop. "Pete and I used to go dancing sometimes, when we were dating. He was awful at it, but we'd go to the dance hall and do the jitterbug until curfew."

Jackie snorts. She's looking up at Claire with what she hopes is affection. "I don't think I've seen the jitterbug since I graduated high school."

"Probably because that's the last time I really got out of the house," Claire says, starting a spirited hand-jive. "Pete and I stopped going dancing after we got married."

Jackie's smile fades into something more somber. It might even be pity, but Claire doesn't care. As long as Jackie is looking at her at all, the world can't be so bad.

"Won't you join me?" Claire says, still bouncing as a new song comes on. It's even jauntier than the last. "It's no fun to dance all alone."

Jackie sets the joint on the edge of an ashtray but doesn't budge from the couch. "I haven't danced like that in over a decade."

"I'll teach you," Claire says. She twirls, splaying out her arms for balance, spinning and spinning until she's dizzy. When the world stops lurching, Jackie is looking at her with one of those half-smiles. It reveals so little of her thoughts, and Claire wonders for the hundredth time what might be going through her mind.

To Claire's surprise, Jackie hauls herself up off the couch. "Fine. Just for you, Claire."

Claire manages not to jump and squeal in excitement, but only just.

"It's all about constant movement," Claire says, demonstrating a few steps. "Momentum. Once you know the basics, you can ad-lib together."

Jackie copies Claire's foot movement easily. It sets her long, flowing hair to bouncing, and Claire is made suddenly *very* aware that Jackie is not wearing a brassiere under her negligée.

The thought doesn't feel as shameful as it should.

"So, something like this?" Jackie says, grabbing Claire's hands. She pulls herself closer, swinging their linked arms as she copies Claire's feet.

"Exactly like that," Claire says. Jackie does a quick spin-out, still holding Claire's hand—their linked arms go taut. "You're better at this than I am."

Jackie laughs. There's something magical about it—her eyes are vibrant, her dimples flashing. "You're a good teacher."

Jackie spins again. This time she turns inwards, and all at once she's pressed tight against Claire's front. Jackie's arm is over Claire's shoulder, her other hand pressed slightly to Claire's upper chest. In her attempt to teach, Claire has inadvertently taken the man's position. It's unfamiliar to be the one holding Jackie's hand, to have her own land on Jackie's waist, but the strangeness of it feels equally good. A natural extension of her altered state.

Having never touched Jackie beyond a light hand on the arm, her sudden closeness is more potent than the marijuana. Jackie is warm, and Claire can feel the pliant softness of her body under the negligée. She can smell Jackie's shampoo over the smoke. It makes her want to lean forward and bury her nose in Jackie's hair.

Thankfully Jackie moves just far enough away to curb that impulse. She follows the moves that Claire lays out and picks them up in a heartbeat. Their height difference is oddly perfect. Claire is used to needing to compensate for Pete, making herself smaller. Now she's leading the dance, and her height is an advantage. Jackie doesn't step on Claire's feet—her bare toes jive perfectly with Claire's stockinged ones, kicking and moving in tandem to the album's next cheerful song.

Claire doesn't feel self-conscious at all.

There's not much floor room to work with in the conversation pit. When a particularly wide spin trips Jackie up, taking Claire with her through their linked hands, Claire only just manages to catch herself on the couch and stumble down onto it. Jackie hits the floor, but she's laughing all the while.

"There, see," Claire says breathlessly, straightening up to sitting, "wasn't that a ball?"

"As promised," Jackie says. She's out of breath too, even more so than Claire. After a moment she climbs up onto the couch, settling on her back and twisting until her head is set in Claire's lap.

Claire's breath catches. Jackie does it thoughtlessly, settling onto Claire's legs and draping her own feet over the opposite side of the couch, but now Claire can't think of anything else.

"I can't believe you picked the steps up so quickly," Claire says. Jackie's head feels heavy, but the last thing she wants is for her to move. It feels as if a treasured cat has chosen Claire's legs to sleep on. "I thought you said you didn't dance?"

"I said I didn't dance *anymore*," Jackie says. She grabs the joint again—it's just a little stub, now. It's a wonder that she hasn't burnt her fingers on it. "I used to go to plenty of school dances before I left home."

Claire can hardly imagine Jackie so young, dancing the night away in some gymnasium. "I bet all the boys fought over you."

Jackie snorts. "And why would you say that?"

"You're smart. You're beautiful," Claire says simply. "You're a catch. Any man would be lucky to have you."

Jackie pauses mid-inhale. The joint drifts away from her mouth. Her eyes are set somewhere on the ceiling past Claire. When she exhales, the smoke rises lazily past Claire's face. Claire can feel it brushing her skin as if Jackie has trailed her fingers there.

"Men have no interest in smarts, in my experience," Jackie finally says, handing the last of the smoldering stub to Claire to finish off instead. "You're quite handsome yourself, you know."

Claire has been getting better at inhaling without coughing, but this time she fails. The paper singes her fingers, and she almost drops the ash onto Jackie. "What? No, I—I mean, I'm not—compared to you? You're the prettiest woman I've ever met."

It's barely a coherent sentence, but Jackie doesn't seem to give it much thought. She reaches up to touch her finger to the tip of Claire's nose. "That doesn't detract from your handsomeness."

That tiny *boop* feels like the funniest thing that's ever happened in Claire's life. She giggles, dropping the remains of the joint into the ashtray. Everything feels floaty, like the couch she's sitting on is made of clouds.

The feeling intensifies when Jackie catches Claire's hand from the air and intertwines it with her own, running her thumb over Claire's palm until it tingles.

If Claire had thought Jackie's head in her lap was unprecedented closeness, this is another level entirely. It isn't brief—Jackie continues the motion, a rhythmic and repetitive rubbing against Claire's palm. She seems entirely focused on it. It gives Claire the opportunity to take Jackie in, observing the little things she hadn't noticed before. She has a small scar on her chin. She consistently paints her toes, but not her fingers—they're bare and natural. The hair on her arms is much thicker and darker than Claire's. It suits her. Claire wonders, lazily, what it feels like. The texture of it. If any of the other hidden places of her body are the same.

She can also see the edges of Jackie's tattoo from this angle. It's more than just a tree branch—it looks like it could have flowers on it, but Claire can't see the whole thing.

"Your tattoo," Claire says. "What is it?"

Jackie makes a small noise. She's still tracing Claire's hand. "This is going to sound strange."

"How so?"

Jackie is quiet for a time. Her thumb continues its path around Claire's palm.

"It's an acacia," Jackie finally says.

She lets go of Claire's hand, turning her wrist so that Claire can see it properly. Inked onto Jackie's skin plain as day is a branch of familiar, puffy flowers. It's realistic, too—it could have come right from the tree in the middle of their cul-de-sac. There's no color to it, but Claire can imagine filling in the lines with bright yellow paint.

Now that Claire has a frame of reference for what Jackie's skin feels like, the curiosity burns ever hotter. Would it feel different to the rest? Her fingers seem to tingle in anticipation of finding out.

"Why did you get it?" Claire says. "You're the only person I've ever known to have a tattoo."

"To remind me of something," Jackie says. She turns her wrist away, taking Claire's dream of touching the tattoo with it. She goes back to tracing Claire's palm, switching to the opposite hand this time. "It's why I pushed to buy this house. I saw the tree there, and it felt like it was meant to be."

"Maybe it was," Claire says.

"Maybe," Jackie murmurs. She traces along the line of scabbed crescent-shaped marks in the meat of Claire's left palm. The shameful remnants of where her fingernails often dig in. "What are these?"

"A bad habit," Claire says. Nobody has ever noticed them before. She wants to close her palm, to hide them from Jackie, but Jackie's tracing is keeping her hand spread open.

Jackie hums. "I have a few of those, too." She caresses the marks gently. It sends a wave of shuddery feeling all through Claire.

Claire's eyes wander to the photographs on the wall. She zeroes in on the one that's so fascinated her since she first noticed it—she stares at the short-haired woman with the cigarette, uncaring now about whether or not Jackie will notice.

She can almost imagine being at the party where the picture was taken. It was probably a lot like Jackie's housewarming. She can hear the music, the kind of loud rock that Jackie sometimes plays, and smell the hazy smoke on the air. Marijuana and cigarettes intermingled.

Claire imagines, in her very floaty mind, what it might be like to be in that woman's place. Confident and relaxed, in tight pants and an ascot with her legs spread. Not a care in the world for who might judge. Relaxed. Claire can't remember the last time she felt truly relaxed, before this moment. Maybe she never has been.

As Claire stares at the photo, Jackie's word strikes her again. *Handsome.*

Claire has never been beautiful. If she stands out, it's for her freakish height. Her bony build, her flat chest. She's always been a fish out of water. Throughout her tomboyish childhood and awkward adolescence her mother always used to say that Claire was just waiting to bloom, until it became clear that she was as bloomed as she'd ever get.

Coming from Jackie, *handsome* doesn't feel like such a bad thing.

"I've never had a friend like you before," Claire says, swiping her hand through the last of the smoke drifting up to the ceiling. It swirls and churns in patterns she can't predict.

"Yes, I'm not nearly as high-strung as Martha."

"Do you think I'm high-strung too?" Claire says.

"I'd say more...buttoned-up," Jackie says thoughtfully. Her feet swing idly, dangling over the arm of the couch. "But I think there's an animal in you, just waiting to break out."

Claire laughs towards the ceiling. "An animal?"

"There's a lion in here," Jackie says, tapping on Claire's chest with a grin. "I know it."

"Ha! More like a squirrel, maybe. Or a rabbit."

Claire's eyes feel sluggish and slow, but still she drags them down to look at Jackie again.

Jackie isn't handsome. Jackie is *stunning*. Jackie has full lips and prominent cheekbones and a lovely jawline. Her eyebrows have a gentle arch, thick and well-shaped where Claire's are light and sparse. Jackie doesn't need to cover up every feature with makeup the way Claire does—she only emphasizes her natural ones. She wears clothes that show off her figure, rather than hiding it. And she has the softest, most silky hair Claire has ever seen.

Claire wishes that she could draw this moment. She aches to commit this image to paper forever, so she can never forget it. If there was anything in the room to sketch with, she might do it right now on the back of her own hand just to keep this feeling a little longer.

"I'm sorry that Acacia Circle doesn't have a beach. But I'm very glad you moved here, Jackie," Claire says quietly.

"So am I," Jackie says. Her brows knit together. "I wasn't expecting to find a friend."

A thrill rushes through Claire, from the roots of her hair all the way to her toes. She doesn't just want to be Jackie's friend—she wants to be her *best* friend. She wants to be the person Jackie comes to with her problems. The person she knows she can trust with anything.

The part of Claire's brain that usually stops her from doing silly things seems to be turned off, and against her usual instincts she gives in to her impulse to touch. She cards her fingers through Jackie's hair, feeling the silky strands tickle her skin, and giggles again.

"You have such nice hair," Claire murmurs. With Jackie's head on her lap like this, it's hard not to wonder how her hair would feel against Claire's bare legs. The thought makes something twinge, deep inside her. "How do you get it so soft? Mine is like a Bichon Frise."

"Your hair is *not* like a dog's coat," Jackie says, chuckling. "It's just curly. Curly hair is lovely. But I use a good conditioner. Hair oil, and no hairspray."

"You don't use hairspray?"

"Nope." Jackie makes a little *pop* with her mouth on the word, and they both dissolve into giggles at it. The laughter makes Jackie curl up a little, but she doesn't let go of Claire's hand.

"I don't think I've ever been this relaxed," Claire sighs. She tips her head back, resting it on the back of the couch to stare up at Jackie's popcorn ceiling. "Do you do this all the time?"

"Rarely," Jackie says, her fingers still tracing patterns over Claire's. "I find it too easy to get addicted to things."

The swirls that Jackie is making on Claire's palm seem to match the nonsensical patterns in the ceiling. With her eyes so relaxed, Claire keeps finding images in the plaster. A cresting ocean wave. A dinosaur, with a spiky back and an open mouth. An airplane with a crooked wing. They look like brushstrokes in thick white oil paint.

Claire keeps stroking Jackie's hair with her free hand. It keeps her grounded—she's a kite, riding the smoke higher and higher to join that airplane, and Jackie is the only thing keeping her from getting lost in the big blue sky. Claire lets the strands of Jackie's hair slide through her fingers, and then she scratches her nails over Jackie's scalp.

Jackie moves suddenly. Her back arches a little, and she makes a noise that Claire has never heard before. It's high, and throaty, and it gets cut off by Jackie clearing her throat before Claire can examine it further.

Jackie's chest is flushed under her robe. She drops Claire's hand.

It sticks in Claire's mind, that little one-second soundbite. She wants to recreate it. Make it longer and louder. Claire is full to the brim with something she doesn't understand, suddenly, and the cloudiness of her mind isn't helping at all.

The movement has made Jackie's negligée shift up her thighs. The hair above her knees is unshaven and dark, like her arms; Claire wonders, as the skirt glides over her skin, what it might feel like to be that scrap of silk. Light and flowing, pressed so intimately to Jackie for as long as she chooses to wear it.

A silk negligée doesn't have to go home to its husband after every visit.

That thought is finally enough to part the clouds in Claire's mind. When she glances up at the clock on Jackie's mantel, it reads 3:47.

The anxiety that's been so blissfully absent for the afternoon comes back in a great wave. It floods her, crashing against every surface, and Claire springs to her feet, dislodging Jackie from her lap.

"Shoot—it's almost four! Oh, I should have been home hours ago. I have to make dinner."

Jackie frowns up at her from the couch cushion. Her hair is ruffled, and she looks like she doesn't quite understand what's happened.

"I'm sorry, Jackie, but Pete will be so upset if he gets home with no supper," Claire says, hopping on one foot towards the door as she tries to get her shoes back on—she doesn't remember taking them off. Her fingers aren't quite working properly.

"Okay," Jackie says quietly.

Claire trips over the two steps leading up and out of the conversation pit. She catches herself, her face flooding with heat, and darts to the door.

She can't look back at Jackie. If she looks back, if she sees the expression that accompanies that *okay*, she might not have the willpower to leave, and she can still remember how Pete reacted the last time she didn't have dinner on the table when he got home. There had been an Arctic chill in the house until he felt she understood not to do it again.

Cooking is twice the chore it usually is. She finds herself forgetting parts of the recipe that she knows by heart. Twice she burns the onions she's sautéing because she's staring out the window at Jackie's front door, remembering the softness of her hair, and she has to start over.

Dinner still isn't finished when Pete's car pulls in.

"Smells like lasagna," Pete calls from the foyer, as if they don't have lasagna every second week without fail.

Claire doesn't answer. She's hurriedly washing the dishes, trying to get the kitchen as clean as she can while the lasagna bakes, and her attention has caught on a stubborn piece of food on the edge of her cutting board.

"How long until dinner?" Pete says, poking his head into the kitchen.

"Forty-five minutes."

"*Forty-five—*" Pete throws his briefcase onto the kitchen table as he passes, and the loud noise makes Claire flinch. "Since when can you not make a lasagna by 5:30?"

"Would you prefer undercooked pasta?"

Pete stops in his tracks. The lasagna bubbles in the oven, marinara sauce sizzling over the edges of Claire's spare casserole dish.

Claire has never snapped back. When she makes a mistake she apologizes, often incessantly, sometimes to the point of annoying her husband further. Something is different today. Today there's a resentment in the pit of her belly that something—the drugs, probably, or fact that she had to abandon a perfectly lovely day with Jackie to come back home—is making manifest.

Today, she hears Jackie's voice in her head.

You should be kinder to yourself.

Pete slams the kitchen door behind himself. "What's gotten into you? I work to put food on the table, and you can't do your job and cook it?"

You're very different, Claire.

In this moment, Claire wants to be different. She wants to be daring. She can't imagine Pete scolding Jackie for not having dinner on the table—Jackie would push back, like she did at the housewarming party. She'd stand her ground.

Why shouldn't Claire?

"I wanted to work, too. Remember?" Claire says. Her voice is thin, but she gets the words out. "I had a job at Anita's arts and crafts store, and you asked me to quit."

Claire had been so proud of herself for getting that job in high school. Anita was a kindly older woman who gave Claire the freedom to sketch in her downtime, and for a time, when Claire's mother had been busy planning her second wedding, Anita had been like the parent Claire was missing. She gave advice, and taught Claire to cook. She'd even allowed Claire to stay the night a few times while her mother enjoyed extended visits at her soon-to-be-husband's house.

"I had you quit so that you could stay home and take care of the house," Pete says loudly. "I gave you a gift, and this is how you repay me? With laziness?"

"Please don't speak to me that way," Claire says, as calmly as she can. Her fingers are tangled in her pearls, but her voice is steady.

Pete steps closer. He peers at Claire, squinting, before rolling his eyes. "Oh, Claire, don't start crying. You know I hate it."

Claire rubs her eyes. They're dry, but she realizes now that they must be red like Jackie's were. She's grateful that he doesn't suspect the real reason. "I lost track of the day. It won't happen again."

"I should hope not. Martha manages to keep an immaculate house, and she's pregnant," Pete says, loosening his tie and throwing his jacket over the back of a chair. Instinctively, Claire picks it up to be hung in the closet. "There's nothing stopping you, is there? My mother raised four sons and she still managed to get a damn lasagna out by dinnertime."

It's a backhanded jab. Another reminder that Claire hasn't given Pete what he wants.

Claire smooths her hand over the soft cotton of the jacket. There's an imperfection in the weave near the collar. The brief bout of confidence that drove her to talk back to Pete is leaking out of her. Pete's voice has been raising for the entire conversation, and the volume has the effect it always does.

Claire deflates.

"Yes, dear."

Fighting is useless. What can she really do besides grin and bear it? Pushing back only reminds Pete of all the ways Claire is failing him. She has no idea why she even tried. Her indulgence this afternoon was a mistake.

Pete is cold with her for the rest of the night. It means a break from some of Claire's wifely duties, at least, and for that she's grateful.

By the time Claire wakes up the next morning fresh and sober it all seems a bit embarrassing. The way she acted. The way she's *been* acting when it comes to Jackie. Disobeying her husband, causing friction in her marriage. She wishes she was as strong as Jackie is, able to buy a house and have a job and live on her own, but she isn't. She never has been.

She's Peter Davis's wife.

Chapter 9

Claire doesn't call on Jackie the following day.

She finally plants the spring flowers. She scrubs the kitchen until the linoleum is gleaming. She goes grocery shopping, glancing around the corner of each aisle as if she's expecting Jackie to jump out from behind the milk fridge in one of her hip designer outfits. It feels unimaginably dull to shop alone, after doing it with Jackie.

She makes it all the way to bedtime without serious incident. She makes dinner and cleans the dishes and tidies the kitchen, and she mends some loose threads in Pete's favorite tie while he watches his evening news. The anchor talks about anti-war protests in L.A., a theft in Tulsa, and a new dance club opening in Fresno.

"Why don't we ever go dancing anymore?" Claire says, suddenly.

"Why would we?" Pete says. His attention is more on the television as the broadcast shifts to syndication.

"Because it's fun," Claire says. She tries to stave it off, but the memory of dancing with Jackie yesterday is clearer to her than the screen she's watching. She can remember how Jackie's hand felt in hers. Her laugh in Claire's ear. The exhilaration of spinning her around the living room like a fool.

It had been silly, and Jackie didn't tell Claire to stop. She seemed to like it that way.

"I'm too tired to dance, Claire," Pete grumbles. "I work for a living. And besides, we won't have time for any of that once we get a family started."

Claire swallows. A second mention in as many days is more than usual, and it sets her nerves on edge.

"You know, Dr. Martin gave me a call at work the other day. He offered the number for some specialist in the city," Pete says, sending cold fissures down Claire's back. He fishes in his pocket, finally producing a business card and handing it over to Claire without taking his eyes away from the television. "Says the man is a miracle worker."

Claire takes the card with an unsteady hand.

Dr. Kirkland, Fertility and Prenatal Specialist.

"I—I don't think I need a specialist. These things just take time," Claire says, pressing her thumb into the embossed letters. Her fingers want to dig into her palms.

"It's time to be proactive, I say," Pete says gruffly. "Get you all checked out. See what's broken."

Claire clenches her teeth. She isn't sure even the best fertility specialist on the planet could identify all the broken parts of her.

She keeps her mouth shut for the rest of the night. She follows Pete up to bed, does her wifely duty, and waits for Pete to start snoring before she starts her routine.

She stares at her own reflection in the vanity mirror—at her freckles, her springy hair, the thin hollows of her collarbone. She removes her pearls, setting them in the bottommost drawer of her jewelry box. She sets her engagement and wedding bands into her ring dish. She unpins her hair, pulling the brush through it in a soothing pattern.

She's just about ready to run a scalding bath when through the adjacent window, Claire sees the flicker of moving shadows in Jackie's backyard.

An intruder?

Claire's heart flutters. She goes to the window, peering down over the fence.

The shadow isn't an intruder. It's Jackie. The shape of her is unmistakable, but it's strange to see her after such a long day of careful avoidance. Jackie is standing by the pool, lit by flickering underwater lights, and she appears to be removing her silky robe. Except that underneath it, she isn't in a bathing suit. She's just—she's in her negligée, but now she's slipping out of that too, and—

And then she's in nothing. Absolutely nothing. Jackie is *naked*, and Claire can't look away. Her hairbrush is suspended in midair and her mouth is hanging open and *something* is happening in the vicinity of her hips as she watches Jackie, bare as the day she was born, dive into the pool.

Jackie's pale form cuts through smoothly from one end to the other. After surfacing she treads water for a second, her limbs looking wobbly and strange under the surface, and then she floats onto her back and kicks her legs lazily to keep afloat.

Claire is standing so close to the window that her breath is fogging the glass. She moves to a different pane, gobsmacked, trying to make out the details—she can just see the outlines of Jackie's chest floating on the surface, the fan of her dark hair around her head, and then a darker patch lower, between—oh, *gosh*, between—

Jackie's feet find the bottom of the shallow end. She stands, the water shifting out from her body in ripples, and then she tilts her head in Claire's direction.

Pete snores loudly.

It's in that moment that Claire realizes her bedroom lamp is on. She's standing in the window, staring at her neighbor swimming naked like some kind of peeping Tom, probably perfectly silhouetted by the light for Jackie to see her shameful spying.

Claire squeaks, in a deeply unladylike way. She ducks below the windowsill, shaking, and presses a hand to her racing heart. She hardly even recognizes herself in the actions of the last few days. The drugs, the argument, the *peeping*—Claire is clearly losing her mind.

She can never see Jackie again after all of this. Never.

All she can do is crawl until she's out of the window's line of sight and climb into bed next to a snoring Pete, her stomach in knots and her bath forgotten. She hardly sleeps that night, tossing and turning until Jackie's pool lights finally turn off in the wee hours.

Claire maintains the distance from Jackie as late April shifts into May.

It's for the best, really. Now that she's not so consumed with spending as much time next door as possible, she gets caught back up with the housework easily. She goes to book club, though once again nobody else seems to want to discuss the book. She even passes a small stationary store on the way home from grocery shopping, and she waffles outside for close to five minutes before she decides to use her last few leftover cents to buy a notebook and a set of drawing pencils.

The first time she opens the book with a sharpened pencil in hand, it all comes back in a rush. The scrape of graphite against paper. The smell of a fresh sketch. The streak of grey lead it leaves along the edge of her hand. It all feels as familiar as her grocery list. Maybe even more so.

She fills the book with meaningless little sketches each day. She makes a rough approximation of the bird nesting in the rafters above Jackie's front door. She jots down cloud shapes and squirrels and anything else she can see from her kitchen window. She draws the yellow acacia tree—she painted it once, just after she and Pete moved in here and before she left her job at Anita's art shop, but all she has now is pencil. The dark grey lines and round flowers remind her of Jackie's tattoo.

And once she's gotten accustomed again to having a pencil in her hand, Claire slides easily back into what she used to do at the park for hours at a time—simple portraits, capturing features in a quick sketch. Since there are fewer passersby in the cul-de-sac than there used to be in the park, Claire is limited to the faces she already knows.

She draws Peter from memory, frowning with his fingers crinkled in his morning paper. She draws Martha dusting a shelf with a hand over her belly, and Walter at his grill. She draws her parents—her mother's face comes easily, but Claire has to work to recall the details of her father's features.

Maybe it's because she hasn't been allowing herself to see Jackie, but it's her face that Claire struggles with the most. Claire starts sketch after sketch, tracing out the lines of Jackie's features in increasing detail—she draws Jackie smiling, and she draws her thoughtful. She tries to commit to paper the magic of Jackie's laugh.

None of the sketches feel good enough. No pencil can accurately capture her, let alone one held inexpertly by Claire, and the constant attempts do nothing but remind her how long it's been since they saw each other.

It doesn't help that every time Claire tries to draw anything below the column of Jackie's neck, she's reminded of what she did.

She gives up after her seventh attempt. She rips out the pages, folding and tucking them into the back of the sketchbook where nobody needs to see them again.

To say it's a shock to answer the front door later in the week to Jackie Callas in a scarlet romper is a vast understatement.

"Jackie!" Claire manages to gasp, swiping at a stray corkscrew of hair that's fallen out of her bun. There are still suds on her hands from the dishes, and she can feel them drying on her flushed forehead. "What are you doing here?"

Jackie's romper is partially unbuttoned. It shows off a truly startling amount of collarbone, among other things. There's a small mole just peeking past the fabric on the swell of Jackie's left breast. Claire hadn't been able to see that detail from her window.

She averts her eyes quickly.

"I haven't seen you in ages," Jackie says, shrugging. "I thought I'd be the one to stop by this time."

Claire bites hard on her lower lip.

Since the pool incident, Claire hasn't been able to clear that strange night from her head. The idea of seeing Jackie up close, talking to her as if she didn't silently watch her skinny-dip like an absolute *pervert*, has filled Claire with unexplainable dread.

"I'm sorry I haven't visited," Claire says, drying her sudsy hands on her skirt. "I've just been…"

"Busy. I guessed," Jackie says. Something sad passes briefly over her face. It's fleeting, but Claire catches it. The idea that she might be the cause is too much to bear.

Perhaps Jackie didn't see her in the window, after all. Maybe Claire is making a mountain out of a molehill like she always does, and ruining something perfectly nice over nothing.

"I'm sorry, Jackie," Claire says, trying her best to relax and speak sincerely. "I really am. I've been a bad friend, lately."

"It's perfectly fine," Jackie says with a careless wave. "If you're still busy, I'll go."

Claire opens the door wider. "You should come in. I'll make us a drink, for once."

Jackie hesitates for a moment, but she steps inside. Her heels click on the linoleum. The linoleum of Claire's house.

Something about it, about glamorous Jackie standing in Claire's entryway in her chic outfit and following her into the kitchen, makes Claire feel hot and cold all over.

Jackie's gaze sweeps the kitchen in that quick, observant way she has. She looks around at the speckled countertops, the wooden table, and the window that faces her own driveway with something sharp and appraising in her eyes, and Claire is reminded suddenly of just how different her house is from Jackie's. Her home has none of the openness, none of the trendiness, and there's so much housework that still needs to be done.

To Claire's horror, Jackie's roving eyes land on the sketchbook sitting on the kitchen table.

"What's this?" Jackie says, tapping the table next to the book. She doesn't make any move to pick it up, but Claire still dives for it, clutching it to her chest.

"Nothing," Claire says. Her voice is a little shrill; she clears her throat, tucking it under her arm. "Just a book."

Jackie arches a brow.

"Just a sketchbook," Claire admits. "I've been doodling,"

"Have you?" Jackie says, breaking into a wide grin. "That's fantastic!" For a terrible, breathless moment, Claire wonders if Jackie will ask to see them—if Claire will be forced by politeness to flip through countless half-finished sketches of Jackie in front of Jackie herself. But Jackie doesn't ask. She leans against the table, smiling at Claire. "I'm glad you're finding your passion again."

"Me too," Claire says. Her voice cracks. She clears her throat, manners outweighing all else even now. "Would you like a tour of the house?"

"I'd love one," Jackie says warmly.

Her kindness doesn't negate Claire's self-consciousness as she guides Jackie upstairs to the bedrooms. Every slightly dusty photo frame and missed patch of vacuumed carpet might as well be outlined in chalk, ripe for criticism.

"The bedrooms are up here, and the master bath," Claire says, gesturing at the open doors. She wishes she'd have thought to close them. "And Pete's home office. Not much to see."

"Is this your wedding photo?" Jackie says, examining one of the frames near the stairs. "You look so young."

Claire's stomach does a funny twist.

"I wore my mother-in-law's dress," Claire says. She fidgets with her pearls, pressing one so hard against her collarbone that she wonders if it might bruise. "It didn't quite fit me."

She's not sure why she feels the need to explain it. Her wedding day hadn't been anything to write home about. Pete didn't want the fuss of a large wedding, so they did it at the courthouse with only family in attendance. She's never felt like she looked particularly nice on the day, either. The dress was too small. Too short by a few inches, too narrow in the shoulders and too large in the waist, and Rita had fussed about making any permanent alterations. In the end Claire had worn it cinched with a piece of white ribbon, and held together in the back with a pin.

"Why Pete's mother's dress? Why not your own mother's? Or a dress you chose?"

"Rita wanted me to wear it," Claire says simply. "All my sisters-in-law did before me."

Despite walking past that photo every day, it's been years since Claire thought about it in such detail. She'd never been one to dream about her future wedding day as a little girl, so when Pete and his mother started overriding her decisions, she'd just accepted it. It wasn't worth the argument. Her own mother put up a bit of a fuss, but Rita's pure force of personality put a stop to that quickly.

She can still remember the shame of not fitting into the dress. Rita had pulled and tugged at the zipper until it almost broke between Claire's shoulders. She'd felt like a painting stuffed into too small a frame, all long limbs and protrusions ruining a family heirloom fitted for a more normal body than her own as Rita and Pete tried to trim her edges away.

Jackie looks closer at the photo. "Was Pete standing on a box? I had the idea that you were taller than him."

Claire can feel her cheeks heating up. Pete has never taken well to that being pointed out, and Claire has yet another reason to be glad he isn't here. "I wore ballet flats. And stooped a bit. Pete and Rita didn't want him to look short for the pictures."

"They had a lot of requests, didn't they?" Jackie says. There's something sharp in her tone that Claire can just imagine Pete bristling at.

"It was easier to let them plan it."

"Did you have a nice honeymoon, at least?"

"Pete doesn't like to travel," Claire says, barely able to look Jackie in the face to see the pity she's sure is written across her features.

After a brief pause, Jackie takes a step towards the closest door. "Is this bedroom yours?"

"Oh, um—Yes. Did you want to—?" Claire says, but Jackie is already ducking inside.

Jackie looks around the bedroom with an interest that Claire can't understand. She runs a hand over the foot of the bed as she glides past, the pristine folding of the duvet wrinkling in a line under her fingers, and she stands at the window to look down into her own backyard in the very place Claire peeped from. Seeing Jackie there makes her feel antsy.

Finally, Jackie comes to the closet, still open after Pete's dressing this morning. She moves Pete's things aside to thumb past Claire's clothes, drab skirt after drab skirt, taking in the breadth of Claire's stiff handmade dresses.

"I can't imagine how frumpy this must feel compared to your closet," Claire says, shifting from foot to foot. "I mean, look at what you're wearing today. You could be on a runway."

"You've said that kind of thing several times now," Jackie says suddenly.

Claire blinks. She does remember saying something of the sort, when they first met. She's only surprised that Jackie remembers, too. "Have I?"

Jackie lets the last skirt fall back into line, turning on her heel and regarding Claire carefully. Claire tries very, very hard not to be rude and stare at the bare skin of her collar.

"Do you remember what I said about being kind to yourself?" Jackie says, one perfect brow arched.

"It's less an unkindness and more an objective fact," Claire counters.

Jackie folds her arms. "Do your clothes bother you? Do you *feel* frumpy?"

Claire sinks down to sit at the end of the bed. She still hasn't gotten used to this aspect of Jackie's personality—the blunt questions, and the seemingly genuine interest in Claire's answers. The intensity. Jackie is looking at her as if she expects a real answer, and inexplicably Claire wants to give it.

"I think so," Claire says. "Frumpy and…and plain."

"Why not buy some new clothes?"

"Nothing ever fits me right," Claire says. There's a thread loose near the hem of her skirt—she pulls at it, even though it means more work in the mending later. "I'm too gangly, I don't fill anything out properly. I've been that way since I was a child."

"There are styles that would suit you," Jackie says. "You say I could be on a runway, but you realize that runway models have *your* body type?"

Claire scoffs. "I look nothing like them. And besides, Pete doesn't like modern styles. There's no point in spending money to pretty me up, Jackie. It's just lipstick on a pig."

"Lipstick on a—Claire, that's absurd," Jackie says. The bed dips just to Claire's right, and she can feel Jackie's shoulder touching her own. "Having different measurements than a department-store mannequin doesn't mean you aren't gorgeous in your own right."

Gorgeous. A word Claire has never heard in reference to herself, and one she has a great deal of trouble believing.

Claire recalls Jackie's word from last week. She called Claire handsome. Claire has never been able to believe anyone—Pete, her own parents, *anyone*—who called her pretty, but something about the word Jackie used then has stuck with her.

Jackie's shoulder feels warm against her own. Claire's skin tingles through the fabric of her dress. She wishes that Jackie would use that word again.

"I should make us that drink," Claire says, springing to her feet. She feels warm, and Jackie's body heat isn't helping any. She turns on her heel, striding towards the stairs, and after a pause she hears Jackie follow.

Claire is only just getting the kettle on to boil when three crisp knocks sound at the front door.

She almost drops their mugs. Instead, she sets them on the table, rushing to the window while Jackie hovers near the stove, not yet sitting down.

Claire can only see a sliver of the front stoop from here, but it's enough to identify Martha's bright red hair.

"Shoot," Claire hisses, letting the curtain fall back. Her heart is in her throat. Knowing that Martha could be watching the frequency of her visits to Jackie's house is one thing but having her actually see Jackie here is another.

What if she tells Pete?

"Is everything okay?" Jackie says.

Claire whirls around. She wrings her hands together, pacing from the window to the kitchen door and back. "It's Martha. Okay, just—I'll just go down there and ask her to leave. It's fine."

Jackie is quiet for a moment, watching Claire pace.

"She really doesn't like me, does she?" Jackie says softly.

Claire sighs. She twists her wedding band around her finger. "She really doesn't like most people."

"She likes you," Jackie says. "And you're worried about her seeing me here." It's matter-of-fact, and it makes Claire's stomach churn.

"Claire?" Martha calls, muffled by the door. Claire can hear the impatience in her voice. "It's very hot out here."

"If you have a back door, I can go," Jackie says. "She won't even know I've been here." She moves as if to head in that direction, but Claire steps into her way.

"That's not—it's not that I don't want her to see you, Jackie, it's—she's just a bit of a gossip. And Pete, he doesn't exactly know—it's not that he doesn't *know*, it's really more that I just don't mention—"

Knock, knock, knock.

"I'll be just a moment," Claire says in a rush. "Please don't go?"

She runs to the door after Jackie's tentative nod, opening it just enough to see Martha's face.

"Finally. What took you so long?" Martha says. She pushes on the door, but Claire holds fast.

"I'm actually a bit busy right now," Claire says, through the crack. "I'm sorry. Could you come back later?"

"Busy? Doing what?"

"Just busy," Claire says. She starts to close the door, eclipsing Martha's shocked face. "I'll call on you tomorrow, I promise."

A dainty foot wedges into the crack just before Claire can close the door.

"Claire Davis, do you have someone in there with you?" Martha says loudly.

Claire reels back. It's as if Martha has slapped her—she stops pushing at the door, which refuses to budge anyway with Martha's shoe in the way, to stare at her with mouth agape.

"If you're stepping out on your husband, so help me," Martha says, her voice getting shrill enough to startle the birds in the acacia tree.

"Don't be ridiculous," Claire says, opening the door wider in an unsuccessful attempt to get Martha to move her foot. "It's nothing like that, nothing at all!"

"Then you'll have no issue letting me inside, will you?"

There isn't much Claire can do. Martha bulldozes her way in, headed straight to the kitchen, but when the door swings open to reveal Jackie sitting at the table she freezes in place.

"Oh," Martha says, as Claire hurries in behind her. "It's you."

"Don't worry, I'm on my way out. I needed a cup of sugar," Jackie says. She rises to her feet. "But I've distracted Claire long enough."

"Wonderful. Be seeing you," Martha says snappishly.

"You don't have to go," Claire says, but Jackie is already halfway to the door. Claire isn't brave enough to grab her arm.

"But I should," Jackie says. She nods at Martha, giving her a smile. "Lovely to see you again."

"And you," Martha says, with none of Jackie's warmth.

The door closing behind Jackie leaves Claire all tangled up like a string of Christmas lights. She's absolutely sure of one thing—that she's just made Jackie feel as if she's ashamed to be her friend.

Claire isn't ashamed. She just can't let Pete find out. If he does, Claire is sure he'll put a stop to it.

"I didn't see her taking any sugar," Martha says. She hasn't yet sat down—she smooths a hand over her belly like it's a worry-stone. "If I didn't know better, I'd think you were making friends with the swinging neighbor."

"Jackie isn't a swinger," Claire says, rather forcefully. "I told you that she invited the whole neighborhood to that party. Are you really spreading rumors over that?"

Martha recoils. The echo of Claire's words seems to ring in the small space. The look of pure shock on Martha's face speaks for itself—Claire has never snapped at her like this. She's never snapped at anyone like this, at least not before the lasagna incident with Pete.

"Sorry," Claire says, hunching her shoulders and trying to lower her voice. "I just think you're being unfair, that's all. She hasn't done anything to you, has she?"

Martha doesn't answer. She purses her lips, and then to Claire's horror, her eyes get shiny.

"I came over to figure out what desserts you're bringing to dinner on Friday night, but it looks like you have a new best friend," Martha says. Her voice cracks on the last word, but she turns on her heel before any tears fall.

"Martha," Claire says, half-heartedly. "Don't be silly. That's not—"

The door slams shut.

Claire sinks into the closest chair with a shaky sigh.

"Well done, Claire," she mutters, folding her arms on the tabletop and setting her forehead on them. "Now *everyone* is upset with you."

Chapter 10

Dinner with Martha and Walter is an awkward affair.

Pete and Walter don't seem to notice at all. They talk just as they usually do, blind to the tension that sits between their wives. Pete swigs his wine; Walter noisily shoves salmon into his mouth. Martha picks at her asparagus, clearly still upset, while Claire makes patterns in the hollandaise sauce with her fork.

Claire is successful in her resolve to put on a brave face for the night until the conversation turns to the other side of the street.

"Haven't seen hide nor hair of that new neighbor since she moved in," Walter says, topping up his own wine and Pete's. "She hasn't come to book club, has she, Martha?"

"She has not," Martha says tightly.

"Wonder how she affords that big house without a man around."

"She's a photographer," Claire says, before she can think better of it. "She...told me at the housewarming."

Martha stabs aggressively at a boiled potato.

"A working woman! She's certainly easy on the old eyes, isn't she?" Walter says boisterously. Whether he doesn't see Martha flinch or he simply doesn't care, Claire doesn't know. "Bet she'd be a handful, though. Big-city woman like that strikes me as one of those bra-burners. Needs someone to tame her."

"The looks aren't worth the trouble, Walt," Pete says, grinning into his wine glass. "I'm glad Claire has nothing to do with her. Don't need someone like that putting any ideas in her head." He says it as if Claire isn't right next to him. He does it often, but tonight it sets Claire's nerves on edge.

It doesn't help that Martha's head perks up for the first time all night.

"Oh?" Martha says, setting her fork down demurely. "I see Claire crossing the lawns pretty frequently to visit her."

Claire's stomach sinks to the floor.

"Don't be ridiculous," Pete scoffs. He turns to Claire, who stares down at her half-eaten salmon. The other half is currently churning in her stomach.

"Claire? Didn't you spend the afternoon with our dear neighbor just the other day?" Martha says. There's a pinched, satisfied sort of look on her face. A small revenge for Claire's emotional slight. Claire has never seen her look quite so vindictive.

Claire's nails find their home on the inside of her palm.

"Is that true?" Pete says. His knuckles are stark white around his fork.

"She needed a cup of sugar," Claire says. She keeps her eyes aimed at her plate. "We had tea. That's all."

Walter piles more potatoes onto his plate. The clatter of the serving spoon against the bowl makes Claire's skin feel itchy.

"Is this why you've been slacking off lately? You're spending all your time socializing with that tramp?" Pete says.

Claire says nothing. Something is bubbling in her stomach. It's hot and acidic, and it makes her want to snap at someone—at Pete's furrowed brow, at Martha's smugness, at Walter and his noisy eating. Swallowing it down is like trying not to vomit all over the dinner table.

"Well, that ends today," Pete says when Claire doesn't answer. He chuckles indulgently, looking to Walter, and his grip on his fork relaxes. "Suffice to say, you won't be associating with her again."

Claire is sure that if she stayed silent, the topic would pass. The spotlight would leave her, and she could put her head down for the rest of the meal. But that hot, bubbling feeling has only gotten worse, and whatever is holding it back starts to dissolve the moment Pete confirms Claire's persistent fear.

You won't be associating with her again.

In a surge of indignance, Claire snaps. "You can't control who I see."

A hush falls over the table. Walter pauses with his fork halfway to his mouth. Martha's eyes go wide, looking back and forth between Claire and her husband.

Pete's moustache twitches. "We'll talk about this at home," he says. Six words. Deceptively simple, and they're just enough to cool whatever mania caused Claire to speak up.

The rest of dinner is even more awkward. Usually Pete would stay to share a few drinks with Walter, but tonight Claire avoids her usual post-dinner chat with Martha and says their goodbyes early.

Pete's demeanor changes the moment they step into their own house.

"You embarrassed me tonight," he says. It's a quiet anger, but Claire doesn't doubt it could get worse at any moment.

"I'm sorry for when and where I said it, but I don't want to stop socializing with Jackie," Claire says, trying to keep her tone even. "There's no reason—"

"This is not a discussion," Pete says loudly. "You should want nothing to do with her, or the people who were at that party."

Claire flinches at the volume, but she doesn't step back. Her heart pounds against her ribcage. This is the second time in as many months that Pete has been given cause to shout at her, and in both instances it's been Claire's fault. Fighting didn't help at all last time. She should lower her head, apologize, and do what her husband says.

But that bubbling, acidic feeling is rising further up her throat again. Here, with no audience, Claire can identify it.

She's *angry*.

"She came over for tea, Pete," Claire says forcefully. She doesn't quite match Pete's volume, but it might be the closest she's ever come to actually shouting. "For Christ's sake, I'm not going to start *swinging* just because we spent an afternoon together."

Pete balks. For once, rather than fearing the fallout, Claire is flooded with a kind of exhilaration. A freedom. Standing her ground with Martha had been one thing, but this is another altogether. She's not going to back down, this time.

"What the hell has gotten into you?" Pete says.

Claire strides past him, heading to the stairs. "Nothing. I just don't see why I can't be friendly with a neighbor."

Pete catches her arm as she passes. He pulls it taut until she jerks back from the first step, his grip tight on her forearm. "Clearly it's getting in the way of your duties as a wife."

"I'll make sure it doesn't," Claire says, yanking her arm away. She storms up the stairs, fueled by adrenaline, and Pete calls after her.

"I don't want you seeing her anymore, Claire. And that's my final word!"

Rather than going into the bedroom where she'll soon have to share the space with him, Claire darts into the upstairs bathroom and locks the door firmly behind herself.

She can hear Pete's heavy steps coming up the stairs. He goes straight to the bedroom, slamming the door, and the house goes quiet.

All the anger that propelled her here leaves Claire's body at once. Her legs seem to quiver—she sinks down onto the closed toilet seat, shaking like a leaf.

She just raised her voice at Pete. She pushed back at her husband. She *argued*. She's going to pay dire consequences for it she's sure, but in the moment it felt good in a way Claire couldn't have imagined.

Maybe Jackie would even approve.

When Claire finally emerges, Pete is already sleeping. He's facing the wall, snoring away as if nothing is weighing on his mind. He's given Claire her rules, and now he has nothing to worry about. She's not to see Jackie again.

Claire sighs.

She sits heavily at her vanity, combs her hair, and lays out her things. Her necklace goes in its box, her hair pins in their dish, her wedding rings on their shiny plate. Every piece of her orderly life accounted for.

With all her layers removed, Claire looks to Jackie's house. There's a light in one of the windows. Claire wonders what it might be like to go there, now. To disobey Pete and show up at Jackie's door and tell her everything that happened at dinner.

Would Jackie be in that robe she wore the other day? Would they retire to the conversation pit, where Jackie would lounge and give Claire whatever bits of wisdom she can spare? Would she bring out that marijuana again, to help Claire relax? Would Claire partake?

Pete snores loudly, startling Claire from her thoughts.

Sneaking over to Jackie's is a ridiculous daydream, and nothing more. But Claire refuses to stop speaking to Jackie just because Pete doesn't like her. If she's very careful not to alert Martha, she can still make their friendship work. She's sure of it.

Taking a slow, deep breath, Claire sets down her hairbrush and climbs into bed.

Monday morning dawns bright and sunny after a rainy weekend. Pete puts on a new tie over a clean, ironed shirt. He reads the paper, grumbling again about degeneracy and shoddy police work as he reads a cover story about some anti-war protests. He eats his eggs, packs up his briefcase, and leaves for work after a quick peck on the freshly-shaven cheek from Claire.

The moment Pete's Cadillac rounds the corner, Claire picks up the phone. Jackie answers on the third ring with a curt, businesslike *Jacqueline Callas speaking*.

"Good morning, Jackie," Claire says, making herself comfortable at the kitchen table. "It's Claire Davis calling."

Jackie's voice warms up immediately. "And my day gets brighter. What can I do for you?"

Claire twirls the cord around her finger, smiling foolishly into the phone. "I just wanted to talk. And to...well, to apologize, in fact. For what happened last week with Martha?"

"Oh, Claire, don't worry about that," Jackie says. Claire can just imagine her waving a casual hand, quick to forgive. "I understand."

"Even so, it was incredibly rude of me," Claire says. "I know I must have given a terrible impression, but I very much enjoy our time together. Martha is just quite..."

"Territorial?" Jackie drawls.

"I was going to say sensitive," Claire says, though not without a smile.

"Of course you were. You're a kind person."

"And you're too kind to *me*," Claire says. "I'm glad you aren't upset."

"Of course not. I'm happy to hear your voice," Jackie says. Her voice is warm and easy. Already it's lifted a weight from Claire's shoulders.

"Any fun plans for today?" Claire says. "Some high-fashion photoshoot you're jetting off to?"

"I'm actually reading a cookbook."

"Oh, dear," Claire blurts.

Jackie burst into laughter on the other line, and Claire laughs with her—the last time she stopped by while Jackie was trying to cook a simple can of soup, Jackie had lit a kitchen towel on fire.

"I know," Jackie says wryly. "I'm a menace in the kitchen, but I can only eat so many bowls of cereal."

It strikes Claire as a terribly lonely image. Jackie alone in her breakfast nook on a beautiful day like today, eating a sad little bowl of cornflakes.

"Why don't I give you the recipe for that chicken casserole you liked so much?" Claire says. She goes to the sink to look out the window at Jackie's driveway, the phone cord trailing behind her. "It's dead simple."

"And risk me burning the neighborhood down?"

Claire laughs again. She laughs so much these days that it's hard to remember what things were like before her foul moods could be solved by a simple phone call. She shifts the receiver to the other ear, drumming her fingers on the countertop.

Martha, Claire remembers suddenly, is at a prenatal appointment in Sacramento this morning. She complained just last week about Walter not being able to get the time off work to accompany her. For once, Martha won't be behind the curtains to see Claire leaving the house. If there was ever a time...

"We could make it together?" Claire suggests.

Jackie pauses for a long moment. "Are you sure?"

"I think you can do it. With supervision, of course."

Jackie agrees quickly. She has to run to the store to get some of the ingredients, but within the hour they're in Jackie's kitchen together with everything laid out on the countertop.

"All right," Jackie says, picking up a block of cheese with a dubious expression. "Step one: make sure the fire extinguisher is handy."

"No fires today," Claire says, laughing as Jackie raises an eyebrow. "We hardly even need to use the stove. It's mostly in the oven."

"I think you're underestimating my ability to ruin things."

"With me here, you'll be perfectly safe," Claire says.

Jackie's smile softens.

Jackie is a good student, though somewhat skittish. It's interesting to see her so out of her element—her usual confidence is reduced to nothing as she raptly follows Claire's instructions, and yet the whole thing is so easy. So smooth. Jackie listens to her, trusts her implicitly, and their conversation never pauses even over the sizzle of pans and the music from Jackie's record player.

Claire can't imagine what it would be like trying to teach Pete something like this. Or Martha, even. Pete would give up in frustration before they even began. Martha would probably have a hundred more efficient ways to do it and end up teaching Claire.

Claire hardly touches the casserole, simply pointing Jackie in the right direction instead. Jackie chops broccoli and cooks chicken, checking in with Claire constantly on its doneness, and when the whole thing is assembled in Claire's old casserole dish and bubbling away in the oven Jackie sits heavily in the breakfast nook with an exhausted groan.

"You do this every day?" Jackie says, her head lolling back against the bench as Claire slides into the opposite side with two cups of tea. "For every meal? *And* you clean, and garden. How do you ever have time to visit me with that much to do?"

"I'm not sure," Claire says, shrugging. "Pete is the one who has a job. I just keep house. I don't even have children to care for."

"Do you want children?"

"No," Claire says, without a single thought.

Jackie hardly reacts, but it hits Claire like the shockwave after a bomb.

Her mouth snaps closed. She's never been asked that question so easily, so frankly, and in her comfort with Jackie she answered just as honestly. Though Jackie doesn't look as horrified as she rightfully should, the shame is overwhelming.

"Not right now," Claire corrects quickly, her tongue tied in knots. "I mean—I'm sure we'll start a family soon. Pete wants to. He's been bringing it up more since Martha got pregnant."

The business card tucked behind the phone in her kitchen tugs at Claire's conscience. She still hasn't called the fertility clinic, and Pete has brought it up twice since he gave it to her.

"You shouldn't have them if you don't want to," Jackie says softly.

Claire's stomach lurches.

The whole wretched process makes her uneasy, from conception to pregnancy to motherhood. It suits her about as well as her clothes do. It all comes so naturally to Martha that Claire is positive she'll be hearing about how she's doing it wrong from the moment any of her children enter the world. And nobody has ever assured her that how she feels is okay. Not her mother, not Rita or Pete or Martha or even Dr. Martin. Not one person has ever made her feel as if her hesitation is legitimate, until this moment.

"No, I will. I will," Claire says. She makes a fist, pressing her nails into her palm. Pressing and pressing until she's sure she's made herself bleed again. "I will."

She will. She'll *have* to.

The record in Jackie's player ended some time ago. As if she can sense that Claire needs a moment, Jackie gets up and rifles through her cabinet in the living room. Claire can hear her carefully removing the vinyl, putting it back in its case, and replacing it with something new.

The voice that fills the house is ethereal. Claire recognizes it, now—it's the same female singer that she heard from Jackie's windows on the day she moved in. Joni Mitchell, if Claire is remembering right. Jackie has shown her lots of new music since they met, but she favors this album. Claire has heard it more than once by now.

For some reason, it strikes her differently now than it ever has before. The simple instrumentation and the deep, haunting tones in the vocals. The lyrics, lamenting over love found and lost. Jackie's quiet humming to match the song.

It's poetry. It's so different from the music Claire is used to, Pete's old country albums or her own favorite cheerful pop songs. It makes Claire ache for something she didn't know could exist.

"Jackie?" Claire says, as Jackie slides back into the booth. With some effort, she unclenches her fist and presses her palm against the tabletop. "Have you ever loved like that?"

Jackie takes a sip of her tea. It leaves a strip of moisture on the crest of her upper lip; she wipes it away, yet somehow keeps the perfect line of her lipstick. "Like what?"

"The way this woman sings. Like it's in your blood," Claire says. The words just keep coming, an unstoppable flow now that she's taken the cap off—she's asking something deeply personal, but it feels as if she *has* to. "Like your whole soul belongs to someone. Like you want them more than anything on earth."

Jackie is silent for a while, tapping the side of her mug. The record plays, spinning and spinning just like Claire's thoughts.

"I always thought that sort of thing was just for the movies," Claire continues. She can't bear to look up from the table, to see how Jackie is looking at her. "Real people don't feel that way. But she makes it sound so sweet."

"It can be," Jackie says. It's so low that it's almost a whisper.

Claire exhales. She wants to cry, and yet she doesn't want Jackie to see her like that. There's so much going on inside her these days that she can't even begin to label what she's feeling. "What's it like?"

"It's...all-consuming. When it ends, it feels like you might die. But when you're in it..." Jackie swallows, so heavily that Claire can hear it. She's let go of her mug, and now she's smoothing her thumb over the center of her own palm, like she once did to Claire's. It's the only part of Jackie that Claire can look at right now. "It can be wonderful. Transcendent."

"What happened to make it end, for you?"

"There's only so long one can be in the middle of a marriage," Jackie says.

Claire looks up. Jackie is chewing on her upper lip. Her lipstick has faded a bit, now.

"You were a *mistress*?" Claire says. She can hardly believe she's heard it right. She's defended Jackie from the ladies at book club, told them a dozen times that Jackie wouldn't steal anyone's husband, and now Jackie is telling her that's exactly what she did.

Jackie makes a noise—like a laugh and a scoff at once. "I suppose you could call it that."

"But that's...that's..."

"I know," Jackie says. "You're already looking at me differently."

Claire tries to school her expression. "I'm not! I swear, I'm only... confused. Why would you do something like that?"

Jackie makes another noise that Claire can't decipher. "I was in love. I was so in love that it made me nuts, I was...I was obsessed. I couldn't see it as anything but a star-crossed romance. I kept convincing myself that if I just stuck it out, eventually...I would get what I wanted so badly."

"Did you?" Claire says. "Get what you wanted, I mean?"

"No. After a few rounds of being assured the marriage was over before everything just went back to status quo, I realized it was never going to happen. I presented an ultimatum," Jackie says heavily. "You can guess what the end result was."

Claire looks down at Jackie's hands again. Jackie won't quite look at her, so they're the best place to guess at her mood. "Is that why you moved here? Why you always avoid the subject when I ask?"

"I needed to get away from my life in the city," Jackie says. There's a stark white mark on her hand where her thumb was. Her fingernails are bitten, the edges of her nail beds a little ragged. "All of it. Carte blanche. I think part of me wanted a slice of normalcy." Jackie sighs, shaking her head. "Maybe a bit of self-flagellation, too. I knew I wouldn't fit in here. I guess I thought I deserved it, after what I did."

Claire isn't sure what to say. She tries to imagine Jackie kissing this handsome, shadowy married man of hers. Being touched by him. Held by him. It makes Claire feel a bit ill. But what's even harder for her to imagine is loving a man so much, wanting him *so* badly, that she would step into someone else's marriage. If Pete had been seeing someone else when they'd met, she wouldn't have given him a second glance. There was nothing star-crossed about their courtship. No maelstrom of desire. He'd asked her to a school dance, and she'd been flattered enough to say yes.

"I wouldn't blame you if you judged me for it. I know it was wrong," Jackie says. There's a shake in her voice. "I'd understand if you don't want to associate with me anymore."

"I don't think I've ever loved," Claire blurts.

It burns in Claire, this sudden knowledge. This certainty. Whatever Jackie is talking about, whatever this music is expressing, this joy and connection and aching melancholy? It's alien.

"Like the songs? Not everyone does," Jackie says. She pauses, and then sighs again. "Maybe that's for the better."

"No. I don't think I've loved at all," Claire says. Something in her is pushing, *pushing*—to talk, to listen, to discuss this terrible feeling with Jackie. To purge it somehow, with someone who might understand. "I don't think I know what it feels like."

A warm hand settles over Claire's. When she finally looks up, the expression on Jackie's face is unimaginably tender. Understanding.

Claire has never been looked at like that before. Not by Pete; not by anyone. The strange feeling she's been wrestling with gives way to something else. It's bigger, taking up even more space, pressing everything else against the walls of her mind.

Panic.

"I'm sorry," Claire says. Her breath hitches. Her throat is getting tight, and the words are getting all tangled there. "I shouldn't be saying that. I love Pete, I do. He's my husband, and I should give him what he wants. I don't know what's wrong with me, I—I—"

"Claire," Jackie says. She squeezes Claire's hands; the balloon recedes enough for her to take a breath. "You're safe here."

It's inexplicable—technically speaking, Claire is very *un*safe here. Even just being in this kitchen is breaking a rule that could cause a fight worse than the one she and Pete have already had, but even so Claire believes her.

The weight of everything comes down on her at once. Her fights with Pete, and with Martha. The reality of a family she doesn't want, looming closer and closer. The endless cycle of her life.

At least with Jackie, she's not alone.

The tears come so suddenly that trying to stop them is a losing battle. Claire buries her face in her hands, choking on a sob, but it's too late. Jackie makes a quiet noise, sliding out from her booth seat, and Claire feels the bench dip next to her instead.

An arm lands around Claire's shoulders.

Claire trembles under the weight. Not because it's bad, but maybe because it's too good. She's not used to crying with anyone else around. Pete hates it when she cries. Usually, she only indulges the urge behind a locked bathroom door.

"I'm sorry," Claire gasps into her hands. Jackie's arm is tight around her, and the pressure of it helps. "I'm so sorry, I don't know what's come over me. Oh, I feel—so *silly*."

"You don't ever need to apologize to me for feeling," Jackie says. The smell of her shampoo fills Claire's senses. It's deeply comforting, though it only seems to make the tears come faster.

"I have nothing to cry about," Claire says, repeating the mantra her mother gave her to get through the tears on her wedding day. It didn't make them stop then, and it doesn't work now. "Nothing at all. I have a good life."

"You have choices, you know," Jackie says, with a strange note of urgency. "Your husband is stuck in the last decade. Things are changing. Things *have* changed."

"What things? What choices? It doesn't matter what I do. This is my life, Jackie."

"I can get you birth control, if you want it."

That's enough to stop the tears. Claire looks at Jackie sharply. "You can...how?"

"I know someone," Jackie says. Her eyes are dark and intense. "People who can take care of it. Is that what you want?"

"It's against the law."

"I know," Jackie says, smiling gently. It softens the strangeness of her eyes. "That doesn't always make it wrong. Remember?"

Claire sniffles. A tissue is pressed into her hands and she blows her nose noisily, wiping furiously at her eyes.

Jackie shifts. Her arm is still around Claire's shoulders, and it's making her feel warm all over. "Maybe this is rude, but...how have you gone so long without it happening if you aren't on the pill?"

Claire balls the tissue up in her fist. That's the rub, really—though Claire is grateful for it, she has no idea how she's escaped motherhood so far. It's as if her dread has poisoned her womb, made it inhospitable for the children Pete wants so badly. Intentionally or no, it's her fault. "I don't know. Pete thinks there's something wrong with me. My doctor wants me to see a specialist."

"Did you ever think that it might be him?"

"Pete?" Claire says. She frowns, distracted now from her own self-loathing. "It's a woman's job to give her husband children."

"No, it isn't. And men can be infertile, too. He shouldn't have you thinking it's all your fault," Jackie says. That intensity is back, tenfold; her arm tightens around Claire's shoulders almost to the point of discomfort. "You don't deserve that."

Jackie is so very close, right now. Claire can see a single white eyelash nestled among the long, dark others. There's a darker ring around the edge of her brown irises, almost dark enough to match her pupils, which are strangely wide. Jackie's scent is so lovely, the warmth of her arm so sweet, and yet her words are so mystifying. How could it *not* be Claire's fault?

The oven timer blares through the kitchen.

Claire jumps. It's enough to bring her back to the present; she takes a few deep, heaving breaths, and Jackie moves her arm away quickly.

"Goodness. There that goes," Claire says, clearing her throat. She wipes her face again, blowing her nose once more and stuffing the tissue into her sleeve, and then she does what she does best. She pushes it all down. "Right. We need to sprinkle some more cheese on for the last 15 minutes, so it gets nice and bubbly."

Jackie doesn't stop her. She's pensive until the casserole is served, and Claire goes home feeling more tangled up than ever.

Chapter 11

Martha and Walter's Memorial Day party is a yearly occurrence. Every year it's the same potluck food, the same conversations, the same neighbor kids running through the same sprinklers. Claire makes the same potato salad, and puts it on the same folding patio table.

What is *not* the same is Jackie Callas strolling across the lawn with an armful of sodas.

Pete, thank heavens, is too busy at the grill with Walter to notice. Claire darts over to Jackie quickly, taking some of the bottles before Jackie drops them.

"Thanks," Jackie says, chuckling a little at what she's sure is a flabbergasted expression on Claire's face. "Trust me, I'm as surprised as you are. I found an invite from Martha in my mailbox. Wasn't sure I should come, but then I saw you were here."

Claire wants nothing more than to preen, but she has more prescient issues. Martha is across the lawn refilling the beer coolers, but more accurately Claire would say that she's holding a bag of ice while staring at the two of them with narrowed eyes.

"Can I find you again in a few minutes?" Claire says quietly, trying to show as little emotion on her face as possible. Nothing that could be interpreted one way or another.

Jackie looks perplexed, but she nods. "Oh. Sure. I'll just…mingle."

Claire heads straight to the coolers. She helps Martha lift the last few bags of ice, distributing more beers throughout, and when Claire is crumpling up all the plastic bags Martha clears her throat pointedly.

"I'm surprised she actually came," Martha says, nodding in Jackie's direction.

Jackie is drifting through the party, looking a little lost—she's very clearly out of place amongst groups of people who already know each other, not wanting to force herself into conversations, and she gives the kids a wide berth.

"I'm surprised you invited her," Claire says.

"You seem to like her so much, I thought I'd give her a chance." Martha's words seem like a peace offering, but her tone says otherwise. This feels less like an olive branch, and more like a test. An experiment to see if Claire is maintaining her now-forbidden friendship.

"I was only being polite. We haven't talked in weeks," Claire shrugs. A careful lie, one more barefaced than she's ever dared before. "We don't have much in common, to be honest."

Claire's suspicion is confirmed when Martha smiles.

"Good. That's good," Martha says, pouring out two glasses of fresh lemonade. "You know, I think I should apologize, Claire."

"You do?" Claire says blankly. In all their years as friends and neighbors, this might be Martha's first-ever apology.

"For that friction with Pete, over dinner the other day. It was for your own good, you must see that now that you've put aside this business with Jacqueline," Martha says. She's strangely earnest as she hands a cup of lemonade to Claire. "You aren't upset with me, are you? I was only trying to help."

Claire takes the lemonade. She takes a sip—it tastes more sour than usual.

"Of course not," Claire says. The words feel hollow. A script laid out for her, as if none of her thoughts matter. "It's for the best."

"I'm glad you've seen the light," Martha says. She pats Claire on the shoulder, her other hand resting on her belly—she's really starting to show, these days. "Now we can go back to the way things should be, after this silly little speed-bump. Right?"

Claire bites her tongue.

Martha looks as if she might say more, but she stops mid-sentence, her eyeline focusing on the group of kids somewhere over Claire's shoulder.

"Miss Jane, is that a *frog* in your hand?" Martha says, pulling out a perfect parental tone that Claire is sure she'll be hearing from across the road for the next eighteen years. "And dirt all over your pretty dress—*where* is your mother?"

Martha bustles off to deal with the situation. Pete is on his fifth beer of the day, loud and boisterous and entirely distracted at the other end of the lawn. Jackie, having probably been frozen out of any conversations, looks like she's heading home.

In this small pocket of opportunity, Claire slips away.

She catches Jackie's arm near the side of the house, pulling her into Martha's well-maintained bushes. Jackie whirls on her, looking ready to defend herself until she sees that it's Claire who pulled on her sleeve.

"Oh. Claire," Jackie says. She looks around them—they're shielded from the party here, but Jackie doesn't seem particularly happy about it. "I was just leaving. This feels rather...clandestine."

"I thought we could have a little privacy here," Claire says, keeping her voice low.

"So you want to spend your Memorial Day in a shrub?"

Claire doesn't answer. She doesn't know what to say—the answer is yes, she'd spend her Memorial Day just about anywhere if it meant spending it with Jackie.

In Claire's silence Jackie seems to sink deeper into herself, averting her eyes and gnawing at her lower lip. The leaves are casting dappled shadows across her face, shifting and cascading over each other in the breeze.

"Pete told you not to see me anymore, didn't he?" Jackie says.

She sounds tired. Resigned. Claire should have known that Jackie would suss it out immediately. She's too smart to have the wool pulled over her eyes.

"He did," Claire says. She lowers her voice as the group of kids sprints by, shouting about starting a game of tag. "But he isn't home during the day, he doesn't know where I go. As long as I can keep Martha from seeing —"

"I don't want to cause marital issues," Jackie interjects. She's pulling away, as if she's going to step out of the bushes. "Or issues with Martha. This is all getting very complicated."

"You're my friend. You're worth it."

Jackie shakes her head. Her brow is furrowed. "I should go. I shouldn't have come, really. You don't need me waltzing in and messing up your life."

Jackie takes a step backward, but Claire reaches out to grab at her hands. She's never been a particularly physical person, in her friendships or in her marriage, but it feels so much more natural with Jackie. Easy. Jackie's soft hands cling to Claire's in return, even as the rest of her tries to leave.

"Mess up my life?" Claire says, aghast at the very idea. "You've made my life better."

"I've gotten between you and your best friend. I've caused fights with your husband," Jackie says. "You're a good person, with a good life. I'm not."

Claire is startled to see tears gathering in Jackie's eyes. She's reminded of Jackie's words from their last visit—*I knew I wouldn't fit in here. I guess I thought I deserved it.*

"I don't think that's true," Claire says.

Jackie only shrugs her off. She won't quite look Claire in the eye, and Claire comes to the uncomfortable realization that she's done it again.

She's made Jackie feel as if she's ashamed to be her friend.

"I want you in my life," Claire says clearly. It's maybe the first time she's ever felt completely sure about something. "Whether that means hiding it from Pete, or fighting with him every day about it. You're—"

Claire's voice falters. What she wants to say is, *you're my best friend, not Martha. I never knew friendship before you. Nothing else matters.*

"You're too important to me," Claire says instead. "I don't want to stop being friends. Do you?"

Jackie's eyes are wide. She looks down at their hands, and then back up; there's something strange in the air between them, an intensity that makes Claire want to move closer. Jackie's skin is so, so soft.

"No. I don't," Jackie says quietly.

"Then let's not stop. Okay?"

Jackie nods silently.

"Okay," Claire says. She squeezes Jackie's hands, but doesn't let them go. She doesn't want to. "Good. That's settled. Now. Hot dog, or hamburger?"

Jackie laughs a little. It breaks the strangeness still hanging between them like cobwebs. "Neither. I really should go. I don't feel like being glared at by Martha all day."

It's understandable, if disappointing. "Will I see you this week?"

Jackie swallows. She glances back towards the party, where Pete's voice can be heard above the others. Her hands are still held in Claire's.

"I'd like that," Jackie says. She finally squeezes Claire's hands, and before she drops them, she flashes a smile that holds at least a hint of her usual vivaciousness. "Give me a call on Monday?"

The fact that Claire never visits, *can* never visit, on the weekend when Pete is home remains unspoken.

Claire stays in her little hidey-hole for a few long, quiet minutes after Jackie has headed home. She can hear Pete calling for her, wondering where she is—that it's taken him this long to realize she's gone isn't surprising. Claire ignores him until a small child sprints through the bushes, barreling into Claire's middle.

"Oh. Sorry, Mrs. Davis," the girl says—it's Jane, the one Martha scolded not long ago. She does have grubby hands and scraped knees at the hem of her skirt. "We're—um, we're playing hide-and-seek."

Jane shifts from foot to foot. There's a hole in one of her stockings, and a toe is poking out. She looks an absolute mess, like she's been tumbling through the dirt with the boys. She also looks supremely nervous. She must be expecting another scolding.

"Don't let me get in your way," Claire says, smiling down at her. "This is a good hiding spot."

Jane relaxes immediately. She's all long limbs and knobbly elbows, scrappy and tomboyish; Claire is sure her mother must be frustrated to no end by it, much like Claire's once was, but Jane doesn't seem to care. She crouches down in the mulch with no regard whatsoever for her nice dress. "Thanks! Don't tell Darren I'm here, he thinks a girl can't win."

"Mum's the word," Claire says, pressing a finger to her lips. She moves to slip through the bushes and back to the party, but she stops just short. "And, Jane?"

Jane looks up at her guardedly. There's a twig in her hair, and a fierce brightness in her eyes. An expectation, maybe, of being told she's too much. Too wild. Too unladylike.

"You look like you've had a grand time today," Claire says. "Keep having fun, okay?"

Jane breaks into a grin, wide and happy. "Yes, ma'am."

Pete is sticking fireworks into the ground with a few other men when Claire finds her way to the party again. He's stumbling a little—usually Claire would remind him to eat something or slow down on the beer, but instead she settles into a lawn chair next to Martha. He can take care of himself for a night.

"Where did you disappear to?" Martha says. She's watching the proceedings like a hawk, ready to give input on firework placement as always.

"I ran back home to powder my nose," Claire says.

Martha doesn't press. She heaves herself up to make her slow way towards the fireworks, calling directions to Walter and Pete, and Claire relaxes into her chair.

All in all, not a bad Memorial Day.

Her mother's phone call comes in early the next morning. She often likes to ring up after she goes to church, and Claire appreciates the earliness with the time difference—Pete likes to sleep in on a Sunday, so the conversation doesn't get interrupted.

"How are things?" her mother asks.

Claire whisks the waffle batter aggressively, frowning at the lumps that won't quite break down for Pete's breakfast. "Fine. How are things for you?"

"Lovely," her mother says simply.

The line crackles. It's not uncommon to run out of things to talk about—these calls are usually short, full of small-talk and random chatter. They don't talk about anything substantial. They never have. If ever Claire tries, her mother changes the subject.

Lately, though, everything Claire has been thinking and feeling has felt substantial. And who else can she talk about it with? Martha is a direct line to Pete. Jackie is the source of most of her ennui. Isn't a woman supposed to get advice from her mother? Passing wisdom through generations, and all that?

"A few things are...less than fine," Claire says carefully. She sets the bowl of batter down, tucking the phone more securely into her shoulder as she turns to slicing strawberries.

Miriam pauses for a long time before she answers.

"Such as?"

"Pete and I have been fighting," Claire says. "On occasion."

"Oh, honey," her mother sighs.

"I know," Claire says.

She can hear movement, as if her mother is getting more comfortable to listen. "What have you been fighting about?"

"A friend of mine."

Another pause. This one is longer and feels heavy with some meaning Claire is still sorting out. She cuts berry after berry, careful to keep the slices even.

"A friend?" her mother says. "Is this friend…a man?"

"No, Mother." Claire sighs. "Her name is Jackie. What do you take me for?"

"I was only asking."

"Pete doesn't want me seeing her anymore. But I have been. I've been going against his wishes," Claire admits quietly. Even if she can already sense the judgement that will follow, saying it out loud untangles one of the many knots in her chest. "Almost every day, now."

"Claire," her mother sighs. "You need to keep Pete happy. Why would you do something so foolish?"

"I don't know why he hates her so much," Claire says in a rush, throwing down her knife. "They all do. They dislike her without even knowing her. She's wonderful, Mother. She's smart, and independent, and so kind. She's my *friend*. Why is that such a bad thing?"

"I'm sure he has his reasons."

"He thinks she's a bad influence on me," Claire mutters. She feels petulant, now, like in talking to her mother she's been brought right back to being seven years old, trying to explain why she ruined her church dress splashing in puddles.

Her mother *tsks*. "It sounds like perhaps she is."

Claire clenches her jaw until her teeth hurt.

"I just want what's best for you," her mother says. It's the same tone she used when Claire expressed doubts on her wedding day. "A happy, secure life. *Safety*. Why would you put that at risk?"

"Why should Pete get to control every single thing I do?" Claire says. The syrup warming on the stove is starting to bubble, and she turns the knob down. "It isn't fair."

"He is your husband."

"But—"

"This is how it works, Claire," Miriam says. "You have nothing to cry about. You're making a mountain out of a molehill. Pete takes care of you, and you stick it out. Things will get better."

Claire is struck dumb, for a moment—it's been years since her mother was so firm with her. The last time she can remember was in sixth grade, when she had chipped one of her teeth playing rough on the playground equipment and almost ruined school picture day by getting blood on her dress.

Claire runs her tongue over the chip, still there on her second incisor. Small, but significant. The remnant of her last act of defiance, before very recently. Her mother had wanted to get it filled with some kind of bonding, but her father had disagreed. He said it gave her character.

"So what's for breakfast?" her mother says brightly, as if the conversation never happened at all.

Claire shouldn't be surprised. Her mother has always avoided difficult conversations, always emphasizing that it's better to look at the positive. But even for her, this is an abrupt pivot.

"I have to go," Claire says. She can hear Pete moving around upstairs, grunting and snorting, and it's never a pleasant morning when he comes down to find no breakfast.

"Oh. Sure. But you'll do what I said, won't you?" her mother says insistently.

"I'll talk to you next week," Claire says. She slams the receiver down harder than she meant to, but it *is* rather satisfying.

Claire sits for a moment in her frustration. She didn't expect her mother to be particularly helpful, but she didn't expect to be scolded, either.

When she hears the upstairs bathroom door open and close, Claire shakes herself out of her thoughts. She puts the coffee on and sets the waffle iron to heating. She makes Pete his breakfast, cleans up the kitchen, and spends the afternoon cutting coupons while Pete goes out golfing with Walter.

On Monday, Claire jets over to Jackie's house as soon as Martha's car pulls out of the drive for her weekly grocery shop.

Claire likes to think she's gotten better at reading Jackie's subtle facial expressions. When the door opens, there's a moment of genuine shock on her face that fades to happiness, though Jackie tempers it quickly.

"I wasn't sure I was going to see you again," Jackie says. She's smiling, but it looks skittish. Not a word Claire would usually associate with Jackie Callas.

"I told you you would," Claire says.

Jackie looks down, fussing at the carpet with her bare toes. Her hair falls like a curtain, concealing her thoughts from Claire. "I know. I guess it was hard to believe."

"Can I come in?" Claire says.

Jackie steps aside quickly. "Of course. I just have a couple things to finish in the darkroom, and then we can have some lunch. I've got leftover pizza?"

"Darkroom?" Claire says. She slips her shoes off at the door, and Jackie ushers her towards the hallway. The door Jackie shows her through is the only threshold in the house Claire hasn't yet crossed—the stairs to the basement. Claire's house doesn't have one, so she's a bit startled by just how pitch black it is—Jackie seems to have blocked the small windows to keep any light from getting in. Claire can't see anything at all until Jackie flips a switch, and the room lights up in a strange red glow.

There's a strong chemical smell on the air down here. Several tables hold differently colored plastic bins. Claire has to duck a little to avoid strings of photos draping from the ceiling like clotheslines. On a sturdy desk against the wall is a large piece of equipment that looks like a microscope. There's a sink in the corner, a couch on the opposite wall, and stacks of differently sized photo paper scattered everywhere.

"This is where I develop my prints," Jackie says. Under the red light, she looks eerie and eccentric.

"You do it all yourself?"

Jackie takes a photo from one of the tables, still shiny with liquid, and clips it to one of the clotheslines. "I like to have control over every aspect of the process. Someday I'd love to have my own gallery too, but that's a bit of a pipe dream."

"What are you working on right now?"

"I just finished up a commercial gig. Advertisements for a perfume company," Jackie says. She moves to a different table, one crowded with six different bins. "But my pet project is in here."

Claire peers into one of the bins. It's hard to see under the red light, but swimming in some kind of clear liquid is a large photo. It's hard to tell if it's in color or black and white—it's an amorphous form, like an ink blotch against a light background. "What is it?"

"Look closer," Jackie says.

Claire squints down at it, trying to see whatever Jackie wants her to see. The liquid makes the shape a little wobbly. She tilts her head this way and that. There's a shape that could be a head, and perhaps shoulders. Breasts below, and flowing hair. "It looks like a woman. With wings, maybe?"

She stares, and stares, and—

"Wait. It's an orchid," Claire says suddenly.

The flower is twisted and shadowed, but the lighter lines that streak up the petals make it clear. Jackie has formed another image with the negative space. Now that Claire has seen it both ways the image keeps shifting back and forth, orchid and then woman and back again.

"I was going for an ambiguous image. I've always been fascinated by them," Jackie says. She trails a finger across the liquid over the photo, sending ripples across the surface. "Finding new images in the negative space. There's no background, and no fore. Just two interpretations of the same thing."

"Like a brain-teaser?" Claire says.

Jackie shows Claire to a string of photos hanging above their heads. "Exactly. I have a whole series on flowers. The patterns you can find in the petals. Playing with angles. Light and shadow."

Claire reaches out, touching the edge of one of the photos. It's still damp. "How do you come up with this kind of thing?"

"I don't know. Hidden things jump out at me, I guess," Jackie says. Claire could swear by the sound of her voice that Jackie is looking at her, not down at the photo, but when she raises her head to check Jackie's gaze is down on the bins again.

"I wish I could see things the way you do," Claire says. The hanging photos make all sorts of shapes using flowers—a tulip shot from above, which looks like a king is emerging from the petals bathed by a golden sunrise. A lily that echoes the shape of a ballerina.

"You see things in your own way. You're an artist," Jackie says.

Claire scoffs, shaking her head. "I told you, I gave it up when I got married. And I could never make anything like this."

"What kind of art did you like to make?" Jackie asks.

"I liked to paint everything I could see," Claire says. She drifts through the room while Jackie pulls the photo out of the liquid with tongs. "And I used to sketch people at the park."

"Really? Just passersby?"

Claire shrugs. "I like to see what I can capture in a single image. I always feel like I can understand someone better after I've drawn them."

"That's how I feel about my camera," Jackie says. She dips the photo into a different bin of liquid, sloshing it around a bit. "The lens is like a filter that helps me see things in a new light."

Claire keeps following the strings of photos hanging all around. "You really like flowers."

"I'm terrible at keeping them alive, but I love to photograph them. My father is a florist. He doesn't talk much, but he'll talk about plants," Jackie says drily. She puts the photo into a third bin and carries it to the sink. "He used to tell me the hidden meanings behind all of them."

"Like acacias?" Claire says. "Your tattoo. Do they mean something special?"

Jackie doesn't answer for a minute. She seems to be washing the photo under the running tap, and Claire has already accepted that her question won't be answered when the faucet turns off.

"They mean hidden love," Jackie says quietly. Her back is to Claire. Her voice sounds strange. "Concealed emotions."

Jackie clips the photo up to dry with the rest. It drips slowly onto the concrete floor, leaving dark patches near Jackie's feet that Claire can see even in the dim red light.

"You said you got the tattoo to remind you of something," Claire says.

"I did say that, didn't I?" Jackie turns around, drying her hands methodically on a towel. Her eyes are fixed on it, her brow furrowed. "You have a way of getting things out of me."

"I do?"

"Yes. Without even trying, apparently," Jackie says. She tosses the towel onto the edge of the sink. "I think I'd tell you just about anything, if you asked."

Claire wishes above all else that she knew what to ask right now. Her mind has gone blank. She wants to know everything about Jackie, any crumb that she can find, and now when she might actually open up Claire can't come up with a single thing to say.

"Does the tattoo have to do with the man you loved?" Claire blurts.

Jackie makes a noise. It's almost like a laugh, but there's something else to it that Claire can't figure out. "Right. The *man*."

It's obvious that it was the wrong question to ask. It's as if an invisible shutter has slammed down between them, and Claire's stomach sinks. "Sorry. I just—you said hidden love, and I thought—"

"I didn't get it for a man," Jackie says. She's tracing over the tattoo with her fingers, brushing over the lines of the acacia branch without needing to look. Her eyes are fixed somewhere to the right of Claire, and totally unreadable—the red light is casting strangely over her features, obscuring some details and sharpening others. She looks like one of her own photographs come to life. Light and shadow.

It all feels significant, and Claire isn't sure why. She takes a step towards Jackie, but stops when her hip hits one of the tables. The mystery liquid splashes up, leaving spots on Claire's dress, and Claire couldn't care less about possible stains.

It seems to snap Jackie out of her strange mood. She straightens up, dropping her arms and stepping out of the direct path of the light. Her face falls into darkness as she shakes her head a little and heads towards the stairs, slipping past Claire in a wave of herbal shampoo.

"Not that it matters," Jackie says. "That's all over, now, isn't it?"

"Jackie," Claire says, but without a follow-up question she's left blinking in Jackie's wake as she climbs the stairs two at a time.

"Are you hungry?" Jackie calls loudly, disappearing into the upstairs hall. "I'm famished."

In the light of day, it's as if their conversation never happened. Jackie is her usual self. The rest of the afternoon passes over pizza and sodas, and Claire tries to set aside the strangeness in the darkroom.

It's startling, how quickly it all becomes a new norm. Jackie's discomfort with the subterfuge of their friendship is clear for the first few days after Memorial Day, but eventually they both slip into the habit—she gives Claire a spare key so that she can come straight inside rather than knocking, to reduce the likelihood of being spied on. If Jackie phones the house, she only does so when Pete isn't home. The ruse of it all becomes second nature.

Claire's mother is wrong. She has to be. If lying to Pete is what it takes to keep this, then she'll do it happily.

Perhaps Jackie is changing her, like Pete says. Maybe it's for the better.

Chapter 12

Something Claire doesn't ever expect when she knocks on Jackie's door is for her to already have a visitor.

Jackie is a solitary person, Claire has learned, whether by accident or design. She seems to have almost no visitors besides Claire. When Claire knocks on the door one very normal Tuesday and it comes with a very loud, very *male* laugh booming over the fence from Jackie's backyard, it seems so out of the ordinary that Claire wonders if she's imagined it until she sees a second, much smaller car next to Jackie's in the driveway. A small white Volvo. It's older than Jackie's Mustang, but in decent condition.

"Claire?" Jackie's voice shouts. Claire can only just hear the words. "If that's you, we're around back!"

Claire is long past being nervous about visiting Jackie, but the introduction of someone new—a man, no less—has her stomach in knots. But she wants to see her friend. In the end, she has no choice but to make her way around the side of the house to the fence gate, beyond which is a yard Claire hasn't yet stepped foot in.

It's a nice space, to be sure. It's well landscaped and decorated. The gardens are empty, but the lawn is well taken care of. The tasteful patio furniture matches the shimmering pool. Looking at the water is enough to make Claire blush these days, with the memory of that night at the window. Today is no different.

It doesn't help that Jackie is sitting in one of the lounge chairs in a pristine white bathing suit, with a drink in her hand.

It stops Claire in her tracks. Jackie is wearing a floor-length flowing sarong over her bottom half, but it's still the least amount of clothes Claire has ever seen her in. The suit is somewhere between a one-piece and a bikini, with cut-outs along the sides to show off the waist. It seems to glow in the bright summer sunshine, perfectly complimenting her dark olive skin.

It takes a mammoth effort for Claire to pull her eyes away from the shapely curve of Jackie's hips to pay attention to the person sitting beside her.

The man to Jackie's left is darker-skinned even than Jackie—in fact, Claire is sure that he's Black. He's well-groomed, with tight dark curls and eyes such a lovely shade of hazel that they almost look golden. He's wearing tiny red swimming trunks, and his shaved chest shines with baby oil. They're laughing together about something.

Claire is overcome by the bewildering and sudden urge to turn around and go home. Jackie is so joyful in his presence. So easy. Who is she to interrupt?

Jackie spots her before she can bolt.

"Claire! Come here—I'd like you to meet Theo," Jackie says, waving Claire over. "One of my oldest friends."

Theo offers his hand. When Claire takes it, he pulls it to his mouth to give her knuckles a dramatic kiss. His full lips are soft and completely whiskerless.

"Charmed," Theo says, with a wink. His voice is deep and rich. "Care to join us for an aperitif?"

"I'm not much for French food," Claire says.

Theo laughs as he lets go of Claire's hand. His head tips back, as if he's never heard something so funny in his life. "It's a *drink*. I told you there was no culture here, Jacks." His accent is different from Jackie's—slightly southern, maybe?

"I know it's a drink," Claire says. Her frustration must be obvious, because Jackie speaks up right away.

"She was making a joke, you ditz," Jackie says, smacking Theo on the arm.

Theo sips at his drink. Based on the jug sitting between them on the side table, it looks like a dark red sangria, and they've almost finished it. "Oh. Well, you can't blame me for assuming. Look at this place. It's where blandness goes to die."

"Be nice," Jackie says. She moves the sangria jug away when he goes to refill, raising a pointed eyebrow. "She's a friend."

"I am being nice!"

"Be nicer," Jackie says.

Theo rolls his eyes. "When you invited me down to your slice of suburban hell, you didn't stipulate that I needed to charm the locals."

"Don't listen to him. I really would love for you to join us, Claire," Jackie says firmly.

Claire sits gingerly on a lounge.

Like Jackie, Theo is unlike anyone else Claire has ever met. He's fascinating to listen to. He commands a conversation easily. Claire can see him easily tripping up someone like Pete, but at the same time there's something about him that's so *different*. Claire's interest is swiftly joined by a sort of irritation at the way Jackie seems so in-tune with him. She tops up his drink without asking, and laughs at all his jokes and stories. He has a kind of sharp wit that Claire can't help but envy.

Theo has no wedding ring, so it's doubtful that he's the married man Jackie has talked about. But he's charming. He's suave, and clever, and extremely handsome. He's affectionate with Jackie, touching her on the arm or even the thigh as he gesticulates with his hands, and Jackie doesn't seem bothered at all. She seems to expect it.

They have an easy intimacy that makes something hot twist in Claire's belly.

Perhaps it's that he takes Jackie's attention so easily? Claire is sure she'd feel this way with anyone else Jackie decided to spend her time with, man or woman. Maybe it's just bitter jealousy, no different than Martha's hatred of Jackie. Maybe Claire is just being petty for no reason at all.

It can't be because of Theo's race, can it? She's never thought of herself as one of those people who gets in a tizzy over inter-race relations, even if Pete has always voiced a vague disapproval. If Jackie wants to see a Black man, that's her business. It's perfectly legal nowadays. She can see anyone she likes. She can marry him, even.

Claire swallows past a sudden bout of anxiety.

"And then he made a move. Right in front of his wife," Theo is saying, and it's enough to bring Claire back to the present. "So I told him, if you want to kiss me, have a cigarette first. His breath smelled like cheap booze, and I had no interest in experiencing it through his mouth."

Claire's brain skips like a scratched record.

"He?" Claire blurts.

Theo raises a brow. He looks back and forth between Claire and Jackie, who suddenly looks pale and pinched.

"I believe that's what I said, Suzy Homemaker," Theo says, draining the last of the sangria.

"You kiss *men*?" Claire says. She feels like the slowest horse at the race, but his nonchalance is so absurd that it doesn't feel real. This isn't the sort of thing one says openly. Theo might as well have publicly announced his intention to commit grand larceny.

"Exclusively." Theo winks again. His confidence is as shocking as the admission itself.

Jackie's foot is twitching. She's looking at Claire as if she's expecting her to explode at any moment, and Claire schools her features to conceal the somersaults her brain is doing.

Theo kisses men. Assumedly, Theo has sexual relations with men. He's one of *those*. One of the types of people Pete complains about over the morning paper—the sex-freaks. The degenerates. Claire is confused and a little unsettled by it all, but it's mixed with a great deal of unexpected relief.

Theo and Jackie aren't together, romantically or otherwise.

Theo laughs, presumably at the expression on Claire's face. He pats Claire's hand as if she's a precocious toddler. "Oh, look at how shocked she is. Jackie, I thought that you—"

"Theodore!" Jackie snaps harshly. Claire jumps at the volume of it—she's never seen Jackie look so grave. So angry. *"Don't."*

A few beats of silence pass. Claire can feel the awkwardness in the air like a mist—Jackie's jaw is clenched, and her knuckles are white around her glass. Claire wonders if she and Theo are about to have a fight, and if perhaps she should leave.

Theo's face falls. He puts his hands up, looking suddenly quite sober. "Shit. I'm so sorry, Jacks. That was—fuck. No more wine for me."

"What?" Claire asks, looking between them. Some sort of secret has passed through the space she's sitting in, and she feels slow for not catching it. "What is it?"

Jackie shakes her head with a smile that looks forced. "It's nothing, Claire. Don't worry about it."

"Just a misunderstanding," Theo says. His blasé tone from earlier is gone.

It doesn't feel like nothing, but the subject changes so quickly that Claire can barely keep up. The awkwardness never quite eases, though, with Theo clearly trying extra hard to carry the conversation and make up for his mysterious blunder, and Claire excuses herself less than an hour after she arrived. Usually, she'd stay until at least two o'clock.

The first thing Claire does when she gets home is dart up the stairs to peer over the fence into Jackie's yard. Jackie and Theo are huddled close together now, in a conversation that looks intense and intimate. Theo is holding Jackie's hands between his much bigger ones. Jackie's shoulders are hunched. Her head falls forward onto Theo's shoulder, and he puts an arm around her. Claire isn't sure she's ever seen a man and woman, especially of different races, so close unless they're going steady.

Jackie looks upset about something. The thing that Theo almost revealed, maybe? Claire is too far away to read their lips, but she shouldn't be spying in the first place, no matter how badly she wants to know.

Reluctantly, Claire lets the curtains fall back across the window.

Theo stays at Jackie's house for two days, from what Claire can tell. She sees them sitting at the pool a few more times through her bedroom window, but she isn't brave enough to visit Jackie again until Theo's car no longer sits in the driveway.

She spends that morning fretting, wondering if the strange conversation by the pool will still hang between them, before she finally darts across the lawns.

Claire's knuckles have hardly touched the door before it opens. Jackie is dressed for driving, her hair wrapped under her silk kerchief, and she has a hand on her hip.

"I have a serious craving for some ice cream," Jackie says.

It's as if the day by the pool never happened. Claire blinks, her fist still raised, trying to re-adjust to the sudden shift in her day. "I think I have some in the freezer?"

"I want to go out," Jackie says. She steps outside, closing the door behind her. "Coming with?"

Claire hesitates. Martha's curtains are closed for now, but who knows if they will be when Claire gets back? "How long will we be gone?"

"I'll have you back before you know it. An hour's break won't make the house fall apart," Jackie says. "Do you know a place, or should we just drive around until we find one?"

Claire does know a place. And isn't it safer to be with Jackie somewhere besides their suburb? Martha isn't one to venture out to get ice cream. If they go to the shop Claire remembers on the far side of Sacramento, nearer to where she and Pete grew up, there's little risk.

The glowing yellow and blue neon sign over Sweetie's Malt Shop is a sight Claire hasn't seen in years. She used to frequent this place with her childhood girlfriends, and then, later on, with Pete and his larger group of pals. She didn't enjoy it as much in the later years—she was usually crammed into the corner of a booth while Pete and his boys talked about sports or teased each other about girls. It was more fun with her own friends, before they all slowly found beaus and lost touch. But she does miss the milkshakes.

Claire gets strawberry, with whipped cream and shaved chocolate on top. Jackie goes for a banana split with extra peanuts. It's just as good as Claire remembers. The day is hot and sunny, and they sit at an outdoor table to soak it in—Claire typically needs to be concerned about sunburn, but Jackie seems to absorb the sunlight and reflect it back out. She's her own little star, warm and funny and delightful to be around. A little sunburn is worth it.

"You know, I used to work at a little store not far from here," Claire says, mixing her melty whipped cream into the last of her milkshake. She wishes she'd gotten two—it's been too long since she had a treat.

"So you weren't always a homemaker?" Jackie says. As if she can read Claire's mind she scoops up a spoonful of ice cream and banana, offering it across the table to Claire. "Try this, it's amazing."

Claire takes the spoon, and Jackie is right—it's delicious. She hardly thinks about the fact that she'd ordinarily never share cutlery with anyone, even Pete. "Pete asked me to quit and stay home not long after we got married. He was tired of it interfering with my duties at home, and it's a long bus ride to get all the way out here."

"And he didn't want you to get a license," Jackie says.

Claire nods. "I loved working there, though. It was the sweetest little art supply shop, over on Cochrane Avenue. Anita always treated me like family."

"Is it still there?"

"I'm not sure. I haven't been this far into town in years," Claire says. "Anita very well might have retired by now."

Jackie hums thoughtfully around her spoon.

Claire bites her tongue before the rest slips out—that she felt so guilty about quitting that she hasn't even been able to bring herself to call Anita and catch up, and now here she is ten years later, having lost touch with someone she once loved like a second mother. If the shop has closed, or god forbid something has happened to Anita, Claire would have no idea.

She spent almost her whole adolescence there, stocking shelves and helping Anita decorate the little art studio in the back room. When Anita bought a pottery wheel, she taught Claire how to throw clay. Claire is sure she still has the vase Anita made as a wedding present in a closet somewhere—it was beautiful, but Pete hadn't wanted to put it out on display.

Claire doesn't think much of it when Jackie takes them on a different route home leaving the malt shop, but when the Mustang makes the turn onto Cochrane Avenue, Claire's suspicion mounts.

"I thought we were going home?" Claire says.

"There are multiple ways to get there," Jackie says slyly. "Point out where the store was for me?"

Jackie slows the car as they pass familiar shops. There's the pet store that Claire used to visit on her breaks to pet puppies. Next to it is the little sandwich shop that often gave Claire free lunch in exchange for her drawing some nice designs on their daily menu board. And two storefronts down, with the *OPEN* sign that Claire once lovingly painted still hung in the window, is the Crafty Corner.

The door chimes when Jackie strolls through it, with Claire trailing behind her. The same nerves that have kept her from giving Anita a call all these years sit in her stomach like a rock. The store smells the same as it always did, like new paper and acrylic paint, but the layout has changed a bit. There's more art on the walls now, some with price tags fixed underneath and others seeming to belong to the store.

Immediately Jackie gravitates to a piece on the far wall, near the cash register. "Oh, I *love* this. It looks just like our tree, doesn't it? Yellow is my favorite color, you know."

Claire is just filing that new piece of information away when she steps around a shelf to see which piece Jackie is talking about, and all her breath escapes in a *whoosh*.

It's Claire's painting.

She'd completely forgotten about it, until this moment. It's the one she painted just before she quit her job here, a month or so into her married life with Pete. They'd just moved to Acacia Circle, and Claire had been quite taken with the tree that was clearly the street's namesake. She'd spent one of her first days as a proper housewife doing it. Pete had come home, and upon seeing supper not on the table yet he'd made it clear what her new priorities needed to be. Claire had thrown out most of her art supplies not long after.

Claire knew that Anita kept it, but she never expected it to be hung in the store. She's never considered herself an expert with oil paints, but she'd been proud of the way she managed to capture all the different shades of green and gold and butter-yellow in the flowering tree. Even now, looking on it with older and less kind eyes, Claire can see that it's not a bad painting.

And Jackie likes it.

The door to the studio behind the register swings open. Claire hears a familiar pleased squeak.

"I'll be damned—if it isn't Claire Fields."

Anita is older and more lined than Claire remembers. She even seems a bit shorter. More stooped, maybe. Her hair is longer, gathered into a messy grey pile on top of her head. Her apron is covered in paint stains, her hands are caked in clay from her pottery wheel, and she's absolutely beaming.

"Anita," Claire says, in a rush of warm feeling. "It's Claire Davis, now. Remember?"

"Sure, sure," Anita says, waving off the mistake. She hurried forward, clasping Claire's hands in her own wrinkled and clay-crusted ones. "Oh, it's so lovely to see you. And all grown up, look at you! I wasn't sure I'd ever see you again after you ran off to get married to that boy."

Claire should never have been nervous about seeing Anita again. She doesn't have a mean bone in her body. Claire doesn't even mind getting clay on her hands. "I was nineteen when I saw you last. Not exactly a child."

"Close enough," Anita says, winking. She turns towards Jackie. "And who is this young lady?"

"This is my friend Jacqueline," Claire says, gesturing Jackie over. "She's an artist, too—a photographer. Her work is wonderful."

"Claire is being very generous," Jackie says, offering her usual brassy handshake to Anita. "It's lovely to meet you."

Anita shakes her hand enthusiastically. Jackie doesn't seem to mind the clay, either.

Anita is just as absent-minded and kind as she was when Claire worked here. She and Jackie take to each other right away, and Claire is reminded of another reason Pete wanted her to quit this job—he disliked Anita, and she never seemed to think much of him, either. Pete thought it was odd that Anita was a spinster with her own business.

"I've had girls in and out working the cash over the years, but none were half as good as Claire," Anita is saying. "They didn't have your work ethic, or your passion for the arts. You were a gift, dear. If you ever want your old job back, the door is wide open."

"You've always been too kind to me," Claire says.

"Only as kind as you deserve," Anita says firmly.

"That's what I've been telling her," Jackie pipes up. "She's too hard on herself. See, Claire, it isn't just me."

"I never should have introduced you two," Claire says, but she can't stop herself from smiling. There's something very calming about having both of them in a room together. Two people who are just *hers*, without the involvement of Pete or the rest of the neighborhood.

"Are you still painting?" Anita asks. "I know you turned down your college acceptance, but your talent is too good to waste."

Jackie tilts her head. "College? Which college?"

"The San Francisco Art Institute," Anita says before Claire can think to answer, with all the gusto of a proud parent. "And she got early acceptance, too."

"SFAI?" Jackie says, turning to Claire with raised eyebrows. "You've been holding out on me, saying you're not a real artist. That school isn't easy to get into. Why didn't you go?"

Claire twists her fingers into her pearls. The answer is simple, but in present company she's ashamed to admit it. Anita encouraged her to apply, even helping to pay for the application, but Pete wanted to settle down and get married right away. Claire sobbed on Anita's shoulder in this very shop the night she agreed to reject the admission offer. Being back here is like a strange reminder of the path she almost took.

"She's a brilliant painter, Jacqueline. She has an incredible grasp of color," Anita says, thankfully interjecting before Claire needs to reveal yet another of her weaknesses. "And such insight—she could capture more about a person in a five-minute sketch than most artists could in a full portrait sitting. Just wonderful."

"Anita, please," Claire says, pressing her cool hands to her warm face. "I only sketch sometimes. I haven't painted in ages."

"That's too bad. I've kept some of your pieces up around the place to liven things up, see?" Anita says, pointing to the painting of the acacia tree.

Jackie's eyes widen dramatically.

"This is yours?" Jackie says. She takes a few steps closer to the painting, raising a hand as if to trace the yellow brushstrokes. "Claire, it's gorgeous. You didn't tell me you could paint like this."

"It was a long time ago," Claire says quietly.

"I have more in the back. Come on, we'll dig them out," Anita says, already halfway to the studio door.

"We really don't need to do all of that," Claire calls, but Jackie is already following Anita with a grin on her face.

"This one got the attention of the Art Institute," Anita says, flinging a dusty sheet off of a rack full of unframed paintings. She pulls out the closest one, holding it up for Jackie to see. It's one Claire remembers well—her first mixed media piece. She'd painted scraps of fabric into the canvas with oils, using the different textures to offset the detailed faces she sketched above them.

"Claire," Jackie says softly. She steps closer to the painting, and this time she does trace the brushstrokes. Her fingers drift across the composition Claire had long forgotten. "*This* is what you called a silly distraction?"

"She won an art competition with this piece," Anita boasts.

Claire is torn between discomfort, and a sudden and fierce rush of pride. Jackie is looking at her art as if it's worth something. The visit ends up being far longer than Claire anticipated. Anita drags out every old painting and sketch of Claire's she can find, from landscapes to portraits to her brief forays into abstracts, showing each to Jackie in turn, and Jackie praises each one in detail. Claire is sure by the end of it that all the blood in her body has moved to her face.

Once Anita has finally let them leave with yet another assurance that Claire is welcome back anytime, Claire buckles into the Mustang with a lighter heart than she's had in years.

"That woman is a riot," Jackie says, chuckling as she checks her mirrors and pulls out of the parking spot. "I'd like to introduce her to Theo."

Claire hums in agreement. She's not entirely sure Anita's view on homosexuals, but she can see her being tickled by Theo's attitude.

"And you," Jackie says, levelling Claire with a pointed look over her sunglasses, "you've been hiding your light under a bushel. Those paintings were amazing. And I'm not saying that to be nice," Jackie says loudly, before Claire can protest. "I'm saying it because it's true. I've seen much worse work hung in galleries."

Claire can't bring herself to accept the compliment, but she manages not to deflect it by pressing her lips together.

"If your sketchbook is anything like those pieces, I'd love to see it someday," Jackie says. "Anita is right. Why would you hide a talent like that?"

Claire's mind drifts to the dozen half-finished sketches of Jackie in said book, and her cheeks burn. "I didn't think it was worth anyone's time."

Jackie sighs. "And who told you something like that?"

The answer is obvious, and goes unspoken.

"Can I ask you something personal?" Jackie says. The car slows to a stop at a red light.

"Of course."

"Do you regret not going to college?"

Claire stares hard at the traffic light. It burns into her eyes, that glowing red spot—it reminds her of Jackie's darkroom. She wishes she were there now, where Jackie might not be able to see the *more than anything* written across her face. "Regrets aren't very useful, are they? I didn't go. There's not much point in wondering what might have been."

It's a lie, of course. Claire has thought a thousand times about what it might have been like to accept the offer. She's never even been to the campus, but she's seen it on the news before. It's been a long time since the longing was this acute.

The light turns green. Jackie usually hits the gas with a lead foot at a green light, but this time the car doesn't move until the Ford behind them honks its horn.

"I'm sorry," Jackie says. It's almost lost to the wind. "For what it's worth, I think you would have thrived."

It's only as Jackie drops her off at home that Claire realizes Anita didn't ask any of the usual questions. She didn't ask after Pete—she didn't even reference him by name, only calling him *that boy* like she always has. She didn't ask if or when Claire was planning to start a family. She only asked after Claire. Her art, her life, and a few questions to get to know Jackie.

Just one whole, lovely afternoon with two people who care more about how Claire is doing than about what color the nursery will be.

Chapter 13

It's not every day that a man lands on the moon.

Walter and Martha host a party to celebrate the grand occasion, of course. Half the neighborhood gathers around their television set, eagerly watching as three men do the impossible. A years-long quest to go where no man has gone before, ending here in Martha's living room over devilled eggs and Jell-O salad.

Jackie hosts a party, too. She invites Claire, though they both know that there's not a chance of her being able to go. Claire can see it ramping up across the road as she and Pete head home to bed at dusk—the music is so loud that it can be heard on the street, and there's splashing and loud conversation coming from Jackie's pool. Knowing that Jackie is in there somewhere makes Claire ache to be a part of it.

Pete's day-drinking catches up with him quickly enough that, to Claire's relief, he collapses into bed as soon as they cross the threshold. Bypassing her vanity, Claire peers out the window into Jackie's yard. The pool lights are on, and the back door is open—music is still drifting up between the houses. The pool is full to bursting, and Claire is sure the house is the same.

Pete is sound asleep, and Claire is still dressed.

It feels as if someone else is controlling Claire's body as she descends the stairs, slipping back into her shoes and opening the door as silently as she can. An invisible hand is guiding her to cross the lawns, dart up Jackie's front step, and enter the party.

It's different from Jackie's housewarming in almost every way.

Last time, Claire had known most of the partygoers. Jackie invited the entire neighborhood, including people Claire knew. Nice, normal couples.

Those people of course went to Martha and Walter's party instead and are now sound asleep in their beds. Claire knows none of the people milling around Jackie's house this time, scattered all over the space in various states of interlocking lips and bodies. The air is thick and smoky with what Claire can now recognize is marijuana as well as tobacco, and Claire can see someone at the coffee table arranging white powder into neat little lines.

Claire can't explain it away this time. Jackie is hosting a swinger's party.

Claire can only imagine what Martha might say. She'd screech about decency, about values and morals. None of that is Claire's concern. The truth is, Jackie hosting a party like this doesn't bother Claire so much as it simply confounds her.

Jackie is smart. She's kind and interesting and *wonderful*. Why would she feel the need to have these people in her house?

Once again, Claire has a hard time finding Jackie in the crowd at her own party. It's a sea of people with a common purpose, but the hostess is lost in it. Claire drifts through the kitchen and out to the backyard, fixated on finding just one person, when she's seized by the shoulders.

Whirling around, she's somewhat disappointed to find that it's Theo.

"I'm pretty sure you're not supposed be here," Theo says loudly, tapping Claire on the tip of her nose. It's significantly less charming than when Jackie did it.

"Does Jackie not want me here?" Claire says. A sudden worry grips her, and she steps back from him.

Theo lets go of Claire's shoulders, which only serves to highlight how inebriated he is—he wavers on his feet, giggling. He's also wearing makeup, dark eyeliner and bright crimson lipstick, which Claire isn't sure how to navigate. "No, she *definitely* does. But I'm told your husband has certain rules that this is in clear violation of."

"My husband is sleeping," Claire says shortly.

Theo's eyebrows raise. "Oh, little birdie's breaking out of the cage. I *knew* it."

"Knew what?"

"Good for you," Theo says, kissing Claire airily on the cheek and turning her around towards the door. "Jackie is sulking on the ottoman. Go get her." He taps Claire lightly on the bottom, before disappearing into a crowd of dancing people on the lawn.

Claire finds Jackie just where Theo directed. She's at the edge of the party, tucked into a corner of the conversation pit, and she's sorting through what looks to be a stack of photos. There's a drink on the ottoman next to her, and one of those instant-print cameras. Claire has no idea how she missed her—Jackie is in a ruffled yellow shirt that crops off just under her ribs, showing a startling amount of soft belly above the waist of her pants. She stands out in the crowd, and yet no-one pays her any mind.

As Claire watches, Jackie sets the photos neatly down next to her drink. She raises the camera to her face, snaps a picture, removes it from the receptacle, and sets it on the stack without glancing at it before holding the camera up again, scanning the room slowly for another shot.

Jackie is so focused on the task that she doesn't notice Claire approaching. When Claire taps her lightly on the shoulder, Jackie jumps so hard that she almost spills her cocktail on Claire's shoes.

"*Claire!*" Jackie exclaims, with far more excitement than expected. She jumps up to clasp Claire by the arms, beaming, and she gets a waft of familiar herbal scent that sends her heart racing. "You're here!"

Like Theo, Jackie stumbles a little when she tries to sit back down on the ottoman, almost taking Claire with her.

"Are you all right?" Claire says, settling Jackie back on the cushion. It displaces the stack of photos—they scatter to the floor, but Jackie doesn't seem to notice.

"I am now," Jackie says, grinning wide. She grabs at the almost-spilled cocktail, draining the glass in one gulp. "I thought you were across the road with Martha?"

"What are you doing all the way over here?" Claire says, rather than answering the question.

Jackie's light dims a little. She holds up the camera with a wry smile. "I'm observing."

"Shouldn't you be mingling? This is your party."

Jackie's shoulders sink, like some massive weight has settled there. She waves a photo idly as it develops, fanning herself with it, and it makes her hair flicker around her face.

"I prefer this," Jackie says, not quite meeting Claire's eyes. Her speech is a bit slurred. "Theo is the partier. I'm never really…happy, at these things. But other people are. And if I can capture it like this, even if it's fleeting, maybe I can keep some for myself. Bottle it up."

By the end of it Jackie is whispering, but Claire hears every word. This level of naked honesty from Jackie, with no addendums or wry subject changes, is rare. To have Jackie explain her method, the reason her photographs are so detached? It's a gift.

It's also somewhat worrying. Claire sits down, taking the spot recently vacated by the stack of photographs. She's never seen Jackie this melancholy or this inebriated, even on the day her mother called. It seems to affect her even more than the marijuana did.

"Why have this kind of party?" Claire says quietly. "If you want to observe happiness, there are other ways. Why invite all these people to your house? These..." Claire swallows, averting her eyes from the couple in the corner whose heavy petting is quickly becoming lewd, "these *swingers*?"

Jackie sighs. She sets her camera down, rubbing tiredly at her face. All the excitement of Claire's arrival is gone. "You're starting to sound like your husband."

The comment hits Claire like an arrow. She flinches, reeling back from Jackie. "No, I'm not," Claire rushes to clarify. "I'm just...I suppose I'm confused. Do you really do this? Do you...have *sex* with these married men, too? Is that how you met the man you fell in love with?"

Jackie moves her arm away from Claire's hand, and snaps another photo. She's not looking at Claire anymore. It's like she's in another world, and now Claire's presence is making it worse.

"No," Jackie says simply, from behind the camera.

"I don't understand," Claire says.

Jackie says nothing, and in the open space Claire's mind runs rampant. The logic just doesn't make sense. Why let all these swingers trash her house and act lecherous all night if Jackie isn't one of them?

Jackie turns. Her gaze finally meets Claire's full-on, and whatever is going on behind it makes her chest hurt. "You really don't understand, do you?"

Claire is lost at sea. Jackie is talking so vaguely, as if there's something Claire should be picking up, but she has nothing to go on. She's missing something, and nobody will explain it to her.

"Help me to," Claire says. "Please?"

Something heavy hits the ground in the distance, from the direction of the kitchen. Claire is torn between relief and despair when Jackie stands up, setting the camera down. She kisses Claire on the cheek, on the opposite side that Theo did; it lands so close to Claire's mouth that her lips seem to tingle.

"Don't you worry about it," Jackie says. Her warm breath brushes Claire's cheek. It smells like whiskey and citrus. "Enjoy the party, okay?"

Jackie is gone before Claire can protest.

Claire grabs at a handful of the spilled photographs as Jackie weaves through the party, not heading to the kitchen but towards the door to the bedrooms. The pictures are all artfully done, even for such a simple medium—there's one of a man that Claire is sure is naked, jumping into the pool. There's one of the conversation pit, blurred with smoke, with couples intertwined on the couch. There's one of Theo, posing like a model on Jackie's coffee table.

When Claire looks up again, Jackie is near the kitchen. She's been stopped by a beautiful woman in a bathing suit. It's not a terribly strange sight, given the pool party outside, but something about it sours Claire's stomach. The woman is leaning close to whisper something in Jackie's ear.

When Jackie smiles at the woman, it doesn't reach her eyes. Claire could swear, in fact, that her eyes have instead flicked over towards the ottoman where Claire is sitting. But Jackie nods, and together she and the woman disappear through the swinging door towards the bedrooms.

With Jackie gone, there's no reason for Claire to stay. She leaves the photos where they are, and with one last look towards the door Jackie disappeared through, Claire flees the house back to her own.

After the party, Jackie's car disappears from the driveway for three days.

It's not the first time Jackie has been gone overnight. She often has photography gigs in the city, and she's told Claire that if they go late, she stays with a friend. Claire now assumes that the friend is Theo. But it's a longer absence than usual, so when Claire finally wakes up to see the blue Mustang has returned to its spot, she's knocking on Jackie's door almost as soon as Pete's car turns the corner.

It takes longer than usual for Jackie to answer. Claire can hear movement behind it, shuffling footsteps, and then the door opens to Jackie squinting into the early morning light. She's dressed in a black turtleneck despite the warm weather, and Claire doesn't quite stifle her gasp.

Jackie has a *shiner*. Her left eye is bloodshot, and the skin around it is a lurid, swollen purple. When she gives Claire a weak smile, her half-healed split lip cracks open.

"Jackie!" Claire says, hurrying forward. Her stomach bottoms out when she reaches out instinctively to touch the bruise, and Jackie flinches. "What on earth—what *happened?*"

"Don't you like my new look?" Jackie says, closing the door behind Claire. Her voice is a little rougher than usual, like she hasn't been sleeping well. "I'm going for devil-may-care."

"You look like you've been pummeled," Claire says.

Jackie chuckles lightly, but then winces, her arm going to her ribs. "That's not too far from the truth."

"What happened?" Claire asks again. Horrible scenarios all crowd her mind, a myriad of ways that Jackie could have ended up in this condition, only to land squarely on the worst one. "It wasn't...Jackie, it wasn't that man, was it? The married one you used to see?"

Jackie doesn't seem interested in explaining herself. She notices that her lip is bleeding in the reflective surface of one of her photo frames, and makes a small noise of frustration. "Nothing like that. Can we drop it, please?"

"Have you been to a doctor? Gotten yourself checked out?" Claire says, trailing her towards the living room. "You could have a concussion. Your lip could get infected, or you could—and what's wrong with your ribs?"

Jackie sighs, sitting gingerly on the couch. Her posture is stiff. "They're bruised, that's all. I already went to the hospital. I'm supposed to take it easy for a while."

Claire sits beside her, careful not to jostle. The curiosity is burning in her—she can't conjure a situation in which a woman could end up in this condition if it isn't by the hand of an angry lover. However it happened, the idea of anyone hitting Jackie sends a surge of anger through her. "At least let me look at your lip. Please?"

Jackie is reluctant, but eventually Claire convinces her to grab the small first aid kit in her bathroom and sit still on the couch. Claire swipes away the blood on Jackie's lip, cleans it with antiseptic, and dabs some ointment, and then she wraps an ice cube in a clean dish towel to hold against Jackie's swollen eye.

"I shouldn't have even opened the door today," Jackie says, leaning back against the couch cushions as Claire presses the ice to her face.

"I have a key. I would have checked on you eventually," Claire says. "Jackie, you look like you were in a boxing match."

"I went to a bar in the city," Jackie says, after a long silence. "There was an altercation. It's really nothing to worry about. He only got a few hits in."

Claire moves the ice away. "He? You got in a fight? With a *man*?"

Jackie looks disgruntled by the sudden lack of ice, despite all of her complaining earlier. "Less a fight than a beating. I'm not exactly a scrapper."

The anger rises in Claire again. It's not like what she feels with Pete, or when the book club ladies speak badly of Jackie—this is deeper. A fierce need to protect. Claire has never even thought about being in a fight, but if someone threatened Jackie in front of her? *Hit* her? Even if it was a man, Claire isn't sure she'd be able to stand back and watch.

"Who would do this to you?" Claire says, pressing the ice to Jackie's face again. It's wet and cold in her hand, but Jackie makes a pleased noise, so there's no way she's going to stop doing it. "And *why*?"

"Claire, please let it go," Jackie murmurs. Her eyes are closed, but her hands are twisting together.

"How can I let it go? Did you at least call the police?"

"Wasn't exactly necessary," Jackie mutters. "Theo is tougher than he looks. He hit them back, and we ran. It's fine."

"Them?" Claire had been imagining some drunk man taking a swing at Jackie in an alley, a one-off freak incident caused by a singular idiot lashing out. Not a group beating. "How many were there?"

"A few," Jackie says tiredly. "It was hard to tell. Everything was spinning."

"How did you get tangled in something like that?" Claire says, before it hits her. When she imagines someone like Theo at a bar, with his biting wit, running into the kind of men Pete works with…if he tossed an insult at the wrong person, someone big and drunk and a little rowdy…

"Was this about Theo?" Claire asks haltingly. "Were the men…was it because he's…"

Claire trails off. They haven't yet discussed what Theo said that day at the pool, and Jackie's face now reminds Claire of how it looked then—her lips are pressed tightly together. Her eyes are open now, and she's staring straight ahead. She barely flinches when Claire presses the ice to her face again.

"And if it was?" Jackie says.

Claire pauses. The question feels like more than the sum of its parts, and she considers her words carefully as she lowers the shrinking ice cube.

"Then...I hope Theo got some good punches in."

Jackie's face softens. Her eyes shift to meet Claire's, and it's as if a wall drops between them. Jackie looks so tired, suddenly. Vulnerable and exhausted. A droplet of water is sliding down her temple, and Claire swipes at it with her finger without thinking.

"I really don't like the idea of someone hurting you," Claire says. Her voice won't seem to rise above a whisper.

Jackie gives a weak smile. "I don't think anyone has ever cared this much about it before."

The cloth has fallen out of Claire's hand, and the ice is melting into the couch cushion. Usually that would make her antsy, but Claire has bigger concerns.

"I care," Claire says. She traces her finger along the cool, damp skin just at the edge of Jackie's bruised eye. "I know it's strange, but I keep wishing I had been there."

Jackie's brow furrows. "They just would have hit you, too."

"Maybe with me there they wouldn't have," Claire says. It feels like a stupid thing to say the moment it leaves her mouth—what could she possibly have done against three grown men? Attacked them with her vacuum cleaner? But it also feels true. If she'd been there, she would have tried to protect Jackie, no matter how silly it looked. "I've never hit anyone, but I'm sure I could learn."

"See?" Jackie says. Her voice is low, her breath dancing across Claire's face. Her pupils are large and dark, just barely distinguishable from the mahogany color of her eyes. It makes them seem so endlessly deep that Claire could tip forward and fall down them like Alice down the rabbit hole. "I knew there was a lion in here."

She taps her forefinger against Claire's chest just over her collarbone, just like the day they smoked together. And Jackie's hand doesn't move away. It lingers, the very tip of her finger pressed against Claire's skin. It feels like there's something moving underneath it, some thrilling feeling coursing through Claire to gather right under the spot Jackie is touching. Something about this moment feels fragile, and Claire finds herself holding her breath to keep from breaking it.

Suddenly, Jackie jerks away. It comes with a hiss of pain.

Claire retracts her own hand from Jackie's face so quickly that it sends a jolt up her arm, her heart jumping. "Shoot. I'm sorry—did I press on your bruise?"

"Do you want to learn how to drive?" Jackie says, standing up abruptly. She snatches up the damp towel from the couch, heading towards the kitchen in a rush. The softness is gone from her voice.

Claire is left on the couch, nursing her conversational whiplash. This kind of thing has been happening with Jackie more frequently lately, the moments of closeness and sudden pivots, and she's not sure why. "What?"

"My eye hurts, and I need a distraction," Jackie shouts from the kitchen. Claire can hear the sink running. "Have you ever taken lessons?"

"In high school," Claire says. The spot on her chest that Jackie was touching is still tingling, and she rubs it absently. "You don't want me to learn in your Mustang, do you?"

"Where else?"

"What if I wreck it? It's too expensive, Jackie, I couldn't." Claire stands up on wobbly legs, meaning to follow Jackie's voice, but Jackie reappears quickly. Her face is damp and shiny, like she's splashed it with water.

"I don't care if you crash it. I only bought it to piss off my mother."

"That's one expensive rebellion," Claire says. "Are you sure?"

Jackie breezes past her, grabbing her keys from the table next to the door. "Come on. We'll find an empty parking lot."

Claire has completely forgotten the strangeness of earlier by the time she's behind the wheel of Jackie's car in an empty Denny's parking lot, learning how to shift it into gear. The vague memory of her school lessons comes back quicker than she expected—after only a few false starts she's cruising slowly around the lot, pressing down on the gas a little more with each lap under Jackie's encouragement. It's all less complicated than Claire thought it would be, and the sense of freedom she's felt in the passenger seat is amplified, even if she's not really doing much besides learning to park.

Even at their slow pace, the wind ruffles Claire's hair. The sun warms her face. Jackie is smiling so much that her lip has cracked open again. For a moment, as she rounds a corner perfectly and Jackie claps in delight, Claire conjures an impossible fantasy. Cruising down the highway with Jackie, fully in control of her life, with the wind roaring in their ears. Headed off on some grand adventure.

After such a wonderful afternoon, Claire's kitchen feels stifling when she comes back home.

Chapter 14

The week goes on like any other. Claire cleans the baseboards and tries out a new banana cake recipe. She calls her mother to give an update on the goings-on at home, entirely incongruous with how she really feels. Rita sends a new dress in the mail, brownish-yellow with green plaid, and Claire shoves it into the back of the closet. She skips book club; the last time she went she'd almost pressed her nails right through the skin of her palm again to keep from snapping at the other ladies as they talked about Jackie.

On Thursday afternoon, Claire picks the phone up on the third ring just after lunch.

"Davis residence," Claire says, tucking it against her ear as she rubs baking soda into the silverware. The forks are starting to tarnish, and the last thing she needs right now is Pete noticing. So long as she keeps up with everything at home, he's less likely to notice her shortcomings.

"Hello, Davis residence," comes Jackie's voice through the receiver, low and warm. "Callas residence calling."

Claire drops a handful of spoons.

"Jackie," Claire says, scrambling to gather the utensils again without getting tangled in the telephone cord. It's rare that Jackie is the one to call first. "How are you?"

Jackie chuckles. "I'm just fine. I'm not interrupting, am I?"

"No, not at all. Nothing important, anyway," Claire says, shoving everything back into its drawer. Polishing can wait. "Sorry. How's your day so far?"

"My day is just fine. It's your day I'm curious about. If I'm not mistaken, it's a special one?"

Claire toys with her pearls. Today is certainly a special day, in the worst way—she called the fertility clinic this morning. She managed to put off an appointment until early December, at least, and she doubts that Pete will question the date so long as there is one on the horizon. "Is it?"

"Did I write down the wrong birthday on my calendar?"

Claire frowns, darting to her own wall calendar. Thursday, July the 31st. In the stress of this week, she hadn't even realized.

"You remembered," Claire says.

"Of course I did," Jackie says, as if that's not something marvelous. "Happy birthday, Claire."

In a humiliating turn of events, Claire finds herself close to tears. She's been worried since the party that Jackie was upset with her—now she seems completely normal, as if it never happened. And she's remembered a special day that even Claire hadn't marked when she woke up this morning.

"Thank you," Claire says, clearing the choked-up tightness from her throat. "Jackie, that's—it's so unbelievably sweet of you to call."

"So, what did Pete get you?"

"Pete? Oh, he, um." Claire clears her throat again, looping a finger through her pearls. "Birthdays aren't really his—"

"He forgot, didn't he?" Jackie says quietly.

Claire lets out her breath. Lying to Jackie on Pete's behalf is a waste of her energy, at the end of the day. "I don't think he's ever remembered."

The line is quiet for a moment. Claire could swear she hears Jackie's fingers drumming on some table surface even through the phone.

"Do you have a minute for me to stop by?"

"Stop by?" Claire squeaks.

"I'll run quick as a rabbit, I promise."

Claire darts to the window, her arm tangled in the telephone cord— Martha's curtains are closed, and her station wagon isn't in the driveway. It looks as if she's out. But if she comes back while Jackie is here...

If Claire gets caught with Jackie again, it's over. She doesn't doubt that Pete would sell the house and uproot them if she disobeys him this time. She'd never see Jackie again.

But it *is* her birthday.

"Um. Yes," Claire says, doubting herself even as she says it. "Sure, yes, I think—that would be lovely."

Jackie turns up at her door not long after with a smile and a large box wrapped in colorful paper.

"You didn't," Claire says, as Jackie steps past her and into the entryway with the box in her arms. "That's not for me, is it?"

"Open it," Jackie says, thrusting it into Claire's hands.

The package is heavy, and Claire holds it against her body nervously. "I can't possibly accept this. I didn't get you a gift for your birthday."

"Mine isn't until November. Open it," Jackie says, grinning wide.

It takes some convincing—at one point Jackie threatens to open it herself—but finally Claire is persuaded to rip the paper off. Beneath it is a cardboard box, and inside that box is—

"Art supplies?" Claire says, hardly believing her eyes as she pulls out a fresh set of watercolor paints. Underneath it is a cup of new brushes, a real sketchbook with charcoal pencils, and a stack of heavy painting paper. The brushes are good quality. Claire runs them over her fingers, and the sense memory chokes her up again. The smell of the linen paper brings her back to her childhood room, learning to find the colors of a sunset in a simple set of twelve watercolor pucks.

"It's a start," Jackie says. "Eventually I'd love to get you some oils."

"Oh, Jackie, this is—it's too much. I don't even paint anymore. I couldn't possibly accept this."

"Anita only let me pay for half of it, so don't go feeling guilty," Jackie says. "You said it used to make you happy." Jackie picks up the sketchbook, pressing it into Claire's hands. "If that's true, you should see if you can't find that happiness again. Don't let it go."

Claire's battle against tears has been a losing one from the start, but she had hoped to delay it until Jackie leaves. It does, however, give cause for Jackie to hug her.

Since the day they shared a joint and Claire stupidly ran her fingers through Jackie's hair without asking, Jackie's physical affection has been a fleeting gift. It always comes as a surprise and ends just as abruptly, like a bolt of lightning in a clear sky, and it usually leaves Claire similarly buzzing with electricity.

The hug Jackie pulls Claire into as she tries not to cry feels like the best birthday present she could ask for. It's tender and comforting, and it lasts long enough for Claire to file the details away in her memory. The smell of

Jackie's hair. The warmth of her body. The way Jackie rocks back and forth slightly, almost imperceptibly, and rubs little circles on Claire's back.

"Do you have anything at all planned for yourself?" Jackie asks, pulling back from the embrace as Claire hurriedly wipes her eyes. "Even one little birthday treat?"

Just you, Claire nearly says. *Just this one indulgence.* She bites down on her tongue to keep the words inside.

When Claire shakes her head silently, Jackie sighs. "All right. It's your birthday, Martha is out, the weather is gorgeous, and your house is immaculate. Do you know what that means?"

"That I should weed the gardens today?"

"No," Jackie says, already heading to the door. "It means you should go shopping today. Come on."

"But…I don't have any money," Claire says, to an empty kitchen.

Claire isn't sure how, but despite her vehement protests she's sitting in Jackie's convertible heading downtown within ten minutes.

She's only been to the department store a handful of times since she and Pete married. There isn't anything for her here—she doesn't shop. Rita makes her clothes, for a fraction of the cost of a brand-name store. Pete gives her an exact amount of money per week for groceries. If they need a piece of kitchen apparel or an appliance, Pete has her order it from the Sears catalogue.

Jackie strolls through the store like she owns the place. She's confident in the crowd, where Claire is nervous. Jackie flicks through racks of clothing and boxes of shoes with the eye of a seasoned shopper, while Claire trails behind her.

The section they end up perusing for the longest time is completely unfamiliar to Claire, not to mention entirely out of a normal price range. The mannequins are dressed in bright colors, polka-dots and stripes and loud prints, a far cry from her own muted palette of dresses. Jackie seems right at home.

Claire feels out of place in comparison. Uneasy. Dowdy. Boring.

"Even if I had money with me, I couldn't possibly afford anything here," Claire whispers, feeling as if every eye in the store is on her as she follows Jackie through the racks.

Jackie has a bundle of outfits already, dresses and blouses and skirts slung over her shoulder and forearm. She grabs Claire's hand, pulling her into the men's section. "Don't be ridiculous. You're not paying."

"What?" Claire gasps. The price tags she's seen so far are absolutely sky-high for a gift, especially on top of the art supplies. "That's absurd, that's utterly—why are we looking at men's pants?"

Jackie rolls her eyes affectionately, grabbing a pair of navy corduroys and a light blue button-down. "Trust the process, okay?"

Jackie paces the aisles, grabbing at garments until her arms are full, and then gestures imperiously for an employee to get them a private changing room. The space they're led into is huge, with a large mirror, a cushioned bench, a coffee table strewn with fashion magazines, and a large folding privacy fan to change behind.

Still, Claire is shocked when Jackie closes the door behind the employee and doesn't leave herself. Instead she guides Claire towards the privacy fan with her armful of clothes, and takes a seat on the bench to wait just out of sight.

This must be what girlfriends do. Claire is simply unfamiliar with it—Jackie is in her element, idly leafing through one of the magazines, and the fan is positioned to give Claire total privacy. Jackie clearly wants to see Claire in each of the outfits she's picked.

Swallowing hard, Claire starts from the top.

The clothes Jackie picked are all over the map. There are a few skirts, a dress or two, and four pairs of pants, two of them in men's sizes. Jackie also chose two men's shirts—a polo, and a button-down—with a selection of ascots.

She's not sure why Jackie is having her try on men's clothes, but Claire doesn't see the harm. They're in a private room. It's a day out of the house. Nobody will see, and Jackie wouldn't pull such a crude prank as to laugh at her. It could be fun.

She tries on the dresses and skirts first. They feel better than her own clothes, more modern and fitting more easily to the shape of her body, but they still give her the feeling she's always had—that something isn't quite right. She no longer feels so frumpy, but she doesn't feel at ease in herself the way Jackie always seems to be.

Jackie nods her approval of both looks, smiling over her magazine as Claire looks at herself in the big mirror, and finally when the ladies' outfits are exhausted Claire picks up the corduroys.

"I'm still not sure why you got me things from the men's section," Claire calls over the privacy fan. "It's not like they'll…"

She says it just as she's pulling the pants over her hips; to her shock, they fasten in a perfect fit. They're snug on her narrow hips, and long enough for her spindly legs without being too big in the thigh. They fit every contour of her lower half effortlessly, ending in a gentle flare at her ankle.

"Just trust me on this. I have an instinct," Jackie calls back.

Claire turns to the side, twisting and staring down in disbelief at the way the pants hug her bottom. They make it look more impressive, somehow, even from this angle. Less flat and more shapely. As she stands in her brassiere and looks down properly at the shape of her own legs for the first time in her life, she suspects that maybe what Jackie has is a superpower.

Claire chooses the button-down shirt, a light blue to match the dark blue of the pants and tucks it into the waistband with a growing sense of excitement. Maybe once she's dressed, she'll look in the mirror and see that she looks ridiculous, but something in her needs to see Jackie's reaction to assure herself she's not losing her mind.

With her shirt buttoned, Claire steps out from behind the fan.

Jackie goes still. She sets the magazine down, her eyes now raking up and down over Claire's body instead in a way that makes goosebumps erupt all over her arms.

"What do you think?" Claire asks breathlessly, doing a little spin in her stockinged feet. She's not quite prepared to look in the mirror yet, not quite ready to face what she might look like, but Jackie's face is telling a story all its own. Claire just wishes she could read it.

Jackie wets her lips. She swallows, her throat gently bobbing. She rises from the bench, circling Claire with a strange look in her eyes.

"Jackie?" Claire says. Her voice is thin and nervous. "I look silly, don't I? Should I change?"

Jackie has come around to stand in front of Claire, now. Slowly, silently, she eases the top button of Claire's shirt open, leaving a gap at her throat. Her fingers momentarily brush Claire's sternum, and Claire twitches.

There's some strange energy coursing through her. Chain-lightning, crackling through her veins.

Still silent, Jackie reaches behind Claire's head to loosen the clip that holds her updo in place. Their faces are mere inches apart, and Claire is tempted to close her eyes as dull brown curls spill down across her shoulders. There's a singular focus on Jackie's face, and in her eyes. She runs her fingers through Claire's hair, loosening the hold of the hairspray, and her short nails scratch lightly at Claire's scalp.

Claire feels as if she might melt into the linoleum. Jackie's nails send a shiver all through her. The touch is shockingly intimate, and it stirs in her a wave of *something*—a surge, a driving force with no objective. She has no idea what it's telling her to do, but it crashes through her nonetheless.

It's the single strangest and most exciting moment of Claire's life, and she can't for the life of her articulate *why*.

"There," Jackie whispers, her voice cracking slightly. Her pupils are wide; there's a half-smile at the corner of her lips as she guides Claire by the hips to turn around. "Not so buttoned-up now, are you?"

A different person is staring back at Claire from the mirror.

Just like she thought, the pants fit her almost too well. They cling to every previously nonexistent curve, fitting perfectly to her too-long legs. She's never felt so exposed, and yet so comfortable. The shirt is the same— the color makes her grey eyes seem brighter, and it feels tight on her arms and shoulders in a way that's strangely satisfying. The buttons don't even strain over her small breasts. She doesn't feel like a badly-framed painting anymore, bulging at the edges and constantly threatening to burst out.

It all just *fits*.

For lack of anything better to do with her hands, Claire sets them on her hips just below Jackie's—they're still sitting lightly just where Claire's pants meet her shirt.

Claire looks confident. Powerful. She looks like the woman in Jackie's photograph.

Jackie's head pokes around Claire's shoulder. Her hands are as hot as an iron.

Claire is suddenly very aware of the fact that this shirt isn't starched and stiff like her dresses. It's a thin, light cotton. The heat of Jackie's touch is more pronounced through it.

The goosebumps are everywhere, now.

"What do you think?" Jackie asks quietly.

"I think…" Claire exhales shakily, trailing off. What Claire thinks, deep down, is that this might be the first time she's ever felt truly *herself* in her entire life.

Pete would absolutely hate it.

Claire licks her lips. She smooths her sweaty palms down the front of her shirt, moving her shoulders and watching the way the fabric flexes to accommodate. She's not too wide for this shirt. Not too narrow for these pants.

"I think the neighbors might talk," Claire finally says.

Jackie laughs. Her hands move away, and the moment breaks like a pebble hitting a still pond.

Jackie buys Claire the outfit, despite her many half-hearted protests. It goes in a box at the bottom of the closet, hidden safely away from Pete, but every so often Claire takes it out and puts it on while he's at work just to look at herself in their bathroom mirror.

Every time she does, she feels like a snake shedding its old skin for something new and raw underneath. Something unfamiliar, something frightening, but infinitely better.

Her mother calls after dinner to wish her a happy birthday. Pete doesn't remember at all.

Chapter 15

August comes with an excruciating heatwave.

Day after day passes by with no relief. Claire's usual cooking and cleaning schedule has to be done in their sweltering house. In these hellish conditions, she's more grateful than ever to take shelter for a few blessed hours in Jackie's air-conditioned living room. Claire often gazes longingly at the pool from her humid bedroom window after their visits, but she never makes the suggestion to swim.

She's seen Jackie's chic swimsuit. Claire's one and only handmade suit looks like a potato sack in comparison, and she'd rather Jackie didn't have to see it.

The heat seems to make Claire's anxieties expand along with everything else. The card with the fertility specialist's number stays next to the phone, with Claire's appointment date scribbled underneath. Every minute she spends with Jackie runs the risk of getting caught, but Claire can't stop. Spending time with her isn't a desire anymore, not even an impulse—it's a need. A requirement just to get through the day. She's like an alcoholic, clinging to the bottle even as someone tries to wrench it away.

When Martha calls with an invite for fondue on a Saturday night, it's actually a relief—Martha has air conditioning, too, and this way Claire won't need to bake along with whatever she puts in the oven for dinner or listen to Pete complain about eating hot food on a hot day.

Martha's belly is bigger than ever when she answers the door. She looks about ready to burst, requiring more help from Claire than usual to get things together even if she won't actually admit it. When they've all sat down around the sizzling oil and melted cheese and Pete compliments Martha on her hard work, Claire bites her tongue.

"Thank you. Things have been so hectic lately, with the baby coming," Martha says, demurely dipping the edge of a piece of broccoli into the cheese. "And that moon landing party was such a delightful time, but the planning and cleanup really took a lot out of me."

"I'm glad we could have a quiet night in tonight," Claire says.

"So are we," Martha says. She sounds as sincere as Claire has ever heard her.

"Did you see that moon landing party across the road?" Walter says, chortling as he spears several pieces of sausage and sticks them all into the oil at once. "Looked pretty rowdy."

Claire's mouthful of bread and cheese doesn't want to go down, suddenly—she chews and chews, while Pete laughs.

"I try not to pay much mind to that house," Pete says. He stabs at a meatball so hard that it splits in half and falls into the cheese. "As does Claire. We're of a like mind about that woman, aren't we, sweetheart?"

Swallowing the bread is like trying to stomach sawdust, but Claire manages. "Yes, dear."

Another lie. Another brick on the stack. It feels as if it's piled so high at this point that she can hardly see Martha at the other end of the table.

Martha's mouth is pinched. She keeps looking back and forth between Pete and Claire, though Claire thanks the Heavens above that she doesn't actually open her mouth until she and Claire are alone in the kitchen doing the washing-up.

"Are you and Pete truly of a like mind about the neighbor these days?"

"She has a name, you know," Claire says tiredly. "Why do you ask?"

Martha quietly washes a plate. She scrubs and scrubs at some imaginary crusted food, rinses it, and hands it to Claire, who wipes it with a towel. A reliable routine.

Walter and Pete's distant laughter floats in from the den.

"After the last time, Claire, I told you I didn't want to interfere anymore," Martha says in a sudden hushed whisper, as if it's an avalanche she's only barely kept at bay until now. "But having just seen you strolling around Macy's with Jacqueline a few weeks ago, I'm starting to think that I might need to. You are *lying* to your husband."

Claire drops the plate. It bounces off the countertop, but she manages to catch it before it shatters.

There's no fib that can get her out of this.

"Were you spying on me?" Claire whisper-shouts back.

"I was minding my business buying maternity clothes, thank you very much!" Martha hisses. "You were the one who was—you were—*cavorting* around the department store."

That word feels like a slap to the face. It brings to mind the changing-room—Jackie's nails brushing Claire's scalp. The absurd, shameful electricity of it all. It felt forbidden, somehow, but inexplicably right.

"Martha, please," Claire says, setting the plate down but clutching the towel in shaky hands. "Don't tell Walter. He'll tell Peter, and then—"

And then Claire really won't be able to see Jackie anymore. The thought is intolerable, now. Untenable.

Martha washes a wine glass with gusto, frantically running the sponge over every inch. "Why cause issues with your husband over a friendship? And with someone like her? There's absolutely no reason, Claire, no reason at all."

No reason. As if Jackie has given Claire nothing in their months of friendship, rather than showing her the most kindness she's ever experienced. As if the balm Claire feels every time Jackie is near is anything short of miraculous.

"Jackie is wonderful," Claire says indignantly. "She's just misunderstood."

"She associates with freaks. That makes her just like them."

The indignation swells into a burst. Claire throws down her damp dishtowel so hard that it *smacks* against the countertop, turning on a wide-eyed Martha. "Do you know it was my birthday?"

"Excuse me?" Martha says.

"The day you saw me with her. It was my birthday," Claire says fiercely. She sets her hands on her hips—the effect is stifled by her dress, but she feels almost as she did when she first wore the outfit Jackie bought her. Confident. Powerful. "You didn't remember. *Pete* didn't remember. But Jackie did. She bought me a gift."

Martha swallows. Suds drip from her hands back into the sink.

"I give you and Walter cards for your birthdays every year. I give Pete a gift for his," Claire continues, letting the anger sweep her up. She can't say these things to Pete, or risk losing Jackie forever. Instead, she's turning the geyser on Martha. "Do you know how long it's been since I got a birthday gift?"

"I didn't...realize," Martha says faintly.

Martha looks as if she might cry. Claire has never taken this tone with her, not once in their years of being neighbors and friends. When Martha spilled the beans about Jackie the first time, when she invited Jackie to Memorial Day out of spite, every time Martha has made Claire feel inferior or small since the start of her pregnancy—Claire has always quietly taken it on the chin.

Claire sighs. She braces her hands against the counter, letting her head drop forward.

"Martha. Please. If you're truly my friend, if you've ever cared for my happiness at all, do this for me," Claire says quietly. "I'll never ask you for anything else. I swear."

When Claire turns to her again, Martha looks stricken.

Walter's head pops through the kitchen door.

"You ladies about finished in here?" he says, blithely unaware of the tension in the room. "We've got a game of parcheesi set up."

"We'll be there in just a moment," Martha says. Her voice is measured. After a few seconds of silence, she bustles out to the den.

Martha is quiet for the whole game. She sends them on their way home without saying a word about Jackie, and though Claire is quite aware that she could blab the whole thing to Walter the moment they leave, she has the strange feeling that her secret is safe, for now.

The house is just barely cooler than it was during the day. Pete is insistent, tonight, on lovemaking, and the suffocating heat makes it more uncomfortable than usual. Claire does her duty, thinking all the while of the appointment on the horizon.

Once he's snoring consistently, she rises and starts her routine—face washed. Jewelry in the case. Hair unpinned.

While she waits for the bath to fill, Claire wanders to the window.

The pool lights are on, and Jackie is in the water. She's in a bathing suit this time, at least, but she's not swimming so much as she's floating underwater, the shape of her body flickering with the surface movement. She's still. Her limbs are splayed, her dark hair fanned around her, and she stays under for a worrying amount of time. Long enough for a pit of fear to form in Claire's stomach.

Claire finally breathes again once Jackie surfaces. She slicks her hair back, her feet finding the bottom, and in a strange echo of the last time this happened, she looks up towards Claire's window.

This time, Claire waves. Jackie only pauses for a moment before she waves back.

After a tepid bath, Claire slips into a night of fevered dreaming.

She's in Jackie's pool. She's not sure how she *knows* it belongs to Jackie, since her eyes are closed, but with the smell of chlorine and the cool water on her skin there's really nowhere else it could be. She's alone, at first, but then she senses someone behind her. Someone moving closer. Currents of water are shifting against Claire's back, warmer than the rest.

Two hands land on her hips. She knows without even opening her eyes who they belong to, and slowly Claire becomes aware of the fact that she's not wearing a bathing suit.

The nakedness doesn't feel the way it normally does. Usually, the only place Claire is entirely naked is the bath, her small private oasis after Pete has gone to sleep. Even in bed with her husband she usually keeps her brassiere on, if not her whole nightgown.

Jackie being here to see her nude body doesn't set Claire's nerves off. She feels calm. Floaty. Almost like she did the day they got high. Jackie's hands are on her skin, and Claire can smell her shampoo over the chlorine. There's a voice in her ear, low and throaty and very familiar.

"Not so unbuttoned now, are you?"

And unbuttoned Claire surely is. Jackie's hands are moving up, sliding around to rest just under Claire's breasts, which feel strange and tingly and bare.

Claire wants to open her eyes. She wants to turn, to do *something*, but she isn't sure what. She isn't even sure what's happening now. She's never been touched like this, with such slow intention, and she's never felt this way before.

Jackie's fingers creep upwards, ever upwards, until they're just about to cup—

Claire wakes to the quiet trill of her alarm.

She heaves herself upright and hits the silence button before Pete wakes up, as she always does. Her nightgown is soaked in sweat, from the heat of the night. Her breasts feel oddly sensitive against the fabric. Something is throbbing between her legs to the tune of her heartbeat.

The details of her strange dreams are slipping through her fingers. She can hardly recall the details, but even that small remembrance makes something strange shudder through her.

Pete grunts, and rolls over. His arm falls across Claire's lap, and Claire is made aware that she's slippery between her thighs.

She jumps out of bed.

The unfamiliar slipperiness is even more apparent as she walks to the bathroom. Claire would never typically bathe in the morning, but today she puts her shower cap on and gives her body a quick rinse in the shower before she starts on her routine. When she washes, everything feels as sparky as a live electrical wire.

Perhaps if it continues, it could be something to talk to that specialist about. For now, Claire puts it out of her mind.

There's no sense dwelling on something so strange.

Once they've started, the strange dreams don't stop.

They always feature Jackie, though they aren't always quite so alarming as the first one. Sometimes they're completely innocuous—often she and Jackie are simply together, existing in the same space. Sometimes they're on Jackie's couch again, Jackie's head in Claire's lap, her fingers tracing tingly patterns all over Claire's hands. But sometimes those patterns drift up her arms. A few times they even move over her thighs, and she's not entirely sure what to think about that.

Even more confusing are the dreams that aren't so innocuous.

In those dreams, Jackie's hands are more insistent. Jackie touches her firmly in places that don't seem friendly. Places that even her husband ignores. Her neck. Her belly. Her breasts. She can feel Jackie's hair drifting across her thighs, long and silky-soft.

The image of Jackie in a cut-out swimsuit from that day at the pool haunts Claire. In these dreams, there's always a sense of urgency, with the knowledge that there's something Claire should be doing. Something she should feel ashamed of. Without fail they end before Claire can make heads or tails of their meaning, and she wakes up sweaty and bewildered. It's maddening.

It's one such maddening morning when Claire, while folding laundry and idly recalling last night's dream, leans into the corner of the laundry basket and feels like a pressure valve in her lower body has been released.

It's intense. It's *good*. So good that Claire groans without meaning to, the loud sound startling her enough that she moves away.

The feeling is gone as suddenly as it came. Claire leans back, her heart pounding, and tries to figure out what on *earth* has happened.

She's doing exactly what she always does—she has the basket upturned, and is using the bottom as a sort of table to fold Pete's shirts. She leaned forward to grab one that fell and unfolded itself, and the corner of the base pressed into her pelvis. And then the *feeling* happened.

Apprehensively, Claire leans forward again. She presses herself into the corner of the basket, reaching and shifting until she finds the same spot.

The feeling returns twofold.

Claire can't stop the loud noise that leaves her mouth. It feels *indescribably* good, like nothing she's ever felt in her life—somehow, the pressing of hard plastic into the cleft between her legs is making her feel like she's going to writhe out of her skin. Claire leans forward harder, rolling her hips, and the feeling seems to crawl up from the point of pressure to wrap around her chest, all the way up to the base of her neck.

Last night's dream unfurls again, bursting back into her mind's eye. She and Jackie were in that changing room again, and Jackie's hands didn't stop after a single button at Claire's throat. They kept going, button after button popping free, and just before Claire woke up Jackie had parted the shirt to reveal that Claire was entirely without a brassiere.

The thought brings a *pulse* with it, centered between her legs. It's similar to the ones she often wakes up to, but more intense. Claire leans harder into the basket, hearing herself whimper as if she's not inhabiting her own body but instead floating above the scene. She's rocking against the surface, chasing that feeling, and *gosh* it feels good, it feels so strange and awful and *wonderful*—

The downstairs phone rings. The harsh trill startles Claire so badly that she upturns the entire basket, and all the folded laundry on top.

For a moment Claire is still, her hand pressed to her chest. The phone rings a second, and then a third time. She can feel her blood pounding through her veins, moving through her body and distributing shame through every cell.

It takes two more rings before Claire hurries down to answer it.

"Davis residence," Claire says. She's noticeably breathless, but she puts it down to the sprint down the stairs to get the phone. She's still trembling all over.

"Claire, it's Dorothy O'Neil," Dorothy says. She's always been one to announce her full name at every opportunity. "There is a strange man parked outside of your house."

Claire frowns. She moves to the kitchen window, peering out at what she can see of the road. "A strange man? Are you sure?"

"Very sure," Dorothy says. Dorothy is known for calling the police over local teens walking through the neighborhood after dark. She can have a hair trigger, and clearly she's been activated by this. "He's been there for nearly half an hour."

Once upon a time, it would have been Martha making a call like this. Claire hasn't heard from her since their confrontation over fondue.

"I'll go see who it is," Claire says. Her racing heart is only now starting to slow down.

Dorothy gasps. "Don't do that! What if he's a hooligan?"

"In Acacia Circle?" Claire says doubtfully.

"He could have a weapon," Dorothy insists. "He could be a criminal!"

"Why did you call me, then? So I can better anticipate my murder?"

Dorothy doesn't have an answer for that.

"Thank you for the warning, Dorothy," Claire says, before hanging up the phone with a firm *click*. A glance out the front window shows that there is indeed a vehicle parked at the curb between her house and Jackie's, but it looks familiar. A small white Volvo.

When Claire knocks on the car window, Theo jumps so hard that he hits his head on the interior roof.

"What the fuck?" Theo says, his voice getting louder as he rolls the window down. "Can a man not roll a cigarette in peace?"

Claire can now see that his lap is littered with loose tobacco. She winces. "Sorry. I'm only here to tell you that the neighbors think you might be a murderer."

"I will be, if I have to stay here much longer," Theo grumbles.

"You might want to—"

"Oh, Christ. Here comes the fucking cavalry," Theo says, his eyes flicking to something behind Claire. She has just enough time to turn around before Dorothy has descended upon them.

"Excuse me. Clearly you do *not* live here, and this is a safe neighborhood," Dorothy says. She's clearly already prepared to swing her handbag at Theo's head, gathering up a head of steam as she storms across the Circle. Louise had her gardens revamped last year, and Dorothy had pulled a similar fit when she saw the work crew wandering around the Circle—Claire should have known she'd cause the ruckus of the decade.

"Of course I don't live here, you old bat," Theo says, rolling his eyes. "I've been waiting for someone."

Dorothy gasps. Her mouth opens and closes, like she can't decide which tirade she'd like to go off on.

"He's not a criminal, Dorothy," Claire says.

Dorothy looks as if Claire has just proposed marriage to Theo. She goes pale when he opens the car door, and she jumps backward.

"You don't know him, do you, Claire?" Dorothy says, as if Theo isn't there at all.

"I do," Claire says.

"You can't be serious. He's..." Dorothy trails off, staring at Theo with obvious distrust.

Claire's mind races. If she says that she knows Theo through Jackie, she has no doubt that Dorothy will make sure their continued friendship makes its way through the neighborhood and back to Pete. She's never been good at lying on the spot.

She's so grateful when Theo intervenes that she almost hugs him there in the middle of the street.

"I'm her interior designer," Theo says smoothly. "She and her hubby are considering a remodel." He turns to Claire. "I know we discussed a green color palette, but based on the exterior, I'm thinking we might veer more towards a rococo style. How do you feel about white and gold?"

It's a smoother lie than Claire could come up with so quickly. Luckily he's dressed nicely—his maroon shirt has a loud paisley print on it, and doesn't have a single wrinkle. He's taller than Claire expected, too. She'd first met him in a bathing suit reclined on a pool chair, but at full height he must be well over six feet.

He cocks his hip with a smile, waiting for her answer as Dorothy steams.

"We can discuss it," Claire says, quickly leading him towards the house by the elbow. Dorothy's eyes are fixed on where Claire's hand is touching his arm. "Dorothy, I'll see you at book club?"

"Ta-ta, Dottie," Theo calls over his shoulder.

Claire is sure that half the neighborhood will know what happened by the end of the day, but Claire's tolerance for the suburban politics of Acacia Circle has waned lately. As long as it doesn't threaten her friendship with Jackie, she couldn't be bothered anymore. If Dorothy's husband happens to mention this to Pete, Claire will just tell him that she was looking into designing a nursery, and Theo was who the design firm sent.

Theo follows her into the house, looking around judgmentally as Claire shuts the door behind them. "You really could use a remodel, you know. The décor is very 1956."

"My husband doesn't like change," Claire says. She leads Theo to the kitchen, putting the kettle on and arranging two cups. "Thank you for coming up with that story. The only lie I could think of was that a neighbor down the road was having her lawn re-sodded again. The crew was mostly colored last time. But that wouldn't explain how we know each other." She pulls the sugar down from a cabinet, dropping a spoon into the jar. "Hopefully Dorothy believes you're a designer. That's possible, right?" When she turns back to him, Theo's expression has changed.

"Yes. But it's more believable that I'm the help," he says.

Claire's stomach sinks. That familiar feeling of stepping wrong in a conversation is worse than ever before, and her pearls are between her fingers before she knows it. "That's...not what I meant."

"It's really impossible for you people to imagine me doing anything besides underpaid manual labor," Theo says. He laughs to himself. "Couldn't be seen with someone like me any other way, could you? Not in this neighborhood."

"No," Claire says. "No, that's not—that isn't it. It's not about—" she swallows hard. The kettle is starting to whistle, and she takes it off the heat. Her tongue is in a tangle. "Oh, I've put my foot in it."

"It's nothing I wouldn't expect from a Suzy Homemaker," Theo says. He smiles, but it's tighter than it was before. More guarded.

"That's not all I am," Claire protests.

"And I'm not a laborer," Theo says bluntly. "Yet your first thought to placate your little friend was *wandering workman*."

"I'm sorry," Claire says again. "My husband doesn't like my friendship with Jackie. I was worried that if I told Dorothy the truth, it would get back to him. She's a blabbermouth. And you salvaged the situation. I really am grateful."

Theo's lips purse together. Claire has no idea what he's thinking, but he hasn't stormed out yet, at least.

"I'm not always sure what to say around you," Claire admits. "I've never known anyone like you before."

"A Black queer?"

Claire hopes she's managed not to flinch. Though Theo is using it to describe himself, it still feels vulgar. "Yes."

"I know better than to expect anything but the same old rules in this hellhole," Theo says. "Say whatever you want. We were never going to be friends, were we?"

"But I'd like to be," Claire says.

One of Theo's thick eyebrows arches delicately. "I don't make a habit of befriending people who look down on me."

"I don't," Claire says. When he raises his other eyebrow as well, she sinks down into a chair. Her stomach is now in a state of uneasy flux. "Do I?"

Theo says nothing. Claire taps her pearls against her teeth until it feels like they're reverberating in her brain. Does she look down on Theo? She was uncomfortable when they first met, but she'd put that down to jealousy over his friendship with Jackie. But she said what she said, and didn't think twice about it until Theo said something. Is she any better than Dorothy?

"You're going to be the talk of the suburb after the stunt you pulled today," Theo says.

Claire crosses her arms across her chest, squeezing tight until the anxious feeling subsides a little. "Probably."

"Does that bother you?"

It's been a long time since she was in school, but something in his voice makes her feel like she's in a cramped desk sweating her way through an algebra test. "So long as I can still see Jackie, I'd rather a little gossip than Dorothy calling the police on you just for sitting in your car."

"Why?"

Claire considers that, for a moment. She can't say she isn't a little bit worried about the potential drama this could cause, but in the end the answer is simple. "Jackie loves you. I'd rather try to be like her than like Dorothy. Even if I don't always succeed."

For a minute, Theo just stares at her. The clock ticks. The refrigerator hums. Claire drums her fingers on her forearms as his eyes drill into her.

"You're an odd duck," Theo finally says.

It doesn't sound derogatory in the same way it did when he called her Suzy Homemaker. If this really has been some kind of test, Claire can only hope she's passed some threshold in his estimation.

"So I'm told," Claire says. She goes back to the stove, pouring the slightly cooled water into two mugs and pushing one towards Theo. "Will you sit down with me?"

Theo seems to consider his options. He looks from Claire to the door, and then from the door to the tea.

"You're not as much of a freak as Jacks. But it's a start," Theo says slowly. He sits down, making himself more comfortable and pulling his tea towards himself.

Claire exhales in one big rush. It's obvious that this doesn't mean she and Theo are fast friends, but it must mean something that he's still giving her the time of day. "Thank you. And that's maybe the first time someone has told me I'm not strange *enough*."

"Trust me, hon. You're barely on the scale," Theo says. "Unlike Jackie, who should have been here an hour ago."

"Is she often late?"

"She was late to her own birth," Theo drawls. "She was supposed to meet me at eleven, after an early shoot. Apparently, there's some record store in Sacramento the likes of which I couldn't possibly find in San Fran."

"That sounds like a nice time," Claire says mildly.

She's not sure how to continue the conversation, but Theo does it for her—he stands up, pointing out the kitchen window where Jackie's car is rolling into the drive. "Look, Jacks is home. Come on."

He abandons his undrunk tea, and Claire blinks in his wake. It sounds like an invitation, but it comes so suddenly that she can't keep up. "You want me to come with you?"

Theo raises his eyebrows, as if she was invited all along and this shouldn't be a surprise at all. "What else do you have to fill the time? Waxing the linoleum?"

It turns out to be a wonderful outing, even if Theo only invited her out of some kind of curiosity. Jackie is in a good mood after her photoshoot, and apologizes to Theo for several minutes about her lateness while they drive to the record store. Theo pokes fun at Claire's music taste, seeming to test her boundaries, but it feels more in jest than genuinely mean. He's strange and often impolite, but he's also clever. He makes Jackie laugh. Above all, he clearly cares about Jackie's happiness as much as Claire does. When they first met Claire never thought she'd come to enjoy his company so much, but she finds that after that strange afternoon she's always quite happy when she sees his car in Jackie's driveway.

If Pete knew she was associating with someone like Theo, he might be as angry about *that* as about the Jackie of it all. And Pete will never understand the pull Claire feels towards Jackie Callas.

Even Claire doesn't fully understand it. All of it, every hour spent listening to Joni Mitchell or shopping with Theo or watching raptly as Jackie licks an ice cream cone, Claire hides from her husband. She's always home with dinner on the table before he's any the wiser. These days, she has it down to an art.

And she'll keep at it for as long as it takes.

Chapter 16

Near the end of August, Martha goes into labor.

Claire has been prepared for this eventuality. She agreed when Martha first got pregnant to check in on the house for the few days Martha will be at the hospital, and she has every intention of upholding her promise even with the strangeness between them lately.

Even so, Claire finds herself taking advantage of Martha's absence. While she's at the hospital welcoming her little bundle of joy, Claire sees Jackie every single day.

Keeping their friendship from Pete is now imperative. Jackie is too important to lose. Maybe Jackie is a bad influence—she encourages Claire to speak her mind, after all. She gives Claire a taste of freedom during her stagnant days. Jackie bought her the first outfit she's ever felt truly comfortable in, just because she could. That fact—the fact that Jackie bought it for her, the fact that Claire feels comfortable wearing it even if she's terrified of being seen in it—is what drives Claire to put the outfit on and go over to Jackie's house in broad daylight.

Sure, she runs there as fast as her legs can take her, but the delight on Jackie's face when she opens the door makes it worth it.

"Claire!" Jackie says, quickly moving aside to let Claire in. Her eyes widen as Claire passes, fully taking in Claire's clothes. "Goodness, you—you look *fantastic*."

Claire gets a unique thrill every time Jackie pays her a compliment, but this one feels different. Jackie isn't her cool, collected self—she trails behind Claire on the way to the kitchen, her eyes wide, and Claire feels exposed by the clothes. Like without the protective shell of a skirt, Jackie will somehow see whatever strange force has been twisting at the apex of her thighs lately.

It brings to mind that moment with the laundry basket. Something twinges behind her zipper, and Claire clasps her hands over her lap when she sits in the breakfast nook.

"You're here early today," Jackie remarks, setting the kettle on to boil. "Not that I'm not happy to see you, of course. And in such stunning duds." Jackie says it jauntily, winking on the last word, but her cheeks are rather pink.

"I have some things to do for Martha later today. She's off having the baby," Claire says. She presses her hands to her thighs—the texture of corduroy is strange, as is the shape of her own legs. "She'll be at the hospital for a few days."

"That's nice of you," Jackie says. She keeps glancing at Claire as she lays out mugs and teabags, and the warmth of her attention is better than a hot bath.

"It means I don't have to worry about her peeping through the curtains every time I leave my house."

"Now it's just dear Mr. Davis that you need to worry about," Jackie says. There's a hint of bitterness to it that Claire finds herself sharing.

"Oh, Mr. Davis can stuff it," Claire huffs.

Jackie laughs abruptly. She looks shocked by Claire's candor, and Claire is honestly rather surprised at herself. Though these kinds of thoughts have been building up in her for some time, it's not often that she voices it. The freedom of it loosens something in her chest.

"Claire, what was your maiden name again?" Jackie asks, suddenly demanding as she slides into the booth across from Claire. "Not your husband's name. Your real name. Anita said it when we visited her shop."

"When I married, my name was Fields," Claire says. It feels unfamiliar on her tongue. "Claire Fields."

"Claire Fields," Jackie says. Her mouth forms the name slowly, smiling around it as if she's tasting it and finding it satisfying. "I like that. It's nice to meet you, Claire Fields."

Jackie holds out her hand. It's oddly reminiscent of their first meeting, but Claire feels as if an entirely different person is shaking Jackie's hand this time. Being Jackie's friend has shifted something that Claire isn't sure she ever wants to shift back.

Their hands don't part until the kettle whistles.

Jackie jumps up, taking it off the burner with a too-quick motion. She grabs the kettle a bit too far down on the handle, and hisses as she drops it back onto the burner. "Ah! Damn."

Claire is out of her seat in a blink. She grabs Jackie's hand, examining the burn—a thin red strip across the palm of her hand, but it doesn't look like it will blister. "Careful! Are you all right?"

Jackie pulls her hand back abruptly. "I'm fine. I forgot my brain today. Don't worry about me." Jackie's laugh is a little strained. She must be hurt, and not want to show it—she busies herself with pouring tea.

"You should put something on it, at least," Claire says. She leans against the counter, and folds her arms across her chest.

Jackie swears again as she pours hot water all over the countertop.

"*Shit*. Goddamn, fucking—kettle," Jackie mutters, chucking the kettle into the sink. It steams quietly, and Jackie takes a deep breath as spilled water drips down her lower cabinets. "Sorry. I'm sorry, Claire. I don't know what's wrong with me today."

"Nothing is wrong with you," Claire says firmly.

Jackie throws a tea towel onto the counter, soaking up the scalding water. "You don't know how untrue that is."

The towel darkens slowly. Jackie throws it into the sink along with the kettle, and after a moment of consideration, she opens a drawer to pull out a pack of Marlboro Lights.

"You don't mind, do you?" Jackie says, rifling in another drawer to produce her lighter. "I need to settle my nerves. It's either this, or make a martini at nine in the morning."

Claire blinks. Jackie is already pulling out a cigarette. "You smoke?"

"Used to. I quit two years ago."

Jackie doesn't wait for an affirmative. She disappears towards the living room, and by the time Claire has followed Jackie is draped over the couch taking her first deep drag.

Claire sits gingerly on the edge of a cushion.

Jackie's gaze flickers towards her, and then back to her cigarette.

"You seem unsettled," Claire says quietly. "Did I do something wrong?"

Jackie sighs. It comes with a cloud of smoke. "No, darling. You haven't done anything," Jackie says. The pet-name makes Claire feel a little better. "I'm just at the end of a very trying week."

"What happened?"

"I learned that I need to change my phone number," Jackie drawls. She takes another drag of her smoke; Claire hates the smell of cigarettes, but she doesn't hate the way Jackie's lips form around it. The sharp, almost rough way she breathes it in and out. It's different from the slow, lazy way she'd smoked marijuana. It's angrier. Like she resents herself for doing it.

Claire gets more comfortable on the couch. Though she's wearing pants, she still sits primly with her legs folded. "Was it your mother?"

"No. I think she got the message last time when I called her a wretched money-grubbing hag."

"Goodness," Claire says mildly.

Jackie laughs. Again, there's a harsh bitterness to it. "Trust me, she's called me worse."

"Was it...that man you told me about, then?" Claire says hesitantly. "The married one?"

Jackie taps her cigarette on the ashtray. She sits back against the couch and sucks at her teeth, taking another long drag. The ash glows orange.

"Apparently I give the impression that I'm a total sucker who will come running back the moment someone snaps their fingers," Jackie finally says.

"No, you don't," Claire says. "If he thinks you're like that, he's—he's an *ass*."

Jackie's head snaps to her. She smiles, and then laughs quietly. The weight of her sudden mood seems to lift.

Claire did that. She made Jackie happier, when this mystery man made her so sad.

"I don't think I've ever heard you swear," Jackie says. She sets the cigarette down, instead picking up the instant camera sitting on the coffee table. "Hold still—I need to document this moment."

As she usually does when a camera is pointed her way, Claire squirms out of the lens frame. Instead, she snatches the camera from Jackie's hands, turning it around and snapping a single quick photo of her own before Jackie can protest.

"You're the photographer now, are you?" Jackie says, her smile wide and genuine now. The cigarette lies forgotten in the ashtray.

"Better than being the photographed," Claire says, taking the photo from the slot. She can just barely see the outline of Jackie emerging from the white square.

"You know, I hardly saw a single photo of you in your whole house besides your wedding portrait," Jackie says. "The rest are of Pete and his family."

Claire waves the photo in front of her face like a fan. "I don't really like having my picture taken."

"What if it was me taking it?" Jackie's posture is relaxed, but her leg is bouncing rapidly.

"You want to photograph *me*?" Claire says. "Why?"

"I think you should have at least one photo of yourself that you like," Jackie says, grabbing the camera back from Claire. "A picture of the real Claire Fields."

Claire has been gazing in wonder at Jackie's photographs for almost as long as they've known each other. Lately she's been caught up on *how* Jackie takes them—since the party, it's become more apparent how detached Jackie is from her subject. Capturing the untouchable. Now Jackie wants to capture Claire, up close and personal.

The thought makes her a bit sweaty.

"Are you sure?" Claire says. "I don't think I'll measure up to the models you're used to."

"Measure up? Jackie says, pulling Claire to her feet and starting to tug the pins from her hair. Her smile is soft. "You'll blow them out of the water."

Jackie sits her on the ottoman, loosing Claire's hair from its coif and arranging the curls around her shoulders. Claire sits stiffly at first, waiting for Jackie to pose her, but Jackie's brief instruction of *'do whatever feels natural'* as she fusses with the light levels in the room leaves Claire at a loss.

Jackie starts out distant, taking pictures of Claire's stiff posture from the other side of the couch. Claire is sure that she's absolutely failing at being a model, but as the minutes wear on Jackie keeps giving encouraging comments. She makes little jokes to make Claire giggle. She assures Claire of her handsomeness, and for maybe the first time in her life, Claire starts to believe it.

Jackie's attention is addictive. Claire has never been looked at this way, with such interest.

In a bold move, she uncrosses her legs and leans forward with her elbows on her knees.

Jackie's eyes light up.

Under Jackie's intense focus, Claire opens up like a flower in full bloom. She's becoming something greater. Her forearms look different, braced against her thighs like this—they look lean, *strong*, and for the first time that seems like a good thing. Claire can feel the defined line of her shoulders pressing against her new shirt as Jackie's eyes drift across it. Her legs feel articulated from her body, not trapped under her usual stiff skirts, and Claire spreads them and relaxes with a lack of shame that surprises her. For the first time, she's completely unframed. Jackie is seeing all her edges, all the parts of herself she usually tucks away, and she seems to like each one.

Claire feels, once again, rather like the woman in the photo that's so fascinated her since the day Jackie hung it. She glances at it—it's across the room, so she can't see the details, but she committed them to memory a long time ago.

Under the flash of Jackie's camera Claire wonders what it would feel like to have Jackie leaning against her arm like the other woman in the picture. Claire can almost feel the buzz of the alcohol; though she has never in her life considered smoking, she can definitely smell the cigarette Jackie would be lighting.

Something inside Claire is glowing like that ashy ember, and Jackie's brown eyes are stoking it.

Jackie snaps picture after picture, each one a closer shot than the last, and when she runs out of film in her fancy camera she switches to the instant-print. When the first few of those fully develop, Claire can hardly believe it.

"It doesn't even look like me," Claire says quietly, looking back and forth between two shots.

Jackie takes them from her, and hands her a few newly developed ones. "It does. Look closer. This is how I see you, Claire. You're...fascinating." Jackie's voice is so quiet on the last word that Claire almost can't hear it.

The person looking back at her, the person Jackie apparently sees, is a stranger to Claire. And yet she's somehow intimately familiar—she's something close to who Claire was once, before time and expectations changed her. It's the person she never thought she could be. Jackie is sitting close to her, all heat and distraction, and Claire never wants to move away.

Jackie is such a good friend. She's such a good friend that it makes Claire's chest ache, like pressing on a bruise.

Claire goes home with three photos. Jackie gives her two of them—one is one of Claire, sitting on the ottoman with a wry smile and looking more confident than she's ever felt. The other is of both of them, taken close up and slightly off-kilter. Jackie had held the camera up and out as far as she could, snapping it blindly. Jackie is laughing, and Claire is looking at her with that emotion she can't explain.

She wonders if that's always how she looks, when she looks at Jackie. If anyone else can see it. If Jackie can.

The third photo is one Claire slips into her pocket before she goes back to her own house to get started on making some casseroles for Martha. It's the one she took of Jackie, before their impromptu photoshoot. She's smiling at Claire with a cigarette between her fingers. Her eyes are soft. Her hair is tucked behind one ear, but there's a stray piece of it falling across her forehead.

Claire puts the photos in her bedside drawer, pressed like flower petals between the pages of her favorite book.

Chapter 17

Claire doesn't hear from Martha for the rest of the month. It's not a surprise given their last conversation, and Martha will need time to recover from childbirth, but it's still strange not to hear from her for such a long stretch. Not even a phone call. Martha's curtains stay closed in the weeks after she returns from the hospital. Claire learns through Pete's occasional chats with Walter that they've named the baby Daniel.

Jackie also disappears for a week around the same time. She has a high-paying extended gig in San Jose, and she's opted to get a hotel rather than driving for hours every day. It leaves Claire with nothing to do outside of the household chores, which she's gotten down to an art at this point to make time in her day for other things.

If only to fill the time, Claire finally sets up the paints Jackie gifted her in the sunniest corner of her kitchen table. She sits in front of the mini-easel, a brush in her hand, poised to start.

Nothing comes to mind. Claire has so many colors to choose from, and yet she can't call to mind a single image that she wants to commit to paper. She flips through her sketchbook, but none of her drawings call to her.

After a whole fruitless hour, Claire dials Anita's number.

"Cozy Corner Arts and Crafts, how can I help you?" Anita says cheerfully. There's a pottery wheel working in the background of the call.

"It's me. Claire, I mean. Davis," Claire says, wincing at her own stammering. "I hope I'm not interrupting?"

The pottery wheel stops abruptly, followed by the *thunk* of what Claire can only assume is a large hunk of clay hitting the floor. "Damn—no, not interrupting. Or if you are, I welcome it. I can't get this goddamn bowl to shape up the way I want."

"I know the feeling," Claire says.

"Happy to hear from you either way," Anita says cheerfully. "I was hoping you'd be in touch after Jacqueline came to buy you those paints."

"I tried to use them today," Claire says. Everything is still set up at the other end of the table, the unused water cup taunting her in the sunlight. "I couldn't do it. I stared at the paper for an hour and nothing came. This used to be easy, didn't it?"

"You're rusty. It'll take time to get back in the saddle. We all change over time, dear."

"I suppose we do," Claire says. "When you knew me—I mean, before I married Pete. What was your impression of me?"

"My impression?"

"Your memory of who I was. Lately I've been feeling...strange," Claire admits. "Like I don't know myself anymore."

Anita makes a thoughtful noise. "My impression of you...you were whip-smart. Honest. Shy, but when someone got you on about art, you'd talk their ear off," Anita says. "And...lonely, I'd say."

"Lonely?"

"Different. You had friends, and eventually you started seeing that boy," Anita says, apparently determined to continue her tradition of not using Pete's name, "but I always felt you only shared the surface with everyone. The rest came out in your art."

"I'm not sure what the rest is," Claire says. Based on the blank white paper she's staring at, the answer is *nothing*. "I saw myself as not much at all, then. A nobody. Waiting to bloom, like my mother always said. I want to think I've gotten past that, but sometimes I think I'm still waiting."

"You were always bloomed then, chickadee," Anita says. "Your petals just looked different than the rest. I think you were waiting to..." Anita pauses. Claire can hear her tapping her fingers against a surface. "To *be*, maybe."

Claire rolls a paintbrush between her fingers. "Waiting to be what, exactly?"

"Whatever you were meant to be," Anita says simply. "Find it, and the art will come."

Claire sits with that, after hanging up the phone. She has no idea what she's meant to be. Being around Jackie has brought out new things in her—is that what Anita means? Under Jackie's camera lens she felt herself became something worthy of being photographed, like one of Jackie's impossible flowers. Claire had put it down to Jackie's talent in finding beauty in the unremarkable, but maybe Jackie was just finding something that was already there. Something interesting on its own.

Claire gathers her supplies and carries everything out to the backyard, setting the mini easel up on the grass and kneeling in front of it. The breeze ruffles her hair. She breathes in the fresh air, and for the first time in years she puts brush to paper.

She ends up with something abstract. It's all shades of blue, ripples and waves interspersed with white. She's not sure what it is, exactly, but looking at it gives her a sense of comfort.

August has turned to a warm September when Jackie returns.

A mere hour after the Mustang pulls into the drive after her week away, Claire is knocking on her door. It's a hot day for early autumn, and Claire can hear movement inside—the back door sliding open and closed, footsteps through the house.

And then Jackie is answering the door in a yellow bikini.

Claire had seen Jackie in a bathing suit that afternoon by the pool with Theo, but this time is different. There's no sarong. It's not a one-piece with cutout sides. It's nothing but skin, warm dark tones against the yellow fabric, and there's just so much of it. It's like someone drew her up in a laboratory in the quest to make a perfect specimen of womanhood.

Claire isn't sure she truly understood the term *hourglass figure* until this moment. Jackie's bust seems more generous than ever with so little fabric covering it up. There's a lovely dip between Jackie's ribs and her hips, a spot that seems to beg for a hand to be resting there, and another between hip and thigh. There's a scattering of dark moles across her torso. There's a thin line of dark hair that trails down the middle of her belly, over the swell under her bellybutton, and disappears under her bikini bottoms.

At the very edges of Jackie's bikini line, Claire can see more dark, curly hair.

"Great timing. I was just thinking of calling you," Jackie says, leaning against the doorframe. She doesn't seem to notice Claire's eyeline, but that doesn't make Claire any less ashamed of it. "I missed you this week. Come on in."

"You're swimming," Claire says loudly, already spinning around to head back towards her own house. Her face is so hot that she's sure her blush must be visible from the moon. "I didn't mean to interrupt."

"Don't be ridiculous," Jackie calls after her. "Why would that stop you from visiting?"

Claire stops, but doesn't yet turn around.

"I...don't know," Claire says, still staring resolutely at Jackie's mailbox. Her heart is beating so hard that she's sure the fluttering can be seen under her dress. "It feels rude to impose?"

"Just go get your suit. We'll swim together," Jackie says.

"I don't have a suit," Claire says, finally daring to look directly at Jackie again. It's a lie, of course, but Claire would rather not swim at all than have Jackie see her in that shabby homemade number.

"Not even one? Do you not like to swim?"

Claire rubs her arms self-consciously. "I don't often have the chance."

Jackie hums. She shifts her weight, cocking a hip, and Claire stares very carefully at a spot on the side of Jackie's house. "At least come sit with me?"

Claire trails Jackie through the kitchen, avoiding the wet footprints all over the linoleum. She's wearing her regular clothes today, rather than the ones Jackie bought, a brown dress with yellow flowers and a low bun, and she kicks off her shoes before taking a seat on a lounge. For once, she lays back comfortably rather than sitting up straight.

"I do like to swim," Claire finally admits when they're settled, staring up at the rainbow pattern on the deck umbrella. She feels a bit like she's in a therapist's office, reclined on one of those couches while she confesses her sins. "I think."

"I thought so. Didn't I see a bunch of cabin photos in your house?" Jackie asks. Her hair is gathered on top of her head in a loose updo, and Claire can't stop looking at the seldom-seen column of her neck.

"Oh, yes. Pete's family owns it," Claire says, looking up at the canopy above to keep from staring at Jackie's neck. "But I don't usually swim there. He goes hunting, and I get to spend the weekend with his mother." Claire can't quite keep a leash on the resentment in that sentence.

Jackie snorts. "There's a story behind that tone."

"She and Pete are very close," Claire says, clasping her hands hard over her stomach. "Rita always has something to say about how I'm doing as a wife."

Jackie hums. "Sounds like my mother."

"Does she also critique your cooking and your body and the fact that you haven't had children yet?" Claire says. She tries to raise an eyebrow—one of Jackie's trademark expressions, and one Claire isn't sure her face can fully manage.

Jackie laughs. "The last point, definitely. Along with every other life choice I make."

"You don't deserve that," Claire says, much more softly.

"Neither do you."

Claire hums. She leans back, turning her face towards the sky again and closing her eyes. "I lied, earlier. I do have a bathing suit. Just one. But it's..." Claire pauses, choosing her words carefully. "Rita made it for me. It doesn't fit very well."

"So she made you wear her wedding dress, and she controls what you swim in?" Jackie asks, not bothering to hide her incredulity.

"She makes most of my clothes. Pete says it saves us money." Claire toys with her pearls. Maybe she's getting too honest now, a little too comfortable in revealing the more embarrassing parts of her life. But if she can't share everything with Jackie, who can she share with?

"Why don't you borrow one of mine instead?" Jackie says suddenly.

Claire's eyes fly open.

Jackie looks a little surprised at herself for suggesting it, but she schools her expression quickly.

"Your...clothes?" Claire says.

"Bathing suits. I have a few. They're all clean," Jackie says, standing up quickly and gesturing for Claire to follow. "You can just wear whichever one fits."

Which is how Claire finds herself in Jackie's bathroom with a selection of suits laid out, trying to find one that will cover everything it needs to.

It's not an easy task. She and Jackie are wildly different sizes—Claire has none of Jackie's curves—but she manages to find a top and bottom set that she can tie tight enough to not fall down immediately.

Claire has never worn so little fabric in her life. Her underwear covers more than this—it at least sits at her bellybutton, where Jackie's bikini feels like nothing but a few tiny scraps of material strung together with twine. Claire's hipbones are jutting out. Without her usual layers she can't hide her wide shoulders, her narrow hips and tiny breasts.

Rita has told her a hundred times while taking her measurements—clothes create an illusion. With the minimal fabric she has on right now, Claire might as well just be baring herself to Jackie's eyes completely naked.

Claire takes the pins out of her hair, wraps one of Jackie's big, fluffy towels around herself, and heads out to the pool.

Jackie is underwater when Claire emerges from the house. Jackie cuts through towards the stairs and then rises up to meet her, water streaming down her body, and for a moment as Jackie emerges from the pool Claire is so overcome by the similarity to the Jackie that she sees in her dreams that she's rooted to the spot.

She can smell the chlorine. She can hear Jackie's voice, low in her ear.

Not so unbuttoned now, are you?

Jackie is so soft. So *feminine*. She's all shapely curves and swells, where Claire is sharp angles. Something about the way Jackie looks right now feels dangerous, like the glowing red spiral of a hot stove element, and a part of Claire that's getting louder by the minute wants to slap her hand onto it to feel the burn.

"The water's nice and warm," Jackie says, in her actual real-life voice. On the patio table is a bottle of soda with a straw in it. Jackie takes a sip, blissfully unaware of how Claire's traitorous eyes track every drop of water that runs down her skin. The bow that ties Jackie's bikini top cuts slightly into the softness of her upper back, leaving divots in the soft flesh, and something swoops low in Claire's belly.

"Just—um, just give me a second," Claire stammers. She pulls the towel tighter. Faced so up-close with Jackie's perfect body, she doesn't want to reveal her own.

Jackie sets her soda down. "You can't swim in a towel, silly."

"I know, I—I need sunblock, first," Claire says, grabbing at the open bottle sitting next to Jackie's drink. She holds it out like a shield, but Jackie only steps closer.

"Sure. Do you need help with your back?"

The idea of Jackie's hands on her body, spreading warm lotion over her skin, is even worse than the exposure of the bathing suit.

"*No!*" Claire yells.

Jackie stops in her tracks. Her eyes are wide, and a little hurt. It pierces the panic slowly rising in Claire.

Claire clears her throat, trying to lower her voice. "Sorry. It's only that I—I burn very easily. Maybe I should just stay up here under the umbrella?"

"We can do whatever you'd like," Jackie says softly.

Whatever Claire would like. What *would* Claire like?

What Claire would like is to feel as comfortable in herself as Jackie does. What Claire would like is to understand her own fascination, her own *fixation*. What Claire would like is to forget her strange dreams and the tension they leave her with, and have a good time with her friend.

Claire drops the towel.

Jackie goes silent.

Her eyes rake over Claire's shoulders, over her stomach and her bare legs, in a way that reminds Claire of how she felt in that department store changing room. It doesn't feel like Claire is being judged, as she feared, but it's certainly more focused than Claire expected. She feels as bare as a newborn.

Jackie's skin has gone rosy. Just when Claire is about to ask what's wrong, Jackie seems to snap out of it. She blinks rapidly, her wide eyes snap up, and in a rush, she sprints past Claire and dives into the pool.

It's out of character for Jackie to do something so sudden, so dramatic, and the water from her dive splashes on Claire's feet in a big wave. Jackie stays underwater, seeming to settle on the bottom of the pool; Claire remembers seeing her do the same thing from her window, once.

That remembrance leaves her hot all over.

Claire descends the stairs into the shallow end at a normal pace. The water is just cool enough to be refreshing, but it does make her shiver as it hits her thighs. She can see Jackie moving under the rippling surface, coming towards her, closer and closer, until Claire is sure Jackie is going to plow right into her.

A hand closes around Claire's ankle, pulling sharply, and suddenly she's underwater.

The water is a shock to her system, but not nearly as much as Jackie's sudden move. When Claire surfaces again, shaking water out of her eyes, her first order of business is to shout.

"Why did you do that?"

Jackie, of course, surfaces perfectly. Her hair slicks back. Water droplets form on her eyelashes. In contrast, Claire's curls are stuck to her face, and the borrowed bikini bottoms are riding up.

"You were taking too long," Jackie says. The strangeness from before seems to be gone—she's her usual self again, cheeky and laughing as Claire finger-combs her own hair.

"So your solution was to try to drown me?"

"You're perfectly welcome to try to drown me in retaliation," Jackie says, grinning as she drifts away in a perfect backstroke. "If you can."

"Is that a challenge?"

"More of a dare."

"Oh, I'm gonna *get* you," Claire says, laughing as she lunges in Jackie's direction. Jackie gets a face full of pool water, and the war begins.

Jackie is a great swimmer, but Claire has a longer reach. They chase each other around the pool, giggling and shouting like children, and Claire forgets propriety. She forgets that anyone could be listening, and that Pete will notice if her hair is wet when he comes home. She swims and splashes and laughs with Jackie, and she doesn't care about anything else. Her sides are sore with pure, undiluted joy when Jackie successfully jumps on her back, playfully shoving her under the water.

Claire surfaces again quickly. She turns to grab for Jackie's legs, pulling her all the way around with the intention to dunk her under the water in retaliation, but Jackie latches on like a koala bear—her legs wrap around Claire's waist. Claire's hands go, instinctively, to Jackie's thighs.

The game stops.

They're pressed together in every conceivable place. Suddenly Claire is very aware of every inch of touching skin, every scrap of fabric, every tiny movement between them. Now it's Claire's fingers making divots in Jackie's thighs, gripping them like a life raft. The water is cool, but Jackie's skin is hot.

Jackie is staring at Claire's mouth with an indecipherable expression. Claire can see every soft, dark hair on her face, illuminated by the bright sun. Droplets of water slide down her temples.

Claire is hit with a thought that goes off like a gunshot.

They're close enough to kiss.

The very idea is like a foreign language deciphering itself before Claire's eyes. Kissing a woman. Kissing *Jackie*. It's unfamiliar, frightening, but something about it resonates somewhere deep inside her. It's like a tuning fork, striking a piercing note that lines up exactly where it's supposed to.

One of Jackie's hands curls around the back of Claire's neck in a hold that makes Claire want to melt and become one with the chest-deep water. Her heart is thrumming like the engine of the Mustang; she can feel warm breath on her lips. They tingle with restless anticipation.

Claire's eyes drift closed. She tilts her head up, letting herself slide into whatever is about to happen, as she feels the slightest brush of warm breath against her lips.

She wonders, suddenly, how her dreams would have continued if she had kissed Jackie in them.

As if she can hear Claire's shameful thoughts, Jackie stiffens against her. She leans away, her legs releasing their hold, and she uses them to launch herself off of Claire's body so hard that Claire is propelled backward a foot or so into the deeper end of the pool.

When Claire opens her eyes, Jackie is standing in the shallow end. She's breathing in quick, frantic little gasps. She's flushed, now, all the way down to her chest.

"I forgot, I—I have a gig in the city," Jackie says. Her voice is unnaturally high and seems to quiver. She's already climbing out of the pool, stumbling up the stairs and wrapping Claire's abandoned towel around herself. "A paying one. Soon. Now, actually. I have to go."

"Didn't you just get back?" Claire says. Her very bones are vibrating. She takes a step forward, still struggling to keep up with the rapid-fire nature of the last few minutes. The water ripples out around her wobbly legs.

Jackie doesn't acknowledge that Claire has said anything. She's fumbling with the sliding door. Her voice sounds choked. "Keep the suit." Finally, Jackie manages to rip the door open, and she disappears inside. "I'll see you later."

She's gone before Claire can respond.

After a minute or two, Claire drags herself out of the water. She drip-dries awkwardly at the threshold of the sliding door, before scurrying to the bathroom to get her own clothes and throw them on haphazardly. Jackie's bedroom door is closed when she passes. The Mustang screeches out of the driveway a few hours later.

Chapter 18

Claire wakes the morning after Jackie's rapid departure to an empty driveway next door, and it stays empty for a stretch of days that start to feel endless.

Claire tries calling, though she knows the house is vacant. She peers over the fence—Jackie's soda bottle is still on the patio table, next to the sunblock. She even goes so far as to peep through Jackie's living room window.

Jackie is nowhere to be seen.

The car is still gone, and the house is dark. Claire starts to worry after the first morning, and she keeps worrying as the days stretch into a week.

Jackie could be anywhere. She didn't so much as leave a note. What if she got in some sort of car accident? What if she was *kidnapped*? Claire's fevered brain invents all sorts of horrific scenarios, each worse than the last, with no way to confirm one way or the other.

Claire can't shake the feeling that Jackie's absence is her fault. She did something that day in the pool, showed a hint of what her mind has been circling around. She'd almost *kissed* Jackie. On the lips. And clearly Jackie was disgusted by it. There's no other explanation for her sudden mood change, and her rapid departure.

The only thing to do is put her mind to other things. Claire throws herself into housework. She puts extra effort into meals, so much so that Pete actually makes note when she serves him a perfect lamb crown roast.

"Is it our anniversary?" Pete says, diving into the meal enthusiastically.

"Our anniversary was in March, dear," Claire says.

Pete chortles. "Well, it's nice to see some initiative in this house. Walt says that even Martha is falling behind lately."

Claire frowns. "Falling behind?"

"Not keeping up with things. Walt says the house is going to hell," Pete says with his mouth full of mashed potatoes. "He had to fix his own dinner the other night. Can you believe that?"

"She has a baby to take care of now," Claire reasons. "Newborns are a lot of work."

Pete scoffs, sawing his lamb off the bone. "Doesn't mean she should stop taking care of her husband. She should be able to manage her time. I really thought Martha would do better."

Claire pushes her potatoes around on her plate.

She would never have imagined that Martha might be struggling. She's been so excited to be a mother, so perfectly put-together all throughout her pregnancy, and now that the baby is here Claire assumed that she would be thriving.

They might have fought the last time they talked, but the idea that Martha has been suffering alone makes Claire uneasy.

The following morning, Claire knocks on Martha's door with a Tupperware full of baked goods.

She gets no answer. When Claire leans close, she can hear the distant sound of a baby crying. She knocks again; this time, she hears movement beyond the door. A muted thump, like something has been tripped over, and Martha's voice swearing.

Claire blinks in the bright sunlight. Martha doesn't *swear*.

"Martha?" Claire calls.

From what Claire can guess is the den, she hears a muffled voice. "I don't have time to entertain today."

"You don't need to entertain me," Claire says, shifting from foot to foot on the stoop. "Will you let me in?"

"I'm busy," Martha says. Her voice sounds hoarse, even behind the door.

"I'm here to help."

"I don't need your help!" Martha says shrilly. "Why don't you go have tea with your *real* best friend?"

Claire sighs. She shifts the Tupperware to her hip. "I'd like to visit with you."

Martha stays quiet. The baby is still crying. Slowly, in the window to the right of the door, Claire sees a curtain shift.

Claire holds the container up to the gap like a peace offering. "I have blueberry muffins."

The curtains flutter back into place. After a few long beats, the door opens a crack. Even through the sliver Claire can see that Martha's eye is bloodshot and puffy.

"The house isn't fit for company," Martha says.

"Mine never is, according to your standards."

The crack widens a little, and then shrinks again, as if Martha is going to shut it on her.

"Please let me in, Martha," Claire says softly. "I don't care about your house."

After a few beats, the door creaks slowly open. Claire steps inside; when she finally takes in the state of the place, she has to stifle a gasp.

The den is a mess. Blankets stained with spit-up are strewn all about, and it clearly hasn't been dusted in at least a week. Martha herself looks absolutely exhausted. Her red hair is limp and unkempt, and there are dark bags under her eyes.

Daniel continues to cry in his portable crib near the couch.

"Everything is just fine. Just fine," Martha says before Claire can ask, hurriedly tidying up. She grabs at a collection of baby bottles, knocking them all about in her hurry. "You can't stay long, though. It's time for Danny's nap."

The baby's cries reach an ear-splitting volume.

"He has colic, you see," Martha says, over the noise. Her eyes are watering. Her voice shakes as she chases one of the fallen bottles under the coffee table. "The doctor says it should clear up by twelve weeks. But until then—"

It's as if the baby doesn't need to breathe. He cries and cries, and Martha's shoulders start to shake.

Claire leans down, grabbing the fallen bottle and helping Martha to her feet. "Walter isn't helping, is he?"

"Why would he? He's the head of the household. This is my job," Martha says fiercely. "Taking care of the house and the baby is my job, and I—" Martha's voice finally cracks open into a sob.

Claire should feel some kind of satisfaction, maybe, that Martha is getting a comeuppance for her recent behavior. That her façade of perfection is breaking apart. But she doesn't. She pities her. She wraps her arms around Martha, and lets her cry.

"He never sleeps," Martha sobs into Claire's shoulder. "He's up at all hours, and he cries constantly, and when he does sleep I have so—so much to do around the house that I can't—and Walt keeps saying—"

"To hell with Walter," Claire says loudly.

Martha reels back. She seems momentarily shocked out of her tears, blinking up at Claire, and Claire takes her by the shoulders.

"Go try to put Daniel down for his nap. I'll clean up down here," Claire says firmly.

"Oh, no, I couldn't. It's my job. I'll get caught up. I could never—"

"Martha," Claire says, interrupting firmly. "Let me help you."

She feels rather like Jackie right now. Calm and in control. Jackie has talked her out of tears before, and now apparently Claire knows how to do it for someone else. It makes Claire's chest ache a little with missing her.

Claire manages to get the living room tidied, the kitchen cleaned, the dishes done, and the ingredients for a decent supper gathered together by the time Martha comes back. She looks a little more put-together—she's changed into clean clothes, and her hair is gathered into a tidier bun.

"He's finally down, for now," Martha says quietly. "Thank you." She takes a seat at the kitchen table opposite Claire, and for a time they sit in silence.

This whole house feels like some kind of horrible vision into Claire's future. The crying baby, and Martha's exhaustion, and Walter's lack of care for the whole situation. She can see Pete being just the same. Raising the baby will be Claire's duty, along with all else. While Claire suffers trying to give him what he wants, he'll be complaining to Walter about how she isn't meeting his expectations.

"I don't know what's wrong with me," Martha says suddenly.

"Nothing is wrong with you," Claire says, automatically.

"I should be living the happiest days of my life, you know," Martha continues. Her voice is getting shriller. "I have a good husband and a nice house, and a beautiful, healthy little boy. But I'm—it's as if I—oh, I don't know how to describe it."

"You feel like you should be grateful for what you have," Claire says. The words come without much thought. "You have everything you should want. But you feel broken. And that makes you feel like a monster. A failure."

Martha's shoulders fall. *"Yes,"* she says, grasping at Claire's hands.

The contact is strange—it reminds her of Jackie, in a way, but it feels so different. So much less fraught.

"Yes, exactly. I feel as if—as if everything good about my life has gone away. I look at my baby and I feel nothing, Claire. I'm so very *tired.*"

"You aren't broken, Martha," Claire says. She squeezes Martha's hands, as Jackie sometimes does for her, and Martha clings to them. "You're doing the best you can. It's not fair that all this pressure is on your shoulders."

"I should be doing better."

"Walter should be helping you," Claire cuts in. "Why is it that he doesn't notice your suffering at all? That he gets to just keep on living his life happily, while you break your back to make up for everything he doesn't do? How is that fair?" Claire is almost shouting by the end. She's surprised by her own vigor, and it's clear as Martha blinks at her with wide eyes that perhaps Claire isn't only talking to her friend.

"What else do you expect?" Martha says, wiping at her eyes. "We grin and bear it, don't we?"

Claire shakes her head. That phrase has been somewhat of a comfort between them for a long time, but it feels hollow now. "Maybe we shouldn't. Maybe we deserve more."

"What more is there, Claire?" Martha says tiredly. She rests an elbow on the table, setting her chin in her palm. Her eyes drift closed. If Claire stays quiet for long enough, maybe Martha might actually get some sleep.

A few months ago, Claire would have agreed with Martha's assessment. What more is there? There was nothing, then. Just the life she had, the routines, the dissatisfaction. But knowing Jackie has changed things. Jackie's life is more. She proves that it can be done.

As Martha looks to be drifting off at the kitchen table, her exhaustion finally catching up with her, Claire misses Jackie with a ferocity that's frightening.

"Come on," Claire says softly, putting an arm around Martha's shoulders. "You should get some sleep. I'll watch the baby."

Martha grumbles half-heartedly in protest, but she's soundly sleeping as soon as her head hits the couch cushion. Claire drapes her in a knitted afghan and spends the afternoon alternating between quiet cleaning and glancing out Martha's front window at Jackie's empty driveway.

Jackie's absence continues for eight days, and then ten, and then two full weeks. Claire compulsively checks the window every day, just in case—she has no way to contact her friend, no hint as to her safety or when she might return, and it's driving her squirrely.

The only clue Claire has about Jackie's whereabouts is that Jackie has mentioned staying with Theo in San Francisco overnight when she has late jobs in the city. And his telephone number is written on a scrap of paper on Jackie's refrigerator, right next to Claire's own.

Claire would never ordinarily abuse her spare key privileges, but this is a special circumstance.

The house is unnaturally still and cold when Claire slips inside. It's as if Jackie is the only thing that fills it with life—without her, it's a mausoleum. The cloudy day outside casts a greyish pall on the kitchen. Claire shuffles through, focused on her goal, but when she reaches the refrigerator and finds Theo's number stuck to it with a magnet she realizes she didn't bring anything to write it down with.

She darts down the hallway, guilt chasing her like a specter, and slips into Jackie's office.

Having not been in this room since the night of Jackie's housewarming party, it looks strange to Claire now. The desk is messy, scattered with film canisters and scribbled notes in Jackie's messy hand. Boxes and camera bags crowd the edges of the room. No less than seven different tripods are leaned in one corner, all toppled over each other. It doesn't look as if Jackie took any equipment with her at all.

The walls are hung with photos. They're not framed like the ones that decorate the rest of the house but stuck into the drywall with pins. They cover all kinds of subjects—some are people, others landscapes, and some are contextless pictures of statues or animals or colorful flowers. It's like getting a peek directly into Jackie's mind.

And there, hung among the photos dead center over Jackie's desk, is Claire's painting.

It stops Claire dead in her tracks. It's unmistakable—the acacia tree that should be hanging in Anita's shop is here, like a beacon of color in the grey of the silent house. Jackie must have asked for it. Or stranger still, she might have *bought* it and found it important enough to hang in her office. She spends a lot of time here, if the empty mugs and food wrappers scattered across the room are any indication.

Claire is still reeling when she finally remembers what she came here for. She bends over the desk, grabbing the nearest pencil—the end of it is chewed to bits—and searches for something to write on. The desk is covered in more loose photographs, but no paper.

Claire forgets her purpose yet again when she notices that the photos all have the same subject. A woman, with light hair. There's a shoebox on the floor next to the desk, the dusty lid upended nearby as if Jackie dumped it out. These photos must have been hidden away. At the bottom of the box are some envelopes, but Claire ignores them for now.

Curiosity burns in her. She really shouldn't be rifling through Jackie's things as well as breaking into her house, but Claire's willpower has been so weak lately.

She sinks into the office chair, squinting down at the photos.

Whoever the subject is, she's gorgeous. Her hair is long and dyed a platinum blonde that Claire is sure most people couldn't pull off. It's almost Marilyn Monroe-esque. Her eyes are a startling blue. She truly does look like she could be on the cover of Vogue. She's effortlessly beautiful, and seems like she lives for the camera. The way she locks eyes with the lens makes Claire feel like she's the one being stared at.

One picture catches Claire's attention above all, though. Jackie is in it.

It's a picture of the two of them together—Jackie is in an armchair, seemingly at one of those parties Claire sees in some of her photographs, and the blonde woman is draped over her lap. Their cheeks are squished together as they smile for the photographer. Jackie looks younger, here. She looks happy. She's beaming in a way that Claire has only seen for brief but wonderful windows of time, when Jackie lets her guard down.

In the angled light from the window, Claire can see the barest hint of raised letters on the surface of the photo.

She flips it over to find an inscription, in Jackie's handwriting.

Sept 14, 1964

Valerie,

You and me against the world. Always. You know I'll wait as long as you need me to.

Endless love,

J.

Claire sets the photo down hastily. The envelopes at the bottom of the shoebox might have piqued her curiosity before, but now she can't even look at them.

As if she's been in a trance since she sat down, Claire realizes the gravity of what she's done. She springs back up, her heart pounding, and backs away. She's just invaded Jackie's privacy terribly. She's not entirely sure what exactly she's invaded, but that photo feels like something she never should have seen. Something Jackie wouldn't want her to see.

Jackie has never mentioned a Valerie. Did Jackie have another best friend, before Claire? Someone she left behind in the city? Is that one of the things she was running from?

Is she running from Claire, now?

Claire does scribble down Theo's number before she runs back home, but her guilt keeps her from calling.

Jackie's Mustang pulls into the drive around noon the next day.

The relief Claire feels when Jackie emerges with her suitcase is enough to give her a head rush. The gloom of yesterday's weather has persisted, but the sprinkling of light rain doesn't bother Claire—she barely remembers to turn the oven off before she sprints outside, catching up to Jackie just as she's fiddling with her keys.

"Jackie?" Claire calls, frowning when Jackie's hand freezes halfway to the lock. "Where on earth have you been?"

Claire was hoping for a smile, at the very least. Maybe even an apology. Jackie is always happy to see her, no matter her mood. Instead, Jackie's expression when she turns around is so somber that it looks like a mask.

"I stayed with Theo," Jackie says quietly.

"You didn't say you'd be gone a week," Claire says, her breath coming fast from the run. She presses a hand to her chest. "I was so worried."

Jackie is uncharacteristically withdrawn. When she takes off her sunglasses her eyes are red-rimmed, though she can't seem to meet Claire's gaze directly. She's staring somewhere near Claire's shoulder.

It all feels off, as if the wrong Jackie has come back from the trip. She's never been like this with Claire, not even that strange night at her moon landing party. After so much time apart all Claire wants to do is spend the rest of the day soaking her in, but Jackie seems to want the opposite.

"I don't think we should see each other anymore," Jackie says.

The words reverberate through Claire, hurting more and more with every echo as she realizes their meaning. Jackie could have slapped her in the face with all her strength and it would sting less.

Claire takes a step back, her hand going to her pearls. Jackie's words land in her and take root.

"If this is a joke, it's not very funny," Claire says. She probably sounds wounded and petty, but she doesn't see a reason to mask how Jackie is making her feel. Those roots are pushing through her lungs, hindering her breathing. "Have I done something wrong?"

The shadow on Jackie's face gets darker. She looks as beautiful as ever, and Claire drinks in her features like she's been stuck in the Nevada desert for a week rather than in her own home. Her skin is paler than usual, as if she hasn't left the house much either, but it makes everything that much starker—her sharp jawline, her expressive brows, her soft lips, the tiny scar on her chin. From being playfully dragged over a heating vent by her brother as a child, Jackie once told her. Each feature perfectly fitted to make a wonderful whole.

"No. You haven't done anything wrong. But I have," Jackie says heavily.

"What do you mean?"

"I shouldn't have done this. Any of this. Moving here, getting close to you, trying to get away from what my life was before, pushing you to—" Jackie stops. Her jaw clenches so hard that Claire worries for her teeth. "I need to stop, before I ruin another life."

"You haven't ruined anything," Claire says. She's having trouble following Jackie's argument—pushing Claire? If anything, she's been the first person to truly support Claire. She can't really regret their friendship, can she?

"I've fucked up your marriage," Jackie says.

Claire tries not to flinch at the strong language.

"I've encouraged you to lie, and sneak, and cross-dress," Jackie continues heatedly. "What do you call that, if not ruining a life?"

"Cross-dress?" Claire says, but Jackie is still talking.

"Please, don't make this harder than it needs to be." Jackie unlocks the door and opens it, shoving her suitcase inside. "It's for the best."

"I'm getting quite tired of being told what is or is not for the best," Claire says fiercely.

Jackie's eyes flicker up to her, going wide before darting down again.

Claire isn't usually so direct, but she's feeling more desperate by the minute.

"Pete is right. I'm a bad influence on you," Jackie says. It's toneless, like she's been rehearsing it in her head but her heart isn't quite in it. "I won't drag you down with me. It's best if we just…" Jackie swallows hard.

Claire can see tears swimming in her eyes. She's never seen Jackie cry before. Not once.

"If we what?"

"If we go our separate ways."

"Since when do you listen to my husband?" Claire says. Her anger is deflating, faced with Jackie's tears. Her voice is quavery now with the effort of holding back her own. "Did he tell you to say this?"

"No."

"Is this because of what happened in the pool?" Claire says, desperate now and not bothering to hide it. "That was—it was nothing, we don't even have to talk about it. We were just having fun. Please, Jackie, don't do this. Please."

The tears slip free, tracking down Jackie's cheeks as she squeezes her eyes shut. She looks pained. But she still turns on her heel, stepping through the doorway and moving the door quickly so that Claire can't follow.

"You have a life to live, Claire," Jackie says. She directs it towards the wall. "A good life. Go live it, okay?"

The door shuts in Claire's face.

She stands on the stoop for a long while, blinking the rain out of her eyes. She grips her pearls, twisting and squeezing, but it doesn't help. The heavy, tangled knot that formed when Jackie left a week ago has grown, swelling and eclipsing everything else.

How could Jackie do this? Just drop Claire like their friendship didn't matter? Insist on not seeing her again for no reason at all? Whatever perceived wrong Jackie thinks she's committed, Claire wouldn't care. She *wouldn't*. And if it's really about what Claire did in the pool, she can make up for that. She'll do anything. Perhaps if she knocks on the door, if she begs Jackie to come out—

The pearl necklace snaps in Claire's hand.

Claire blinks, looking down at her feet as pearls cascade over her shoes. She's vaguely aware that real pearls shouldn't scatter like this, but the idea of being hurt by something so inconsequential as Pete's inability to buy a decent necklace is ludicrous right now.

She should feel something, shouldn't she? A gift from her husband lies broken on the concrete. Pearls are rolling across Jackie's doorstep, shining and opalescent even in the rainy gloom. But no sadness manifests. No disappointment. Nothing. Just a rapid fading of all color from the world. Everything settles into a bone-deep numbness, and Claire can't even summon tears.

She doesn't bother to pick up the pearls. She turns on her heel and walks back home, her feet squelching in the wet grass, and when Pete gets home, he doesn't even notice that she's not wearing the necklace.

Jackie's curtains stay closed.

Chapter 19

Numbness becomes a comfort in the days that follow.

To distract from the conversation that keeps playing in her head like a scratched record, Claire throws herself back into her old patterns. The house has never been more sparkling clean. She scrubs every inch of the bathroom and kitchen until her fingers are raw. She cooks, and she cleans, and she hardly eats a morsel.

Pete has seemed relieved by the change. He hasn't noticed Claire's weariness, or her dissatisfaction. He hasn't noticed that she's dropped almost a full dress size from her already thin frame, or that she's always filling her hands with some kind of activity to keep herself from thinking too hard. He seems pleased, in fact.

Even the things Claire used to enjoy are harder than they were before. Working in the gardens to curb the summer plants and encourage autumn growth used to be one of the household tasks she didn't dread. Now she's elbow-deep in mulch, ignoring the soreness in her body as she tears out weeds and prunes flowers, and all she can think about is Jackie.

There's an empty place inside her, now. She's gotten so used to having Jackie as a break in her long days that it feels impossible to go back to a Jackie-less world.

It must have been that day in the pool that made Jackie push her away. Claire goes over and over it in her head as she resists the urge to look over the fence, dissecting every detail. They'd been having fun, hadn't they? Jackie had been so close, and then she'd been running for the hills. Claire knows empirically that there's no chance Jackie could have actually read the strange thoughts Claire has been having, the dreams and the unexplainable urges, but they still fill Claire with shame.

This must be Claire's fault. Her unnatural feelings have driven Jackie away. Unless Jackie suddenly decided Claire truly wasn't worth all the trouble. But then why did she run away so suddenly? Wouldn't she have—

Claire hardly feels the wasp land until she looks down to see the stinger buried in her hand.

It buzzes away, apparently satisfied with its work. Claire can see the spot starting to swell up already, but the pain feels strange. It seeps up her arm, radiating to each of her fingers, but it's as if the sharp throbbing has sliced through the numbness she's been suspended in. The wasp's venom seeps into her bloodstream, casting smoky pulses of pain through her nerves, and for the first time this week it feels like Claire can breathe.

How strange.

The back door opens and closes somewhere behind her. Pete has been out this afternoon doing some kind of errand he wouldn't explain, and Claire couldn't start dinner until he got back, lest it get cold.

"Come on inside and get cleaned up, hon," Pete calls. "I've got a surprise."

Claire stands. She leaves the gardens in their chaotic state, following Pete inside. She turns the bathroom tap as hot as it can go, viciously scrubbing the dirt from under her fingernails with an old cleaning toothbrush. It's only when she's dried them on a towel that she sees the state of her hands.

They're an alarming mix of pale skin and crimson splotches. The skin between her knuckles is dry and cracking. When she clenches her fists, she can see the fault lines filling with red. Her nail beds are chewed beyond recognition, and both of her palms are a minefield of scabbed nail-marks. The wasp sting on the back of her hand has swollen to the size of a quarter.

She's reaching in the medicine cabinet for some ointment when Pete calls for her again.

"Are you coming?"

Claire's arm drops. She swallows down whatever the wasp sting has released, and she joins Pete in the living room.

Pete is grinning ear to ear. There's a box next to him on the carpet, wrapped in brown paper.

"What's this?" Claire says.

Pete is puffing hard. The most exercise he usually gets is mowing the lawn, so carrying the box inside seems to have taxed him. "A present."

"For who?"

"For you!" Pete slaps the top of the box—standing upright, it reaches his hip. "Call it a birthday gift. Open it, go on."

Claire's curiosity stirs. It might be several months late, but Pete hasn't gotten her anything for her birthday in recent memory. This is a nice step in the right direction. Maybe he really has noticed all the work she's been doing.

Claire reaches for the paper, but Pete is too excited—before she can open it he's already torn the wrapping off, presenting the gift like it's a shiny NASA rocket.

Claire tilts her head to read the box. *Electrolux: Luxomatic, Model 1205.*

It's a new vacuum cleaner.

"See all the attachments?" Pete says, popping the box open to pull the thing out. It's a pale blue that reminds Claire painfully of Jackie's Mustang. "This way you can get all the nooks and crannies you usually miss. And it has different settings, see?"

Claire stares uncomprehendingly as Pete points out the new-fangled features. He holds up the hose and various attachments as if they're everything she could have ever wanted, the perfect gift for his old lady. His ball and chain. He's talking animatedly, but the words aren't quite registering in Claire's brain.

The wasp sting throbs.

Claire thanks him with a kiss on the cheek. She makes him a gin and tonic, cutting lemon slices with numbed fingers. The juice stings in her mangled nail beds. She pushes her tuna casserole around on her plate at dinnertime and cleans up the dishes while he turns on the evening news. Then she climbs the stairs, and shuts herself in their darkening bedroom.

The evening has turned cloudy. It looks like it might rain again, and Claire sits in the dim room as the last minutes of dusk cast shadows across the floor.

The walls feel too close. The duvet is too scratchy. The room smells like Pete's cologne. And the whole room is Pete's, really, isn't it? Claire's vanity is in the corner, but the room is laid out the way Pete likes it. The photos on the walls are of his family. Even Claire's clothes hanging in the closet are from his mother. Where is Claire, in this house? Is she in the book on her nightstand, the next novel chosen by Martha for book club? Is she in her new vacuum cleaner? Everything that's hers is hidden away. The outfit Jackie bought for her. Her sketches, her paintings, her photos with Jackie.

Every night before she goes to sleep, she's been taking the photos out of their hiding place in her vanity drawer, just to feel something. Now she feels too much. She feels so much that it won't fit inside her. It fills every space in her body.

The low tones of the television drift up from downstairs. Rain is starting to patter on the window. There's a knot in Claire's chest, growing bigger by the moment. She's digging her nails in so hard that her hands are numb.

Grasping desperately across the bed, she presses her face into the nearest pillow and *screams*.

It's maybe the loudest sound she's ever made, and yet the pillow muffles it to all but her own ears. She screams until her throat is hoarse. It wrenches loose the knot in her chest, but when her breath finally runs out it leaves her feeling completely hollowed. It isn't just her hand that hurts, now—it's everything. Her stomach. Her throat. Her heart.

She can feel a sob coming. It's rising in her throat, making her eyes sting—

"Claire, honey?" Pete calls, just barely audible from downstairs. "Another drink?"

With a heaving effort, Claire chokes it back. She grits her teeth, wipes her eyes, re-applies her mascara, and somehow wills her hands to stop shaking as she fixes Pete his drink.

<hr />

Claire had held out some hope that book club would be a welcome respite, but it hardly helps at all. It's at Dorothy's house this time, Martha having finally loosened her grip on being the only host, and for once Claire is glad that it always devolves into gossip. She's been so distracted lately that she didn't finish the book, and the quick sidetrack into the usual chitchat is welcome.

"I haven't seen Susan Wilson here for a few meetings," Dorothy is saying, raising her eyebrows as she refills everyone's teacups. "Do you think she's decided she's not a fan of literature after all?"

Martha shakes her head. Her little Daniel is in the crook of her arm, and she's having trouble balancing him as she sips her tea. "I'm not sure. I've sent the invitations, but she hasn't shown up since the spring."

"I heard she's having troubles with her husband," Louise says.

The baby makes a squeaky kind of noise, and Martha readjusts his swaddle. "And where did you hear that?"

"The Wilsons live a few doors down from me," Louise says. There's a smugness to her voice—she's clearly relishing being the first to reveal a new and juicy piece of information. "I heard that he's *swung* a bit too far, if you know what I mean."

"You're not saying they're..." Dorothy says, making a vague gesture with her hands.

Louise grins. "Like a saloon door, from what I hear. And Susan is no saint, either. Did you hear about what happened at that big housewarming party, back in March?"

Claire's head snaps up. She'd barely been following the conversation, but her attention is lassoed effectively with just a few words. "Jackie's party? What about it?"

"What I heard is that Susan and the hostess were *very* preoccupied," Louise says.

Claire scoffs, sitting up a little straighter. "Preoccupied with who? Mr. Wilson? Don't be ridiculous."

The mention of Jackie makes her stomach hurt; the idea of her with Mr. Wilson, a tall and insufferably loud man with a penchant for bad jokes, makes it roil. Jackie can do miles better than him. She wouldn't give him the time of day, Claire knows it.

"No," Louise says, leaning closer and grinning like she's sitting on the biggest exclusive the neighborhood has ever seen, "with *each other.*"

It might as well be a gunshot. Claire's ears start to ring.

With each other.

The words go together to make a complete sentence, but it's a sentence that doesn't make sense. It's absurd. It's—

With each other.

With only three words, Louise has set off a series of firecrackers in Claire's brain.

Jackie and Susan had spilled out of the bathroom together that night at the party, looking rumpled. Claire has hardly thought of it since, but when she starts to think harder about the source of that rumpling, her thoughts echo with conversations she thought she'd forgotten. Jackie at her kitchen table, rolling a joint and saying *lots of things are illegal, Claire.* Jackie promising illicit birth control, putting her arm around Claire's shoulders and saying *that doesn't make it wrong, remember*? Jackie in her darkroom, tracing the acacia on her wrist and murmuring *I didn't get it for a man.*

Jackie standing in the rain, all the light gone from her eyes. *I'm a bad influence on you.*

"I should have known someone like Jacqueline would be spreading that lifestyle through the neighborhood," Dorothy says. It sounds muffled to Claire, like she's hearing it from underwater. "It's too bad that she's infected Susan."

The firecrackers have set off an avalanche. Understanding hits Claire in a great tumbling mass, and one by one she follows the chain reaction.

Claire has always felt like she was missing something when it comes to Jackie, some final puzzle piece that would bring the whole picture together, and here it is. The vagueness in the way Jackie has always talked about love—never saying too much, never giving specifics. The lipstick mark on her neck at that first party—Susan's shade, while Susan had looked at Jackie as if she was a delightful plaything. The woman at the moon landing party that Jackie led towards her bedroom by the hand. That strange conversation with Theo at the pool, where Jackie got so angry at whatever he came close to revealing. It must have been this.

Jackie denied sleeping with strange *men* at her parties, yes, but she didn't mention women.

Claire's world shifts on its axis. It's like one of Jackie's ambiguous images, a change from a photo negative to a positive image—she's been looking at Jackie a certain way for so long, and with no warning, everything has flipped.

"I can't say I'm surprised," Louise says, seemingly unaware that Claire's entire world is moving from under her feet. "That woman has struck me as a freak since she first moved here."

"Claire lives right next to her," Dorothy says. "Did you ever suspect she was like that?"

All eyes land on Claire.

Claire's mouth has gone dry. There's sweat pooling at the small of her back. There's too much going on all at once, too much to think about, too much to possibly come up with an answer, and she's grateful when Martha cuts in.

"Maybe we should get back to the book," Martha says.

Louise pays her no mind. "Susan has been bragging about the whole thing, apparently, to make her husband angry. She seems to think it makes her look sophisticated, experimenting like some kind of homosexual."

Claire flinches.

Intellectually, she knows what that word means. *Homosexual.* A man who does things with other men. Like Theo. Or a woman, who—

Claire swallows hard. The reality of it isn't quite connecting with Jackie. Those people are the ones she sees on the news, protesting and rioting with what Pete calls the *freak parade*. He's been saying for years that they're part of why society is declining. She's gotten very used to Theo, but Jackie? If Jackie is one of them, what does that mean?

And what does it mean that Claire had wanted to kiss her in the pool?

Little Daniel, God bless him, lets out an ear-shattering cry just then. In the sudden fuss of shushing him and getting a bottle, the subject drops. When he won't settle down after feeding, Martha ends the meeting early.

Claire tries to dart for the door before anyone accompanies her home, but before she's even reached the sidewalk, she hears Martha's stroller catching up behind her.

"Are you all right?" Martha says, rolling up on Claire's left.

"Fine," Claire says. She's still thinking about Susan's lipstick on Jackie's neck.

"I'm sorry you had to hear that about your friend," Martha says.

"No, you aren't," Claire says shortly. "You hate Jackie."

Martha's steps falter.

"I did. You're right," Martha says. She looks rather ashamed of the admission, when Claire turns around to wait for her to catch up. "You've been so reclusive since she came to town, and I thought...well, it doesn't matter now, does it?"

Claire can tell Martha is trying. It's a big step forward for her, and normally Claire would be grateful for it. Now it's all she can do not to sprint to the quiet safety of her own house. The marks in her palm are still fresh from a bout of frustration last night, and when her nails land there again it sends spikes of pain up her wrist. "Did you know?"

"That she was a homosexual?" Martha says.

Claire twitches again as the word spills out so carelessly. "Yes."

"Not as such. I knew she was odd, but I never would have thought she and Susan…" Martha trails off, clearing her throat as they reach Claire's driveway.

Claire can't bring herself to accept Martha's invitation to chat. She needs time alone more than anything. Time to think, to reconcile what she's just heard. To re-align herself in this new world, where Jackie and Susan Wilson—where they—

Claire's head feels like it's about to split open as she closes the front door behind herself and sinks to the floor with her back pressed against the sturdy wood, but no amount of Anacin Pain Reliever will ease it.

Chapter 20

The following days can only be described as one great prolonged crisis.

The numbness is gone, replaced now with something much worse. Claire can't stop thinking about Jackie and Susan. They stick in her mind like a stain, like those stubborn droplets that spilled on her dress in Jackie's darkroom. She's scrubbed them three times over, and they still persist.

The way Susan had giggled, and touched Jackie's arm with such familiarity. The flushed, gratified look of them when they spilled out of that bathroom. How had Claire not seen it? How had she been so blind? She tries to picture what it might be like, whatever they did to each other in there that left Susan so giggly, but her experience of intimacy is limited to being bedded by her husband. His rough hands, his scratchy kisses. Try as she might, she can't imagine Jackie in that scenario.

Jackie must be different. She must *know* things. She'd be talented, Claire is sure. Soft. Confident, like the characters in the romance novels that Louise sometime tries to suggest for book club.

The thought exhilarates Claire as much as it makes her head spin. It brings to mind the dreams, which Claire is still having regularly. It's impossible to deny now that the way Jackie touches her in them is how she should want to be touched by Pete.

Pete's touch doesn't even light a spark. She's never looked at any other men with much desire, either. Yet when Jackie so much as puts a hand on Claire's wrist?

Fireworks.

Cycling through these thoughts without anyone to share them with is excruciating. What would anyone else in her life think if they knew? She saw firsthand what the neighborhood ladies think. Claire can't even begin to imagine what Pete's reaction would be to the newest piece of chatter.

In a whirlwind, Claire digs up the scrap of paper with Theo's phone number on it.

"Ronny, I've told you a hundred times," Theo's voice says on the second ring. "You can beg as much as you'd like, but this station is *closed* until you shape up. I won't play second fiddle."

"Theo?" Claire says, after a pause.

"...who is this?"

"It's Claire Davis."

Theo makes a little noise that reminds Claire of a chatty feline. "How on God's green earth did you get my number?"

"It was on Jackie's refrigerator," Claire says in a rush. "I was wondering if you could talk for a moment? Please?"

"Talk?" Theo says. He pauses. "What about? From my understanding, you and Jacks aren't speaking anymore."

If Theo's words were daggers, they'd be buried in Claire's gut right now. She grits her teeth, willing herself not to choke up. "I know that. But I hoped that maybe you...I realize that you're Jackie's friend, and not mine. But you know things."

"I *know* things. How cryptic," Theo drawls. "But unlike dear Jackie, I have a stacked social calendar. Clock's ticking. To what do I owe the unexpected call, Mrs. Davis?"

Claire could swear that he's put an emphasis on the *Mrs*, but it's hard to tell over the phone line.

"Right. Okay. Well, um. You're a..." Claire takes a deep breath. It's somewhat steadying, but she still feels shaky. "Theo. You're..."

"Out with it, Suzy Homemaker," Theo says.

"You're a homosexual," Claire blurts. "Correct?"

Theo laughs a little. "Hm. Interesting way to start a conversation. I think I've made that quite clear."

Claire breathes out all at once. It leaves her light-headed. "Yes. So, my question is," she says, drumming her fingers on the table, "I suppose, how you...knew. That you were...like that."

"I hit puberty and wanted to fuck men," Theo says simply. "Is that all you wanted to know?"

Claire tsks, pressing a hand to where her pearls used to sit. "Theodore!"

"Only Jacks can call me that. You phoned *me* up. Don't get shy now."

Claire's stomach flips. She did call Theo up. She dialed his number to ask an absolutely ridiculous question, and the absurdity of it makes her stomach lurch.

What is she *doing*?

"You're right. I don't know why I did this," Claire says. She's pressing the phone so hard against her ear that it's starting to hurt. "Cripes. I'm sorry, I shouldn't have—please don't tell Jackie. Don't tell her I called."

Claire has almost hung the phone up when she hears Theo's voice, loud and clear.

"Wait."

Claire's hand hovers over the cradle. She wavers for a moment, the receiver hovering over the cradle, but curiosity gets the better of her—she puts it to her ear again. "Yes?"

Theo sucks at his teeth. "Why do you ask?"

Claire's breathing has gone heavy. Her palms are sweaty, slipping on the plastic phone. Her line is private, but it feels like anyone could be listening.

"Because," Claire says, her voice thin and warbly, "I have been having some...doubts."

"About?"

"Everything," Claire says. "My marriage, my—my whole life. All of it. I'm lost, Theo."

Theo takes a long pause. He says nothing for so long that Claire wonders if maybe he's hung up on her.

"Why do you feel the need to have this conversation with *me*?" he finally says, with none of the snark she's come to associate with every word that comes out of his mouth.

Claire clings to the phone cord. Her fingers are all twisted up in it, wound into the tight coils until they get snarled with little tangles. "Who else could I ask? Who would even hear me out without sending me to the psychiatrist? Jackie trusts you, and I thought—oh, I don't know what I thought."

Theo sighs. "I really did not want to get caught up in Jackie's little burst of temporary mania."

"I'm sorry. I didn't know where else to turn."

For a few beats, there's nothing but the crackle of the phone line. Fingers drum on a surface, and then he lets out a long sigh.

"It's simple, really. I always felt different," Theo finally says. "I didn't want to do the things boys were supposed to. I never measured up. My father liked to point it out, before he left my saint of a mother to start his little white family."

"Your father is white?" Claire blurts. "That's—"

"That's all you need to know about it," Theo says, cutting clear through Claire's pity. "Don't trip over yourself again. Do you want to know how I fell in love, or not?"

Claire's stomach is still flipping. She wants to know about that more than anything. It's as if she's filling with helium and floating away, as something complicated happens in the larger part of her brain. Her body is the front in a war between two feelings. "I do. You fell in love with a man?"

"I was seventeen," Theo says. "We ran away together. I found community. I never looked back. That's when I met Jacks. She dug me out of my hole when that relationship ended."

"How did you know you were in love?"

Theo sighs. "It was obvious. Just looking at him set my heart off. Every song felt written for him. I didn't know what love was supposed to feel like, but he taught me. And touching him, it was—it was like his skin was magic. I wanted to be closer to him, no matter where we were. No matter who was watching."

"Right," Claire says, needlessly. It's hard to say anything more meaningful when her thoughts are all of Jackie. How it feels to look at her. How it feels to be touched by her, whether it's a simple squeeze of the arm or Jackie's fingers brushing against her chest as she unbuttons Clare's shirt in a changing room.

Magic might be just the right word.

"I'd make up excuse after excuse to be near him. Eventually they got so flimsy that I couldn't deny it anymore," Theo says, his voice softer now. "I kissed him. And it was incredible. He just felt...right."

Claire could count the number of times she's felt *just right* on one hand. She's lived a life of *just fine*. A life of *not quite*. The only moment that might have risen above it was that afternoon in the pool, when she had the thought of kissing Jackie. When the very idea of it had set something in her ringing like a bell.

Claire doodles on the pad of paper next to the phone. A heart. A spiral. A great, sweeping cursive J.

"The ladies at book club said that Jackie slept with Susan Wilson," Claire says.

She's not sure how she expects Theo to react, but an irritated groan was certainly not on her list. It's long and loud and ends in a sort of shout that makes Claire jump.

"Christ. I fucking *told* her," Theo says. "Don't get tangled up in the goddamn suburbs. Which one is Susan? You housewives all look the same to me."

"Has there been more than one?" Claire squeaks.

Theo sighs. Claire hears something scratchy, like he's rubbing his face but hasn't shaved in a while. "That's not my place to say. But it is my place to make sure Jackie doesn't get given the run-around by some curious suburbanite who doesn't care about her."

"I *do* care about her," Claire says hotly. "Very much. She's the one who walked away from our friendship."

"And are you in love with her?"

Claire's argument dies on her lips. No matter what she's starting to suspect, saying it out loud is another thing entirely.

Theo makes an amused noise. "Right. How about attraction? You asked me what it felt like. Do you feel that for her, at least?"

"I..."

Theo keeps pushing. "What about your husband? How do you feel about him? Does he make you hot?"

"Hot?" Claire says faintly.

"Under the collar. In bed. Do you like kissing him? Fucking him? Does his touch get you hot, or do you lie back and think of England?" Theo says, either ignorant to or uncaring of Claire's growing discomfort.

Claire can't describe anything Pete does as making her *hot*. Lovemaking is a wife's duty. She's never exactly enjoyed it, but then she's not meant to, is she? That's for the husband to enjoy. It's her job to make sure he's satisfied.

But then, what about Claire's dreams?

She doesn't have them every night, but it's often enough that she can't put them out of her mind. Jackie is the only constant in them. Jackie in the pool, in the changing room, in the conversation pit, sitting on Claire's bed.

Claire usually loses the details when she wakes up, but they leave Claire sweaty and trembling when her alarm trills.

The warm, slick evidence she cleans up between her legs every morning—is that the kind of *hot* that Theo means?

Theo clicks his tongue. "Saying it out loud helps, trust me. Share with your favorite homosexual."

"I..." Claire says. Her voice is dry and croaky. She closed her eyes tight, letting her forehead fall onto the table. "Theo, I don't know what any of this is supposed to feel like."

"Then you should figure it out before you try to involve Jackie. I'm not letting her get hurt again."

Again.

Claire sits up straight. She's struck by remembrance, now, of something she hadn't connected before—the married man that Jackie loved. The one she's been so broken up over. If Jackie really is like Theo, then maybe it wasn't a man at all. It must have been a *woman*.

The beautiful blonde woman from the pictures on Jackie's table rushes into Claire's memory. The inscription Jackie had written—*you and me against the world. Always.* A sentiment for a lover, not a friend.

I'll wait as long as you need me to.

They were pressed together so intimately in that photo. Claire didn't think to look, but she'd bet a hundred dollars that if she had, there would have been a wedding ring on the woman's finger. Just like Claire. Jackie promised to wait, but all her waiting ended in heartbreak.

"Valerie," Claire says softly.

Theo makes a startled noise. "Now how in the hell do you know that name?"

"Oh, my word," Claire breathes. There's too much happening at the moment to bother with explanations. "I'm right, aren't I? The person who broke her heart isn't a man at all. It was Valerie."

"Someone's a little snoop."

"It was an accident," Claire protests. "The photos were—I didn't mean to."

"Sure you didn't, Nancy Drew," Theo says. "Look, figure yourself out. Fuck her over, spread this around your little suburb in some twisted attempt to pretend you're not tangled up in it, and I will personally take a monumental shit in your favorite kitchen appliance."

Claire is left with a dial tone, and far too much to think about as she relies on muscle memory to prepare an angel food cake in the afternoon. Rita's fifty-fourth birthday party is tonight, and Pete's entire family is going to be there. It's the last place she needs to be thinking about the fact that Jackie apparently cares enough about her to be given the 'run-around'.

Does Jackie mirror Claire's feelings? Does she too lie awake at night, thinking about how close their lips had been? Does she dream of Claire, and wake up shaking?

The thoughts persist as Pete drives them to his parents' house, and as Rita comments that she prefers chocolate cake over sponge. They spiral through Claire over dinner, where thankfully everyone is too preoccupied feeding and calming down the kids to pay much mind to the fact that Claire has barely touched her beef bourguignon. Theo's words stick with her when everyone gathers in the family room to take a group photo.

Is she attracted to Pete? It's not a question Claire has ever been asked before. It's not something she ever thought to consider. Looking at him, red-faced from the wine and laughing at some joke with his father, Claire doesn't feel a stirring of anything Theo talked about. Heat. Desire. She's not sure she's ever felt it for him, even when they first met.

Their courtship hadn't exactly been electrifying. He asked her to a dance in junior year, and Claire said yes, flattered by his interest—nobody had ever expressed any in her before. She'd always been the tallest girl in her class, a tomboyish childhood turning into lanky awkwardness in her teenage years. But people looked at her differently when she was with Pete. Having a man by her side made all of those shortcomings ease, back then. She blended in.

But if this life is what it means, does she want to blend in? What was it that Jackie said, when they first met? *Don't bother with the background.*

Wondering if it might just be Pete she isn't stirred by, Claire considers his brothers, too. Handsome men, all. His oldest brother John has always been kind to her, kinder even than Pete. He's broad-chested, with a neat beard and a wife who by all accounts seems to adore him. He looks like the perfect father, bouncing his youngest son on his knee. Is that attraction? Noting his nice qualities, his good looks?

Pete's youngest brother Alan is clean-shaven, with hair almost to his shoulders that Rita continually tells him to cut. He's jovial and quick to smile, but he doesn't make her laugh like Jackie does. And Bill, two years

Pete's senior, is so similar to Pete that Rita often jokes they're simply twins who weren't born together. They even have similar moustaches.

They're all strapping men. Perfectly acceptable. So why, in looking at them, does Claire feel nothing? *Less* than nothing? In comparison to the feeling that grips her when Jackie smiles at her, let alone the day in the pool when they'd been close enough to kiss, those men might as well not exist.

It's only later when Pete is sound asleep and Claire is alone in the bath that she allows herself to consider the obvious conclusion.

If attraction really is the way Theo describes it, then she isn't attracted to her husband at all. She's never met a man who sparked that in her. But Jackie?

Even the slightest memory of that day in the department store changing room, of Jackie's breath against her face and her nails scratching Claire's scalp, sends a tingling through her. An excitement that Pete has never stirred. That antsy, restless feeling in her gut when Jackie smiles at her—is that attraction? Or the tightness in her chest when she saw Jackie in a bathing suit for the first time? When she leaned against the laundry basket and felt that explosion of sensation, conjuring memories of her dreams—is that what Theo means?

What would it mean to embrace whatever she's feeling, and step into this great and terrible unknown? Jackie and Theo would be her only life-rafts, and she hasn't even spoken to Jackie in weeks. If this is really who Claire is, if she's like them, she'll lose everything. Her house, her marriage. Her friends, such as they are. Pete has made it clear what polite society thinks of those people.

But why, Claire thinks suddenly, should she only be listening to Pete's opinion on the topic?

Jackie is a good person. One of the best Claire has ever met. She doesn't put on the same airs of fake kindness that Martha and the other neighborhood ladies do—she's genuine. And Theo isn't the downfall of society. He's funny and witty, even if she rather wanted to hit him at first. He put effort into helping her today.

Why shouldn't she want to be like them?

The idea of a life without Pete, stranded on her own with no husband to provide, has always terrified her. Divorce always seemed like a death sentence. She can't drive, and she has no savings. It would be an end to life as Claire knows it. But maybe if she had the kind of community Theo talked about, that wouldn't be so bad. She could find a job somewhere, make her own money and support herself. She could come home after a hard day not to a husband demanding dinner and drinks, but to someone like Jackie, who makes her feel more at ease than anyone she's ever known. She could hold Jackie close when she needs comfort.

She could kiss her. Fall asleep in her arms. Even take her to bed.

The very idea fills Claire with a longing so sharp that it kick-starts a gut-wrenching sob. And then another. They feel good, in a way. Rather than holding back Claire lets it happen, lets herself fall apart in the downstairs bathtub until every confusing emotion she's been trying to quash has been wrenched out of her.

It's a cleansing sort of cry. An all-out sobbing mess, the kind that leaves her exhausted and dehydrated and blissfully empty in the lukewarm water. It's strange to be relieved by something so life-shattering, but she is. Finally, after months of confusion, there's an *explanation*. She's not losing her marbles.

She's just like Jackie. She's gay. She's a *queer*.

What she doesn't know is how on earth she's supposed to decide what to do about it.

Chapter 21

Usually, Pete spending a Sunday at the golf course would mean Claire gets a rare weekend day to herself. She'd listen to music, or more often these days sketch or paint. Once, she might have visited Jackie. Now it seems she's destined to do nothing but spiral over the same worries.

Instead, Claire seeks out company.

"I'll be back to pick you up in the afternoon," Pete says. The car is idling in the library parking lot, and Claire is already halfway out. "Don't get too many books, I don't want to have to haul them back here to return."

Claire doesn't kiss him goodbye. He doesn't seem to notice—he zooms off, intent on catching his tee time. The moment he turns the corner she veers in the opposite direction, crossing the street and heading off to her real destination.

The bell above the door of Anita's shop jingles as Claire pushes it open.

"Just a moment," Anita calls, busy reaching on her tiptoes for a stack of canvases on a top shelf. It reminds Claire so starkly of her first impression of Jackie, reaching fruitlessly for a box of cereal, that the hollow space in her chest aches.

Is Claire cursed to forever be haunted by Jackie Callas at every turn?

Claire hurries to grab the canvases for her. When Anita turns to thank her, Claire finds herself wrapped in a tight, motherly hug—for once, with Anita standing on a stool, they're of a similar height.

"So?" Anita says, breaking into one of her beaming smiles. "Did you manage to paint again?"

Claire winces. She hasn't picked a brush up since she stopped speaking to Jackie. "I can't stay for too long today," she says instead. "Pete is picking me up in the afternoon, once he's done golfing."

"Pete, schmete," Anita says, waving a careless hand as she hops down from her stepladder. "He can wait."

"He thinks I'm at the library," Claire admits.

Anita pauses, halfway through moving the stepladder behind the desk. "Oh. This is a clandestine operation, then?"

"I was hoping you might give me some more advice."

Anita wastes no time. She hurries to the front window, flipping the *open* sign over to *closed* and locking the door. "Come on. Back to the studio."

Claire chews at her thumb as Anita unlocks the studio door. Anita gestures for her to sit on the sagging old couch, but Claire can't. Instead, she paces. She's practically wearing a track in the carpet by the time Anita sits down. Her own paintings are looming down at her from the storage shelf as she struggles to find the right words.

"Claire, what's going on? You're running around like a racehorse," Anita says. She follows Claire with her eyes, her wrinkled brow furrowed.

Claire wrings her hands. The effort of maintaining a calm façade all morning while her mind races has exhausted her. She needs to tell *someone* about her doubts. Her conversation with Theo only tied the knots tighter. She needs just one person to either tell her it will all be alright, or to talk her out of this insanity. Anita was a confidante in her youth. And who else does Claire have?

Abruptly, Anita stands. Her expression is one Claire has never seen before—it's soft, and serious. She steps into Claire's path, stopping her in her tracks, and takes Claire's hands in her own.

"Claire. Has something happened?" she says gravely.

The answer should be automatic—*of course not. Everything is wonderful*! But Claire bites down on it.

What's the honest truth? That she's miserable? That she's just realized she's a homosexual? That every good thing she's managed to claw out of her life disappeared when Jackie closed the door on her?

Tears spring to Claire's eyes.

"Oh, chickadee," Anita says softly.

The tears come full-on as Claire sinks down onto the sofa, and Anita follows.

"I'm sorry," Claire gasps, graduating quickly to sobs as her Anita's arms close around her. "I'm—so sorry to come to you like this."

"It's all right," Anita murmurs. She strokes Claire's hair, giving comfort even while she's entirely in the dark as to why Claire needs it. All the unhappiness of the last six months is spilling out at once, and poor Anita is simply the rock Claire is clinging to. "You're all right. Just tell me what's happened."

It takes Claire a minute or so to get herself together. She takes the tissue Anita offers, wiping furiously at her eyes.

"I'm sorry, I—shouldn't. Things are fine," Claire says, blowing her nose loudly. "I shouldn't complain. I have a nice house and a husband who provides. We're starting a family. I have nothing—nothing to—"

Claire's voice breaks in another sob.

Anita looks oddly pensive as Claire weeps into her lap. She hands over a fresh tissue, stroking Claire's back in a rhythmic motion. "Would you like to talk about it?"

Claire doesn't have the energy to hold it back anymore. She talks into her hands, hoping that by muffling the words they won't come across so harsh.

"I'm not happy," Claire says, with a surety she now feels utterly confident in. Her voice is warbly, but the conviction is true. "And I think I want to leave Pete."

Theo was right. To say it out loud is like a sigh of relief that runs through her whole body. She can't take it back, now. She can't ruminate any longer in the prison of her own mind. She's spoken it into existence.

Anita's response is blessedly pragmatic, just as Claire hoped. She keeps rubbing those circles on Claire's back. She doesn't even sound surprised. "May I ask why?"

"Because Pete doesn't love me," Claire chokes out. "And I don't love him."

Anita is quiet. She rubs Claire's back until the sobs have stopped trying to rise up Claire's throat. When Anita speaks, it's with a calm kind of authority. "I feared you'd never realize how much more you deserve," she says, once Claire has controlled herself. "I'm glad you're starting to see your worth."

Claire isn't sure that's true, but it's nice to hear. She twists her hands together. "My mother thinks I should just deal with it. Focus on keeping Pete content."

"And why should you stay for his sake?"

"Because the alternative is…" Claire trails off. She swallows past the lump in her throat.

"Divorce," Anita says simply. It's as if the word has no effect on her at all. "It's not the end of the world, Claire."

"Isn't it?"

"No," Anita says. "It's the beginning, if you allow it to be."

The beginning. But the beginning of what, exactly? Pursuing something with Jackie? Theo implied that Jackie might return her feelings, but Jackie has made it clear that she doesn't want Claire in her life anymore. She ended their friendship. And Theo had been adamant that Claire figure herself out before involving Jackie, anyways. So, is divorce the beginning of a life alone? She feels alone already. At least without a husband, she'd only need to take care of herself. It's not impossible. Jackie does it, and so does Anita.

Claire bites down so hard on her nail bed that she tastes blood.

"I don't know what to do," Claire mumbles, around her thumbnail. "If I leave, I have nothing. Nowhere to go. My whole life has been with Pete."

"You'll always have a place under my roof," Anita says.

"That's kind, but I couldn't do that to you."

"I'm offering," Anita says firmly. "I have a sofa upstairs, dear. If you decide leaving is what you need to do, you come straight here. Okay?"

It's the same kind of selfless thing that Anita used to do for Claire when her mother went out of town for days at a time. But Claire hadn't been hiding a secret like this, then. The *Jackie* of it all is pushing at her chest, hammering on her ribs, fighting to get out. If Claire reveals the full truth about herself, about who she is and who she really wants, and Anita doesn't accept it—what then? Where can she go? Would she be trapped with Pete, living this lie? Will she be sent away somewhere to be fixed?

"What if I did something that you didn't approve of?" Claire says.

Anita snorts. "What right do I have to control anyone's life but my own? Judgement does nothing but lock a woman inside herself."

Locked inside herself. It's an apt description for what Claire has been feeling—as if some part of her that was shoved out of sight long ago is elbowing its way in again, insistently tearing down Claire's whole life.

"I know you're different," Claire, Anita says softly. She puts an arm around Claire, which is impressive given their height difference even while seated. "It's all right. You always have been."

"More than you know," Claire says, leaning into the warmth of Anita's hug regardless.

Talking to Anita helps to settle Claire's mania, but it doesn't leave her with a decision one way or the other. After drinking three cups of Anita's herbal tea and having another good cry, she scurries back to the library in the afternoon. She takes two books out just to justify the trip, and Pete honks the horn from the parking lot an hour or so later.

The first half of the car ride home is silent. Pete doesn't even have the radio on—he seems perfectly content with his own thoughts. When he strikes up a conversation, his voice ringing out into the quiet makes Claire jump.

"You know, once we have kids, I won't be able to take you to this part of town anymore," Pete says, drumming his fingers on the steering wheel. "I can't be carting you back and forth with children at home."

Claire's already uneasy stomach churns.

"I could get a driver's license," Claire says.

"You don't need a driver's license," Pete says. It's the same thing he's said since she first asked for one, after they moved to Acacia Circle.

Claire sits up in her seat. "It would make life easier for both of us. Getting out for groceries and errands would be easier, and—"

"And a car would be an extra cost, especially if you crash the thing. Don't argue, Claire," Pete says. The car turns into their driveway, shuddering to a stop. "It's tiresome."

Claire can see light shining in Jackie's front window. She stares at it as Pete turns off the car, unmoving in her seat until she sees a figure pass across it.

Claire has never really put much stock into the term *heartbreak*, but something in her chest is aching. There's a deep, physical pain that could only be a broken heart as she considers what her life is hurtling towards.

Motherhood. Spending her days trapped in the house with no way to get around, which will only get harder when she's lugging a baby around like Martha. Living next to Jackie, watching her shadow pass by the window and knowing what she might have had a chance at if she'd just been a little braver.

Pete has already gotten out of the car, letting the door slam behind him, but Claire stays where she is.

"Claire?" Pete calls.

Claire grips the armrests. All the worry of the last few weeks, all the anxiety, all resentment and fear and guilt, has settled into something cold and hard and angry right in the middle of her chest.

Pete appears at the window. He taps hard on the glass. "Did you hear me? We're home."

"I heard you," Claire says distantly. "I'm coming."

The next morning, Claire puts two dollars out of the grocery money into an envelope and hides it in her vanity.

Chapter 22

Slowly, carefully, Claire plans her exit strategy.

She gathers her few precious belongings together, and the bare minimum of clothes she might need—undergarments, pajamas, and a few of her old dresses that Rita didn't make for her. Photos of her own family, always tucked away in an album rather than on display with Pete's. A few of her favorite books, including the one where she hid Jackie's three photos. A few precious knickknacks, and her art supplies.

Everything else can be left behind. Her makeup, her kitchen tools, her jewelry. The baubles that Pete has bought her as gifts over the years. All of it is dust to her.

She starts to put away as much of Pete's grocery money as she can into that envelope to use as an emergency fund, pinching pennies and cutting coupons to keep him from noticing. She digs through the couch for forgotten dimes. The weeks press on, and what was at first a contingency starts to become a reality.

The straw that breaks her back is surprisingly mundane.

Martha's Halloween party is a mainstay of the neighborhood. Claire half expected it to be cancelled this year, what with the baby, but apparently, he's sleeping better these days—Martha has his little pumpkin costume all sewn up by the time the day comes. Helping in the party planning gives Claire something to direct her energy toward. She helps to decorate. She washes and irons her usual costume (a black dress and little homemade cat ears) and Pete's (he refuses to dress up any more than a tie with tiny bats on it). She gives out bags of homemade cookies to trick-or-treaters, and when the kids have retired, she brings her potato salad across the road on Pete's arm, trying not to think about the fact that there's clearly also a party going on at Jackie's house and she hasn't been invited.

Sure, Pete wouldn't let her attend, but Jackie always used to invite her.

The evening seems to drag by. Claire feels as if she's having the same conversation over and over again—*how are you? How's your husband? Is the bathroom renovation going well? Oh, yes, he's getting so big, last I saw him he was crawling—no, Pete and I aren't expecting any time soon—no reason, just not the right time—Sharon's Swedish meatballs are delicious, what's the recipe?*

It's exhausting. A never-ending performance that she's not sure she can keep doing.

Where Martha's party gets more subdued as the night presses on, Jackie's seems to ratchet up in intensity. Claire can see the activity from Martha's front window, where she takes up residence to get away from the excruciating conversations. There are lights in the windows, bent by the shadows of dancing people. She can't hear the music, but she can imagine what it sounds like. Not the Monster Mash currently grating on her ears, but loud rock and roll. There are even some people out on the front lawn. Claire is sure someone in a Dracula costume is vomiting in Jackie's hydrangeas.

Pete's cologne fills Claire's nose before she hears his voice.

"Why are you sulking over here? It's not very sociable."

"I'm not in a very sociable mood," Claire says flatly. A woman with dark hair is stumbling down the street arm-in-arm with another woman, and Claire watches them intently until they pass under a street-lamp and it's made clear that it isn't Jackie.

Pete lowers his voice. "Then get in one. This is a party."

Claire squeezes her fist until pain shoots up her arm. "I've been on all night. I'm tired."

"What are you talking about? *On?*" Pete says, his volume rising a little. "How hard is it to make conversation? Stop embarrassing yourself and come back to the party."

Someone is comforting the vomiting Dracula across the street, rubbing his back and pulling his long hair out of his face. It looks to be a tall woman with an impressively voluminous hairstyle. Claire isn't doing anything embarrassing like that, is she? She's not vomiting in Martha's rose bush or drinking too heavily. She's just asking for a minute to compose herself.

Claire has been actively trying not to bring Jackie to mind too often lately—it hurts too much. But Jackie's words come back to her now. *There's nobody to embarrass here, Claire.*

Claire runs her tongue along her teeth, finding the familiar groove of the chip on her incisor, and she whirls around.

"I said *no*, Pete," Claire says loudly.

All heads turn towards them. It isn't just a small dinner party with Martha and Walter, this time—half the neighborhood is here. At least, the half that isn't at the party across the street.

Pete's neck turns fuchsia.

"We'll talk about this later," Pete says, as always. He's still speaking quietly, but Claire is done with being quiet.

She's been quiet her whole adult life. She's put on masks, always adding new things to her repertoire, assuring herself that someday, it would get easier. It would become natural. But meeting Jackie changed everything. With Jackie, she didn't need to perform. Claire got a taste of what a maskless life might be like, and she wants it back.

"I'm tired of talking about it," Claire says, not bothering to quiet her voice even as Pete fumes. "I've been about as perfect a wife as I could these last few months, and it's still not enough for you, is it? Will it ever be?"

"Claire," Pete hisses.

"When will it end? When I finally have your children and give you what you really want? When I'm old and tired and used-up and you still get to live your perfect life at my expense?" Claire says. Her voice is getting louder with every word, and Pete is starting to look a little panicked.

"Stop this," Pete says. "A tantrum at home is one thing, but this is just immature."

But Claire can't stop. It's all bubbling over, everything that's been building in her since Jackie froze her out—since before, even, since the moment Jackie stepped foot in Acacia Circle and gave Claire a glimpse of what things could be like outside of this. Like a school science project Claire is finally erupting, spilling all over Martha's pristine carpeting and not bothering to hold it back.

And Pete sees it as a tantrum. The temporary outburst of a spoiled child. No matter how she talks to him, he'll never understand her discontent. For as long as she stays in this marriage, she'll be alone.

"I can't do this," Claire says, with a clarity that hits her all at once. "I won't. I'm done." To have the last straw be something so simple is somehow fitting. She laughs, a quick and quiet thing that builds as a wave of relief hits her all at once. "Oh, I'm *done*."

Claire turns on her heel, tears the cat ears from her head, and marches out the door.

She's halfway across the lawn when Pete catches up. The air is humid, but she hardly feels it as Pete grabs her arm to turn her back around.

"Where do you think you're going?"

"I'm not doing this anymore."

"Doing what?" Pete says, letting go of Claire's wrist when she wrenches it out of his hand. "What the hell has happened to you lately? I've never seen you act the way you have been in the last year. What happened to my wife?"

"Your wife never existed, Pete!" Claire shouts. It feels good to air it all out, not in the stifling hallways of their house but here under the open sky. The people milling about Jackie's front lawn are watching, and she doesn't care a bit. "Your wife wasn't a person. She was a paper doll that you plugged into your perfect life and didn't expect to have her own thoughts and feelings. But, I do. And I'm not happy. I've never been happy."

"Happy?" Pete says, his voice rising to match hers. "Have you ever not had a roof over your head, or food in the fridge? Have I ever not provided for you?"

"Don't you see that I need more than that?"

"What more is there?"

Claire takes a breath. She tilts her head towards the sky, closing her eyes. "There's partnership. Understanding. There's love."

Pete scoffs. "Now you sound like one of those hippie freaks next door."

"Maybe I am one of them. Did you ever think of that?" Claire says, opening her eyes again.

Pete's coiffed hair is in disarray.

"You are my *wife*," Pete says. He says it as if it's an anchor, a single solid truth in a sea of uncertainty, and perhaps for him it is.

But Claire doesn't want an anchor. She wants to float away.

"You're not happy, either," Claire says.

"I'm perfectly content."

"You married me because I was the first girl who said yes. Do you even like me, Pete? Don't you want to be married to someone whose company you actually enjoy?"

"What does that have to do with anything?"

It's never been more obvious that Pete will never understand. He looks more baffled than angry, standing on Martha's lawn in his Halloween tie, and in looking at him Claire feels nothing but pity.

"I deserve something more," Claire says. She takes a step toward him, now, but for a single reason—to twist her wedding and engagement rings off her finger, and press them into his hand. "I deserve to love and be loved properly."

Pete holds the rings in his palm, staring down at them with a furrowed brow.

Claire has never felt lighter.

"Claire, this is—this is absurd," Pete says. He tries to shove the rings back into Claire's hand, and when she doesn't take them he slips them in the front pocket of her dress. "You're getting overexcited. Go home and get some sleep. We'll talk about this properly in the morning, when you aren't feeling so hysterical."

Uncharacteristically, Pete leans in to kiss Claire's cheek. He smells of familiar aftershave and hair oil. His whiskers are scratchy. He pats her awkwardly on the shoulder, and then he heads back into the party. Back to the judgement and the snippy comments and the boring conversations.

Ordinarily, that would be that. Claire wouldn't have anywhere to go, or any money to get her there. But things have changed.

She goes first to her own house—she digs the clothes Jackie bought her from the bottom of her bag, the only outfit she owns that didn't come from Pete or Rita, and changes into it. She washes the makeup from her face, and shakes her unruly hair out of its updo. She leaves behind her jewelry and her beauty products. And in the middle of her vanity, on top of one of Pete's handkerchiefs, she sets her rings.

The person who looks back at her from the mirror is brand-new. It's the first time she's been brave enough to shed every vestige of her old life without clinging to something. Without the makeup, her freckles are prominent in the bathroom light. She feels taller, even though she's abandoned her chunky heels—she's wearing the loafers Jackie bought her.

Everything she used to be is scattered across her vanity like a discarded snakeskin.

Claire marches back outside to stand on the front lawn with the bag slung over her shoulder, contemplating what to do. It'll be hours before the bus routes start that can get her out to Anita's. She could call a cab, but she doesn't want to spend up her cash too quickly, and who knows if they even run at this hour? She's never really called one before.

The vomiting Dracula on Jackie's front lawn has disappeared, but the woman who comforted him is still there. By the tiny orange glow near her face, she's smoking. Now that Claire is closer she can see the woman is tall. Maybe even taller than herself.

"Going somewhere?" the woman calls out. Only it's not a woman's voice. The cigarette is flicked away. When the person steps into the light of a streetlamp, Claire's confusion shifts into relief.

"Theo?"

Theo grins. He's got a full face of makeup on, and he's decked out in women's clothing—heels, a white off-the-shoulder dress, and a towering ginger wig with what looks like a paper mâché bone stuck through it—but he's unmistakable. And, oddly, very beautiful. In Claire's opinion, he suits women's clothing more than she does. "I heard your little argument with the husband. I was wondering if you were going to get up the courage to follow through."

Claire laughs a little. Some of the boiling tension in her chest eases off. "So was I. Nice dress, by the way. Wilma?"

"Indeed. Made it myself," Theo says, winking. "This is my favorite time of year. Nobody questions a little fruitiness on Halloween."

Claire shifts her bag to the other hand. "And you're not afraid to wear it in public? Here?"

"It turns out Sacramento has more of an underbelly than Jackie thought," Theo says. He gives Claire a long look, up and down. "And I should be asking you the same thing. That doesn't look like a ladies blouse to me."

"It isn't," Claire says. Behind Theo, two people spill out of the front door, giggling as they stumble towards a car parked on the street. "Jackie got it for me."

Theo nods. He crosses the lawn to where Claire is, his voice low and much softer than Claire is used to. "Where are you off to? You do have a place to stay, right?"

Claire really isn't sure about anything right now, but she nods. "A friend. I'm just not sure how I'm going to get there at this hour."

"Come on. My car is just down the street," Theo says. Before Claire can insist otherwise, he holds up a hand. "I feel somewhat responsible for this, if I'm being honest. It's the least I can do."

"Haven't you been drinking?"

"Tragically, no," Theo says, heading off down the road and clearly expecting Claire to follow. "I've been taking care of Jacks all night after she drank herself into a stupor."

Claire's stomach lurches. She takes off after Theo, jogging to catch up. "Is she alright?"

"Depends on your definition of the word," Theo says. He doesn't elaborate, and Claire isn't sure how to politely ask the question that's on her mind—*is it because of me? Does she miss me? Does she hate me?*

Will she ever want to see me again?

Theo climbs into his car in full costume. It's smaller than Jackie's, and his wig presses against the roof as Claire buckles herself in and he zooms out of the cul-de-sac.

"How are you feeling?" Theo asks, once the sign for Acacia Circle has disappeared in the side mirror.

"Better," Claire says. And she means it. She feels lighter as the brighter lights of Sacramento start to appear ahead of them. "It's funny, I should be terrified. I have twelve dollars to my name, and I'm going to be sleeping on a couch for the foreseeable future. But it's on my terms, for once."

Theo hums quietly. The radio is playing an energetic song that reminds Claire of the song she and Jackie danced to, once. The Supremes. If she closes her eyes, she can still feel Jackie's body against hers. Their hands clasped together. The bright, eager look in her eyes as Claire spun her around. She'd been so beautiful that day, still in her pajamas with messy hair and visible blemishes.

It must say something that Claire feels sadder thinking of that moment than she does about leaving her husband.

The car jerks as Theo takes a corner hard. He drives the same way Jackie does—with a flagrant disregard for his own safety. But he gets them across town in one piece. The car is quiet except for Claire occasionally giving Theo directions until he pulls up in front of the Cozy Corner. The upstairs windows are all dark—Claire is probably going to have a time waking Anita up.

"Here we are," Theo says. "Your new life awaits."

"My new life," Claire echoes. She's not entirely sure how to feel about that. She knows this is her cue to leave, but her legs feel heavy.

"Go on. Find your feet," Theo says. He pats Claire's thigh, like Claire has seen him do to Jackie on occasion. It should seem very silly, considering he's in a wig and a dress, but Claire has already become accustomed to it. "You've got my number."

"Thank you, Theo," Claire says quietly. She opens the door, finally willing her legs to move. "For everything."

Anita answers the hammering on the door in her nightgown after a few minutes, groggy and squinting. When she sees the bag in Claire's hand, her eyes widen.

"Did you?"

"Is your offer still open?" Claire says. Maybe she should be feeling emotional, in tears, even, but instead she feels buoyant. Filled with purpose.

Anita gasps. She clasps Claire's face between her hands—it's as if Claire has just told her the Beatles are in town. "Thank god."

Claire laughs, her face squished between Anita's palms. Her excitement makes the whole thing feel a little bit less insane. At least one other person besides Theo doesn't think she's a madwoman for walking out on her life. "That's not the reaction I'd expect from anyone else."

"You know how I felt about that boy. He dimmed your spark," Anita says. Her eyes widen dramatically. "Oh! That means you'll need a job."

"Yes. So I was hoping that—"

"When can you start?" Anita says.

She doesn't say a thing about the clothes.

Chapter 23

For the first time since she was a teenager, Claire sleeps in.

She wakes around nine thirty on the first of November. Usually by this time she'd be up and dressed, have breakfast made, and be busy with the first of the day's chores. Now she rises in her nightgown only when she hears the sizzle of pancake batter hitting a griddle.

"Blueberry pancakes?" Anita says over her shoulder, when Claire has poked her head up over the back of the couch. "Orange juice is in the fridge—could you pour us some?"

Claire never gets blueberry pancakes anymore. Pete prefers chocolate chip or banana, so she digs in with gusto. She feels ravenous—where normally she'd stop after one, she devours six pancakes easily with a glass of juice and a coffee.

"I think I want to start looking for a place to live," Claire says, once the plates have been cleared. "I don't want to be in your hair for too long."

"I don't mind having you here," Anita says. "Don't feel any pressure to leave on my account."

"I can't tell you how grateful I am that you're allowing me to stay," Claire says.

Anita re-fills Claire's coffee. She pushes the cream and sugar towards Claire without her asking, and while Claire mixes them in, Anita watches her with a smile.

"You know," Anita says thoughtfully, "I hardly recognize you today."

Claire doesn't doubt it. Having not brought any of her products with her, her face is bare. Her hair is unbound in its natural curly state, and tangled from sleep.

"I'm sure I look a bit of a mess," Claire says. She fiddles with the ends of her hair. It's been so long since she wore it in anything but an updo that she hadn't realized how long it had gotten.

"Not at all," Anita says. She leans across the table to clasp Claire's upper arms, squeezing them tight. "And that's not what I mean. You're taking up space again."

Claire isn't sure what that means, but Anita is beaming, and it makes Claire feel as if she's finally done something right.

"I'm not really sure what my next step should be," Claire says, cupping the warm coffee mug in her hands. "I don't even know what made me leave, in the end. I just snapped last night. I don't even know anyone who's gotten divorced."

Anita stirs sugar into her own coffee. She methodically taps the spoon against the rim of her cup, sets it on the table, and takes a sip. "You do, actually."

Claire looks up from her mug with a start. She's always known that Anita isn't married, but she'd assumed that she was a widow. "You? Really?"

"How do you think I could afford to start this business without a husband?"

"I always thought it was life insurance."

Anita snorts. "If only. No, in my case it was infidelity. Pretty cut and dry. Your case will be a lot harder, unless you wait to file until the new year."

Claire frowns. She hasn't put much thought yet into the legalities of it all. "Why the new year?"

"Haven't you read the papers? Some family act is coming in on the first of January," Anita says. She shuffles to a kitchen drawer, pulling out an address book and flipping through it. "Starting then, you won't need to prove abuse or infidelity. You can divorce for any reason. They're calling it *irreconcilable differences*."

"And...how exactly would I do that?"

"You call a lawyer," Anita says. She stops at a page in her address book with a victorious noise, and scribbles something onto a piece of paper. "I'll get you in touch with mine. He'll get you started with your dissolution petition and summons. And you'll need a bank account." Anita brandishes the pen in Claire's direction. "I assume you don't have one? I can pay you in cash for now, but you'll want somewhere to put your money eventually."

"Summons? Will I need to go to court?" Claire says. She'd thought that the hardest step would be making the decision to leave, but it's becoming clear that it's only the beginning. And she can't imagine that Pete will take it lying down.

Anita hands her a scrap of paper with a name and number on it. "Only if Pete won't settle things the easy way. And if you want to get out on your own right away, there are little apartments like mine above every shop on this street. I'll help you look," Anita says.

Claire nods. She taps a quick rhythm on the table, chewing on the inside of her cheek. "How did you do it? Start over after your marriage fell apart?"

Anita sips slowly at her coffee. "You know, my marriage might have fallen apart, but my life really came together afterward. I've got my shop, and my little place. I've got friends and family."

"Friends," Claire says. The hollow place in her chest where Jackie used to live feels bigger than ever. "I guess I don't have many of those, now."

"What about that Jackie?" Anita says, blithely unaware that it's the worst thing she could possibly say in this moment. "She's been by a few times to buy supplies, you know. She even bought one of your paintings."

Claire is sure that if she opens her mouth, she'll start to cry. She clenches her jaw, staring down at the table, and Anita makes a soft noise.

"A story for another time," Anita says quietly.

Anita leaves Claire to her own devices for the morning. In the afternoon, Claire joins her in the shop to start her new life in earnest.

⚜

The job turns out to be the best possible distraction. It's easy to throw herself into helping Anita run the store as November marches onwards—Claire learns how to order supplies and do inventory. Anita even lets her help with balancing the books. It turns out that Claire has an easier time with the mathematics of it. When the shop is quiet Anita encourages her to paint, and Claire gets brave enough to break out the oils again. Her first few tentative pieces are nothing special, but she can feel the rust shaking off.

One thing Claire is sure of is that Pete has no idea where she's gone.

So, Claire works. She tucks her money away. She meets with Anita's lawyer and gets the ball rolling on divorce paperwork. She puts a deposit on a shoebox apartment above the sandwich shop a few doors down from Anita's, which will let her move in just before Christmas. Brick by brick, she builds something new.

When in early December Anita gives her a weekend off, Claire finds that the sudden lack of purpose feels unnatural. There's no cleaning to be done, no cooking, no grocery shopping. She has so few clothes with her that there's nothing to mend or iron. She doesn't have much to do besides lie on Anita's couch.

"I'll be with you in a jiff," Anita says when Claire pushes the door to the shop open, not looking up from her notes. "My damn accountant wants a record of every time I've so much as passed gas this month, and I'm in the middle of a thought."

"Take your time," Claire says.

Anita sets the pen down, sighing heavily as she looks up. "Claire. Did I not tell you to take the weekend?"

"I have nothing to do," Claire says, already drifting towards a box of paint palettes that needs to be priced. "At least here I can be helpful."

"That's the point of it. You need to stop being so helpful," Anita says. She rises from her stool, shooing Claire towards the door like she's an unruly raccoon raiding the garbage bins. "Get out there and make friends. Get a hobby. Rob a bank."

"You want me to commit a felony?" Claire says.

"If that's what it takes," Anita says, shoving Claire out the door. "I don't want to see you in this store until Monday. Understood?"

Claire is left on the sidewalk, blinking confusedly in the morning sunlight.

She goes back upstairs and paces the apartment. She picks up three different books, but none hold her attention. She gets out her sketchbook, but she's too antsy to draw.

Instead, Claire goes to the phone.

"Considering it's nine in the morning, this *must* be Claire," Theo says, after four rings.

Claire smiles. Theo's sharp edges might have unsettled her when they first met, but now she suspects that it's a token of affection. "Do you ever just say hello?"

"Not a chance," Theo says. "Haven't heard from you in a while. How's the single life?"

"I'm doing what you said. I'm finding my feet," Claire says.

"And?"

"Pete always made me feel like I'd never make it without him. But it turns out that it's much easier to be on my own. I have all this free time, and nothing to do with it."

"Get a bus ticket to San Fran," Theo says breezily. "We can hit the town tonight. Shake the suburbs out of you."

Claire's eyebrows shoot up. She's never ridden a Greyhound bus, but she does have some money to spare, now. "You want me to visit you? Really?"

"Against my better judgement, I've grown somewhat fond of you," Theo says. "And I never could ignore new blood in need."

The two-hour bus ride is shockingly comfortable. The seats are plush, and the bus is air conditioned. Nobody sits beside her, which gives her the entire journey to look quietly out the window and wonder at her new sense of freedom. A few months ago, she wouldn't have dreamed of taking a bus to the coast. She'd have had to ask Pete first, and not only would he have said no, just asking probably would have caused a fight. Now she's trundling along the highway on her own, with 25 dollars in her pocket and a friend waiting at the end of the road.

Stepping out of the bus station in San Francisco is an assault on Claire's senses. It's loud, the air rent with bus engines and car horns and the laughter of a large group of teens across the street. People pass her without a second glance—some are in suits, others in fashionable outfits of the kind that Jackie might wear. Very few look anything like the people Claire knows in Acacia Circle. The air smells like warm pavement and cigarettes and the slightest hint of urine. It's new and bright and fast-paced.

It's all terribly exciting.

"Look what the cat dragged in," drawls a voice to her right. Theo is leaned against the side of the building, dressed in fitted white pants and a violet striped shirt that stretches tight across his shoulders. "Suzy Homemaker, in the big bad city."

At this point, it feels natural to run to him for a hug. He squeezes her tight, leaning back so that her toes leave the ground.

"You looked better on Halloween," Theo says, setting Claire down to take in her clothes. "Did you take all those ugly dresses with you when you left your husband?"

"Only a few," Claire says, grinning. She plucks at his collar. "Do you have any shirts that fit you properly?"

Theo gasps, but he sounds more delighted than anything. "Kitty has claws."

"I learned from the best."

Theo's apartment is located over a Mexican restaurant, and on the way up he orders a quick supper. She helps him carry the bags up the three flights of rickety stairs to his unit. It's small, but he's clearly put so much effort into decorating it that it feels nice and homey, with worn furniture and a few big windows that look over the busy street. The walls are hung with eclectic art and framed photos that Claire is sure are Jackie's. He seems to own just about every musical instrument Claire can imagine. She drops her bag near the couch, next to an open case with a saxophone in it.

"I can't believe I've never asked this," Claire says, taking in the record collection that spans several stuffed bookshelves, "but are you a musician?"

"Composer, performer, occasional disc jockey, choose your poison," Theo calls from the bedroom. "Get in here, I might have something for you to wear tonight."

Claire finds him digging in the back of his closet to reveal an impressive collection of dresses. It's less surprising than perhaps it should be.

"Some of these might fit you," Theo says through a mouthful of their shared crunchy tacos. "We need to get you out of those frumpy housewife uniforms. How about this?" He holds up a garment that Claire is sure would look stunning on Jackie. It's a rosy brown evening dress, made more pink by the shininess of the fabric. The puffed skirt is scattered with a little black leaf pattern. It has halter straps and a big bow over the chest, and it at least looks made for a bustline as small as Claire's, assumedly because Theo is the one who wears it.

Claire bites her lip. "I don't know."

"You don't want to wear that old thing to the bar, do you?" Theo says, waving his hand at Claire's dress.

"No," Claire says. She drifts towards Theo's closet, but rather than thumbing through the dresses, she lingers on his regular wardrobe. She tugs at the long sleeve of a shirt, white fabric printed all over with a yellow sunflower pattern.

Slowly, Theo puts the dress back. Instead he takes out the shirt she's looking at, grinning as he holds it up against her. "Interesting choice. I think it'll fit, if you want to brave it."

"Where we're going tonight," Claire says, taking the shirt from him, "will it be...people like us?"

Theo's smile softens. Claire could swear that he looks a little bit proud of her. "Yeah. One of the safer places to be ourselves."

Theo's pants fit well enough if Claire wears a belt, though his shoes are so big that she has to wear several pairs of socks to keep them from coming off. The shirt has a deep v collar when Claire puts it on, deep enough that it reminds Claire of the jumpsuits Jackie sometimes wears, and it means she can't wear a brassiere without it poking out. Instead she goes without, and Theo gives her a necklace to wear that sits just over her bare breastbone. She ties her hair back into a low ponytail, not bothering to fuss with the curls that spring free.

Looking in the mirror, it feels as if she's looking at whatever real self Jackie unleashed all those months ago. She's not crammed into a tiny frame anymore. She's not blending into the background. She's ready to face the world.

The sun is starting to set when they hop on a trolley headed across town. It's almost full, and Claire is only half-listening to Theo telling her all about the neighborhood they're headed to as she takes it all in. She expected to feel like the odd one out, but not to this degree.

The bus is packed to the gills with the breadth of humanity. There are mothers and children. There are mixed couples, and men heading to night shift work. There are students who reek of their parents money, and people who look like they could use a good meal.

A group of young people crowd onto the car a few stops in, all dressed in what Pete would call *hippie clothes*, and one of the boys grins at her and flashes the peace sign as he passes. He has a colorful bandana tied around his head, keeping his long hair in check, and his shirt has a big yellow sunflower on the front to match Claire's.

Pete would have laughed in his face. But Claire isn't with Pete. She's out in the city, on her own, with her own money in her pocket. After a moment she grins, and makes a peace sign back.

The street they disembark on is bustling, but Theo cuts an easy path towards a nondescript brick building with a tall, flickering sign that says *The Harbor*. She can hear pulsing music inside, and the small group of people passing around a cigarette outside the door all straighten up and shout when they see Theo. Theo shouts back, speeding up his pace, and for a minute it's all hugs and airy cheek-kisses between him and his friends.

"This is Claire," Theo finally says once everyone has been greeted, pulling Claire forward by her lapel. "She's new around here."

"I'm LeAnn. Where ya from?" one of the women says. It's hard to see anyone's features in the dim light, but she looks to have long, dark hair and a pretty face, and she's wearing bright red lipstick. Her accent says Boston, loud and clear. She looks oddly familiar, but Claire can't imagine where she might have seen her before. "Let me guess: Midwest?"

"Sacramento. She and Jackie were cellmates in suburbia," Theo says.

LeAnn nods, smiling at Claire. "Welcome to the club. We miss Jackie around here. How's she doing?"

Claire wishes more than anything that she could answer that question. Thankfully, Theo comes to the rescue.

"She's having a New Years Eve bash. She's inviting everyone out to come rustle some suburban feathers," Theo says, accepting the shared cigarette from someone whose gender Claire can't quite parse and taking a long drag. "You should see if you can make it."

They all assure Theo they'll see about coming, before heading back inside. Claire moves to follow, but Theo stops her with a touch to the wrist.

"You're invited too, you know," he says.

Claire bites at the inside of her cheek. She's quite sure that she isn't invited, actually, but Theo moves past her quickly, and she follows him inside.

The bar is so dark that at first Claire can barely see where she's going. She's already lost track of Theo's friends, and she's only sure of Theo's location because his shirt seems to glow under the occasional strobe lights. What she can see, though, is that the dance floor is packed. It's a crush of people, all dancing to the shabby jukebox in a way she's never seen before. They're all pressed close together, moving in swinging, grinding motions. Big, unselfconscious movements.

Theo hands her a drink, but she's too busy trying to take everything in to take a sip. The woman behind the bar is built like a brick house, and dressed entirely in men's clothing. She has a buzz cut, two thick arms full of tattoos, and a very comforting energy. There's a stage at the far end of the room, where currently several people are putting on some kind of performance—their hands are whirling around their faces in controlled but totally unpredictable ways.

It reminds Claire of the ocean videos she once watched back in school. The camera had lingered at first over the calm and familiar sea surface before dipping underneath to reveal the vibrant chaos hidden in the reef. This bar is teeming with life in the same way. Strange, beautiful creatures drift past on the current of the music, and Claire isn't in a submarine or in front of a television. She's part of it.

Theo seems to know everyone. Claire half-expects each person she meets to know that she doesn't belong here, but they're all unbelievably kind. When they hear she's new to all of this, they congratulate her on her bravery. They buy her drinks that she can't finish fast enough. They pull her to the dance floor to lose her inhibitions among the sweaty mass of people.

It's a sense of belonging like she's never felt before. For once she's not the tallest, not the loudest, not the oddest person in the room. She even catches a few women looking at her with what Theo calls *bedroom eyes*. Even if Claire has no idea how a courtship might go with a woman, it's exhilarating to feel like an object of desire, rather than just a receptacle. The women who look at her are beautiful. Claire can almost imagine herself dancing with them.

But they aren't Jackie.

As the night goes on, Claire's thoughts drift to Jackie so often that it feels like she's in the room. She sees women with dark hair or olive skin, and her throat tightens. She sees women coupled up on the dance floor or kissing at the edges of the room, and wonders what it would be like to be here with Jackie on her arm. Dancing. Drinking. Laughing together, like they used to.

All at once, the force of missing Jackie hits her square in the chest.

Jackie introduced her to this world, put her in clothes that felt right, awakened something in her that she can't turn her back on, and now they haven't even spoken in months. What is Jackie doing right now? Is she still drinking herself into a stupor? Or is she moving on? Has she found someone else to occupy her, like Susan Wilson? Does she still have Claire's painting hung in her office?

Suddenly, as Claire's thoughts take a turn for the morose, the music stops. A red light above the bar starts to flash, and the energy in the room shifts.

"Shit," Theo hisses. He grabs Claire's arm tightly, pushing her in front of him towards the back of the bar.

"What?" Claire says, stumbling a little when he pushes her harder. Her drink slips from her fingers, spilling all over the sticky floor. "What's going on?"

"Cops, Theo says tersely. "We have to go. Now." The crowd has started to push and shove; the bartender is forcing her way to the front of the crowd, towards the police that Claire can now see are spilling through the door. The lights keep flashing.

"Why are the police here?"

Theo doesn't answer. He's got a fist bunched in the back of her shirt, pushing her forward, but she digs her heels in.

The police have pushed their way into the club now. The officers at the front are grabbing patrons left and right, pulling handcuffs from their belts and patting people down. The performers on the stage, dressed mostly in skirts or dresses, are being yanked down to the floor. The bartender is arguing with the police at the door, blocking their way into the club.

Near the bar, Theo's friend LeAnn pushes at an officer's shoulder while he pats down someone that looks a lot like Theo did on Halloween. The officer shouts to a colleague, and quickly LeAnn is pushed face-first against the wall with her arms twisted behind her back. Her face bunches up in pain. When she turns it away from Claire, her dark hair and stature bring someone else to mind.

Claire sees not LeAnn, but Jackie. Jackie with a black eye, a busted lip, and a maddeningly persistent refusal to explain how she was beaten up.

Even Claire is surprised at her own strength when she tears away from Theo, making a furious beeline in the opposite direction. All the rage and helplessness she felt that day seeing Jackie beaten up is propelling her forward at full speed until she barrels into the police officer shoulder-first, sending him flying over a barstool and into a group of three other cops who are struggling to cuff the bartender. They scatter like bowling pins.

The hit reverberates painfully up her shoulder, but it comes with a rush of adrenaline. It doesn't make up for not being there to protect Jackie, but it feels good. It feels right to help LeAnn. She's never thought to do anything to a police officer besides thank them, but right now she feels like she could take on every cop in the place.

LeAnn turns around, flexing her shoulders back into their right place, and when she sees Claire she breaks into a grin.

"Look at you. My hero!" LeAnn grabs Claire's face, planting a firm kiss to her cheek. "Thanks, sweets. Let's get outta here."

Theo appears at Claire's elbow. He's more insistent now, and LeAnn follows them towards the back of the bar. There's a door near the bathrooms that looks like a supply closet, but Theo rips it open to reveal a large storage room.

Claire spills into it with LeAnn on her tail. All around them are crates of alcohol and boxes of tiny straws, and there's another door nearby that looks to lead to the back alley outside, but there's a big padlock on it.

"Why are the police here?" Claire says again. Her heart is pounding— she can hear shouting from behind the closed door.

Theo doesn't answer. He looks to be searching for something, peering into crates and moving things around.

LeAnn plants her back against the door. "Hey, help me hold this closed?"

Claire anchors her shoulder against the wood. Something slams into it on the other side, but the handle doesn't turn. "Theo? Shouldn't we –"

"Shut up for a second," Theo says. He doesn't sound angry, though— he sounds scared, for the first time since Claire has known him. Finally he reaches into a crate of tequila bottles, his hand rattling around while the noise behind the door gets louder, until he pulls out a tiny key. In a practiced flash he unlocks the padlock, and pulls Claire and LeAnn through the open door.

Immediately he's off down the alley at a sprint, and Claire tries to match his pace in her too-big shoes. She can see red and blue flashing lights at the opposite end of the alley, behind them. A man's voice shouts, but Theo grabs her elbow and pulls her hard to the left as soon as they reach the street. Claire bowls someone over, scraping her hands against the sidewalk, but LeAnn grabs her arm and pulls her to her feet again to keep running.

"How did you know where that key was?" Claire pants, once they've weaved a few streets over.

Theo slows his pace down to a jog. The back of his shirt is stained with sweat, despite the cool night air. "I used to hook up with one of the bouncers."

"Why were the police there?"

"They raid the gay bars. Usually it's not until the end of the month, when they come to collect their money," Theo says darkly. "I thought we'd be safe tonight."

"Their money?" Claire says. Theo is still jogging, and Claire finally slows to rip the loose shoes off her feet—hopefully the double socks will keep her soles relatively safe. "Shouldn't we have stayed to help your other friends?"

"Normally I would. But I doubt you want to spend your first night of freedom in lockup," Theo says. Once it's clear that they aren't being followed, he slows to a quick walk with Claire hopping to keep up.

"None of them are in drag tonight," LeAnn says, her heels clicking frantically to keep up with the pace. "If they get caught up, they'll be out by morning."

Claire stumbles, one shoe on and the other off. She knows, of course, that homosexuality is a legal grey area. But she's never seen so many people being so open about it and consequently punished. "Drag?"

"They arrest anyone wearing the wrong clothing. The queens and the butches," usually, LeAnn says.

Butches. The word is just as foreign as *drag*, but it settles somewhere in Claire that doesn't feel unnatural. For now, she tucks it away.

The trolley ride home is less comfortable than the one they took to the bar. LeAnn leaves them after a few stops, headed back to her own place, but she gives Claire a grateful squeeze before she hops off the car.

Once they're safely inside Theo's apartment, sweaty and sore, Theo pulls out a chair for her at his tiny kitchen table. While she sits down, he opens a cupboard and produces a bottle of vodka.

"This is part of it," Theo says heavily. "I didn't mean for you to see it this early, but this isn't an easy life, hon. We're all deviants. You have to decide if being yourself is worth it."

Deviants. Claire frowns, toying with the necklace Theo gave her. It's a long string of wooden beads, with a large amber pendant. "Have you ever been arrested?"

Theo pours two shots, pushing one towards Claire. "Our existence is a crime. They've got nicknames for me at the station."

She can't stomach the idea of more alcohol right now, so she pushes the shot back at Theo. "Has Jackie?"

Theo takes his shot, and then Claire's. He makes a face, and coughs. "Yes."

"What for?"

"Being at a gay bar during a raid. Homosexual conduct. Once for assaulting an officer who was trying to arrest me for wearing a skirt."

"Is this why Jackie pushed me away? Claire says. "She was trying to protect me from this?"

Theo sets his elbows on the table, leaning forward to massage his temples. His eyes are squeezed shut. "That's part of it."

The frank answer is a little surprising. Claire glares at him, poking his shoulder. "Why wouldn't you just tell me that? Why wouldn't she? That changes everything."

"It's her business."

"But—"

Theo raises his head. He looks Claire in the eye, and he claps his hands together loudly. "Okay. I'm going to say this once, and whatever you do with it is up to you. Agreed?"

Claire frowns. "Alright."

"And you never tell Jackie that I told you this. Agreed?"

"Yes, fine," Claire says impatiently.

Theo takes a breath. He rolls his neck and pours himself another shot.

"Jackie never quite forgave herself for all the sneaking around and lying she had to do with Val, and now she's convinced that she corrupted you," Theo says. "That if she hadn't influenced you, you'd have kept on in your happy little suburban bubble, and now she's coaxed something out that will make your life harder. She feels guilty."

"But I wasn't happy," Claire says.

Theo takes the shot. He doesn't wince this time. "Most women aren't happy. They just don't have the gall to do anything about it. Valerie isn't happy with her husband, either, but she chose him in the end. Jacks can't imagine anyone choosing her, so she leaves first, and she stays away."

Jackie doesn't expect to be chosen. Claire's first instinct is indignation—that Jackie didn't even give her the chance to make that choice, and instead chose to hurt them both. But it makes a certain kind of sense. It took Claire time to come around to how she feels, and identify that she's—

Claire almost laughs. Isn't she proving Jackie's point, by not even being able to comfortably think the word? And Claire knows that she's not going back to Pete, but Jackie doesn't.

Actually, Jackie might not even know she's left in the first place. Would there be any indication from the outside? They already weren't speaking, so how would Jackie know that Claire isn't just spending more time indoors?

"Do you think she still wants me to choose her?" Claire says.

Theo stands up. He digs through a box near the couch, pulling out a few blankets. "Sorry, that's the end of Theo's Sharing Circle. It's time for me to clock out."

"Come on, Theo," Claire says. She catches a blanket when Theo tosses it at her. "Help me."

"I've already told you far more than Jacks would be comfortable with," Theo says. He throws a pillow onto the couch, flicking off the overhead light. "Go to sleep, Claire."

Claire tries to do as he says. She tosses and turns for hours. She thinks of her mother, wishing Claire had chosen an easier path. She thinks of what her life was just a few weeks ago. Maybe that life should have been easy, but it wasn't. This, even with the danger and the fear, is still easier. There's a joy here like she's never known before.

Sleep comes eventually, but not for long. Claire's early schedule is still engrained in her, and she's up by seven thirty while Theo still snores. While he sleeps, she tidies his kitchen and does the dishes. She gives the place a dusting. She wanders to the windowsill, where several framed photos sit—two of them feature Jackie.

By ten o'clock Theo is still asleep, and Claire's wandering leads her to his telephone. Her fingers punch seven familiar numbers on their own.

"Hello," Jackie says, after six rings. She sounds tired, and not just because it's early. It's a haggard kind of tired. Even so, just hearing her voice is almost enough to bring tears to Claire's eyes.

Silence crackles over the line. Claire knows she needs to say something, anything at all, but nothing is coming. What could she possibly say? What words are enough to sum up the last few months of her life?

"Hello?" Jackie says again, with a hint of impatience.

Claire can feel the threat of her hanging up the phone, and finally a single word crosses her lips. "Hello," Claire murmurs.

Claire strains to hear anything besides Jackie's sharp inhale. The phone line buzzes over the frantic beating of Claire's heart.

"Claire?" Jackie says softly.

Claire nods, before realizing that Jackie can't see her. She's gripping the phone receiver so hard that her hand shakes. "It's me."

Jackie is breathing heavily. Claire is on the edge of a knife, and she blurts out the first thing that crosses her mind.

"I miss you," Claire says.

"Claire..." Jackie says. It's muffled, for some reason. Like she has her face in her hand.

"I have so much to tell you," Claire says. "Can we talk? Please?"

"Fuck. Don't do this to me," Jackie whispers. "This is hard enough already."

The sound of it snaps Claire's heart in two. "Please just let me talk," Claire says. She feels frantic, suddenly. Her voice cracks. "I think I know why you pushed me away. And it's okay, I—I left—"But the line has already gone dead.

She's not sure how to get Jackie to hear her out, if not over the phone. Would a letter work, or would Jackie just leave it unopened? Should she march to Jackie's door, and risk being caught by Pete or Martha and forced to come back to Acacia Circle before she has her separation paperwork in order?

She calls Jackie once more, but it goes straight to her answering machine.

Chapter 24

Claire's new apartment smells like freshly baked bread.

It's completely bare of furniture when she gets the keys. Anita finds a mattress for her, and a trunk with a clasp for her clothes. Claire shares a phone line with the sandwich shop. There's a hot plate and a refrigerator and a folding table with two chairs. She can hardly fit into the bathtub without folding her legs up like an accordion.

It's perfect.

She hangs the walls with art. She has Anita over for a simple Christmas dinner—split pea soup, and some bread from the shop downstairs. Anita gives her a toaster oven, far outstripping Claire's gift of a new set of clay sculpting tools. By Boxing Day, her new routine has become so normal that looking back on the last ten years of her life feels like she's watching it at a drive-in. She can see the memories, can feel the echo of despair, but it feels like someone else's story, seen through a foggy windshield.

She picks up her first set of divorce papers from the lawyer on New Years Eve.

Her steps feel light on the way home. And her new apartment does feel like home, now—calling her old phone number in Acacia Circle feels odd in comparison. Now, standing in the kitchen of the sandwich shop clutching a yellow envelope full of paperwork postdated to the first of January, she waits for Pete to pick up.

"Davis residence," Pete says gruffly, after so many rings that Claire has almost hung up in frustration.

His voice over the phone brings none of the excitement or tension that Jackie's did. It doesn't even bring guilt. Claire's only feeling now is that she wants to get this over with as quickly as possible.

"Hello, Peter," Claire says.

"Claire?" Pete says. He lets out a loud breath, but unsurprisingly he sounds more angry than anything. "Where the *hell* have you been? How could you just run off like that? You realize it's been almost two months since you've been home?"

"Yes," Claire says simply.

"You missed your appointment at the fertility clinic," Pete says. "They charged good money for that. And everyone's been asking about you, and the house—"

"I told you I was leaving," Claire interrupts. "It isn't my fault you weren't listening."

Pete doesn't address the correction. "When are you coming home?"

"I'm not."

"I'll come pick you up. I doubt you have money for the bus fare," Pete says, before Claire has gotten those two words out. "Just give me an address."

Claire takes a deep breath. She clutches the envelope, holding it to her chest like a shield. She repeats Anita's advice in her head—*it's not a request, chickadee. Phrase it as a statement. Don't let him refuse.*

"We're getting a divorce," Claire says loudly.

Pete's line buzzes.

"I have the papers," Claire says, when enough time has passed without Pete speaking. "I need you to sign them. Will you be at home tomorrow?"

"We're not getting a divorce," Pete says.

Claire pushes on. "You have the option of refusing to sign the papers, but I can file them either way starting next week. It's better for both of us if you just sign."

Pete grunts. "You're being ridiculous. I don't know where you're holing up, but it can't be pleasant. Come home tonight for Martha and Walter's party. We can get you settled again in the morning."

It's as if Claire hasn't been speaking at all. Pete is bulldozing over everything, pushing onwards the way he always does. Claire is tired of being bulldozed.

"I'm not coming home, Pete," Claire repeats, her voice rising almost to a shout. "I'm filing for divorce."

"I haven't been unfaithful. And neither have you," Pete says, with utter confidence. He speaks with the tone of a teacher telling his student they can do extra credit to bring their grade up. "You have nowhere to go.

There's no need to disrupt our lives. If you come home tonight, we'll forget this ever happened."

Claire looks down at the paperwork in her hand, searching for some way to make Pete accept the truth. There's nothing in the typewritten letters on the page, but she does notice something else—the perpetual nail-marks in her palms have finally healed. She can still see the scars, but they're a faint silvery-pink instead of an angry red. Somehow in the last few weeks she's broken the habit. She hardly noticed that she hasn't been clenching her fists lately.

Strangely, that's the thing that makes Claire hang up the phone while Pete is still fruitlessly arguing. She's sure he must still be expecting her to turn up at Martha's party tonight with a brand-new happy attitude, ready to ring in the New Year together.

It's not unexpected, but it is exasperating. After thanking the shop owner for the use of the phone she stomps up the stairs to her apartment, tossing the papers onto the table and flopping backwards onto her mattress with a groan.

If she does go to Martha's party tonight to give Pete the papers, he's going to corner her. She can feel it. He'll talk over her, involve other people to make her feel guilty, and in the end probably won't accept the papers anyways. The lawyer told Claire that the proceedings can continue if Pete refuses to sign them, but it'll get more complicated and expensive. Should she just shove them in the mailbox? Leave them at the house while Pete is at work after the holidays? She doesn't want to wait that long.

But Pete won't be home tonight, will he? He'll be at Martha's party. Claire still has her old house key. Nobody will see her if they're all busy celebrating the New Year. She could go tonight and leave them on the table for Pete to find on the first day of 1970.

Claire is slow and careful while getting ready. She takes a hot bath. She rubs hair oil through her damp curls and lets them air-dry. She pulls the clothes that Jackie bought her out of her bag, and irons out most of the wrinkles by heating up the bottom of her frying pan. When she puts them on, still slightly warm, she can see her reflection in one of the windows. She looks tall and confident. It's encouraging—she needs the extra boost tonight.

The sun is down and both parties are in full swing on either side of the street when her taxi rolls into the cul-de-sac, and Claire directs the driver to stop in front of her former home.

The acacia tree is barely blooming, its flowers falling to the grass in preparation for the coolest months. If there's one thing from this neighborhood besides Jackie that she'll miss, it's this tree. *Secret love,* Jackie had said about acacias. *Hidden emotion.* Claire picks up one of the wilted puffs, rolling it between her fingers until it comes apart into yellow pulp.

How fitting.

The lights are all dark. Pete hasn't changed the locks, so Claire slips into the house and through the darkened hall. She stops in her tracks when she flicks the kitchen light on.

The place is a disaster. The countertops are filthy, and the sink is piled with dirty dishes. The trashcan is full of packaging for TV dinners, the table so scattered with papers and bits of trash that Claire isn't sure where to put her envelope. It looks as if nothing has been cleaned in two months.

Out of curiosity, Claire goes upstairs. In the bedroom, the laundry basket is so full that it's spilling onto the floor. It looks like Pete has bought new clothes rather than figure out how to work the machine. The bed is unmade. All of her things are untouched. Her engagement and wedding rings have been moved, though—they're sitting on her dusty jewelry tray, instead of out in the open where she left them.

Claire is surrounded by her things, the trappings of her old life, and yet it feels as if they all belong to someone else. She's been so changed now that she can't imagine ever slipping into this ill-fitting role again.

Claire picks the rings up, letting them sit on her palm. They felt like heavy weights when she first took them off. Now, they feel light as aluminum foil. They're nothing at all, really, are they? Just two pieces of cheap metal and a tiny stone.

Claire makes the bed. She tucks the top sheet in, fluffs the pillows, and smooths out the wrinkles in the duvet just like she used to. Then she leaves the papers on the bedspread, in plain view. Over her own signature, she sets her rings.

Locking the door behind her feels more final than it did last time. She's strangely aware of the fact that this is probably the last time she'll ever do it. The decisiveness of it makes her feel more confident than she did going in, and once it's sealed behind her she turns towards the loud music coming from Jackie's house. She's weighing the pros and cons of going inside when she sees the white sign on Jackie's lawn.

For Sale.

Claire's stomach lurches.

Her feet take her across the lawns in a daze, and soon she's staring down at the sign as if it's going to explain itself to her. Where is Jackie moving to? And why? The listing date on the sign is only a few days ago.

What if Jackie leaves Acacia Circle, and gets a new phone number and address that Claire can't find? What if she disappears, drives off into the sunset and isolates herself even from Theo, and Claire never sees her again?

Claire can hear footsteps clicking on the pavement somewhere behind her, but she doesn't turn until she hears her name called.

Thankfully, it isn't Pete. It's Martha. She's hurrying across the street, looking at Jackie's front door as if someone is going to come barreling out of it to steal her jewelry.

"Claire! There you are—why haven't you called?" Martha says, pulling a shawl tighter around her shoulders against the cool air. "Everyone's been talking. Is your mother all right?"

"My mother?" Claire says absently.

"Pete said you'd been away in Florida caring for her, and that you'd be back tonight. And here you are," Martha pauses, her eyebrows raising. "In such...interesting clothes. You know it isn't a costume party, right?"

Of course. Pete wouldn't let anyone think something was wrong. She does feel somewhat guilty for not calling Martha to tell her what's happened, but the idea of explaining and justifying her decision was exhausting. Now she doesn't have much choice.

"I'm not back," Claire says. She crosses her arms, grounding herself in her *interesting clothes*. "I'm leaving."

Martha blinks. She touches Claire's arm lightly. "You're going home? It's nearly midnight. Can't you wait a tick until the New Year?"

"I'm leaving Pete," Claire says, more clearly.

The music from Jackie's house seems louder in the ensuing silence.

"You're..." Martha shakes her head, as if those three words are unintelligible. "Claire, that's just wacky. I know you've been having little tiffs, but..."

"It's not the fights. It's every moment of our relationship since the day he asked me to the homecoming dance when I was sixteen," Claire says, looking again towards the music. "You're not going to convince me otherwise, Martha. I'm done with this."

"You don't really mean *divorce*, do you?" Martha whispers. "Did Pete step out on you? Is there some other woman?"

Claire can't help it—she laughs. The irony of it is simply too much.

There is another woman, as it turns out. It just isn't Pete whose eyes have strayed.

"It doesn't matter why. I've told him about it already. I have a place to live, and a job," Claire says. "And I imagine you and the others won't want to associate with a divorced woman."

"Well, I—I—" Martha stammers. Her cheeks have gone pink.

"It's alright. You don't need to explain yourself. I don't fit into your life anymore when I'm not part of the couple across the road. And that's okay," Claire says, more gently. "Pete will remarry. Probably quickly. You'll make friends with his new wife, and life will go on."

"Why can't you stay?" Martha says, shivering against the cool breeze. "I'm sure things will work themselves out. We just have to grin and bear it, right?"

It seems to float between them, that sentence. What used to be a bond that held them together has become a gulf. Martha is planted firmly on one side, and Claire is heading in another direction.

"Someday, I hope you find someone who appreciates you properly," Claire says softly. "I truly do."

Claire looks to Jackie's house again. The party has only gotten louder. When she turns back, Martha's eyes are shining in the light of the streetlamps.

"You've been..." Martha's voice wavers. She clears her throat. "You've been a good friend."

It's probably the closest to acceptance Claire will get from Martha. A sudden surge of affection hits her, and in this last moment together she pulls Martha into a hug. It's brief, but tight.

"Goodbye, Martha," Claire murmurs.

Claire leaves her on the lawn. She's being propelled by something intense to walk up the three steps to Jackie's front door. She needs to see Jackie. Whether the door will be closed in her face again or not, Claire needs to know one way or the other where she stands. She needs confirmation. Closure.

The party is riotous. The air is smoky from the moment Claire pushes the door open. People are in various states of undress all around, and there are at least two strangely-contorted foursomes in progress in the conversation pit. The door leading to the bedrooms is swinging off the hinges with couples coming and going.

It makes her a little bit ill to think that Jackie might be off somewhere doing that, too.

Claire doesn't recognize anyone this time, from either of Jackie's previous parties. She doesn't know a single person until she runs headlong into someone on her way into the kitchen. They're evenly matched in stature, of a similar height, and Claire stumbles backward a little.

"Sorry, I—" Claire starts, but the moment she sees the person's face she loses her train of thought. "Oh, my goodness."

It isn't Jackie. It isn't even Theo. It's the masculine woman whose photo on Jackie's wall Claire has been staring at for months, as if she's walked straight out of the frame and into real life. She's just as striking as she is in the picture, short-shorn hair and all. She has a scar that bisects her right eyebrow that wasn't there in the photo. She's in tight pants, like Claire, and a brown suede jacket. She regains her balance with an easy confidence.

"Woah there. Something got your feathers ruffled?" The woman says, grinning and steadying Claire by the shoulder.

Claire can hardly find words. Her focus is split; for the first time in a while, Jackie isn't the primary thing on her mind.

"You're real," Claire blurts.

The woman looks at her quizzically. "Do I know you?"

Claire winces. She's probably coming off like a maniac. She points quickly to the frame on the living room wall just to their right, her face burning hot. "Sorry. Sorry, it's only—your picture is on Jackie's wall."

"Is it?" The woman says. She looks delighted as she follows Claire's finger. When she sees the photo, she grins wider and leans closer to peek. "Damn! So it is."

A second person pops up at the woman's elbow. She's shorter, with long auburn hair and a bold red lip to match her daring scarlet dress. She winds her arm through the short-haired woman's, leaning into her, and in an instant Claire recognizes her in more ways than one.

"LeAnn!" Claire says. She laughs, too full of this strange, amorphous joy to keep it in. Now that Claire can see them side by side, it's obvious that LeAnn is the other woman from the photo—the feminine one, lighting the cigarette. It's almost too perfect.

"Look who it is—my hero," LeAnn says, giggling when her beau presses a kiss to the top of her head. "Darla, this is the woman I told you about. The baby butch who tackled that cop for me, remember?" LeAnne tucks her arm more securely into Darla's. Her lipstick is exactly the same shade as a smudged mark on Darla's collar.

It brings to mind the pink lipstick mark on Jackie's jaw at that first housewarming party, and where it came from. The reminder burns in Claire, hotter than her own blushing.

"You're kidding?" Darla says, grinning wide at Claire. She holds out a hand, much like Jackie always does. Fearless. "In that case, I owe you one. I was working that night, and when I heard about the raid, I can't tell you how happy I was to see LeAnn come home. I'm Darla."

"Claire," Claire says, accepting the handshake. It's firm and spirited. Darla's hands are calloused, like maybe she does some kind of manual labor. "Claire Fields."

"You a friend of Jackie's?" Darla says.

"Something like that."

"Claire pointed out that we're on the wall," Darla says to LeAnn, pointing at the photo.

LeAnn gasps in delight. "Would you look at that. We look great, baby. We should talk to Jackie about buying it."

Their easy affection with each other sings through Claire's veins. The touches, the pet names. They couldn't be clearer about their relationship to each other. They fit together as naturally as anything.

Claire wants that. She wants it with Jackie.

"I'm actually looking for her," Claire says hopefully. "Have you seen her around?"

Darla claps a strong hand on Claire's shoulder, tilting her until she's facing the sliding back door. "She's out by the pool."

"In this weather?"

LeAnn shrugs. "She's seemed out of sorts all night. I think she wanted to be alone."

Claire's heart pounds away in her chest. Jackie is just through those flimsy doors, after almost two months of distance. Once Claire opens them, there's no going back.

Darla and LeAnn start to head towards the conversation pit, but after a few steps Darla stops and turns back around.

"By the way, I like the shirt. Very sharp," Darla says, winking. "Let me know if you ever want a haircut. My barber knows the deal. She'll do it for free, if it's your first."

Of all the things that have happened in the last hour, this is the one that has Claire's eyes stinging. Darla is open and friendly with hardly a single conversation between them, offering her preferred lady barber as if she's inviting Claire into some kind of exclusive club. A club where Claire can have short hair and wear the clothes she wants to. Where she can walk arm-in-arm with the woman she loves.

Some kind of community.

Claire surges forward, pulling Darla into an even tighter hug than she gave Martha.

"Thank you," Claire whispers. Darla doesn't hold back, either—she seems to sense that Claire needs this, wrapping her shockingly strong arms around Claire and giving her a good squeeze and a hearty pat on the back before they part.

"Good luck, sweets," LeAnn says, giving Claire a wink and a gentle tap on the hip before she heads to the conversation pit with her girl.

Claire steels herself, takes a deep breath of smoky air, and she steps through the sliding door.

It's like stepping into a different world, crossing that threshold and closing the door behind her. The noise of the party muffles. It's darker out here, just the pool lights flickering white and blue, and the stuffy heat cedes to fresh night air.

Jackie is alone. She's sitting in a lounge chair at the edge of the pool, bundled in a blanket with her bare knees drawn up to her chest. She's not wearing any shoes. There's a martini in her hand, but it's largely untouched.

Jackie doesn't turn when she hears the noise of the party spill through the door, or when it closes again. She's staring listlessly at the water. She's not wearing her usual makeup, either, and her hair is flat and un-styled—she looks small and sad and beautiful.

Claire's foot catches on a patio chair. It skids loudly across the stones, and Jackie starts to turn.

"I told you all from the start, no swimming this time. Go back—"

Jackie's eyes fall on her. There are bags beneath them, dark and heavy, and her cheeks look hollower than the last time Claire saw her, but she's still utterly gorgeous. For one perfect moment, Jackie's face brightens.

"Claire," Jackie breathes.

Chapter 25

"I need to talk to you," Claire says, before Jackie can say another word.

Jackie's face falls quickly from joy to the same aching sadness Claire heard over the phone.

"I don't think that's a good idea," Jackie says. She's wringing her hands, now, and her eyes dart around the yard like she's looking for an exit besides the one Claire is standing in front of.

"Maybe it isn't," Claire says. She's breathing hard, not from exertion but from the fact that her heart is beating a mile a minute. She surges forward, sitting in the chair next to Jackie's and grabbing gently at her blanket. "But I'm here anyways."

"It's almost midnight. You should be with your husband."

"I know what time it is," Claire fires back. "I'm exactly where I want to be."

"Claire…" Jackie whispers. It's a broken sort of sound, this time, cracking right in the middle of Claire's name; she looks past Claire through the door, as if she's expecting someone to call out in protest. As if Pete might be lurking in Claire's shadow.

The door slides open. The party noise spills back in, and a group of five or six people stumble towards the pool. Jackie protests half-heartedly, but they pay her no mind—they tip into the pool, clothes and all, while more partiers follow in their wake. The cold is apparently not a deterrent.

Claire doesn't particularly want to have this conversation in front of the entire party, so she takes Jackie's hand amidst the splashing and laughter, pulling her up. The blanket falls from Jackie's shoulder as Claire guides her insistently into the crowd in the living room. She starts towards the bedrooms, but Jackie pulls her arm taut.

"Where are we going?"

"Ideally somewhere private," Claire says.

"The bedrooms are all occupied," Jackie says. She looks utterly exhausted. "They even took over the basement."

Claire holds fast to her hand. If the bedrooms and darkroom are occupied, what options are there? The bathroom, maybe, or...

Casting around for anything at all that might be her saving grace, Claire's eyes land on Theo.

He's watching them with interest, with a drink in one hand and a cigarette in the other. She doubts that he can hear their conversation, but their body language must be obvious. He raises an eyebrow, and with his drink in hand he points to an option Claire hadn't considered. The walk-in coat closet next to the front door. It's just big enough for two.

Claire nods at him, and with a wry smile he disappears into the crowd.

Jackie doesn't protest being dragged there, perhaps because it's so unexpected. Claire guides her inside first, closing the door quickly behind them, and it's a tight fit. There are coats hanging to the right and left, leaving just a narrow corridor to stand in, and Jackie is mere inches away. Claire grabs for the cord to turn the single lightbulb on; even lit so harshly, Jackie is still breathtaking.

"Were you ever going to tell me you were moving?" Claire asks bluntly. So close up, she can hear Jackie's sharp, surprised inhale. "Or were you just going to disappear?"

"I can't talk about this right now," Jackie says. She reaches for the door handle, but Claire is in the way.

"Then when? When will you talk to me?"

"We've already talked," Jackie says, crossing her arms tightly over her chest. "I'm a terrible friend, okay? That should be the end of it."

Jackie's eyes get wide as saucers when Claire moves closer. Their chests are almost touching, and in the close, stuffy air of the closet Claire can feel her warm breath. "Jackie, please. Just this once, even if you never want to see me again afterwards, can you listen to me?"

Silently, Jackie nods.

"I've been so scattered since we met," Claire says. "I didn't know which way was up. But I think I know now."

Jackie makes a tiny sound. A small, nearly inaudible expression of pain.

"You're just confused. I shouldn't—I *can't* do this," Jackie says.

There's such an ache in Claire, one that she's almost sure is echoed in Jackie, but something is holding Jackie back.

"I'm not confused," Claire insists, before correcting herself. "I mean, I was. But then I talked to Theo."

Jackie freezes like a deer caught halfway across the road. "Theo? How? What did he tell you?"

"I figured it out on my own," Claire says firmly. "I just needed someone to set my head on straight."

Jackie's arms un-cross. "Whatever Theo said, Claire, you shouldn't listen to him. He's a meddler. I should never have—"

"The person you loved," Claire interrupts. "The married person. It wasn't a man, was it?"

Jackie says nothing, stunned into a silence that's somehow more illustrative than any verbal confirmation. The moment feels still, like the heartbeats before a jump, even with the muffled music and the sounds of the party behind the door.

"It was a woman," Claire says, in a single terrifying breath. "You loved a married woman."

Jackie's hands are fisted in the fabric of her own dress so tightly that her knuckles are white. It's a deep maroon, under the navy-blue jacket.

Claire is afraid. *God*, is she afraid, but she can't stop now. Not when she's this close.

"And I've seen you, with other women. At parties like these," Claire continues, barely above a whisper. She pries Jackie's hands from her dress, holding them in her own.

Jackie swallows hard. The tendons in her neck flex, and somehow the sight of it—how it makes Claire want to press her lips there, her teeth, her tongue—makes her feel brave.

"You're a lesbian," Claire murmurs. "Aren't you?"

The question hangs in the air between them, a curtain between their bodies that one word could pull down. Jackie's jaw is so tense that Claire worries about her teeth.

Slowly, probably aware of how her answer fundamentally shifts everything between them, Jackie nods.

Claire has known it since the moment Martha told her about Jackie and Susan. Her conversations with Theo have made it clear. This isn't a surprise. But the admittance makes it real, and it's difficult to get her next words out.

Claire smooths her thumbs over the backs of Jackie's hands. Just under the fingertip of Claire's left pointer is Jackie's tattoo, that branch of acacia flowers; it's warm and soft, like the rest of her. Smooth. Not raised or textured at all. It's just a part of Jackie's skin.

"I think I might be, too," Claire whispers.

Jackie's breath all comes out in a *whoosh*. Instead of the positive reaction Claire was hoping for, she deflates like a popped balloon.

"Claire, we can't." Jackie's voice cracks again. Her eyes are shiny when she pulls her hand from Claire's, reaching for the doorknob again, but Claire is still in the way.

Jackie's word choice is so important. Not *won't*, not *don't want to*.

Can't.

"But you want to?" Claire says.

"Yes, but..." Jackie cuts herself off, biting her lip, "but it doesn't matter."

Claire hardly hears that second part. The first is what's most important—the *yes*. Whatever Claire is feeling, whatever she's embroiled in, Jackie is in it, too.

"Why? Why can't we do this?" Claire says. She doesn't bother to mask her desperation. One hand goes to Jackie's hair, then to her beautiful face, tracing the outline of her jaw as she's secretly ached to do all these months.

Jackie leans into it, pressing her cheek into Claire's palm even as she denies her. "You're married."

"You slept with Mrs. Wilson," Claire protests. "And others. Like that woman the night of the moon landing—you went to the bedroom with her."

"They were different. Their husbands were sleeping with other people in the next room. Everyone was aware of the circumstances. Your husband isn't a swinger, Claire." Jackie's eyes threaten to spill over, and she bites at her lip so hard that Claire can see the little indents left behind. "I can't do it. Not like this. Not again."

Though Jackie is denying her, Claire's heart still soars. Once more, Jackie's words are telling.

Not again.

Claire is different than those two other women, because Jackie sees her the way she saw Valerie. Someone who will ultimately choose safety over love.

Claire has already made the opposite choice, but Jackie doesn't know that yet.

"I left him," Claire says simply.

For a moment, only the music from the party is audible. Jackie's brow furrows. She shakes her head a little, as if she's letting the information filter through her brain; when Claire raises her hand, Jackie's eyes fix on her bare ring finger.

Claire agonized over it for months, but now that she's here, the choice seems easy. She feels more just from standing close to Jackie than she ever did for her husband. He's harsh where Jackie is soft, thoughtless where Jackie is kind. He's a pair of shackles, and Jackie is a car on the open highway.

"That's..." Jackie whispers, seemingly tongue-tied. "You're...no. That's absurd."

The crease between Jackie's brows is deep. Claire wants to press her fingertip against it, and so, for once, she does. She does what she wants to do. She smooths out the wrinkle, letting her finger drift down the arched bridge of Jackie's nose. "You know, that's what Pete said. And Martha. But here I am. I think absurd suits me."

"You told them? You actually..." Jackie's eyes are still fixed on the spot Claire's wedding ring used to be, following Claire's hand. "When?"

"I left on Halloween."

"That was months ago."

"I know. I've started over," Claire says.

Jackie's eyes have finally stopped darting to the doorknob. "You left your whole life?"

"It was barely a life," Claire says urgently. "I've been miserable since before we even got married. I just...I didn't know there was another option."

Jackie's mouth is in an anxious twist, her teeth pulling at her lower lip. When Claire moves her hand to cup Jackie's face again, Jackie catches her wrist.

"Your palm," Jackie says. There's a quiet wonder in her voice.

Claire follows Jackie's eyeline to the silvery scars. Jackie has only seen them red and irritated.

"No more bad habits," Claire says.

Jackie's thumb traces over the lines. Mixed with the smoke in the air, it brings back a memory so strong that Claire can feel the weight of Jackie's head in her lap, and soft hair cascading over her thighs.

"I'm working at Anita's shop. I'm living on my own. I've given Pete the papers," Claire pushes on. "I'm never coming back here, now that I know who I am. *What* I am. Now that I know how I—" Claire's voice quavers, and she swallows hard to control it. "How I feel about you."

"And how do you feel?" Jackie whispers.

Claire closes the scant distance between them. Jackie's breath is coming quick, almost as quick as Claire's, and it's up to her to make the final leap.

"That I want this," Claire says, all in a rush. "I want you. More than I've ever wanted anything."

The pause after Claire's speech is heavy. Jackie is still as a statue, her face unreadable, and Claire has done all she can do. Jackie has to meet her the rest of the way.

Finally, Jackie's shaky hand comes up to rest on Claire's breastbone. Her hand is scorching hot through the cotton of Claire's shirt.

"I want you, too," Jackie murmurs.

Claire could power a small town with the force of the feelings those words provoke in her. She's a hydrogen bomb. A rocket about to take flight.

And then Jackie's hand turns into a fist, and she pulls.

The moment their lips meet, Claire understands what Theo meant when he said that it *just felt right*.

It's something that Claire can't explain in words. Any and all kissing experience she might have had before this is nothing—nothing compared to Jackie's lips against hers, the heat of the hand on her chest. The kiss is gentle and tentative, like Jackie is giving her the opportunity to run, but all Claire wants is more. More kissing, more touching, more skin contact, just *more*. She wants what she sees in her dreams. She wants to take all of their clothes off, press against Jackie like that day in the pool, and see what happens if they don't stop.

As soon as Claire leans in more, pushes deeper, makes it absolutely clear that she isn't going anywhere, Jackie seems to lose her inhibitions. And, Claire learns, the introduction of tongue to kissing is absolutely life-changing.

With an almost pained whine Jackie slots their mouths together properly, and with that shift their kisses turn messy and frantic. Claire's heart is beating so hard that she can hear it in her ears, can feel her blood whizzing through her body as Jackie's tongue meets her own, and that unfamiliar feeling from her strange dreams has returned in full force. Jackie is panting into her mouth, pressing her into the closet door, and all Claire's years of discomfort seem so far away as to be another person's life entirely. She's finally at home in her body, doing exactly what she was meant to do.

Jackie is hot and vital. The coat slips from her shoulders as she trails kisses up Claire's neck, her tongue breaking ground on places Claire had no idea were so sensitive, and in a fit of unbridled wanting Claire slides her hands down to grip Jackie's perfect waist and pull her closer.

Every sense is tuned in—Claire is fixated on the shape of Jackie's body under her hands, the taste of her lipstick, the smell of her perfume. Jackie's moan is musical. It strikes that same tuning fork in Claire and makes it sing.

So much is happening that Claire can't possibly keep up. She's running on instinct, following the pattern of her impulses for the first time in her life, and with Jackie's hands sliding under the collar of Claire's shirt to smooth along the hot skin of her chest, one instinct is loud enough to break through the din.

She wants Jackie's hands everywhere. She wants to be one of those couples she saw in the living room, or heading to and from the bedrooms.

She wants to see and be seen.

In a fit of inspiration, Claire's fingers move to the buttons of her own shirt. One by one she slips them free, as Jackie trails her mouth down a scorching path over each new piece of bare skin until Claire parts the shirt to reveal herself entirely.

It's in that very moment that Claire remembers she chose not to wear a brassiere with this outfit.

It had felt right, at the time. Her breasts are small to begin with, nothing to write home about, and she'd gone bra-less when she went to that club with Theo. It had seemed a fitting decision for this new sense of self.

Now, Jackie is staring at Claire's bare chest like it's the ninth wonder of the world.

"Are you sure about this?" Jackie says, her hands landing and anchoring near Claire's hipbones. It's just about the most chaste place Jackie could touch her right now, and yet Claire feels the ghost of Jackie's fingers higher up, where she wants them.

"I've spent my whole life obeying," Claire says. She takes Jackie by the wrists, moving her hands up until they rest on her ribs. "This is the first time I've ever wanted."

Jackie's breath shudders over Claire's sensitive skin. Hands inch upwards, moving closer and closer to Claire's exposed nipples just like in every strange fantasy that's haunted her for months, but this time she's not going to wake up before they reach their final destination.

"I've had so many dreams like this," Claire can't stop herself from blurting.

Jackie makes a noise—it's something like the one she made the day they smoked together, when Claire had massaged her scalp. She bites down gently on Claire's collarbone, and Claire's whole body arches forward and tingles in anticipation.

"Me too," Jackie murmurs against her skin. "Tell me about yours. Tell me what you dreamed of."

Her fingers are tracing just under the curve of Claire's breasts, tracing up and over the sides but not yet daring to really touch, and Claire understands suddenly what it is those dreams were telling her. What she wants. What she *needs*.

Words aren't required. With a sudden burst of confidence, Claire grasps Jackie's hands again and puts them over her breasts.

Claire's suspicions were founded, it turns out. Jackie *does* know things.

The way Jackie touches her is different than anything Claire could have imagined. She cups Claire's breasts with her clever hands, pressing just enough to make her gasp as she kisses Claire senseless. Her fingers dance around Claire's nipples, tracing and flicking and evoking a feeling that Claire never could have imagined. She feels it in her whole body. She feels it between her legs.

When she screws up her courage enough to slip a hand under the hem of Jackie's dress, caressing the warm skin of her bare thigh, everything accelerates. Jackie's hands are everywhere, and Claire wants them to be even *more* places, and she barely has time to process the pleasure of it all before they move south, shaking with want.

And Claire doesn't have a single idea what she's doing.

Once that thought hits, it stays like a burr lodged in Claire's hair. She doesn't know what she's doing. Sexual relations are a foreign language to her—with Pete it was always easiest to think about something else until it was over. With Jackie, the last thing she wants to do is disengage. Claire wants to be aware of every single second.

"I've never—" Claire gasps. Jackie's hands are smoothing over her stomach, tracing each bump of her ribs, slipping just under the high waist of her underwear. "I want—I want this, but I don't know how."

"I'll show you," Jackie whispers. She's sinking to her knees for reasons Claire can't fathom, trailing a hot line of kisses as she goes. "Please, let me show you."

As if Claire could refuse her anything.

At Claire's vehement nod, Jackie unbuckles Claire's belt and pulls it from her waist with a *snap* that makes her shiver. She slides the button from Claire's corduroys, then the zipper, easing it all down her legs underwear and all.

Claire assumes that maybe Jackie will stand up again once the task is done, but she doesn't. She just guides Claire to step one leg out of the garments, and then presses her lips just below Claire's bellybutton, looking up at her with dark eyes.

"Spread your legs for me?"

Claire feels a thousand things at once. There are nerves, but also excitement—she feels exposed, raw as a new cut as she eases her legs apart to reveal herself to Jackie's gaze. She feels a chest-tightening, breath-stealing affection for the woman currently nuzzling the coarse hair between her thighs. And, above all, Claire feels anticipation—something is about to happen, something new, something transformative. She's too distracted by sensation to understand what it is until Jackie finally moves lower, spreads something with her fingers, and takes Claire into her mouth.

The feeling that arises from a single swipe of Jackie's tongue is euphoric.

It's gentle at first, softness against softness, but at the tail end of it Jackie's tongue brushes a spot that makes something deep inside Claire jolt awake. It's like that day with the laundry hamper, put under a magnifying glass by Jackie's touch, by her tongue, by her eyes never leaving Claire's.

Claire spreads her legs wider, gasping as her head hits the back of the door. Jackie eases herself under one until Claire's knee is over her shoulder, opening her up, and Claire steadies herself with a hand on the top of her head.

"Goodness," Claire manages to choke, knowing that her words can't fully explain exactly what she's feeling. Nothing could. It's beyond her comprehension. "Jackie, I—*gosh*. That's—you—can you do that again, please?"

And Jackie does. She does it again and again until Claire is quaking with the contained force of it. There's something magical happening at the intersection of pressure and friction, and Claire wants to chase it down.

Somewhere beyond the closet door, a chorus of voices begins the countdown to midnight.

"*Twelve! Eleven! Ten!*"

The knowledge that it's Jackie's tongue that's doing this to her, her *mouth*, that she's drinking Claire in like wine and moaning at the taste, her fingernails leaving little crescents in Claire's hips from the attempt to keep her close—it's almost too much. Claire squirms in her grip, eagerly following the rhythm of Jackie's mouth like a woman possessed—

"*Seven! Six!*"

She's on a train hurtling towards the edge of a cliff, and there's no jumping off now. She can't, she *won't*. Jackie's deep brown eyes are seeing Claire across the wide plain of her body, truly seeing her, as it all mounts to an inconceivable height—

"*Four! Three! Two!*"

Claire grasps for Jackie's hand, lacing their fingers together over her own thigh. The unknown is opening up under her feet; it's not a yawning chasm but a bright stretch of warm, blissful ocean, shimmering and waiting for her to land—

"*Happy New Year!*"

Jackie's hand squeezes, her tongue doubles in its lashing over that blissful spot, and Claire's body seizes as everything comes to its obvious conclusion.

1970 dawns with raucous cheers. There, in Jackie Callas's coat closet with the muffled notes of the Rolling Stones playing over a rowdy party behind the closed door, Claire has her *eureka*.

It's like nothing she's ever known, those seconds of suspended feeling. It's a pot boiling over—it rises and rises until it spills over the sides of her, uncontainable, intense and yet brief. Claire couldn't stop herself from crying out even if she wanted to. It's involuntary, unstoppable—she's so full to the brim with base, primal *pleasure* that her voice can't fit anymore. She bursts past the boundaries of herself, and it rolls in waves, lapping against brand-new shores.

Jackie groans. She buries her face deeper between Claire's legs, her tongue still making sloppy circles as Claire's world is reshaped entirely.

"Jackie," Claire finally gasps, as the feeling tapers off into something less consuming. Her legs are shaking. She's sure she's only kept standing by the grace of Jackie's shoulders holding her up. "Holy hell."

"That's the second time I've heard you swear," Jackie mumbles into Claire's pelvis, trailing wet kisses over her inner thighs and then upward.

"This situation called for stronger language," Claire says breathlessly as her leg slips back down to earth. "I mean...Jackie, my *goodness*."

Jackie rocks back on her heels, looking up at Claire with an expression more vulnerable than Claire has ever seen on her face. "I've wanted to do that for a long time."

Jackie stands up slowly, pressing herself against Claire again, which helps immensely with the shaking legs. Jackie's mouth is wet and shiny with that between-the-legs slickness Claire has been waking up to for months, and it makes her throb as if the last five minutes never even happened.

"I've never—I didn't know that was possible," Claire says, clinging to Jackie's shoulders. She feels bare as anything with her pants around her ankles and her shirt unbuttoned, while Jackie is still wholly clothed.

"And you liked it?"

"Are you kidding?" Claire says, absolutely giddy with whatever remains of this new feeling. "Can I...I mean, can you show me how to..."

Claire waves inarticulately at Jackie's lower half. She *wants* even more than before, in a way she doesn't have words for.

Jackie swallows hard. Her eyes are dark, not their usual warm mahogany but practically black, like deep pools Claire could dip her hand into. Jackie's lip slides harshly through her teeth. "If you'd like."

"Oh, I would very much like," Claire says, with an eagerness she can't bring herself to be ashamed of.

Jackie's breath comes out in a rush. She tugs Claire closer by her open shirt, and then they're kissing again. Jackie tastes like something deep and unfamiliar. Sharp and salty, but undeniably good.

Jackie tastes like Claire.

The thought lights Claire on fire. Silently, she curses every single day she spent not knowing that this was something she could do.

Remembering how good it felt to have Jackie press her into the door, Claire takes initiative. She grabs at Jackie's hips and spins them both until they've switched positions, and Jackie's reaction is overwhelmingly positive—she groans into Claire's mouth, low and deep, and digs her blunt nails into the base of Claire's neck. Claire's shirt is still hanging open from her shoulders, and she wishes more than anything that Jackie was in a similar state.

"Teach me," Claire pants, biting down on the soft skin of Jackie's throat and feeling it vibrate with a moan. "Tell me what to do."

Jackie moves one of Claire's hands from its place on her hip down, under her dress, and between her legs. Her underwear is damp and sticky. Hot to the touch. Claire presses down firmly, and Jackie whimpers.

"You're sure you're ready?" Jackie says. "You want this?" She looks almost wild, her lips swollen and shiny. She looks desperate, truly desperate, but still her first thought is for Claire.

Claire has never been more ready in her life.

"I want you," Claire murmurs. That new, fresh part of her thrives on how Jackie reacts to the words with bucking hips and breathy sounds. She presses her fingers down harder on the wet fabric, not knowing if it's the right thing to do, but she's gratified by Jackie's breath hitching. "I want you."

With that confirmation, Jackie puts a guiding hand over Claire's again and slips it past her underwear.

Claire is a bit lost, at first. She can feel warm skin under her fingers, and then dry, curly hair, and then a hint of wetness—and then Jackie pushes at her knuckles, and Claire's world narrows to slick heat and Jackie's breathless gasp.

This is completely unfamiliar terrain. Claire has never so much as touched herself here, except for washing—whatever magic Jackie did when she was on her knees, Claire was too overwhelmed to pay attention. But Jackie's hand is still firm on hers, guiding, and Claire does her best to listen.

She wants to make Jackie feel it, too.

Jackie is warm and welcoming, coating Claire's fingers and opening to her exploration; when Claire's fingers slip over a swollen spot, a raised bump near the crest of her, Jackie's hips jolt like she's been shocked.

It's so startling that Claire almost pulls her hand away, worried that she's done something wrong, but Jackie only presses her harder. Two fingers spread over the spot and then come together again.

"That's—my clit," Jackie gasps. Claire can feel it shifting under her fingers. "Feels—feels *amazing*."

Clit, Claire thinks distantly. *Good spot. Remember that.*

Claire slides her fingers across it again, back and forth, and Jackie's eyes roll back as her head hits the door with the thud.

"Claire, *fuck…*"

"It's good?" Claire asks breathlessly.

Jackie's reply comes before she can even finish the short question. "It's so fucking good."

She's heard Jackie swear casually before, but not this often, and not this vehemently. It makes Claire feel hotter every time another word falls out of Jackie's mouth—it's as if she can't help it, like the movement of Claire's hand is forcing the vulgarity out.

The power Claire feels at being the source of Jackie's pleasure is more potent than anything she's ever experienced. She nips at Jackie's earlobe, and is rewarded with a breathy sigh; she shifts her fingers, swiping a wide and messy circle, and Jackie's whole body rocks readily into her as if Claire is the puppeteer pulling her strings.

Back and forth her fingers trace, up and down, trying new pressures and patterns and mapping the results until finally Jackie's shaking hand guides Claire's lower.

"Want you inside," Jackie gasps.

Claire wants to bite at her red lip like a ripe strawberry. When she remembers that she *can*, it lights a firework inside her.

"Where?" Claire asks, capturing Jackie's lip between her teeth and cataloging the frantic sound that results. "Show me."

"My cunt," Jackie whispers.

That word makes Claire blush harder than anything so far. It's a word she's only heard a few times, and certainly not in polite conversation; it's something she's sure her mother would have washed her mouth out with soap for saying in her youth. But it seems to fit here in a way she can't explain. It's harsh, and dirty, and…*hot*.

Jackie pushes at Claire's hand, and her fingers slip through what feels like an absurd amount of wetness until she finds a spot that *gives*. When she presses up and into it, sinking into Jackie to the knuckles, everything slows until Claire is hyper-aware of every sensation.

It all quiets. The party, the music, her own heartbeat in her chest—everything narrows to Jackie, just long enough for Claire's world to shift once again.

She's surrounded by Jackie, inside her, *within* her. They're breathing the same air, sharing the same body. Claire is as close to Jackie as it's possible to be, and she only wants to be closer.

Claire is at least vaguely familiar with this, from the other way round. This is what Pete was always questing for, and she's starting to understand why—for Claire, receiving this has never been anything special, just something to endure until it was over, but Jackie seems to be deriving a pleasure from it that Claire never did. Being the source of that pleasure is a heady rush.

The rush turns dizzying when Jackie grabs the hem of her own dress, pulling it up and over her head. Her brassiere is a silky-soft black thing, with lace at the edges and underwear to match. She props a foot up against the shoe rack, opening herself up to Claire's hand, and pulls Claire's mouth to her throat.

Jackie is mostly naked, and Claire is mostly naked, and they're pressed together skin to skin, and Claire is *inside* her. Nothing has ever felt more right.

Here, at least, Claire has some idea what to do.

Jackie makes a tiny noise of protest when Claire withdraws her fingers slightly, but it turns into a shout of pleasure that Claire is sure the whole party must hear when she plunges them back in, her knuckles pressing hard into the flesh of Jackie's *cunt*.

Just thinking the word, so new and forbidden, makes Claire shiver in the best way.

The rhythm of the motion, in and out, gaining speed and force until Jackie is shaking with it, is enough to drive Claire mad with want. She can feel Jackie approaching that *moment*, the one she herself just felt, and she'd do anything to help her along.

Thankfully, Jackie seems to have no problems giving directions.

"Another," Jackie pants, one hand wound tight into Claire's hair. "*Please*, Claire, another finger."

Claire almost dislodges them both in her rush to comply. She slips a third finger inside, and Jackie clenches around them; every time Jackie makes one of those satisfied sounds, it's as if Claire can feel her own actions in an echo against her own newly-discovered clit, a spot she hadn't even known existed until three minutes ago.

The thought reminds her of how Jackie reacted when she dragged her fingers across it. She's sure that, if she stretches her thumb at just the right angle, it would be—

"*Claire!*"

There.

Claire is running on instinct the way a car runs on fuel. Jackie seems to struggle to give instructions now, her free hand clawing at Claire's bare back under her open shirt. Claire's wrist is starting to cramp, but she can't fathom stopping. Jackie's vocalizations are getting high and whimpery. She's getting tighter around Claire's fingers, and somehow wetter than before; she's on the absolute razor's edge of something that Claire is determined to see through.

Jackie's hand in Claire's hair clenches into a fist. It doesn't hurt, despite the tension pulling at her scalp—it makes Claire *throb*.

"Bite down, and—and curl your fingers," Jackie whimpers, her voice high and tight as she uses that fist to pull Claire's mouth to the right position.

Claire bites down gently on Jackie's neck, and shifts her fingers. Jackie moans, but there's an edge to it—like she needs more.

Claire can give her more. She'll give Jackie whatever she needs.

"Like this?" Claire murmurs. She sinks her teeth into the curve between Jackie's neck and shoulder, harder this time—she can feel muscle flexing, skin shifting, as Jackie cries out and arches into her curled fingers.

"*Yes!*"

The pace reaches a fever pitch. Jackie is clinging to her, and every moan is musical to Claire's ears. She can imagine tracing each sound with a paintbrush, filling out the cadence of Jackie's pleasure with electrifying color. The tension Claire felt when Jackie was using her mouth is around her own fingers now, getting tighter with every second, every thrust, every whimper.

In the moment Jackie finally snaps and releases around her hand, sighing Claire's name into her own mouth, Claire is sure she could take on the world. A missing piece of herself has just slotted into place, lighting up her whole world; there's no more dim corners or shadowy places. Her old life is greyscale, and now the world is dazzling watercolor, illuminated by Jackie fluttering and pulsing around her fingers. This is what life is supposed to feel like. Somehow, making Jackie feel this way is even better than feeling it herself.

Jackie is crying, Claire notes distantly. Maybe Claire is, too; their kisses taste like salt. How did she ever live without this? Without Jackie pulsing in the palm of her hand, her tongue in Claire's mouth, pressed together as tightly as two people can be pressed, like two vines twisted into one?

"Claire..." Jackie whispers brokenly. Both hands cup Claire's face as she presses her lips to every inch of bare skin she can reach. "Please stay."

Claire isn't sure if Jackie means not to pull her fingers away, or something more meaningful. Maybe she means both. Either way, Claire doesn't plan on going anywhere.

"I'm so sorry I didn't see this before," Claire whispers back. Her fingers are still buried deep in a heat she never wants to leave. Her voice is shaky, but sure. "I feel like I've been blind my whole life."

"You have nothing to be sorry for," Jackie says. She tilts her head forward until their foreheads are pressed together. "I should have explained it to you. Instead, I just left you to do it on your own."

"I know you've been hurt before," Claire says.

"I didn't want to ruin another life. I was so scared you would hate me if I dragged you into this." Jackie sighs, stroking her fingers down Claire's temple and across her jaw. "It's happened before. All because I—"

Jackie cuts herself off. Though she doesn't finish the thought, Claire's heart soars at the mere thought of what might have been the end of that sentence.

"I thought I could keep my distance with you," Jackie says instead. She's gnawing at her lower lip. Claire can just see the imprint of her kisses there in Jackie's faded lip balm, and it's entirely distracting. "Keep things light. Just a stupid little crush. But it grew. That day in the pool I realized it was more. And I got the feeling that..."

"That I wanted to kiss you," Claire finishes.

Jackie traces over Claire's lips so gently that it almost tickles. "That made it real. Suddenly it hit home that I was doing exactly the same thing I did last time."

"With a better result this time," Claire says. She nips at Jackie's fingertips, making them both smile.

Jackie's face brightens, but it dims again as she casts her eyes downward. It's as if every time Jackie really feels this, lets this happiness course through her, she stamps on the brakes.

"I'm not Valerie," Claire says softly.

Jackie looks up sharply. The shock is brief, changing quickly into suspicion as she glances backward as if she could glare at Theo through the wood. "Honestly, *what* did Theo tell you?"

"When you were gone, I..." Claire swallows, her mouth suddenly a little dry. "I was worried about you. I went into your house to find Theo's phone number, so I could check on you, and there were photos on your desk."

Jackie sighs. She toys with Claire's shirt, smoothing the rumpled collar. "Ah."

"And then Louise said something about you and Mrs. Wilson, and things started to make sense."

"Who the hell is Louise?"

"She's in Martha's book club. It doesn't matter," Claire says. "But it's true, isn't it? You and Susan were together, at your housewarming party."

Jackie bites her lip. "And if it was? Would you be upset?"

"No. It made me realize that I love you," Claire says, with hardly a thought.

Jackie goes still. Her grip on Claire's shirt goes tight again. She's tense against Claire, and the shock in her eyes is palpable.

Claire can't help it. She lets out a sound, half-laugh and half-sob, at just how *true* those words feel.

Ten years of marriage and years of dating prior, and she and Pete have barely said those words to each other. No matter what Jackie told her about it, romantic love always seemed like a thing that was made up for the movies. That squirrelly, desperate, lets-go-to-Niagara-Falls-and-elope love always felt like a lie. The love from the songs didn't exist.

"You love me?" Jackie says, with a quiet wonder.

Pete's angry face flashes in Claire's mind, full of the confusion and rage that the morning will bring. She sees her mother, pale and worried about Claire's future. She sees Martha, assuring Claire that her relationship with her husband can be worked out. *Grin and bear it.*

None of them hold a candle to Jackie right now, flushed and hopeful and nervous. *Jackie* is nervous. Jackie, the very embodiment of confidence. It makes Claire feel braver.

"I think I fell in love with you the minute we met," Claire says.

Jackie's breath shudders. It's as if she's deflating, sagging against Claire and throwing her arms around her shoulders.

"Oh, thank god," Jackie mumbles, muffled by Claire's shirt.

Claire laughs. She's full to the brim with happiness, overflowing with it, and it's spilling out of her now. "Does that mean…"

"Of course I love you, Claire," Jackie says, tightening her arms around Claire's shoulders. Her voice is quavery. "Part of what scares me is how *much*. Meeting you, knowing you, made me realize that what I had with Val was shallow in comparison. And if the end of that broke me…"

"So you pushed me away?"

"I was trying to let you go. I wanted you to be able to keep your normal life. To be happy."

"My life wasn't happy before," Claire murmurs into her hair. "But now I think it could be."

In an effort to hug Jackie back, Claire finally slips her fingers free from the warmth they've been buried in this whole time. She was so content there that she'd almost forgotten, and Jackie did too, based on her surprised intake of breath. Claire runs her wet fingers briefly through the hair between Jackie's legs, and remembers how Jackie had nuzzled at Claire's before she took Claire into her mouth.

It makes her want to drop to her knees, like Jackie did, and keep on learning.

Punch-drunk on love, Claire kisses her.

It's a soft, unhurried kind of kiss, a kind Claire has never had before. She's never felt the need to kiss Pete outside of the necessary times—a peck on the cheek in the morning, a kiss or two before or after lovemaking. Quick and to the point. Tongue was never a factor.

This kiss is exploratory. Claire follows every whim, sliding her tongue along Jackie's and letting herself learn by example. Her hands explore every bit of Jackie's body she can reach, and Jackie arches into her with a contented noise. She's so very soft—soft lips, soft skin, soft curves. No whiskers or harsh noises. She smells good. She tastes good.

There's not a thing in the world that could make Claire turn her back on this.

Outside the door a telltale *thump* and *crash* bursts the bubble of the moment, followed by a chorus of drunken laughter.

"What now?" Jackie whispers, against Claire's mouth.

Claire knows what she doesn't want to do. She doesn't want to leave this closet yet. She doesn't want to face the real world, with all its harshness. She wants to stay right here, letting contentment fill her up with every soft meeting of their lips.

But the party still rages outside. Pete is probably still at Martha's, completely unaware that Claire is truly leaving, and there are things that need to be dealt with. Everything else can come after.

Many, many times after.

"We could go to my place," Claire says, punctuating it with one last kiss to the tip of Jackie's nose. "It's not much, but it's mine. I don't think staying here tonight is a good idea, with Pete next door."

"Or we could take off," Jackie blurts.

Claire loses her train of thought entirely. "Take off? To where?"

"Anywhere. We can see the country. Go north, or east. We can get a motel," Jackie says, all in a rush. "Anything you want."

Claire's smile threatens to split her face in two. She tucks a strand of Jackie's hair behind her ear, tracing the line of her lovely cheek with the backs of her fingers. It feels as if she might die if they aren't touching in every place they can be. "Are you asking me to run away with you?"

"I want some time with you, before everything kicks off. To figure out what we want and what to do next before the world catches up." Jackie gnaws at her lip, pitching the idea like Claire might refuse. Like Claire wouldn't follow her to the ends of the earth if she asked.

"How long?" Claire says, letting the reality of what's happening fill her up like warm tea in a mug. "I think Anita would give me whatever time off I ask for."

Jackie's smile is radiant. "As long as you want. Wherever you want to go."

This is perhaps the most control over her own life Claire has ever had. She's not one to like making decisions, always aware of the judgement she'll get for making a bad one, but this feels different. Natural.

"I could go for a vacation," Claire says. "Like a honeymoon?"

Jackie's grin widens. She scratches gently at the base of Claire's neck, just at her hairline. "I've got a full tank of gas, and nowhere else I want to be."

"What about your party? You can't just leave," Claire says, though she's already making a list of the few things she needs to pack. "They could trash your house."

Jackie laughs a little. "I'm selling the house. I don't care. I bought it because I was running from something. I never belonged here."

Claire leans back into Jackie's hand—it sends pleasant shivers down her spine. "Neither did I."

"So let's leave it in the dust," Jackie says, a hint of excitement coloring her tone. Perhaps finally she's begun to understand that Claire is in this, just as much as she is. "I'll get Theo to lock it all up tomorrow. He's staying the night."

"Are we really doing this?" Claire says, gripping tight at Jackie's waist.

Jackie nods. She's a little breathless. "I'm all in it. As long as you are."

When Theo sees them come out of the closet together, quite obviously ruffled and glowing, he lets out a squeal of delight so loud that Claire is sure the neighborhood dogs must be howling.

"Fucking *finally*," he shouts, pulling them both into a hug before addressing the rest of the party from over their shoulders. "Okay, party's over. If you're staying, find a spot to crash. Everyone else, get the fuck out."

Eventually people follow Theo's instructions, though not without grumbling. While Jackie packs a suitcase Claire paces the kitchen like a woman possessed, full of manic energy. She's a battery charged up by Jackie, full of lightning and love. NASA be damned, she could jump high enough to hit the moon. And Pete is still across the street, clueless through the most earth-shaking night of Claire's life. He's going to come home to a whole new world, where Claire will be gone forever.

She's ready for her new start.

The house has mostly emptied when Jackie drags her suitcase across the foyer. When she sees Claire, her smile is brilliant—as if she wasn't expecting Claire to still be here. She practically runs into Claire's arms, and Claire picks her up a little in a sweeping hug. She's always tried to hide her strength, her height, her whole self to fit into a role—with Jackie, she doesn't need to.

"Where do you want to go?" Claire says.

Jackie giggles in a giddy, girlish way when Claire sets her down that makes her want to do it again. "I think I need to see the ocean."

Claire grins, pulling in Jackie—her girl, her sweetheart, her *lover*—until they're close enough to share breath. Until she can press their lips together, losing herself in the softness of Jackie's mouth again.

When they part for air, Claire smiles her first fully free smile.

"Santa Cruz?"

It doesn't feel like a vacation, once they've stopped at Claire's place to pack a bag. They hit the highway with the convertible top down, Jackie's hair tucked under a headscarf and Claire's curls blowing loose in the wind. The stars get brighter the further they get from the suburbs, and the wind is cool and bracing. Jackie is smiling full-stop, their hands are intertwined over the gearshift, and every few minutes she looks over at Claire like she can't quite believe she's really here.

No, it doesn't feel like a vacation. It feels like, after a lifetime of being kept away, Claire is finally heading home.

Other Books from Ylva Publishing

www.ylva-publishing.com

Shifting Gears

Jazz Forrester

ISBN: 978-3-96324-984-6
Length: 256 pages (88,000 words)

Workaholic Eleanor blows into rural Canada laser-focused on her new real estate development project. Then her car breaks down. Sweet, smart mechanic Dani is so laid-back—all rumpled flannels and cheeky grins.

What starts as a whirlwind summer fling might turn into more...except Eleanor's secrets threaten to tear everything apart.

The Love Factor

Quinn Ivins

ISBN: 978-3-96324-377-6
Length: 215 pages (75,000 words)

A smart student-professor romance filled with nostalgia, politics, and the forbidden thrills of lesbian love in the '90s.

Molly is almost thirty, bored, and less into her PhD than her sexy, closeted statistics professor, Carmen, an icy woman with strict standards and no interest in dating students.

As they work together to expose a scandal, the chemistry builds, making for a dangerous equation.

The Music and the Mirror

Lola Keeley

ISBN: 978-3-96324-014-0
Length: 311 pages (120,000 words)

Anna is the newest member of an elite ballet company. Her first class almost ruins her career before it begins. She must face down jealousy, sabotage, and injury to pour everything into opening night and prove she has what it takes. In the process, Anna discovers that she and the daring, beautiful Victoria have a lot more than ballet in common.

The Brutal Truth

Lee Winter

ISBN: 978-3-95533-898-5
Length: 339 pages (108,000 words)

Aussie crime reporter Maddie Grey is out of her depth in New York and secretly drawn to her twice-married, powerful media mogul boss, Elena Bartell, who eats failing newspapers for breakfast. As work takes them to Australia, Maddie is goaded into a brief bet—that they will say only the truth to each other. It backfires catastrophically.

A lesbian romance about the lies we tell ourselves.

About Jazz Forrester

Jazz Forrester spends her days getting lost in research rabbit holes over insignificant details. Growing up in rural Ontario, she spent her life constantly reading and creating stories in her head without ever thinking to write them down. Once she started putting pen to paper in 2018, she never looked back. When she's not writing, she spends her time with fandom nonsense, gaming, playing D&D, and trying out new recipes on her partner.

Jazz currently lives in Niagara, Ontario, and enjoys her day job talking to people about history.

Breaking from Frame
© 2025 by Jazz Forrester

ISBN: 978-3-69006-097-4

Available in paperback and e-book formats.

Published by Ylva Publishing, legal entity of Ylva Verlag, e.Kfr.

Ylva Verlag, e.Kfr.
Owner: Astrid Ohletz
Am Kirschgarten 2
65830 Kriftel
Germany

www.ylva-publishing.com

First edition: 2025

We explicitly reserve the right to use our works for text and data mining as defined in § 44b of the German Copyright Act.

For questions about product safety, please reach out to:
info@ylva-publishing.com

No part of this book may be reproduced, scanned, or distributed in any printed or electronic form without permission. Please do not participate in or encourage piracy of copyrighted materials in violation of the author's rights. Thank you for respecting the hard work of this author.

This is a work of fiction. Names, characters, places, and incidents either are a product of the author's imagination or are used fictitiously, and any resemblance to locales, events, business establishments, or actual persons—living or dead—is entirely coincidental.

Credits
Edited by Michelle Aguilar and Lenir Costa
Cover Design by Ilona Gostyńska-Rymkiewicz
Print Layout by Ylva Publishing

Image rights cover illustration provided by Shutterstock LLC; iStock; Dreamstime; Canva; AdobeStock
Graphics provided by Freepik

www.ingramcontent.com/pod-product-compliance
Lightning Source LLC
LaVergne TN
LVHW052246060226
831064LV00037B/529